"For you," he said.

She cried out in awe and joy. Never did she believe Cress would offer her his beads. "Why are you doing this?"

He lowered his arm. "I'm not quite sure. But will you accept my beads?"

Her gaze lifted to his. "With pleasure."

She leaned close to his side and nuzzled his neck. A low moan of pleasure vibrated up his throat. Teasing him with her movements, she unplaited several inches of her braid and with shaking fingers, picked up a glowing orb. Rolling it between her forefinger and thumb to admire, she saw a tiny hole pierced its center.

He never looked away. Not until the last bead had been strung and she replaited the braid did Cress move.

He reached over and stroked the glowing orbs in her hair. "I thought beads were worn afterwards."

"I'm making a statement."

"Can we not stay and continue this…this conversation?" he asked softly.

She grunted in frustration. "Duty calls. For a male, you are unduly correct too many times for my comfort. On the other hand, you possess many attributes I find admirable. The contradictions are confusing."

Cress gathered her into his arms and smiled down at her. "Poor Becca, you have much to learn about men."

Praise for Darcy Carson

First place winner in the Oak Leaf Award of Excellence

~

Third place winner in Heart of the West

~

WIZARD CRESS came out in the top three of
Romance Through the Ages

Woman in the Woods

by

Darcy Carson

Dragons Return, Book 2

Woman in the Woods

Cover Art by *Abigail Owen*

The Wild Rose Press, Inc.
PO Box 708
Adams Basin, NY 14410-0708
Visit us at www.thewildrosepress.com

Publishing History
First Fantasy Rose Edition, 2020
Print ISBN 978-1-5092-2985-7
Digital ISBN 978-1-5092-2986-4

Dragons Return, Book 2
Published in the United States of America

Dedication

To my dear friend and critique partner, Pam Binder.
Thank you for all your wise comments and sharp eye.

Chapter One

She smelled smoke.

Becca d'Firn followed a tree-lined game trail up the mountain slope. Great stands of pine, fir, oak, and maple spread out over the rich land. A slight breeze rustled through branches with varying shades of green, allowing little sunlight to penetrate their dark foliage. Though the going became rough, she kept up her brisk pace. The responsibility to find and fetch the Wizard Cress fell upon her shoulders. Her village counted on her.

She stopped in the tinder-dry underbrush and inhaled deeply. An acrid stench of wood-smoke teased her nostrils. Lightning streaked across the sky, followed by a loud boom of thunder. The earth shook, but not a hint of rain fell. The woods were tinder dry—far too dry for late springtime.

Another bolt of lightning hit nearby. Again the earth rattled, followed by another loud clap of thunder. A few minutes passed, then Becca saw flames leap to lick and fondle the towering trees.

In a heartbeat, the crackle of trees and brush being consumed grew louder and overshadowed all other sounds. The wind picked up. The blaze spread hotter, brighter, feeding on everything in its path. If she didn't do something soon, only blackened sticks and barren ground would remain.

Becca studied her surroundings. A rocky hillside flowed down to a river's edge and provided a natural firebreak. She gave a small sigh of relief. The wide ribbon of sparkling water should slow the fire's destructive path.

It would be difficult to defeat the fire single-handed, but by using the water as one break, and if she could create another, even a small one, then maybe the fire would burn itself out.

Three white-tailed deer, brown eyes huge with fear, leapt out of the woods and dove into the wide, slow moving river. They swam to the other bank and bounded away.

Becca had to act fast to save the creatures of the forest. The Goddess Luna would never forgive her if she didn't attempt to give them time to escape.

Seconds later, a pack of wolves raced out of the woods where the deer first appeared, all consideration for the hunt overshadowed by thoughts of survival.

She could not stop the fire alone. It was presumptuous of her to think she could.

But she had to try. Nothing less would be worthy of her as the Chosen One of her people.

The reminder jarred her into action. Slipping the straps of her pack off her shoulders and down her arms, she tossed the pack, along with her bow and quiver of arrows, to the ground near a stand of willows. Her bow, a prized possession, was constructed of fine-grained yew, the best wood because of its great pliability and strength, and she wasn't about to let flames consume something she had taken such care and many long hours to create. She kept her hatchet tucked into her belt in case she needed it.

When twigs snapped behind her, Becca turned to see a mature sow with striped piglets in tow rush out of the brambles. The little family raced along the water's edge, snorting and squealing in falsetto.

Dragging a pile of evergreen boughs over to the river, Becca jumped into the water. The shock of snow melt water stole her breath away, but once soaked, she climbed out to smother small fires with moistened branches, thick with foliage.

Again and again she returned to the river to wet her clothing and the boughs. Smoke obscured everything. Heat blistered her face, and cinders burned her hands. Those landing on her wet clothes sizzled and winked out. In the distance massive limbs crashed from the canopy to the forest floor. The sound reminded her of a giant predator chewing on the bones of its kill.

As she spared a look at the sky, she saw the smoke part and a flock of birds curled into balls, their feathers scorched, the inferno sucking them down.

Gulping great breaths of smoke-clogged air caused her to cough, and she dared to glance around. Between the rocky area, the river, and her break, she held the inferno in check. Her sole worry became a crown fire erupting.

"Can't give up." She breathed the words, too tired to speak any louder. "I have to try. If not me…who?"

Becca slumped into a crouch and supported her head on her knees to steal a moment of rest. Reason demanded she not waste a precious moment. When she looked up, her worst fears materialized. All her efforts soured. In those few seconds of distraction, flames danced from treetop to treetop.

Jumping to her feet, she grabbed water-soaked

boughs with both hands and beat the ground like a windmill, taking her frustration out on the glowing embers dotting the ground. She would suffocate every fiery spark—even if it was the last achievement she did in her life.

And then in the blink of an eye, the fire poofed out of existence. Like...*magic*.

She swallowed painfully. The roar of destructive flames disappeared, replaced by a pervasive silence that allowed her to hear the loud beat of her heart.

A twig broke. She whirled around, pulling her hatchet free, ready to step forward and face the new danger.

A tall, lean man stood with his arms raised in the air, the sleeves of his brown robe falling back to his elbows—a wizard. His arms shimmered with golden light that faded so quickly Becca decided tiredness made her hallucinate.

The man carried no weapons. Most strange. Then again, what wizard needed ordinary weapons?

Let him be whom she sought—the Wizard Cress. *Please*.

Becca stared at the male. Knife-thin odds fueled her doubts. She sought a legendary wizard, a man many times this one's age. This male appeared to be in his early thirties, which made him a few years older than she. His long, dark brown hair reached clear down his spine and was tied back with a rawhide cord at the base of his neck. The hint of stubble darkened a masculine face with intriguing angles, and Becca felt her body quiver with attraction. The effect surprised her, and she blurted out the first thing that came to mind.

"You're a wizard?" she asked, trying to swallow

the groan warbling in her throat. The statement seemed foolish after what she'd just witnessed.

Straightening, the man stared at her as if he'd never seen a hunter. "I practice a few of the arts."

His deep voice, soft and sensual upon answering, reverberated with a commanding air. "Aye...I would say you do. Very well, indeed."

"I merely suffocated the fire by depriving it of an important element—air."

She brushed off the odd sensation his steady gaze had upon her. "I'm looking for a wizard who lives somewhere around here...the Wizard Cress."

His hazel eyes widened, then narrowed. "I've heard of him."

"You have?" Hope flared within her. "I would be indebted if you took me to him."

The man cast a suspicious glance in her direction. Becca barely managed to wonder at his reaction when he said, "He doesn't much care for visitors. If you are only following a trail of gossip to satisfy some silly—"

"I don't take much stock in gossip," she interrupted, spotting dragonflies, or dragon lights as the iridescent insects were called in The Wilds, flitting around the man's head.

He noticed the focus of her attention. "You're not from Brenalin. Who are you?"

The thought of asking a man—even a great wizard—to save Froy seemed disloyal to the Goddess Luna. Indebting her village to a male was a totally alien concept to everything Becca believed in, but the Council had voted, and she volunteered to find him.

"Becca d'Firn of Froy." Her reply came instinctively, but she sensed she faced a man accustomed to having his orders obeyed.

He held his hands palms up. "I've not heard of your village. Where is it?"

She tucked her hatchet into her waistband. "In The Wilds, along the River Kelt."

"The Wilds?" A frown pulled his brows down in disbelief. "The far Wilds?"

She stared at him, taken aback. "You have heard of The Wilds?"

"It is a kingdom far to the west," he replied. "Both swamp and desert divide it from the civilized world. No one lives there except monsters and savages. Few travel to it. Even fewer return."

How presumptuous of him. She expected more from a wizard. "Do I look like a monster?"

Dark brown brows arched. "You know what they say about appearances."

"They're dangerous?" She decided to go along with him. If he were just another male, his impudence would be swiftly punished, but this one might lead her to Wizard Cress.

"They are deceiving."

His response caught her off guard and made her laugh. She wondered what the Council would say if they learned they were considered savages in this part of the world.

"We are as human as you," she ventured. "My people trace their lineage back more generations than we can count. At one time we might have belonged to a vast civilization, but I cannot say with surety. Nor do I care. It doesn't matter where we originated. That is in the past. We have flourished in The Wilds. We are who we are now."

The man crossed his arms, a sure sign of resistance. "A fine speech," he said, "but of little import to me."

Fury rose within her.

With good reason.

Cold, motivating willpower took hold of her. The Goddess Luna favored the bold, and Becca vowed to never disappoint her. "Do not mock me, wizard. I was bid to find the Wizard Cress because he is our last hope. I have been traveling many moons and must find him."

"Why do you seek Cress?"

"Plague haunts my village. We need his assistance."

Chapter Two

Cress wished he could heal the exhausted woman's burns. No amount of soot hid the blisters on the sharp angles of her face or could veil the smell of singed hair. The bright beads and feathers in her braid were in dire jeopardy of falling off altogether. She dressed like a man in leggings and a studded leather tunic.

A warrior woman from The Wilds.

Incredible. He kept his face impassive to hide his surprise. None of the rumors he'd ever heard mentioned how breathtakingly appealing these women were. He'd only been told they were skilled hunters and true mistresses of the bow.

She eyed him uneasily, and he swore despair crossed her face, making her appear vulnerable. A trick of light? Or his imagination toying with him?

Fatigue dulled her blue eyes, and she dropped to the ground. She licked her lips, a simple motion, yet he found himself imagining what it would be like to shower this woman with soft kisses.

Kisses? His heart pounded at the thought. The crazy thought had no place in his head. His response to this warrior woman astonished him.

Walking over to the river's edge, he pulled a cup from his robe. A simple spell on the robe's pockets allowed him to retrieve nearly any small item he required with a thought. It saved much time in the course of a day.

Time. He almost laughed aloud. It was the one commodity he possessed in abundance. Years. Decades. Centuries. He'd already spent over a thousand years within the heart of the great forest comprising Demit Woods.

Clutching his sleeve to keep it from getting wet, he scooped up water.

"Here, drink this." He handed her the cup, their fingers brushing as he passed it to her. "You must be parched."

She grasped the container and greedily emptied it. "Thank you."

"My pleasure. You did a brave thing, fighting the fire."

"I could do no less." She glanced at the blackened woods.

He followed her surveillance of the area. Benefits still existed in the midst of disaster. The seedbed of ash and mineral soil would allow a mosaic of vegetation to grow anew in the coming season.

"Still, you took a great chance," he answered. "Many would have fled, thinking only of their own safety. Your kindness came at a high price. Your hands and face are burned. Let me take you to my home to properly tend them. I don't live far."

"If you can strike down a whole forest fire, why not just heal me with a spell or something?"

"You need a healer, not a wizard. Magic cannot heal."

Surprise widened her crystal blue eyes. "Why not?"

Cress paused, amused. Her question must stem

from ignorance or stress. "It cannot cure illnesses. Take my word for it. Salida, my housekeeper, can provide proper care."

"My injuries can be tended later. I must locate Wizard Cress," she protested, yet a small smile lit her face.

He smiled back, realizing with mild amusement she failed to recognize the very person she sought. Then again, he couldn't blame her ignorance. Few people had glimpsed him in eons.

A sow with a litter of piglets approached the river's edge on the far side to eye them with caution. Cress heard the gobble of turkeys in the underbrush. Already creatures returned to forage on the bounty dropped to the woodland floor.

He turned back to the warrior woman. She stood and strode over to a stand of willows. There he spotted a bow, full quiver, and travel bags. "Tell me how you heard about this wizard?"

"Everyone has heard of the renowned wizard."

"Renowned, is he?"

"Most definitely," she tossed back. "Can you aid me in finding him?"

He remembered the days he once roamed the land, performing magic for anyone who bid him. Centuries of watching friends age and die had proved outright depressing. Only his sister now remained, and he'd failed her, too.

Now he craved solitude and lived in an enchanted dragon circle by choice with Salida...and the occasional visit from Brenalin's Master Wizard, Einer, who'd ventured deep into Demit Woods to find the ancient circle and in the process found a friend as well.

"I recall hearing he's over a thousand years of age," Cress answered. "Do you believe someone, even a powerful wizard, could live that long?"

She waved her hand in dismissal. "Embellishment is expected when a male is involved. He probably trained disciples who took his place upon his death, then they trained more to repeat the cycle over and over. Still…where there is speculation, truth can also be found. My people need his services."

"I've already told you, magic cannot heal."

"Dozens will die if I do not find him before summer ends. His magic can save them."

The woman's eyes shifted away from his. She kept information from him. Now that made him curious. "I'm sorry, Becca. Death and dying are the natural order of things."

"Old age and accidents I accept. Not plague. His magic can find the cause. Or create a spell to make sure it never returns. But why all these questions? Do you wish to accompany me to Froy in his stead?"

"By the gods—no!"

She didn't say anything for a moment or two. "Think of it as an adventure to tell your family before the winter fire when you grow old."

Cress dared not let sympathy influence him. Besides, he would never grow old while his sister remained trapped within the dragon circle. "I'll be fair with you, Becca d'Firn of Froy—I know Cress." Curiosity prompted him to ask, "Tell me…what are the symptoms of the illness?"

"What good will it do to tell you?"

"Becca," he said, inhaling deeply, "have patience with me. Remember, I can lead you to Cress. Now, tell me about this plague."

"It is a wasting sickness with headaches, fever, chills. When it reaches the point of rapid breathing, few recover. It starts with the most vulnerable—the children and elderly. The Council refused to take any more chances. They called for volunteers to find the great wizard. As leader of the hunters, I stepped forward because it was my responsibility."

"How do you know this plague will return?" Cress asked as he adjusted the front of his robe.

"I don't. Nor am I willing to gamble with the lives of people I care about."

Cress's gut rolled. A mission of mercy. That he understood and empathized with. If she learned his identity, he feared she would attempt to persuade him, try any ploy to gain his agreement. Many others had tried in the past and failed.

Several individual voices united as one in Cress's mind. *"We think this human is a stubborn human female."*

Countless ages had passed since the last dragons of Feldzvelt offered comments about another human. No one knew the Guardians of Secrets existed, believing all dragons had been destroyed in the Great Dying, what the tiny creatures called the devastating war between dragons and humans.

"Begone," he quickly mindspoke in defense.

"We are observing. You cannot refuse us."

Tiny and deadly sharp teeth clicked with insistence near him. *"I do. Leave before I do something we all will regret."*

"We favor her. She put her own safety last to save the forest. Few humans would act with such bravery."

His tormentors' doggedness was indeed a rare phenomenon. That alone made the occurrence worthy of his consideration.

He stared at Becca's wide blue eyes and wondered what it would be like to find favor within them. "You need to rest."

"I will rest after I find Wizard Cress."

Looking at this proud woman from The Wilds, he realized she affected him like none before. It didn't take magic or insight to figure that out. Something more powerful than magic awoke inside him. "Good luck, then."

"No luck is necessary." She retrieved her items from the ground. "I have found him. You are he."

Chapter Three

The male's silence confirmed Becca's suspicion. She should have realized it sooner, but battling the fire stole all her reserves. She dropped to her knees, for her need of his services called for a show of respect. "I should have comprehended your identity at once. Only a powerful wizard could have put out a forest fire as easily as you did."

"Get up," he said. "I am not your master and require no obeisance."

His steady gaze weighed on her as keenly as a touch. She had to think clearly. Keep her focus. She rocked back on her heels, her knuckles digging into the soft loam. "I've never met a real wizard before. Do you require a different form of homage? Forgive my ignorance."

No doubt existed in her mind about the man being a great wizard. Handsome, too. Emotions stirred such as she'd never experienced since reaching womanhood. She needed to convince him to return to her beloved village. But how?

"No apology is necessary." He stared down at her, the tiniest smile curling his mouth. He offered her a hand to rise. "I should be thanking you. Your efforts slowed the fire and saved many creatures."

Luna help her. Every time he smiled, a flutter erupted in her belly. She put her hand into his and warmth shot up her arm. "How did you know where I was?"

A three-point stag slipped out of the woods and crossed the river. Cress looked away and overturned a small branch with his boot toe. It landed near Becca's foot.

"Wizards sense things. Smell them. Hear them." He shifted from foot to foot. "Stop looking so serious, Becca d'Firn. I'm teasing you. I saw the smoke. It led me here."

"Oh," she said, unsettled, but too curious not to inquire. "What if the wind had blown the smoke in the wrong direction?"

"You would have died."

A threat? He dared to try and frighten her. She almost laughed. Little he knew of the hunters of Froy. They faced dangers every day without flinching. "I was going to cross the river."

"I thought as much." He kicked another branch. "That would have been a fatal mistake. The crown fire was about to dance to the other side. You would have been forced to stay in the river. It's fed by snow melt. Eventually the cold would have sapped your strength and dragged you around the bend. There, the river becomes dangerously swift because of the waterfall. The plunge would have been deadly."

Becca eyed the wide river. It appeared harmless enough. Cress remained silent, letting her grasp the danger she'd escaped. "Then it's a good thing you came along in time. You saved my life. And you can save my village."

The wizard laughed, as though grateful for her bluntness. "I think you have too high an opinion of my abilities."

"Are all wizards as modest as you?"

Leaning forward, he studied her with a piercing hazel stare. "I can't speak for the others. Only myself. My offer of hospitality stands. Mend and rest."

"Fair enough." She sighed and nodded her head. "I accept your offer to have my wounds tended. There, we can continue our discussion."

She took a step to follow the wizard. The leather bag tied to her belt and equal in size to a plump rabbit bumped against her leg. It contained gemstones of blood red rubies, cornflower blue sapphires, and huge river pearls gathered over eons. If gratitude proved insufficient, perhaps she could purchase his services.

They crossed the barren, rocky hillside into the woods untouched by the fire. What else did Froy possess as inducement? Even though male, whatever her village owned would be his for the asking. All he need do was make the request.

If only he'd been the wizard she had anticipated— elderly and bent with age, his face a riverbed of wrinkles, sprouting a long, wispy white beard, and squinting at her through milky eyes. This man did not come close to that image. In fact, he interested her very much.

Her attraction to him took her aback. Surprise. Delight. Wonder. She'd never given any thought to what Wizard Cress would look like, how she would recognize him—but now she could honestly say pleasure filled her that he had found her. Following behind, she smelled his scent—pine and male—and it made her curious. She couldn't help but wonder what it would be like to mate with such an appealing male.

The scent of scorched trees lessened as they left the woods behind them. The wizard called a halt, pursing his lips, giving her time to catch her breath. The trek wasn't difficult, but she'd spent nearly all her energy battling the fire. The cool shadow of the forest helped her ignore the sting of her burns.

Cress swatted at pesky dragon lights swarming around him. They were different from the ones in The Wilds. Those were tiny, transparent illuminations that winked on and off in the air. These were larger, solid looking creatures with constant glowing bodies that seemed to reflect the rays of the sun. They flew so fast, catching a simple look at them proved nigh impossible.

They entered a part of the forest where old-growth behemoths, thicker than the arm span of six men, reached for the sky. Pushing through a curtain of low-hanging boughs, they entered a small and dark clearing where patches of grass battled to grow among the needle infested ground. Soft forest duff smelling of decomposing needles, moisture, and dirt mixed with pine and rose up to tease her nose with each step she took.

The verdant beauty of the setting became a sharp reminder of how the people of Froy depended on her succeeding. The Wilds, an unforgiving harsh land, didn't compare to this green oasis. Only the strong survived, and she wasn't giving up. Not by the hairs on Mother Asa's chin—the oldest woman of her village. Becca visualized the woman's round face wrinkled like a withered apul.

Sweet Luna, aid me now. Give me strength. A wave of inescapable despair rose, and she stumbled.

As pebbles scattered, Cress glanced back as though

to check on her. She pushed forward. Salty sweat had dried on her skin. The acrid stench of smoke permeated her clothes. Every breath pulled at the raw pain radiating from her hands and face. She would gladly tolerate far worse for those she loved. Worry had been her faithful escort for so long, she could not visualize being without it. Her family and friends depended on her, and thinking of them now, Becca never felt more alone. She must succeed. Failure was unacceptable. Determination worked through her anew.

Becca refused to slow despite her exhaustion. She was a hunter, not a weakling like a male who needed coddling. The wizard would find no cause to complain about her.

A breeze rustled the treetops. Birds trilled to each other, and once a squirrel vented his disapproval with loud squawking of their progress through his part of the forest.

She eyed Wizard Cress's broad back. Wizard or not, no male had ever refused her. She would convince him to travel with her. It was her right.

After all, the natural way of things was for males to obey women.

Chapter Four

Cress recognized his bad mood by the time they arrived at the ancient dragon circle deep in Demit Woods. He shouldn't have invited the warrior woman here. Now, he didn't have anyone to blame except himself. He owed her because she had tried to combat the fire, and duty compelled him to repay her.

Nor did her silence fool him. Her perseverance became evident in the leagues she'd already traveled. If he knew anything about human nature, she bided her time and meant to try to persuade him later.

"We concur. Good observation for a mere human."

Cress moaned at the dragons' voices. Becca peered at him questioningly. He shook his head and headed for the hut, pretending nothing unusual had happened.

"How many times do I have to tell you? Stop reading my thoughts," he demanded in mindspeech, clenching his fists at his sides.

"We were not doing so. Some thoughts are more obvious than others by your expression or actions. Do not fault us when your human face reveals your mind."

"Well, I don't like it."

"Whether you like or not doesn't matter. We know many things that humans do not."

"Such as?" he had to ask like a fuzzy-cheeked boy.

"How to be patient, for one. If you'd like, we can teach you much."

"I've taught you a few things, too. One being, intruding on a person's private thoughts is rude. Wait until I grant you permission or ask for your opinion."

"We know you, wizard. It has taken eons for you to admit weakness or request our assistance. You are as stubborn as the female. Meanwhile, we will observe and learn."

"Fine. Who am I, a mere wizard, to try and stop you? Just keep your opinions to yourselves. I'm really not interested," Cress answered. The argument would be impossible to win.

His chest rose with a weary sigh when he stopped before the door to his home. Through a casement window cracked open, the aroma of fresh baked bread and ham stew wafted in the breeze. Inside, pots clanged together. His housekeeper, Salida, would be pleased to see him and he her. He lifted the latch and pushed the door inward. The metal hinges squeaked in protest.

"Come. My housekeeper is a bit gruff, but she is harmless enough," he told Becca, who froze to stare at the circle of giant trees—the dragon circle. He motioned for her to enter, only to have her stand and gawk, her eyes as big as saucers. "Surely you have seen trees before?"

"Of course, but something is here." Her tone contained awe. "I cannot say what. Something I sense."

He nodded toward the door again. This time her bright blue eyes widened at the dozens of symbols adorning the floor—magical symbols, capable of trapping an unwelcome visitor or repelling malicious magic. His three favorites were the large pentagram done in red with the male figure in black, a multicolored ring of circles interwoven in bands, and the interlocking two triangles that formed a star.

He smiled at Becca as they entered. She raised her gaze, and her mouth opened when she found herself inside a tower instead of a hut. High overhead, the sun poured through arched windows that could only be seen out by climbing the winding, circular stairs jutting out from the walls. Nature's design at its finest, most efficient, and potent shape.

Proud of his home, Cress cherished the true strength of his tower. He'd constructed it from all nature offered. Air, land, fire, and sea were woven together in a harmonious way to create natural energy.

"Becca, this is Salida." He introduced a silver-haired woman with deep blue eyes that were smooth pools of calm in her wrinkled face. "Salida, this is Becca."

The warrior woman bowed politely. "Hello, Mother."

A smile rose on Salida's face. "Thank you for the respect, dearie. Be welcome." She turned to Cress. "You put the fire out?"

He gestured toward the warrior woman. "With Becca's help. That's where we met."

"Ah." Salida nodded. "Makes sense. A woman usually spots trouble long before a man. Don't know how you'd manage without us." She winked at Becca before turning to face him again. "Now, make yourself useful. Fetch me a bucket of water. I'll see your guest settled."

Cress knew his housekeeper's gruffness covered a soft heart. He'd learned long ago to keep his lips sealed and follow her instructions without argument.

His mouth lifted in a smile when he turned to Becca. "She believes her years of service gives her the right to bully me all the time."

Salida harrumphed and shot him a look suggesting she put up with far worse, then gasped. "Look at this child's poor hands. We stand around jabbering while she suffers. What a terrible hostess I am. Fie on you, Cress Langois, for not immediately telling me she was hurt when I have salve to fix those burns."

The housekeeper hurried over to the far wall and lifted a ceramic jar off the shelf. Scooping out a citrus smelling mixture with two fingers, she carefully carried it back, keeping the gooey concoction from dripping to the floor. Cress never told her he'd performed an enriching enchantment on the jar because she would have chastised him for trespassing in what she considered her domain.

Salida slathered the viscous mixture on Becca's skin. "Praise the gods, none of your injuries appear third degree. Your skin didn't blister, and you shouldn't scar. You'll feel better in seconds."

"It's not bad. Really," Becca insisted.

"Bad enough. Make haste with that water, Cress. I need to clean her hands, and then this good miss can have a bath. I'll reapply the salve afterwards," Salida instructed him. "And you can clean up, too. The smoke in your clothing is smelling up my house."

Becca pushed her braid back. "I'll help fetch water."

"You'll do no such thing. Not until your hands are healed," the housekeeper said with a determined smile. "Be off with you, Cress."

"Salida?" he heard the warrior woman ask.

"Aye?"

"Does everyone do as you tell them?"

"I should hope, although, there is only Cress and me."

Cress picked up the bucket sitting on the floor near the door and left the warrior woman in Salida's capable hands. A dozen trips later, his housekeeper grunted her satisfaction with his efforts and ordered him to leave to give Becca privacy. He didn't argue.

He stripped off his brown robe to reveal plain leggings and a sleeveless tunic, then walked across the clearing of the dragon circle where a towering Ossa pine climbed several hundred feet into the air. At the base of the tree, a slight depression had formed from the hundreds of times of him sitting in the exact spot. Sinking to the ground, he leaned back against rough bark grooved with criss-cross flakes. On warmer days, the scent of vanilla emanated from the bark to perfume the air.

"I met a woman today," he said without preamble. "She has an air about her. I can't explain it. I haven't met anyone like her in ages. If ever..." His voice trailed off.

A tree branch loaded with tiny pinecones dipped down to touch his shoulders.

As he stroked the long blue-green branch, rust colored pine needles dropped off. He remembered the first time this color change occurred. He had been young, naive. Panic nearly frightened him to death, believing the tree suffered some terrible disease and would die. Eventually, he'd learned the annual browning and dropping of needles was a natural development.

He circled his fingers around the branch. Tiny pinecones were nestled in clusters, reminding him of brown speckled eggs. Hefting them in his palm, he took comfort from their familiar texture and feel.

He eyed the tree. "In some ways she reminds me of you, Trell. Oh, I don't mean she resembles you." Sometimes his sister's exact image blurred, and that squeezed his heart. "You were much shorter. Though there is nothing wrong with that." He chuckled to himself. Trell never considered herself short and always acted amazed, if not slightly miffed, when people pointed out her short stature. Even now, reaching for the light, she wasn't the tallest in the dragon circle, although she might be one of the oldest.

A heavy pinecone hit his shoulder. Picking it up carefully, he avoided the prickly ridges on the end. Had Trell guessed his thoughts? Probably. She'd always been perceptive, a talent all good healers possessed. And, while young, Trell had been one of the best, if not *the* best.

He gestured with palms up. "Becca d'Firn of Froy, that's her name. Her village needs help against pestilence. Her problem is compelling. She is…I find her compelling." The reaction and his confusion turned into a new experience for him. He tilted his chin to look straight into the dark green canopy of boughs. "If a simple spell would work, I would have gladly done so, but I cannot cure. You know I speak the truth. Your healer skills would have been better suited to aid her." He sighed. "Becca wants me to travel with her to her village, to leave you."

The large crown of branches swayed. Sometimes

he swore his sister's voice mingled in the swishing, rustling branches, but the words were always out of range.

"I must do what I must," he said, still staring up. For some reason he needed to explain his rationale. "Twice this season fast moving blazes scorched the woods. There hasn't been enough rain. If anything happened to you while I was away…I can't take the chance. I simply can't. You have suffered enough."

All because of him…Cursed because of a prank gone disastrously wrong, she suffered the consequences.

"Fear not for your kinswoman's safety, human. We will protect her." Dragon voices rose together in mindspeech. Several tiny glimmering dragons flitted before him. The rapid beating of their wings filled the air.

"What if a firestorm developed in the enchanted circle?" Cress answered aloud for Trell's sake. The dragons heard him, but his sister could not hear mindspeech. "You cannot perform magic. At least not the kind capable of putting out a wildfire."

"We control the Fire element," the dragons said. *"Your kindred are safe with us."*

He took a deep breath. His favorite element was air. He preferred to work with it more than any other type of magic. "I appreciate the offer, my friends. I do, but I can't abandon Trell."

"The female warrior appeals to us. We sense something about her that cannot be explained."

"Fine. Talk to Becca yourself. I'm sure she'd be thrilled to learn of your existence. Just leave me alone."

"It would be unwise to reveal ourselves." Golden

25

dragons zoomed in and out around the large Ossa, their tiny wings beating so fast they were barely visible.

"Can't you be adventurous without involving me?" Cress asked.

A solitary dragon settled on his shoulder. Slight pin pricks of tiny claws dug into his flesh when the creature cocked its head to stare at him. Golden scales went from variegations of light to dark. He stared into luminous red eyes. Over the ages, he'd submitted to the dragons' whims. This time he refused to give in.

"What about you, Torka?" he asked the creature on his shoulder. "You're clever. What say you?" The dragon remained silent. "If you are unwilling to go alone, ask Parr to accompany you. Your mate is usually up for a little adventure. Approach the warrior woman yourself."

"Colony will rules. We must consider the safety of all."

Cress shrugged. "I regret Becca's difficulty. There is nothing I can do. My own family comes first."

Branches creaked overhead. It sounded like someone wept, and his heart broke.

Chapter Five

Becca woke early, another consequence since leaving home. In Froy, women hunted game at night, so she'd always slept late. A woodpecker's exotic call broke the morning's silence, followed by the chatter of other birds.

The image of the wizard without his robe filled her head. His muscular arms and long legs were worthy of countless, pleasant dreams.

Her sleeping quarters were the finest she'd ever enjoyed. She rolled over in the soft ticking. That night she'd noticed the raised bed contained room for storage beneath, a far more comfortable place than her sleeping furs in Froy. A thick carpet of checks and squares in vibrant reds, black, and lighter yellows and blues covered the floor. Also, far more sophisticated than what waited for her at home.

Sunlight pierced the room from a window, giving her an unobstructed view of the woods. Sitting up, she automatically searched for her bow. She spotted it propped against the wall within easy reach, along with her oil-skinned travel bags. Grasping the weapon, she stroked the smooth wood along the long edge. Out of habit, she drew back the string and tested its readiness. Only inferior hunters weren't vigilant with their bows. Muscles strained against the weight of the draw. She trusted in her skill, strength, and hours of practice to hit her target every time she released an arrow.

Setting the bow down, she inspected her hands. The blotchiness had disappeared. She flexed her fingers. No stinging made her wince. No swelling affected her fingers.

She tamped down growing appreciation as she slipped on her buckskin leggings and tunic, only to realize someone, more likely Salida, had restored them to their buttery softness. She should have predicted the thoughtfulness—the older woman's eyes were the same blue as her mother's.

The reminder stabbed at her heart. Those left in Froy depended on her, and she refused to dwell on the possibility that they might be sick or dying. She had not traveled all this way to take no for an answer from a male. She couldn't. Wouldn't.

Determination welled up in her as she braided her hair into a thick rope and slung her bow and quiver over her shoulder. Emerging from the bedroom, she found herself in a wide hallway. Moisture in the air and a deep rumble led Becca to believe moving water existed inside. Nothing would surprise her in the amazing structure. Loud sloshing barely covered the clanks and clicks that accompanied the sound of machinery.

Her simple hut in Froy, set along the cycles of the moon, seemed primitive compared to the wizard's home. Hers contained a cooking pit in the center where smoke escaped through the hole in the roof.

Following her nose, Becca entered a sun-flooded cooking chamber. All around the room carefully positioned crystals collected the light to add brightness inside.

"Good morning, Salida. If that's bacon, it smells

delicious."

The housekeeper looked up and smiled. "It is. Sit down, dearie, and I'll fix you a plate. How do you feel? Your hands?"

Becca lifted her arms to show how well she'd healed. "I could wrestle a bear this morning with no ill effects."

"You slept well, then?" The housekeeper set a plate heaped with a rasher of bacon, steaming eggs, cheese, and rough black bread on table.

Becca settled into the closest chair and propped her weapons against the table. She hadn't seen such fare in ages, and her belly responded with a growl. "Wonderfully. Although I don't remember taking to my bed."

"You fell asleep out here. You were exhausted from your ordeal. Cress carried you to your room."

Becca paused midway with a spoonful of food. Embarrassment burned her cheeks. Hunters weren't conveyed to bed like a child. She narrowed her eyes. How dare the male treat her so?

"Where is the wizard now?"

"Outside. He usually takes a walk in the morning."

"I'll join him after I've eaten," she said. "Unless there is something I can do you for all the kindness you've shown me?"

Salida ladled water from a bucket. "Go, dearie. Work is what keeps me happy."

A few minutes later, her belly full, Becca went outdoors. The grove of three-hundred-foot evergreens looked natural enough, but since a wizard made his home here, qualms arose.

She looked around. Dappled sunlight fell on the

thatched-roof hut and nearby outbuildings. From this vantage, the structure did, indeed, give no clue to the amazing tower hidden within.

A branch snapped. She turned toward the sound, pleased to see Wizard Cress sitting at the base of a giant Ossa pine talking to someone. She pushed her disappointment away at seeing the wizard in his robe, covering up his well-defined arms.

No individual could be seen, yet the trace of a young woman's voice drifted on the currents.

"Hello." She looked around. "May I join you?"

The wizard scrambled to his feet. "Of course. Sit. You are looking recovered."

She blinked in surprise. For a man to comment on a hunter's welfare sounded unfamiliar to her ears. "You know the purpose of my mission, but I haven't made a formal request. Let me rectify the situation." The wizard frowned, but she pressed on. "Come with me. Save the people of my village."

"I can't leave."

Her heart beat faster. She tamped down a burst of anger. In Froy, males obeyed a woman's order immediately. She had to sway the impudent wizard's mind for her family. For her friends. For Froy. "Surely a powerful wizard can do whatever he desires."

"It's not that simple, Becca," he said, his tone grave. "I cannot leave the forest. I am already protecting my sister. Unguarded, her life is in danger."

"One for so many? My people are dying."

"I can't keep them from dying."

She gritted her teeth and shoved her face in front of his. "Shall I tell you about little Reba? She's five seasons old with bright red hair. Her laughter is like a bubbling spring, and she runs like the wind for one so small." Her voice cracked with emotion, but nothing would stop her. "Or, do you prefer to learn about Adilas, a young woman carrying her first child? Or Gette, my younger sister? Then there's Hallie, Nella, Epper, Kasha, Romy. The list goes on and on. They will all suffer unimaginable agony if—"

"Stop!" He held up his hands, revealing muscular forearms when his sleeves fell to his elbows. "I'm sorry, Becca. Magic cannot heal."

"You don't have to heal the sick. Use your magic to find the cause of the plague and end it," she argued when an awful sense of dread coiled around her chest and squeezed. "You cannot deny my people or let them die."

He sighed. A warm gust blew between them. "My sister, Trell…"

Becca called upon the same well of patience she used when hunting to push aside her anger and focus on her duty. "How can I help? I do not see her. Where is she?"

Cress looked away as though unable to face her scrutiny. "You cannot speak to her. There is nothing you can do."

She inhaled a deep breath. The odor of forest fire smoke hung heavy in the air, a mordant reminder of the wizard's power. "I am no diplomat, nor do I profess to understand the ways of wizards. I only know Froy." She swallowed the lump developing in her throat. "Many would call this an impasse. Allow me to begin anew."

Cress's brows lowered over his eyes and he grumbled, "Begin what?"

"Negotiations. It is common between two factions when they find themselves at odds with each other," she answered him. "I refuse to quit in the face of a little opposition."

He shook his head. A glimmer in his hazel eyes seemed to defy her. "I cannot grant your request. When I offered to tend your injuries, it was as thanks for attempting to save the woods, nothing more."

"Caring about your sister's welfare is an honorable trait, and I fully empathize with your concern." She pulled the leather bag looped on her belt and loosened the ties. Dozens of brilliant, sparkling jewels poured out into her palm, some tumbling to the ground like colorful stars. "Allow me to offer you these. Take them. They're yours. Consider them partial payment for your services. I know wizards value natural gemstones above those conjured with magic. Many more await you in Froy."

Glowing dragonflies appeared out of nowhere and buzzed excitedly. Swift and precise in their aerial skill, some landed on the fallen gemstones; others hovered so close the air stirred with the movement of their wings. The insects acted like bees, and the jewels a heady pollen.

Cress's visage turned grim, his gaze darkening. "I cannot be bought like a ram at market. Going with you is out of the question. I do not make this decision impetuously. Please, Becca, understand."

"No!" She grabbed his wrist. A shock of longing rushed up her arm when she stared into his bottomless eyes. The sensation grew so strong he must have felt it, too.

He peeled her fingers off his arm and stormed

away, his long robe flapping between his legs.

The bag of jewels tumbled from her hand and onto the ground as though it contained nothing but worthless glass.

She despised not being in a position of authority.

Without the wizard, all hope was lost. Innocent people depended on her. Fear brushed across her nerves like poison nettles and she winced in pain.

At home, if this type of problem arose, she would have slipped away and sought the sanctuary of her cave high up the spear of limestone. Her special hideout. Cool in summer, dry in winter, it was the perfect place to find peace and quiet. She always felt an odd, compelling sensation when in the cavern. Since seeking a respite inside her cave was out of the question, she needed to think of another way to bring the wizard to her side.

Before time ran out.

Chapter Six

Cress stomped to the edge of the dragon circle, his temper raging as he stepped two feet beyond the perimeter—an act of defiance, for within the circle time stood still. He'd lived there for nearly a thousand years and vowed to continue for another thousand.

Or, for eternity to save Trell.

He refused to accept the mantle of responsibility for more people.

Then why did the pain of Becca's disappointment cut him so deeply? She'd turned her head away, but not before he glimpsed misery flash across her face.

At least, the Guardians granted him some privacy. They'd remained behind with the gemstones, their desire for treasure stronger than their craving to torment him.

He kicked fallen pine branches in frustration. Cress knew he must remain aloof—if not outright cruel to Becca—something he found abhorrent. He told himself he would have to take a firm hand to dissuade the warrior woman.

Whirr. Thwack! Whirr. Thwack! Whirr. Thwack!

Cress frowned at the unfamiliar noise. Silence fell upon the forest like a heavy drape trying to smother the life out of the woods.

Whirr. Thwack!

A flock of crows took flight from a tall evergreen

as if frightened. They flew to a different tree.

A pang of urgency jabbed at him. He whirled and spurred his feet back inside the border. Becca stood with her bow in hand and poised with an arrow nocked. Fear turned his blood cold. She freed the shaft and it raced toward its goal high in the tree. A dull thud sounded when the arrow struck against solid wood. The tree shuddered from the impact, and the arrow tumbled earthward to clatter where two more lay on the ground at the tree's base.

He'd told Becca he couldn't leave because of his sister, but he hadn't confided that Trell was a tree. The same Ossa Becca now aimed at.

With a gasp, he yelled in desperation, "Stop!"

Too late. Her arrow flew fast and straight at a knot high on Trell's trunk.

He blinked, his lips moving, chanting an incantation.

Arrow heed my call.

Arrow drop.

Arrow fall.

In an instant, the deadly shaft slowed then drifted harmlessly to the ground. Cress stomped forward, quivering in anger. "By the gods, what do you think you're doing?"

Becca turned toward him, her face flushed with confusion. "I am target practicing. It helps me think and is calming. That arrow would have hit dead center. It's very hard to strike something shooting straight up. That's why those knots make perfect popinjays."

"You dare shoot birds within the ancient circle?" he asked, incredulous.

"A popinjay is a wooden parrot. Normally, it sits

atop a pole, and the objective is to get close enough to knock its feathers off. Or, if you're really lucky, actually knock the bird off the pole."

"This is a sacred place. You have no right."

Her backbone stiffened. "I'm not hurting anything."

"Not yet," he countered.

"For your information, Wizard Cress, archers stand directly under the popinjay, and arrows tend to fall straight back to the ground." She walked to where three or four arrows littered the ground. She scooped them up and extended her arm for him to better see what she held. "For that reason, arrows in this game have flat ends. They are harmless. I have steel and stone arrow heads, too."

"Still," he said, the tips of his ears warming with embarrassment, he created a stipulation on the spot, "weapons are not drawn within the dragon circle. It is forbidden."

"So you say."

Cress knotted his fists. The warrior woman challenged him at every turn. He could hardly wait to see her gone. "That's right! Because I say so. Go home. Practice in Froy. It would be best for all."

She slipped her bow over her shoulder. "I'll be happy to return home as soon as you agree to accompany me."

After only a single day Becca already turned his life upside down. "Begone!"

He pointed toward the forest and waited for Becca to leave. With a huff, she stormed away.

Alone again, he sank to his favorite spot at the base of Trell. "You see what I have to put up with. She's impossible. I swear she knew I thought her target practice was putting you in danger."

A branch, heavy with pinecones, creaked downward. He expected the needles to play with his long hair, but they didn't. Instead, the branch nudged his back with the lightest touch as though to say "go".

"I know. I know," he said. "I understand you wouldn't care if I traveled with her. But my life is dedicated to freeing you."

Chapter Seven

Becca left the tree grove with a spring in her step. Cress's reaction had been predicable—protective outrage—and proved her assumption about the Ossa pine correct. Strange as it seemed, the tree held an important place for him.

Her short-lived triumph soured with her next thought. What if she'd antagonized the wizard? In her limited experience, few males appreciated being reminded of obligations. She doubted he would prove any different.

Then again, if he did agree to aid Froy, she would be indebted to him. The thought repulsed her until determination filled her. No, desperation quickly took over. She was running out of ideas, and she feared what came next.

After half a day of searching for answers and uncovering none in the woods, she returned to the wizard's hut.

Salida glanced at her with a huge smile. "Sit your pretty self down, dearie. It's nice to have a woman visit. You remind me of a friend I once knew."

"Do not many visit here?"

"Most fear this place. They consider it haunted. Cress ventures out to acquire necessities that we need." The housekeeper stepped to the trestle table. "I'll fix you a plate of biscuits and honey. I assume you found

Cress."

Becca smiled. "He seems to have a knack for finding me. I was target practicing."

"That's nice," the housekeeper murmured, burying her hands into a bowl of dough. "I'm in the middle of fixing meat pie. Would you like to help?"

"I would be honored, but my cooking skills are very limited. In my village, I am leader of the hunters. Males do most of the cooking."

"Different customs for different folks, I say." Salida shrugged. "We're having a visitor for dinner tonight."

Becca raised her eyebrows. "Who comes?"

The housekeeper laughed. "A no-account, know-it-all wizard named Einer."

"What magic does he perform?"

"What do you mean, dearie? Magic is magic. It's what makes 'em wizards. They're masters of the realm where reality ends and illusion begins."

"I know little of magic and wizardry. The Wilds has none."

The older woman's white brows rose. "No magic?"

Becca shook her head. "None."

Salida nodded toward a thick-billed raven sitting on the windowsill. "Einer sent a message via his usual courier. He likes to show off, I'm afraid, and the birdie is his way of saying he'll want a meal. He's trained his pet to remain until I've fed the nasty creature."

Becca touched the opalescent moonstone draped around her neck. Every Froyan woman wore a similar amulet in honor of the Goddess Luna, and every night she prayed for assistance. Her goddess must be hard of hearing, for none came…

Until now.

Becca stared at the pitch-black raven. If Wizard Cress refused to accompany her, maybe the owner of this bird would. The inspiration kindled a volley of optimism within her. "He must be highly skilled to teach a raven to do his bidding."

"Bah!" The housekeeper slapped the ball of dough down on the table. A puff of flour exploded into the air. "He doesn't hold a thimble to Cress. All wizards share certain commonalities, but there are good ones and not so good ones. Stay long enough, Becca, and you'll see for yourself what I am talking about."

Becca swallowed the barrage of questions forming on the tip of her tongue. Perhaps one or two well-chosen ones better suited her purposes. "Is his family near? Where does he hail from?"

Salida rolled the dough flat and thin, lifted it deftly into a deep cast-iron pan, dumped the bubbling mixture from the hearth into it, and pinched the crust's edges. "You might say we're his family."

A vague answer, and Becca declined to press her luck by seeking clarification. She took her questioning in a different direction. "Why does Wizard Cress always sit beneath that Ossa pine?"

"Ask him yourself, dearie."

"I did," she admitted. "I mean...sort of. I don't think he wants to tell me."

Sympathy spawned furrows on the older woman's aged face. "He asked me not to tell you either."

A pang of frustration stabbed at Becca. "If you can't tell me and he won't, how am I to learn what's going on?"

The housekeeper left the table and returned with a

pot of tea and an earthenware plate containing biscuits slathered with butter and heaped with honey. "Why is it important to you?"

"I haven't time to waste," she answered. "I seek his assistance. The lives of many people are at stake."

"Your village," Salida said, sinking into the chair next to her. "I know, dearie. Cress explained the situation to me this morning. Take heart. He's a man, you see, and sometimes they need a bit of coaxing."

"Coaxing? In Froy, males dare not disobey."

Salida shrugged a plump shoulder, then tittered like a young girl. "I'll tell you one thing if I can have your promise."

The housekeeper's tone held a conspiratorial tone. Becca leaned forward. "You have my pledge."

The older woman raised her hand. White flour outlined three of her fingernails. "A word of caution."

"About what?" Becca picked up a biscuit still warm from the oven. She cut it in half and heaped a dollop of honey that oozed over the sides before taking a bite. Her one weakness was a sweet tooth.

"You would be wise to cease teasing him," Salida said. "I may be prejudiced about his abilities, but Cress wields vast power. He is not someone to toy with."

Becca smiled, but the inside of her mind seethed. "Why not?"

"His calm surface is an illusion. He worries much beneath it," the housekeeper explained. "He grieves to naysay your request."

The response snaked right to Becca's heart. It left her filled with hope and despair yet wondering at the same time what to do next.

"He refused me for no good reason," she replied,

realizing she would beg for help. "Please…If you possess any sway over him, talk to him. Urge him to accept."

Salida pointed at Becca's chest with a biscuit in her hand. "I've been watching him. He looks at you." The housekeeper's expression brightened. "Keep working on him—you might gain his cooperation."

"Really?"

Salida took a bite, chewed, then swallowed. "That's what I see, but don't tell him I said so. He'd have my head."

"I'll not utter a word." Becca gave her promise and meant it with all her heart. A hunter didn't break their word.

She excused herself and went outside with no specific destination in mind. Pinecones littered the ground. In spots, she walked on bare land. In other places, the long needles were so thick and abundant that her steps sank into a mushy loam.

Everywhere sweet pine with the hint of vanilla freshened the air.

She worked her way around the grove, sensing a prickling of ancient magic. Tranquility dwelled within the dragon circle, like her cave—a place of contentment and balance that always filled her with serenity.

Walking along, she realized this place made her happy, but staying remained out of the question. She would have to head back to Froy before the first snows came. Duty, deeply ingrained in her, could not be set aside for her own desires.

She stopped in her tracks at the sound of voices.

Cress talked with someone again—a woman. The same one? His sister? His deep voice sounded troubled, hers soft and distant.

Becca peeked through tree limbs, hoping to catch a glimpse of the shadowy woman. What she saw ended up being stranger yet. An Ossa branch dipped close to the wizard's head with no breeze in the air to cause the action.

A lump stuck in her throat when Cress lifted his hand and his fingers played with the tree's long needles. "What am I going to do with her, Trell?" he asked. "She has spirit, and I admire her, but she asks the impossible."

"*Not impossible. You just fear making a mistake.*"

The words, part husky whisper and part gentle wind, lured Becca to emerge from hiding. A strong sense of approval emanated from the tree.

"This is truly a magical place when trees can talk," she found herself saying.

"*You can hear me? No one ever has. I'd given up hope.*"

The strange voice stopped Becca in her tracks. "You really are a talking tree."

Wind rustled through evergreen boughs like a giggle.

Cress leapt to his feet, a frown twisting his handsome face. "What are you saying?"

She ignored his disapproval and sat on the ground, pulling her knees up and wrapping her arms around them. She quietly took in the glen. "I am talking to the tree. I heard you…and her."

The air around the Ossa sang to Becca. A sad song, one of loneliness and grief, but within the rustlings, she clearly heard, "*Forgive him.*"

"I just heard her voice again. Can you not hear

43

her?"

His lips tightened, like a man forced to obey an order he found objectionable but had no other choice. "You heard someone? Tell me precisely what you heard?" he demanded in a choked voice.

"A woman's voice. She said, 'Forgive him.' I am assuming she meant you."

"Are you certain you heard a voice?"

"Very," Becca told him. She'd heard voices in her cave and always assumed her imagination did it to keep her company, but she wasn't in a cave now. Wasn't alone. "Although a talking tree seems farfetched even for a wizard's homeland."

Cress stared at her, wordlessly. In slow degrees, his expression softened, the earlier anger dissipating. A decision was being made behind those twinkling hazel eyes of his.

Did he waver? She could only hope as she turned away.

Chapter Eight

Warm sun blanketed Cress where he settled into the spot vacated by Becca, but inside icy coldness crept through his veins. He hadn't answered her. He didn't know how.

The play of light and dark slicing through the canopy of Trell's boughs undulated in a light breeze. Had Becca really heard Trell? How could the warrior woman accomplish what centuries prevented him from doing—hear his sister? Why her? Why not him?

His mind raced as fast as the tiny wings of the Guardian dragons flying about his head.

"Go after the female human." A dozen voices intruded on his thoughts. *"Inquire about the jewels."*

Cress's mood mellowed. *"I wondered when the subject of gemstones would come up."*

Moving sunlight made the Guardians appear as shimmering fireworks.

"Treasure such as hers has not been seen for centuries. We wish to learn where she found so many," they said, their tiny red eyes aflame. *"You must learn more. It is vital you comply."*

"Do your own dirty work," he answered.

"You disappoint us, wizard."

"You cannot play on my sympathies."

"We wish verification. That much variety of gemstones in one place is most unusual."

"You're not fooling me," he said. *"You want those gems. All dragons desire caches of treasure."*

"We are Guardians of Secrets. Knowledge is our most valuable treasure. Not baubles. Do you doubt us?"

"Doubt? Most certainly. You're dragons," he shot at his tormentors.

Guardians buzzed with anger at his resistance. *"A sacred place exists. Among the jewels of Feldsvelt the greatest treasure exists—our lost kindred."*

"And you want my help to find this treasure?"

"He agrees," boasted the voice of Parr, one of the bolder dragons, as his position of mate to their dragoness leader permitted, rose above the others in his head.

"Hold on!" Cress snapped. *"I made no such agreement."*

Swiping his long hair out of his eyes, he wished the pesky creatures left him alone. Had the warrior woman's arrival with a bagful of precious gemstones been mere chance? Maybe the Guardians caused the fire all along. As a test.

Cress shuddered when the sun passed behind a cloud, chilling him. He scanned the sky to discover the tiny dragons gone. Another coincidence?

He rose and stomped across the ground with much to consider. His steps faltered, hearing Salida grumbling inside his home, clearly unhappy about something, and Becca giggling.

The arresting sound of her voice brightened the day. The warrior woman looked far too attractive for his peace of mind. He shook off the unexpected realization, walked inside, and stopped when he the two women suddenly went silent.

"What trouble are you two brewing?" he asked, suspicious.

"That old fool Einer is coming," Salida answered first. "As usual, he times his visit for a meal."

Maybe things would work out after all. An ally against the two women might resolve his dilemma. "Don't begrudge him a hearty meal. It's a long journey from Brenalin, and he knows you're a master at turning simple food into a feast. Besides, we haven't seen him in ages, and he's always good company."

The housekeeper blinked in doubt. "So you say."

Events spiraled out of control within his own home, and Cress willed his pipe full of cherry flavored tobacco into existence. At feeling a slight weight, he dug into his robe's pocket. His fingers curled around the wooden shank and bowl worn smooth from his touch. The chair before the fireplace beckoned him, and he headed there.

He settled before the fire in his comfortable chair and lit his pipe. The tobacco glowed red, and smoke corkscrewed through his lungs. Muscles, long tense, relaxed. He closed his eyes to clear his mind.

In the next instant, the door banged open.

Salida cried out in surprise. Pottery crashed to the floor.

Unworried, for only a friend could traverse his protective symbols, Cress twisted to see the small frame of a man with a shock of white hair and a long white beard standing under the lintel. He wore a multicolored robe that shimmered, the colors increasing in intensity, as though alive. Once seen, one never forgot the amazing robe belonging to Master Wizard Einer of

Brenalin.

A quick check showed Becca standing ready with an arrow fixed in her bow. He signaled her to lower the weapon before addressing the newcomer. "What took you so long?"

"Just in time for dinner, I see." Salida grabbed a broom to sweep the broken shards into a pile.

Einer entered—scurrying on thin legs, his rainbow cape rippling with movement, and tiny silver bells jingling from his staff. "Salida, my beauty." He enveloped her in his arms and smacked loud kisses on her puffy cheeks. "I swear you get prettier every visit."

"Spare me your praise." The housekeeper twisted away in a huff. "You made me break my favorite piece of pottery, old man."

"I see nothing broken, woman."

Salida, eyes narrowing with skepticism, glanced down. Cress followed her gaze to a round platter with deer painted around the rim, perfect and whole.

Cress stole another look at Becca. She stared at his friend with the beginnings of a smile on her lush mouth. The smile floored him—hopeful and tentative at the same time, yet genuine, too.

"Einer," Cress said, "a pleasure to see you."

The older wizard stopped before him and peered into his face. "Salida really likes me, you know. Now, let me take a look at you, boy. You haven't aged a bit. Why, I'd swear you've grown younger."

Boy? Cress grinned, amused. "You've been invited to stay here and not age, too."

"Duties to the king and the prince prohibit me from accepting your offer."

"Mayhaps someday," Cress answered, indicating a

chair. "What brings you this time?"

Einer raised snow-white eyebrows. "Good tidings. I found a reference in an ancient tome which might provide a clue to the spell binding Trell."

"Who is Trell?" Becca spoke up, breaking the momentary silence.

Cress deliberately ignored the warrior woman, eager to hear about Einer's discovery. "What have you found?"

"Trell. Trell is the tree?" Becca repeated as if stunned.

"Trell is my sister," he countered.

Einer glanced at Becca, then returned to him. "First, introduce me to this lovely creature."

Grim realization swelled within Cress. He'd never receive an answer to his question until he complied. "This is Becca d'Firn of Froy from The Wilds."

Surprise passed over Einer's face in a flash. "The Wilds, oh my. An amazing place…or so I've been told. Delighted, good miss."

"An honor to meet you, Master Wizard," Becca replied.

Einer's gaze danced from Becca to Cress. The older man beamed when Salida set a pitcher on the table with a clatter. A sweet, earthy aroma rose from it.

"Tea, woman?" Einer said, eyeing the pitcher with contempt. "You know I prefer a kick in my refreshments."

"Fie on you, old man," Salida snapped.

Einer winked at Becca and patted her hand, a gesture of compassion as well as friendship. Cress couldn't help but snort. So much for the old wizard becoming his ally.

"Becca is a lovely name." Einer tottered to the table and poured tea into cups already on the table. "Is it true what they say about The Wilds?"

The warrior woman cocked her head, her blonde braid falling over her shoulder. "What is that, Master Wizard?"

He waved at her. "Polite as well as pretty, but that title makes me feel aged beyond my years. We're among friends. Call me Einer."

Cress extinguished his pipe and tucked it into his pocket. "Einer...don't encourage her."

The older wizard scowled at him. "Ignore him. Speak freely, Becca. Many contradictory things have been said about The Wilds. Too much to know what to believe. I'm eager to hear what you have to say. There is mysticism about the place."

"At last, a wise human," a quartet of Guardians mindspoke to Cress. *"Heed his words."*

No one except Cress noticed the dragons fluttering beyond the window. He flicked a glance in their direction. *"You're just irked because I won't do your bidding."*

Becca stared at Einer with a puzzled expression on her face. "You want to know about The Wilds? I'm not sure where to begin."

Cress understood her reluctance. He felt as though a full moon shone brightly on him on a dark night, forcing him to see Becca in a new light. Being considered different from others was a trait they shared in common. While nearly every man, woman, and child in Brenalin knew of the dragon circle, none dared to enter. Legends claimed the place haunted, inhabited by monsters and savages. Just like The Wilds.

"Begin wherever you please," Einer encouraged, as if positive the warrior woman trusted him enough to confide in him.

Becca took a chair across from the old wizard and began answering his gentle prodding about her homeland and Froy. She explained the name d'Firn meant daughter of Firn, though that first Firn had long ago died, told him of her family, and herself. Cress wondered if Einer cast a spell on her to speak so freely in front of strangers, for he found himself drawn into the tale of a new land and its people's struggle for survival. Even Salida slowed in her chores to listen.

Outside, the sun traversed the sky.

As she concluded, a shadow fell across Becca's sharp but compelling features. She had endured a terrible ordeal, and his heart ached to help her. He fought the temptation to reach out and rest his hand on her arm as Einer did earlier.

Salida broke the enchantment by bringing a steaming kettle of food topped with a golden-brown crust to the trestle table.

Einer helped himself to the tasty-looking food without waiting for permission. He spooned a mouthful as though a starving man. "Hmmm," he mumbled, smacking his lips, "a bit bland. Could use more salt."

"Ha! Little you know. You're losing your ability to taste." Salida glanced at the others seated around the table. "He says that to vex me. His fondness for my pies grows each year like that waist of his."

Einer scraped his chair back to stand and clasped a hand over his heart. "Your insult crushes me. I'll have you know my waist is as trim as it was in my youth."

"You forget, Einer, I knew you back then," the

housekeeper pointed out. "As I recall, you were a tad on the soft side."

Becca spread her arms. "I know a way to remedy that. Since Wizard Cress refuses to journey to The Wilds, you could join me. The journey is long and strenuous and will toughen you up."

"Me? Oh my. I am honored you think me worthy, but unfortunately, my dear," Einer rambled on, "I'm far too old to travel any great distance."

"Surely age is no impediment for a great wizard such as you," she countered.

Einer dipped low in a bow. "Your flattery makes me wish I were decades younger, but alas I am not."

Cress seized the opportunity. "Sit down, old man. I would hate to see you fall over in your acute dotage."

Laughter erupted around the table.

The sound died, and Cress continued, "Really, you should consider her offer, Einer. She's been badgering me since I met her. If you accept, it would solve my problem. What kind of brother would I be if I didn't remain here to protect Trell? She needs me. I can't leave her."

Einer stroked his long beard several times as he sat back down. "I can see how you'd worry, but I might have a solution."

Becca sat straighter at Einer's announcement. Even Salida stopped working to listen. Cress narrowed his gaze as he suspected he wasn't going to like the old wizard's next words. He waited while Einer scooped a second serving of meat pie onto his plate. The women stared at him as he chewed his food.

The delaying tactic left Cress's enthusiasm waning. "This better be something I want to hear, but I doubt

I'm that fortunate. You might as well spill what's on your mind. You will anyway."

Einer swallowed, his cloudy eyes peering at them. "How well you know me. It is no easy thing I suggest."

"Still, you suggest," Cress pressed.

Einer ate another spoonful. "I do, because my idea has merit. I'm sure Trell won't mind. Remember love never fades, and I would be helping the fair lady and you."

Cress doubted the elderly wizard had a point. "Out with it, Einer. What do you propose?"

"Peace reigns in Brenalin. The king does not need my services at the moment. The prince is busy with his new bride. Let me remain here temporarily while you go off on this mission."

Salida lifted an eyebrow. "I hate to admit it, Cress, but the fellow's got a point. Leaving won't hurt you, and it might do some good."

"What about Trell?" he asked. "She can't leave."

"No, she can't," Salida rebutted, "but she'll be safe when you return. Einer and I will make sure of it."

"I may not be strong enough to travel long distances," Einer seconded, "but my wizardly abilities certainly can protect your sister."

Cress fought to restrain his shock. "Have you two lost your wits? You'll be at each other's throats by nightfall."

A grin of hope stretched across Becca's face. He caught his breath. The sight reminded him of the brilliance of a summer sun.

He hated to dash her hopes and wracked his mind for an easy way to let her down. He almost felt like choking the older couple. Almost.

Chapter Nine

At last, an ally. Becca dreamed of success.

Sweet Luna, let Wizard Cress accept.

She kept her prayer silent and glued her attention to the table covered with plates and platters of food. Never had her appetite disappeared so fast.

Salida stepped forward, glaring at Cress. "Listen to us. We're right, and you know it."

"You can't be serious!" he snapped. "How can either of you suggest such a thing? Trell needs me."

"How do you know?" Einer asked. "Has she spoken to you?"

"No," Cress admitted, "but Becca's heard her."

Einer straightened, his white brows pulling together over his eyes. "Is it true? Trell speaks to you?"

Becca hesitated, debating how much to reveal. These people were strangers. But success of her mission depended upon their cooperation. "Since arriving here I have heard sounds—giggles and a whispered voice. At first, I thought my imagination was playing tricks on me. Then today the words were clear."

"Let's go outside." Einer stood again and reached for his staff. Tiny bells tinkled when he adjusted his stance with his staff. "I want to see this for myself."

Cress tossed down his spoon, making it skitter across the wooden table. "I don't believe this. How can we trust her? She could be making up the whole thing."

"Then why ask me what she said?" Becca demanded.

Cress shook his head. "Your announcement caught me off guard."

Salida stepped forward, the wrinkles on her face deepening. "I raised you and your sister. If someone is using Trell's words, I'll know."

With that declaration, the four stepped into the cool night air. They trekked over to the Ossa and stopped.

Cress flashed Becca a dark look and straightened his posture. He waved toward the Ossa pine, "Prove yourself."

Clouds thinned, and a pale moon broke through. *Sweet Luna*, Becca prayed, *guide me*. A silver beam struck the tree, and Becca believed the sign came from her goddess. Craning her head upward, she stared at the tall pine. A tingling prickle reminded her of when she sat in her cave. So quick did the sensation come and go, she dismissed it.

"Hello, Trell," she said. "Will you speak to me again?"

A deep hush settled on the grove of evergreens.

Wishing for an instantaneous reply, a horrifying thought struck Becca. What if Trell refused to cooperate?

Sweet blessed Luna, what else could she do? Plead? Beg? Pray?

Cress shrugged, a smug I-told-you-so expression on his face as he glanced at Einer and Salida. "You see. Nothing. I told you she lied."

Becca gasped at the insult. "I do not. It takes time."

"So it appears," he said, fumbling in the pockets of his robe, "but how long do you propose we wait? The night grows chilly, and I am weary of this farce."

She would wait for as long as it took. Shifting her weight from one foot to the other, Becca saw Salida and Einer exchange a glance with worried expressions.

The Ossa swayed, and branches dipped to brush Becca's shoulder.

Salida gasped.

"Hello, Becca. What would you have me say?"

Guilt washed over Becca for being dubious. "I'm sorry this happened to you, Trell. Can you tell me something that will convince these people I speak the truth?"

Einer stepped forward. His cape shimmered. Bells jingled. "What does she say?"

Becca cocked her head, listening to the odd voice emanating from high overhead. "Her voice is sad, but she says Cress has a jagged scar on his big toe. Left foot. He received it as a child."

Eyes rounded with surprise, Cress stepped backward. "Salida confided that to you."

"I did no such thing," the housekeeper said.

A pinecone hit his shoulder and bounced to the ground. The tall wizard winced. He flicked a glance at the tree.

"I am repeating your sister's words." Becca paused to listen. "Now, she's saying, 'I blame you not. You have stood watch over me all these years. Do not use my predicament to waste your life.' "

A gray-faced Salida swallowed. "That would be Trell. She always put the welfare of others first. I would bet my life on it."

Cress gawked at his housekeeper. "You believe this wild tale!"

He wasn't alone. Becca had trouble accepting it herself. A talking tree seemed a stretch, even for her. "You once cared for others, too! Remember Nolta. Let that not happen again."

A brief moment of stunned silence held everyone in place, Becca more than anyone else. A presence filled her—young—friendly—determined.

"Who told you about Nolta?" Cress demanded, his tone low and deadly.

Becca's gut tightened. She refused to cower. No male spoke to her in such an authoritative tone. This was a disaster in the making. Bringing a wizard to Froy might be a bad idea. "Trell. I swear."

"It's all right, dearie," Salida said, scowling at Cress.

Cress stepped closer. "Tell me about this communication? How does she speak to you? Explain."

"I can't tell you how it works. When I'm near, I hear her. It's as though a sweet voice drifts among the tree branches and I understand the words."

He snorted. Grumpily. "All I hear is the wind."

"*For shame, brother. Are you worried that I will reveal more of your secrets?*"

Amusement laced the words. The situation called for tact.

"She thinks you're worried that she'll reveal your secrets. But I doubt she will. Something tells me she is just teasing," Becca told the people around her. "And I doubt you will break your word, Wizard Cress, if you agree to come with me."

Cress swept his arm out. "Flattery will not work on me as it does on old fools."

"*Look who's talking! Cress wasn't always this*

way. He used to be a loving, caring person. The first to volunteer when the need arose."

"He's changed," Becca mumbled under her breath.

Branches bent down. *"A true shame. What happened to me is not his fault."*

"What did happen?" she asked.

"Ask Cress."

"What's she saying?" Cress demanded.

"Trell does not blame you," she told him. "She says you should tell me about her."

"It's none of your affair," he said.

Pinecones rained down on Cress.

A muscle jumped in his jaw. "Stop! I will do as you wish."

Becca wasn't sure who he spoke to—her or the tree—but if he explained, she wasn't about to interrupt him.

He stood in a wide stance as though to brace himself. "It was right in this spot, over a thousand years ago, when Bonner O'Fray and I were practicing our magic. We were trying to outdo the other when things escalated," he said in a trancelike voice. "I no longer remember who started the contest. Bonner and I were best friends. I forced a wild lilac bush to bloom. He made a pinecone sprout into a sapling with the snap of his fingers. Then I turned a chunk of granite into carbon and created a diamond. Back and forth we tried to outdo the other. We were both cocky in our youth, confident in our skills. It was a disastrous combination. Tragedy struck when Bonner enchanted Trell. I'll never forget it."

Becca squeezed her eyes shut, trying to visualize the pain these people suffered. Cress let out a deep sigh before reciting a spell:

Sacrifice your sister
Sacrifice not her life
Sacrifice your blood
Sacrifice not your pride

"He created a fast-moving vapor to seek her out. The instant it found Trell, she screamed, her face blanched, her eyes widened in fear, then life faded from them.

"She struggled as shoots wrapped around her legs. The strange growth hardened on her body, transforming her skin to rough bark. I tried to cast a counter spell but failed. Trell's arms turned into bulky limbs. Her hair swirled and twisted around her head, hardening, thickening, taking on the appearance of branches. My sister had turned into an Ossa pine."

Becca swallowed, her throat dry. How horrible for him to witness that transformation. Defenseless, unable to protect his sister. Then it dawned on her, she'd never heard of a male trying to save a female. She eyed him from under her lashes. Of course, he'd been concerned. In this land, siblings were raised in the same family unit. In that instant, Becca wondered about her own reaction to the man.

"Its very simplicity made the enchantment complex," he added.

Becca refused to lose the opportunity for understanding. "Why would a friend do such a thing?"

Cress spread his hands wide and gazed at all three standing around him. "Bonner probably meant to teach me humility, but nothing can remedy what he did. He actually held a fondness for Trell. I never imagined he would harm her. He cast the enchantment, but I am the cause of its continuation."

"*We loved each other.*"

The faint words made Becca nod her head. She kept the information to herself for the moment. "Why didn't he reverse his spell?" she asked, still puzzled.

Tears formed glistening pools in Cress's hazel eyes, and he wiped them away with a swipe of his hand. "Because he died."

Becca hadn't seen that coming. "How?"

"I killed him," he answered, his voice flat. "Anger made me crazy. We fought, and I hit him. He fell and struck his head on a rock."

Becca's glance shot from him to the elderly couple, then back to him. "That must have been awful for you," she said, even though sympathy had no place in their tentative alliance.

"More for Trell," he answered her. "She was a healer, and even as a tree twisted her branches to reach him. To save him. Now this development. I'm in a real quandary."

"I made a promise, too," Becca replied. "To help my village. To bring you back."

"I must be losing my sanity." He released a heavy sigh. "I gave my word to follow you into The Wilds if Trell spoke to you, and she has. I will fulfill my promise. But I have one condition."

Her fragile hope wavered. "Conditions were not part of our arrangement."

"They are now. If I save your village, you must return and be my translator with Trell until she is freed from the spell."

Becca sputtered with disappointment. He dashed her prospect for happiness.

Leave Froy again? The wizard had the advantage. What choice did she have?

Chapter Ten

The next morning, Becca swept outdoors, toting her traveling pouches, bow, and arrows over her shoulder. Cress led two horses and a pack mule from the barn. She caught herself admiring his long legs in brown leggings and the easy play of his muscles in a sleeveless tunic. They would be alone for weeks. The time together might prove interesting. Maybe even entertaining. The prospect made her smile.

One of the horses nickered a welcome. She walked over and stroked its velvet nose, causing a quick shiver to run through the sleek roan mare. "Which mount is mine?"

The wizard tossed her a bored look. "Take your pick."

"I'll take this one. Mares are more agile and often smarter." She patted the horse, letting the animal become accustomed to her scent and feel. Running her hand over its rump, she tied her traveling pouches in place and lifted the stirrup to undo the buckle.

"What are you doing?" Cress asked, watching her.

"Raising my stirrups. We're traveling in dangerous territory. Hazards exist everywhere—bears in the forest, hunting cats in the mountains, and great water lizards in the swamp. Raising my stirrups allows me to stand higher if I need to shoot in any direction. It's a precaution. I believe in being prepared. My vigilance will keep you safe."

Cress's brow furrowed, and then he tied his bags behind the saddle of the other mount. "You underestimate me, Becca. I can take care of myself. My magic can protect us well enough."

"You use magic. I'll use my bow. It has stood me in good stead all these years."

Becca boosted herself up into the saddle and contemplated the wizard. His irritation came as no surprise. She'd expected as much, if not more from him. He accompanied her against his will and probably sought fault to cancel the journey.

Salida and Einer approached from the hut. Becca had uttered her goodbyes inside, pledging to return after Cress saved her village. She waited for Cress to hug Salida and shake Einer's hand. Her mount whinnied and shied, flicking its ears when a dragon light appeared near its head.

Cress donned his wizard's robe and swung into the saddle with ease. "If I don't return, promise me something."

Einer faced the mounted man. "Anything, boy."

"Train another wizard to take care of Trell." He held up his hand when the older wizard started to protest. "Let me finish. You will not live forever. Not even here. Promise me as long as Trell lives, she will never be alone."

"You have my word," Einer replied.

"Bah!" Salida ridiculed. "You'll be back in no time."

Becca saw Einer squeeze the housekeeper's hand. "Keep well," he said. "Stay alert, and take care of each other."

"Don't forget your promise, my friend," Cress said. "I am counting on you."

Einer laughed. "So, I am a friend again. Earlier, I was old man. I'm happy to be back in your good graces."

Becca cocked her head. A whispy voice filled the ancient grove.

"*Farewell and good luck. Keep safe. I look forward to your return.*"

Becca caught Cress staring at her.

"What is it?" he asked.

Doubt chiseled on his strong, clean-shaven jaw brought her erect in the saddle. Her face grew warm. It happened every time he looked at her. "Trell bids us 'Farewell and good luck.' Do you wish me to say anything to her?"

"I said my goodbyes last night. She knows my feelings. Lead the way."

Becca dug her heels into her horse's ribs, and the mare leapt into a spine-jarring trot. She had a hundred reasons to hurry—all the people of Froy.

Rain began an hour later—one drop, five drops, then too many to count. The drizzle fell in a steady rhythm until every rock, tree, and bit of ground became soaking wet. They rode for hours, hunched over their mounts with chilled and dulled senses, their shoulders rolled forward against the dampness.

Near dusk, she shot a probing glance at Cress. "I wish we had better weather to begin our journey."

The wizard glared at her. "We could turn back. Just give the word."

"And give up? Not on your life. My only regret is magic cannot control the weather. We're going to have to pitch camp and divide the chores," she said. "Can you cook? Mine's not the best."

"Afraid not. Salida packed several loaves of bread, cheese, and dried fruit. Even a pudding of honey and oatmeal, one of my favorites." He licked his lips as though anticipating eating the treat.

She licked her lips as well. "You have a sweet tooth, too?"

"I confess, I do. Salida makes the best treats." He sobered and continued, "I can take care of the animals."

Dismounting, Becca took her bow and quiver in hand. "I will hunt for fresh meat. That'll stretch our supplies. My night vision is excellent, and I'm used to hunting in the dark. Meanwhile, you can set up camp and tend the animals. Sound fair?"

He wiped long strands of wet hair out of his face. "I wish you quick success. I'm starved."

Their routine became set. After a week the clouds parted, and that night, Becca glimpsed a moon Froyans called Luna's Delight. It hung full in a dark sky with sparkling stars. The sight raised her spirits, and she took it as a sign the Goddess guided them.

She crouched beside the campfire to watch tiny flames leap and beat back the darkness. Three rabbits roasted on a spit and crackled when fat dripped into the flames.

Cress settled his long form before the fire.

Wet and tired, Becca felt miserable and huddled closer for warmth. "Tomorrow we abandon the great woods and start climbing the mountain," she informed Cress.

He covered his mouth when he yawned. "You said it took three months to reach Demit Woods. Barring accidents, how long will it take us to reach Froy?"

"Hopefully not as long as it took me to find you. Remember, your location was unknown to me. My route went in circles." Her wet braid clung to her back. "More importantly, summer begins soon, and I worry we will not reach my village in time."

He snorted. "All I can do is focus on learning the cause of this pestilence. If I fail, no cure will be found. Magic is merely knowledge. I am being honest with you. The worst expectation is everyone is dead."

That pulled Becca up short. Her gut twisted. It was one thing for her to worry about friends and family, another for Cress to voice consequences aloud. "I refuse to accept your scenario. The Great Mother shines down on me. She doesn't forget the faithful. I'm confident she will grant us success."

He held up his hands, then wiped them on the sleeve of his robe. "Only a fool refuses to consider the worst possibility or not prepare themselves for it."

Becca fed a piece of wood into the fire. "Let's take one day at a time."

Rising, Cress filled the space before her. "Mayhaps this weather will improve tomorrow."

"Let's hope, although you'll wish for its return soon enough when we reach the swamp. It'll be the most dangerous part of our journey."

"Why dangerous?" he asked, his tone sincere.

"It's a blackwater swamp. We have to cross it and stay alive."

These were the last words they exchanged until the rabbit was thoroughly cooked. Becca sliced off thin strips and passed a portion to Cress.

She rubbed grease off her chin. "I should probably

tell you something of Froy."

He tossed a log on the fire, causing a shower of sparks to race upward. "Talking might make the time go faster, and I'm all for speeding up this journey."

"Froy is governed by a council of twelve wisewomen," she began. "Six of them are elderly and six are of childbearing age. One for each cycle of the moon. That way there is no dissention among the various ages. The Council votes on all major decisions affecting the village." In her mind's eye, the moon's eerie light beamed down through the archway upon the Council's hut.

"What if this Council evenly splits their votes?"

"The leader of hunters breaks all ties. I am that leader."

He leaned forward, bringing with him a nice male scent. "What if someone objects to these decisions?"

"Why would they do that? The Council exists for the benefit of Froy. It takes into account the best interests of all females." She looked at the sky, letting a light mist bathe her face. "No hunter challenges the Council's decisions because they know we are right."

One of the wizard's sable eyebrows rose. "Your entire village follows these rules?"

"Of course. We believe in fairness."

He leaned back, bracing himself with his palms, his long legs out in front of him. "You've mentioned women only. What of the men?"

Confused, Becca felt positive he jested. "What of them?"

"What role do they play in the governing of Froy?"

"None. They are only males."

Chapter Eleven

Cress longed to scoff aloud, yet one look at Becca's cold-eyed expression and he concealed his own reservations that men meekly agreed to such a life. He had no right to tell her how to run her village. "That doesn't explain why they have no say."

"It is simple. Males cannot discuss anything of importance without digressing into an argument or coming to blows," she said, frowning. "The Council handles matters concerning Froy, and the women vote. The males obey."

He uncrossed his legs. "It doesn't make sense to me. I would be bothered if I did not have any say in my life. The men never complain?"

She let out an exasperated sigh. "Aye, some have…"

"Do you blame them? Who willingly lives like that?"

Her chin went up, and conflict narrowed her blue eyes. "Obeying the Council is our way. The only way."

Again the temptation to dismiss her way of life rose. Then he remembered she'd risked everything to find him. "What have you experienced to view men in a negative light?" he asked, tossing another log onto the night's fire.

She studied him for a long moment, stroking her braid adorned with limp feathers and chipped beads.

"Not all males are bad."

He couldn't help himself. A smile emerged unbidden. "That is good to hear. I did not mean to challenge your way of life. I meant no offense."

"None taken. But mayhap now I can ask a question."

He saw no harm in answering. "Certainly, and I promise to respond to your satisfaction, if possible."

She leaned forward. "I want to know how you will battle the plague. Will you weave a protective spell to aid us?"

"Becca, I don't know what I'll do. Or if anything will make a difference." Magic was familiar ground despite his answer. "What you have asked might be unachievable, but I have a few ideas."

A smile brightened her face. "Such as?"

He liked seeing her smile. "It's too soon to say. Whatever I say now is pure speculation. It would only raise your hopes. I agreed to come with you because of my sister. I promised to try. I didn't promise to succeed."

Poor Becca. At his words, a grim line tightened around her mouth. He knew she wanted a guarantee, and that he could not deliver.

Their meal finished, they fell back into their normal routine of cleaning up, tending their mounts, and bedding down for the night.

She had no inkling of how magic worked, and he had no intention of telling her. Wizards were always in contact with the environment around them. In fact, he hadn't been totally truthful with her. He'd caused the storm to constantly drench them in hopes she would give up, but she surprised him with her stubborn resolve. Now, his manipulation seemed no better than this council of wisewomen. He hated to admit the truth.

Becca curled on her bedroll with her back to the glowing coals of the dying fire. Within moments her even breathing seemed in sync with the soft crackling of the fire.

Sleep eluded him.

He waved his hand and muttered a spell reversal. Tiny golden dragons soared into the night. With their permission, he had placed an invisibility spell on the two dozen Guardians traveling with them. Dragons were immune to human sorcery unless they agreed. The secrecy protected them and stopped the flow of questions their presence might cause. He'd seen Becca staring at them the day they met and suspected her sharp mind might wonder if the creatures followed them.

The mule hew-hawed and the horses nickered. Sensing the dragons, the domesticated animals grew nervous. The Guardians could cause harm, if they so desired.

"So, how do you like travel so far?" he asked through mindspeech in case Becca awoke and overheard him.

"How long will this journey take?" they asked. *"We are eager to find these new lands."*

"We have leagues to travel before we reach our destination." Though ancient creatures, at times the dragons acted very childlike. *"Return home, if you wish."*

"Human!" dragons gasped in a collective voice. *"Do not assume to dissuade us. Never. We will comment, but you'll hear no complaint from us."*

Accustomed to their combined voices acting as a single entity, Cress shrugged. *"Why come along, anyway? This quest does not concern you."*

"Why, indeed? We value knowledge and new experiences. It has been eons since such an opportunity has arisen. We are the Guardians of Secrets; yet we know little of the world outside the ancient circle. Do not begrudge us this chance."

It made sense. Still, Cress worried. *"Be careful Becca doesn't see you."*

"She has already noticed us," a cacophony of voices drowned out his thoughts. *"We wish for you to inform her of dragon history."*

Scratching his head, Cress wondered what tricks the tiny dragons played. They never did anything without a good reason. *"Is that wise? I thought you feared discovery by humans. If seen, they would seek you out and attempt to destroy you as they did others of your brethren."*

"Foolish human! Not all your kind. Only Becca. We sense a good heart and wise mind is within her. We like her." Dragons darted back and forth among the trees and campsite, their bodies resembling sparks escaping the fire. *"Dragon tales are worthy of being repeated. Begin at the beginning."*

He shook his head. *"If I relay your past, she'll either think I'm crazy or she'll figure out you are real."*

"Think on it. Consider the idea." A dragon flew over Becca's slender, sleeping form, its red eyes aglow. *"When have we asked a boon?"*

Cress took a deep breath and scanned the campsite. *"Let's say I'm the suspicious sort. Your motives deserve questioning."*

"For shame, wizard. You judge us unfairly. We ask little."

"I don't know. I wish I had a better feeling about this."

"Do it."

The urgency in their mindspeech elicited a frown. Glowing creatures congregated in front of him, waiting for his answer. *"No, I'll not act rash. However, I will take your suggestion under consideration."*

"Fair enough." Several dragons clicked their teeth and offered up toothy grins. *"We know it's impossible to tell a human what to do. You require time. This is an important decision. We will not pressure you."*

Cress chuckled low and deeply. Gentle persuasion seemed a new tactic for dragons. This had definitely turned into a day and night of surprises. First learning women ran Becca's village, then Guardians wanting him to reveal their past to her.

"I can only hope. I remember a time…"

Chapter Twelve

The next day they rode north. Becca took in the lay of the land as it changed, collecting her bearings. The thick forest thinned. Flat land disappeared, replaced with gentle foothills. She knew what to expect on their journey—hardship and danger.

"We've pressed through the woods. The easy part is behind us," she announced. "Are you ready to tackle the high peaks?"

"I'm in your capable hands," Cress answered.

What did the wizard mean? Becca mulled over his words as they made their way up steeper terrain. He appeared to trust her abilities as a hunter. It was unexpected praise, indeed.

"I wish you had thought that when I first met you."

"Circumstances changed. I didn't know you well enough then," he said, flashing her a disarming smile.

Becca's fast hold on her emotions kept her from revealing surprise. *And you do now?* she wanted to ask. She studied the ground, hoping her silence would prompt him to elaborate.

"I made a mistake."

He nudged his horse alongside hers, only to be forced back as the game trail narrowed when it ascended sharply. Hooves scattered loose rocks. The climb took them up a near vertical cliff. One misstep or slip and all was lost. A chill rippled down Becca's spine. An odd moodiness pressed down on her.

The mule, its lead rope tied to her saddle, slowed when it kept slipping in the decomposing granite. Mules were intelligent creatures known for surefootedness and the only males Becca placed any faith in.

Her mare nickered. Every time she urged her mount forward, the short-legged mule dug his hooves into the ground, living up to his stubborn reputation.

Something spooked the animal. A hunting cat? She glanced at the sheer rock. No place existed for such a creature to ambush them. Whatever disturbed the mule slowed her progress, and that irritated her.

The unmistakable sound of gravel pinging off the mountain side momentarily preceded the pack animal's tether cutting across her thigh, pinning her to the saddle. She tried to make sense of the setback an instant before she realized the mule had lost its footing.

No! No! No!

The mule dragged her horse backward. She dug her heels into the mare's sides, urging it forward.

Braying, the mule scrambled for a foothold, but with each step, hooves slipped closer and closer to the edge and a deadly drop.

Becca refused to panic even as her heart thumped against her chest. She wondered if she had only minutes to live. The rope on her leg trapped her in the saddle. Praying furiously to Luna, she stretched to reach the knife tucked into her boot. She needed to cut herself free. Or be pulled over the edge, if the mule failed to regain his footing.

Her fingers brushed the leather top. So close. So far. This couldn't be happening to her. Not now. She didn't have much time.

Come on. Come on, she urged in desperation.

Coarse rope bit deeper into flesh and muscle. Leaping was out of the question. She could not bear to think of Froy, her family and friends. If she did not escape, she would die.

"Becca." Cress cried out her name in a guttural roar.

Another jerk on the tether and she looked over her shoulder at the mule's front legs flaying against the cliff's edge, sharp hooves striking rock with loud clicks. Over the din, came Cress's voice, a low murmur of hope.

In slow degrees, the pressure on her thigh eased. Hope surged through her limbs. The wizard had cast a spell, and magic lifted the mule back onto the trail. A quiver ran over the animal's hide.

She didn't know who had been more shaken—the mule, Cress, or her. Twice now he'd performed magic and saved her.

"Thank you. That was amazing," she said, a quiver curling through her. "Can all wizards perform magic like you? Or do wizards have limits?"

"Everyone has limits. Even me."

His meekness amazed her. "But you saved me. Twice."

He shrugged off the praise. His easy acceptance confused her. Males of her village would have boasted of their deed, strutted around their village with their chests puffed out. It seemed strange that he didn't swell up with pride.

Hours later, they breached the top ridge where the land leveled off. Snow lay in patches of protected shadows. Massive boulders dotted the landscape, and sun-warmed evergreens scented the air with a clean and fresh smell. Trees were twisted and stunted from the weight of continuous snowstorms throughout the winter. Tracks in the melting snow revealed animals had stopped at a shallow pool to quench their thirst.

"We'll camp here for the night," Becca said, dismounting. She felt exhausted. Surely, she suffered from side effects of the near fatal fall. "The animals are weary, and their hooves need to be picked before we start out again. I'll start a fire."

Cress nodded his accord. Soon she heard the jingle of equipment as he tended the horses and mule.

"You look tired," he said when finished.

Her defenses dropped at his concern. "That's because I am. I nearly died back there. I did little, but the event took a lot out of me."

"We could stay here for a few days and let you rest. There's enough water and plenty of forage for the horses and mule," he said as night snuck up on them.

She yawned. "While tempting, I'll rest when we reach Froy." She glanced around the flat area. "Does this place have a name?"

"I doubt it. It's just a pass. Although these mountains are called Dragon's Teeth."

She looked at the summit soaring above them. White snow covered each peak, accenting their sharpness. "Somehow that seems appropriate, but this pass is too beautiful not to have a name."

He tossed a branch onto the fire. "Give it one then?"

"Me?" She spun from Cress to catch the last rays of the sun turning the tall peaks a vibrant orange and yellow. In her village, decisions were made by majority rule. By letting her decide, the wizard granted her a special honor. "Are you serious?"

"Why not? You have as much right as anyone who has traveled them. You nearly died getting here. Who better than you to give it a name?"

"It's so quiet here. Almost like a dream." She wasn't exaggerating. "How about Dream Pass?"

He looked around, smiling. "Dream Pass. I like that. It does feel like a different world up here, full of peace and quiet and tranquility." His voice dipped low, as if speaking in a normal tone would be profane.

She fingered the ends of her braid. The chipped beads and feathers were dull and limp. She should discard the feathers and keep the beads. Maine, her favorite lover, had gifted her with them. After mating, if satisfied, a hunter braided them in their hair to let others know she'd spent the night with the male. No mistaking the language of the beads. Beads did not exaggerate or lie. The number spoke for themselves. "I agree," she said aloud, wondering to herself what kind of beads the wizard would offer.

That night, warm and cozy, she fell into a sound slumber. Waking refreshed and feeling far better than the day before, Becca looked forward to descending the opposite side of Dream Pass.

The snow disappeared. By midday, the season changed, this time for the better. Aspens grew among pine saplings. Tiny flowers sprouted in bushes that would yield sweet, juicy berries in late summer. The river, swollen from melting snow, swirled and raced toward the valley. For miles, the chatter of chipmunks complaining about the invasion of their territory accompanied them.

Oddly, time on the rugged mountain brought a sense of harmony between them. The danger and beauty they'd shared drew them closer together.

Days later, they reached Wisent Flats, named after the great prairie beasts that traveled over the grasslands. Few trees sprouted along the floodplains of streams, suggesting the land received little moisture.

An eagle glided high in the thermals in a circle, while on the prairie a covey of reddish-brown bobwhites fluffed themselves. At their approach, the birds lifted straight up with wing beats, scattering leaves on the light wind. Then they were gone, frightened away.

A subtle vibration that seemed to germinate in the earth and rise into the air made Becca rein to a stop. "Do you hear it?" she asked.

"What?"

"That noise. It's like pounding hail on hard ground."

Cress cocked his head, then nodded. "What is it?"

She smiled. "The wisents."

Saying the name seemed to produce the beasts on the horizon, singly at first, then in twos and threes, trotting down breaks in short strings along narrow trails. Their huge shaggy heads and humped shoulders sprouted new hair, dark and shiny while the rest of their bodies were as nude as badly scalded pigs.

As wisents moved closer, the ground trembled. Their hooves rattled, and low gruntings heralded their approach. The pervasive noise settled in Becca's bones. The main body became a dark cover—an undulating robe stretching from horizon to horizon.

She watched the massive herd break into smaller bunches to feed into the wind, a characteristic of the animals she noticed on her way to find the wizard.

"Come," Becca instructed, and after only a moment's hesitation, Cress hurried to follow her. "Let's get a closer look. I'm in the mood for something other than the rabbit or fish we've been eating. With Luna's blessing, I can pick off a calf."

"Is that wise?"

His concern had merit, and she appreciated how fast he grasped the danger. "I think so. Keep your voice down though. Wisents spook easily, and once a stampede starts, nothing stops them."

Becca prodded her mare closer. She looped her reins around her saddle horn, nocked an arrow in her bow, and sighted down the shaft.

Several dark heads lifted and stared in their direction. Two cows started a low bellowing in their throats; one trotted away, picking up speed.

Cress eyed the herd, then her. "Mayhaps we should put some distance between them and us," he said in a low voice.

"A good suggestion. I'll try later. Caution might be prudent at this time. Something is bothering them. They look ready to spook." Safely away, she patted her mare's neck. "Well, what do you think of the wisents?"

"They were fabulous, simply amazing. Seeing them makes me feel insignificant," he said, smiling broadly.

"I felt the same way the first time I came upon the herd." Something tingled inside her at the joy on his face. "It was a good thing we were down wind. Smell is their keenest sense."

An odd look passed over the wizard's face. "Not keener than a dragon's."

Becca dismounted near huge protruding boulders comprised of pink crystals and glassy quartz. She wondered why the wizard made the comparison. It seemed odd.

"There are no dragons," she said, compelled to answer. "They were wondrous creatures destroyed by greed eons ago."

Cress glanced at her, as if more than curious about her response. "Then you believe they were once real?"

"Why wouldn't I? Dragon tales are the most popular stories among the people of my village. As a child, I spent many nights listening to our storyteller relay tales of magnificent red, blue, and green dragons. Even black and silver ones.

"In Froy, we worship the Goddess Luna. She is our Great Mother and is associated with dragons. Like her, dragons are related to life-giving. They used to bring maternal blessings."

Cress patted his horse's neck. "Few can weave a good yarn. Your storytellers are to be commended. Still, do you accept all myths as truth?"

"A myth led me to you."

"True," he admitted.

Becca closed her eyes as a kernel of obligation formed to clarify her position. "As a wizard you traffic in magic. Salida explained to me wizards are masters of the realm where reality ends and illusion begins. I would expect someone with magical powers to accept strange and complex occurrences easier than most. All myths have their origins in age-old traditions."

He tied his horse to a stake and began loosening

the cinch on his saddle. "What else do you know of dragons?"

She considered his expression for a moment. So handsome. A twinge of desire warmed her insides. "They were wondrous, magical creatures. Once they lived all over the world and had a great, orderly society. Nothing compares to them in power and beauty."

Finished with his horse, he moved on to tend the mule. "Tonight I'll tell you some things about dragons that you probably never imagined in hundreds of years. Would you like that?"

Talking about her beliefs relaxed Becca. She glanced at the hill where they'd ridden, suddenly feeling like smiling. "All my life I've heard the same tales over and over. New ones would be a welcome change."

"Good," he said. "Although the dragon tales I know might fill several evenings."

The sweet scent of grass wafted over the land. Becca always enjoyed the smell, for it reminded her of carefree summer days before the plague turned it into a time of fear.

"Dragons are potent symbols of luck and power. I wish they were still alive. All I have is my amulet to protect me from evil and unseen dangers." Grinning, she pulled her moonstone from her studded leather tunic. It warmed in her hand. "Silver encircles it to help gain those qualities. See."

Chapter Thirteen

Cress growled to himself. Damn Guardians. He should never have listened to them. They planted the seed about discussing dragons, and now he wondered if they had influenced his decision in some way. He wouldn't put it past them.

His gaze went to the moonstone amulet with its mysterious shimmer. Becca clutched his arm, squeezed, and drew him closer. The back of his hand accidently brushed the swell of her breasts. The contact, far too brief, piqued his arousal, and then the sensation vanished with his next breath—replaced with the cold sensation of dread.

No denying the faith and devotion in the warrior woman's voice. Such deep-seated belief deserved the truth, and Cress vowed to tell her of the dragons at the appropriate time.

"Move aside, wizard," dragons ordered in his head. The air vibrated from their wings flapping rapidly. *"We must see this amulet."*

He cursed again. The Guardians were reading his mind.

Becca canted her head as though she saw them as well. Sometime the dragons were really annoying, always interfering.

"Go away. She didn't invite you to inspect her necklace."

"We underestimated humans once. They were bloodthirsty. Jealous of our jewels. They craved our power. This female human holds us in high esteem without knowing of our existence."

"That could easily be resolved."

Silence greeted his threat.

He leaned forward for a better look at the oval shaped moonstone. A carved dragon circled a waxing moon on its hard surface. Becca's unique fragrance clung to the amulet—sun with the hint of a spice he couldn't name. He inhaled the scent that acted like a drug to cloud his mind. Visions of them together in a tangled heap of arms and legs filled his head. The imagery jolted him, and shame rose momentarily at his thoughts.

He shoved the impression aside only to admit meeting Becca had changed him. He might be a thousand years old, but he knew little of life beyond the ancient dragon circle. The possibility of exploration both elated and worried him.

"Beautiful," he whispered. Genuine astonishment filled him because he wasn't sure if he meant the pendant or the woman. He dug into a pocket for his pipe. He needed to hold something familiar to calm his racing heart.

She gave him a grim smile and backed away. "I'm going to flush some quail in this tall grass. They'll be good eating, as they are feeding on the nuts and seeds that abound here."

"Would you teach me to hunt?"

"You're a wizard. Why do you need to hunt?"

"What if something happened to you? I was born on a farm, but I was sent to Brenalin for wizardry at an early age. It has been eons since I picked up a weapon in self defense." He puffed several times on the pipe. "Wizards don't kill for sport, but I should know how to fend for myself."

"Not until we reach Froy," she said, stomping off.

Shrugging, Cress put his pipe away and gathered bits and pieces of wood for the campfire. All too soon the Guardians returned to harass him.

"This woman is special." Dragon voices intruded on his quiet. *"We are pleased with your decision to share our tale with her."*

He picked up rocks and set them in a circle. *"Did you know of the link between her goddess and dragons?"*

"An ancient tale tells of an alliance between female humans and dragons. We suspect their descendants are in this village."

"That's why you wanted to accompany us. What else aren't you telling me?" Cress rubbed his hands clean on the front of his robe, more out of habit than anything else. *"Who were these people?"*

"We believe they were priestesses to the last dragon king."

"Why haven't I heard about them before now?" He took a moment to scan the horizon for Becca. No trace of her could be seen.

"It did not involve you. Knowledge of them was not required."

The Guardians meant to deflect his attention, but they failed. *"Nonetheless interesting."*

"You dare to test us?"

Cress glanced at the grazing horses and mule. *"Not at the moment. If the situation were reversed, I expect you would demand such a test. Meanwhile, this is not finished. I reserve the right to bring the subject up another time."*

"Annoying human," several flickering, golden dragons united to complain. *"You displease us."*

Cress freed a rusty laugh as he turned the dragons invisible again. The sound of tiny leathery wings echoed in his ears, but he ignored them. Instead, he concentrated on the sweet night, the soothing rustle of prairie grass, and the chorus of frogs. In spite of the distractions, Cress wondered what other surprises awaited him in the wide, unexplored world.

"What about a story while our meat cooks?" Becca asked upon returning with a half dozen quail already gutted and defeathered. She staked Y-shaped twigs on either side of the fire, then shoved the birds on and balanced them over the flames.

Her curiosity wrapped around him like a blanket, keeping the night at bay. "Your storyteller was correct about dragons having a structured society. I doubt if our highest civilization reached their heights. Human beings must have been jealous to persecute them. How much more do you know of them?"

"Many things," she answered, "but I thought you were going to do the telling?"

A nice riposte. Her quickness never ceased to amaze him. "We'll start with the dragon circle. The first dragons of Feldsvelt came from the heavens. They wove the circle to hold their conclaves. Since dragons were longwinded creatures, they wanted a place where they could take their time and remain unaffected by its passage. It is spelled against time."

"Is that why you haven't aged?" Becca asked.

Another observation by Becca that pleased him. "I do whenever I leave the circle, but we're not talking about me. You wanted to hear about dragons." He paused until she nodded, then continued, "It was there the conclave elected their first queen, Selena, a gigantic white elemental dragon. She chose—"

"This is heresy!" Becca leapt to her feet. "Her name was Soluna."

Puzzled, Cress stopped to find the rebuttal mildly evocative. He picked up a stick and poked at the fire with it. Sparks erupted into the air. "You asked to hear my tale. Sit down and listen."

She glared at him but sank down with a grunt of disgust. "I only meant to correct an error."

He wondered how widely different their tales would vary. The Guardians had told him their tales. His belief in the accuracy of his version was deep-seated. "Names easily change over time. Selena chose her kingdom in the far north where the snow caressed her great body." He covertly glanced at her for a reaction. Nothing. "A wise dragoness capable of blending the elements of earth, air, fire, and water together, she proved a good choice, bringing balance to the beginning of the dragon kingdoms. She reigned for many thousands of years and was followed by the mighty red dragon, Realgar."

"Another lie," Becca said in a defiant tone. She tossed a pebble into the fire. "His name was Regal."

Cress chuckled. People always fought change.

"This isn't funny," Becca said, scowling. "You can't do this. Your faith isn't being tested. Mine is."

"It is not my intent to shake your beliefs," he replied, meaning it.

Becca adjusted the meat over the flames to keep it from burning. "You speak blasphemy. All my life I accepted the words of our storytellers. Your version has to be wrong. They would be appalled to discover they failed in their duty."

"No one is at fault. Minor mispronunciations happen all the time. Do you wish me to continue or not?" he asked and went on without waiting for her reply. "I admit not much is known about him except he enjoyed collecting treasure. During his reign, the dragons learned it was the gemstones of Feldsvelt who called them to our world. They revealed their stone magic to the dragons. A dragon isn't fulfilled until he finds the right gemstone."

Her expression softened. "Stone magic? I am unfamiliar with the meaning."

"The dragons sensed an energy in the gemstones and somehow connected with it."

"That is so," mindspoke the Guardians.

Cress went on without responding to them. "This was an anxious period with many dragons vying for the favor of certain gemstones. Realgar, being king of the dragons, selected first and picked the ruby as his keystone."

Becca stretched her legs. "There is a drawing of a small red dragon on a smooth rock near Froy. He is depicted carrying a pigeon-blood gemstone far too heavy for him. Each year, berry juice is used to maintain the color."

This time, Cress checked the cooking birds. They were ready to eat. He slid a quail off and broke it into two pieces and handed half to Becca. She leaned forward, her blonde braid tickling the back of his hand.

The sensation recreated his licentious vision when he held her amulet.

To shove the memory aside, he sank his teeth into the juicy quail. In no time, he licked the grease off his hands and wiped them dry on the grass. "Shall I continue, or have you heard enough?" he asked.

"I am enjoying listening to your tale, but choose your words with care."

Cress needed no further encouragement. Her willingness to hear more pleased him. "The third leader of the dragons was Gallein, a clear, dark green who settled in the ragged Tahoma Mountains. Greens usually like to be near water sources, but not him. Dragons normally live for hundreds of years, but a few much longer. Gallein was one such. He ruled for thousands of years, nearly as long as Selena. His chosen stone was prasiolite, a green amethyst. Gallein liked his wine and, though placid most of the time, he enjoyed stirring up disruptive energies such as earthquakes when he imbibed too much alcohol."

Becca shot him a glare so dark and intense that he almost laughed.

"At least we agree upon his name," she growled, "but I was taught Gallein cured drunkenness."

Cress didn't offer a reason for the difference. "Another female dragon, Zaffer, a pure blue who favored flying in stormy weather, became dragon queen after Gallein. Her stone was not a stone at all, but fossilized tree resin—amber—which can become imbued with power. Some believe she was struck by lightning while attempting to increase her stone's power. During her reign friction developed between humans and dragons. Her lack of attention might have been the reason the seeds of unrest grew."

"Enough," Becca said, yawning. "I am tired and need to rest and digest your fabrications."

Cress adjusted his robe. Her accusation didn't insult him. "I'm nearly done. Human existence on Feldsvelt changed the dynamics of the world. We befriended the dragons, then learned of the treasure they hoarded and couldn't resist temptation. At first, a few dragons were killed, supposedly by accident." He stopped to let her absorb his information. "Next to rule was a rare bronze, Oriole."

Becca touched her fingers to her mouth. "Olla," she said in a low voice, some of her previous belligerence gone.

He acknowledged the name difference with a nod. "A diamond was his chosen jewel, said to promote inner searching and seeking. Unfortunately, this magnificent beast was lazy and overconfident, the latter tendency common among many dragons." Indignant buzzing droned around his head. The Guardians disapproved of his negative characterization of their kind. "Oriole refused to heed the warning signs—even more so than Zaffer—that the humans sought to steal dragon treasure."

Becca's eyes softened with sadness and regret. "Our storyteller usually dips her voice to a whisper when she tells Olla's story. She will shudder and cover her face to emphasize this terrible period. Everyone leans forward, afraid to miss a single, muffled word. It is the beginning of the dark times."

Cress couldn't agree more. "The other dragons established idyllic kingdoms of their own, leaving the ancient circle to the smallest called Guardians of

Secrets, golden insect-size dragons who documented the deeds of their brethren. They were nosy busybody creatures who put every leader, feat, and fact, including the Great Dying, the devastating war between humans and dragons, to memory."

A small smile lifted the corners of the warrior woman's mouth. "It is well known dragons came in various sizes, but I've not heard of tiny ones."

The hour grew late. Cress unpacked his sleeping blanket. "I see no reason not to believe in them. Humans come in all sizes. Why not other creatures?"

"True."

Her easy acceptance of his rationale pleased him. "On another matter…Bonner, Trell, and I found the circle while on break from our studies in Brenalin. No human had set a foot inside it in hundreds of years, if ever. Once we found it, though, it became our favorite spot to practice our magic." He paused to stretch. As he moved, he looked over at Becca and into the depths of her weary eyes. "I'm sorry. You suffered a shock today and are now tired. It's late, and this is a good place to stop."

Becca snuggled down on her bedroll. "Your tale leaves me much to consider, Cress."

She said his name without his title, and he liked the sound on her lips. He stared at her face, amazed at how close he felt toward her.

"A fair telling." The whisper of dragon voices came easy enough, even though the Guardians were invisible. *"Next time stress our intelligence, bravery, and great deeds."*

"You received a fair rendition, I'd say," he responded, beaming like a fool into the night. *"I turned*

you into heroes."

"Justly deserved."

Sitting silent, Cress suspected the tiny Guardians withheld specifics, and the lack of knowledge made him fear what lay ahead. In fact, he despised himself for thinking he did more of their bidding than Becca's.

Chapter Fourteen

Even though she'd enjoyed the timbre of Cress's deep voice, Becca experienced a hard time believing his fabrications. Only because he corroborated part of her own village stories did she allow him to continue. The similarity made it possible for her to believe.

And wonder.

Yet fear.

How could he be aware of so much history which belonged solely to the people of Froy?

Froy.

Thinking the name elicited a flood of haunting memories. Had the plague struck again? Which villagers were carried off to join Luna in the great afterlife? She squeezed her eyes tight to chase away the images her thoughts created.

At dawn she struggled free of her tangled bedroll and turned to face the grasslands. A silence permeated the morning, and the lack of low grunting and thud of hooves unnerved her.

"The wisents are gone," she said when the wizard stirred. "For our safety, it's wise to know where a herd that size is. Can you sense them with your magic?"

Cress closed his eyes. "They departed during the night for better grazing. They're over the next rise. They'll remain in the area until the grass is gone."

"We might as well get a move on, too."

He shrugged and took a step closer. "We can depart any time. Give me a few minutes to saddle the horses and ready the mule."

She appraised Cress, keenly aware of his closeness and the warm scent of male unique to him. She fingered her braid. He hadn't offered any beads, yet she wondered what would he say if she proposed they mate?

"Mayhaps you would like to hear a story of the wisents," she said.

A gleam shone in his hazel eyes. "I'd be delighted."

"My tale is about a herd whose leader was a rare, white cow." Becca helped break camp and saddled her mare. She mounted and gently urged the animal away from the safety of the boulders.

Cress followed. "An albino?"

She glanced at him in contemplation. "No, a true white wisent. They have long been sacred symbols of optimism and prophecy. They—"

"What prophecy?" he interrupted, demanding.

She shifted in the saddle, mildly irritated by the unexpected interruption. The men of Froy knew better than interrupt a female. "The one about a white wisent turning all the colors of humanity—white, black, red, yellow, brown, and then back to white."

"Symbolism is often used as a means to explain faith."

She burst into laughter, the sound driving skittish prairie dogs fleeing into their burrows. "The white cow I referred to roamed the great plains for nearly three decades, a normal lifespan for wisents.

"She died in the dead of a snow-white winter. The

herd drifted onto the ice of Legacy Lake, and their combined weight and sharp hooves broke through. Every creature went to the bottom. The water turned gray so no man or woman would drink it. Legend claims only white birds would settle on the water—gulls, geese, and majestic swans."

"Not quite the same as dragon tales."

Typical male, trying to outdo her. In response, she nudged her mare into a ground-eating lope with a huff. While her story contained no heresy, she refused to let a male outdo her.

Or did something else bother her?

No answers came to comfort her.

After days of steady riding, wispy plumes of steam rose in the distance.

"The thermal hot springs," she informed Cress, seeing him frown. "Most consider the scent repulsive, but not me. It reminds me of my cave."

Cress arched a brow, a silent request for her to elaborate. She didn't. Nor did she tell him it brought her closer to the place she loved.

That evening, they stopped where a slow-running stream bubbled and a geyser erupted to the height of a tall man every few minutes. The gushing water shimmered like a rainbow, even in the dying light of day.

Becca stood within a foot of the wizard. She liked the smell of leather and man that wafted from him. "Mayhaps tonight, you would tell more of the dragons."

He barked a laugh. "Why didn't you ask sooner? I assumed you had no wish to hear more because you considered it sacrilege."

Becca laid a gentle hand on his arm, and a tingle

ran up hers. "My mistake. I didn't want to pressure you and kept hoping you would volunteer."

Cress moved off to stake his horse. "I guess we should take that as a lesson learned. We both assumed wrongly."

Becca followed suit, doing hers and the mule. "I concur." To her astonishment she realized she agreed with the wizard's train of thought. "I apologize for jumping to a conclusion when a simple request would have cleared the air."

"Since that's settled, I'll help finish setting up camp, then I'm going to bathe." He reached into his robe's pocket and drew out a bar of soap strongly scented with pine and vanilla. "Afterward, I'll be happy to continue the tale."

"Sounds good to me," she replied, happiness lifting her spirit. "Once I return with our evening meal, I'll bathe as well."

So saying, she set off to hunt game while Cress went to the stream. She returned with several rabbits cleaned and gutted. Cress had finished his bath. His long, dark hair hung wet and straight to the small of his back. A tingle of...desire bubbled up from her center—warm, tempting, and definitely inviting. The close proximity made Becca aware of the unique maleness of the wizard. She found him appealing—even though fully clothed in leather boots, woolen leggings, tunic, and a brown robe.

In the blink of an eye, Cress stood before her. "Here. You might like this."

She looked at what he dropped into her palm—a square bar of soap, smooth, greasy like beeswax, and smelling of roses. "Thank you," she said, clutching his gift as though priceless. It wasn't beads, but it was a start. "I'll be right back."

"Take your time. These rabbits will take a while to cook."

A short walk to the spring, and she found a deep, natural cauldron where steam rose from a pool. Laying her bow and quiver down, she undid her braid and fingered Maine's beads. They'd chipped and cracked with age. With a flick of her wrist, she tossed them away. Amazingly, they were easier to discard than she imagined. She tried to visualize her lover, Maine, and realized his image had faded to a distant memory. No sadness rose to torment her.

She stripped off her dirty tunic and leggings and turned the garments inside out so the clean side showed. Dare she wash her clothes? Maybe the wizard would dry them with magic. Or maybe they could cuddle together for warmth. She sighed with frustration. In her village she could choose any man, but the wizard…

Dipping a foot into the water, she found the temperature ideal and slid deeper in with a grateful sigh.

Glancing up at the full moon, she sent a prayer to her goddess. *Bless you, Luna. Without your help I would never have found the wizard or been able to convince him to accompany me. I was so afraid of failing.*

"Fear not, child," a multifaceted voice said in her head.

She gasped as if the ground beneath her had opened up. Water splashed in her face when she jerked to regain her balance.

Was she dreaming, suffering hallucinations? Not

once in her life had the goddess deigned to speak directly with her. Others aye, although never her.

"Luna? Great Mother? Is that you?"

"Do not doubt me, child."

The great honor of the goddess speaking to her caused Becca to bow her head, humbled. "No, no, Great Mother."

"Excellent. Do not lose faith," the strange voice spoke. *"Your speedy return pleases us…er…me."*

"Is something amiss in Froy? My mother? My sister?"

"Do not worry, child. I am at your side with every step."

She stole a peek at the gleaming moon overhead and directed her words toward it. "I am honored, Great Mother, with your confidence in me. I pray I can live up to your expectation."

"You have greatly pleased me. Success will come. We have united goals."

Confidence welled up inside Becca at Luna's words. "Thank you," she whispered in gratitude.

"Rest easy, child, and know we…I am with you."

She submerged deeper in the warm water, and calm descended upon her. Becca would have enjoyed soaking until the water cooled, except in this case, she doubted the hot spring ever would, so she forced herself to stand and dry off.

Gathering her bow, a prized possession that she'd spent hours creating, brought a wave of homesickness for those she loved most. Her mother put her first bow into her hands at the age of seven. Over time, thick calluses grew from long hours of practice. Luckily, her fingers hadn't misshapen as happened to other archers.

Her goddess had not deserted her or the people of Froy as she feared lately. Luna traveled with her.

As she headed back, a whistle lifted her spirits.

Chapter Fifteen

Cress dried his hair before the campfire and waited for Becca's return. She walked back from her bath with a spring in her step and riffled through her belongings. He swore something appeared different about her. A small change, yet significant.

Then he noticed—her beads were gone. She pulled out a bone comb and sat cross-legged before the fire.

"You need to know the truth about the dragons," he began.

Becca continued to comb the tangles free. "What truth is that? You're referring to the different names of their rulers."

"I think learning more about the Guardians will clarify misconceptions," he answered, determined to teach her.

"Those are the little ones, correct?"

He let a friendly smile rise on his lips. Her sharp memory came as a pleasant surprise. "The Guardians survived the Great Dying because they hid well. Rumors about the dragon circle put fear into the hearts of men. There the Guardians flourished when all others of their kind were destroyed by our ancestors. A senseless eradication of innocent lives."

"Are you saying what I think? That dragons still exist? Your heresy will not sway me."

"I don't intend to try." He smiled and stuck his

hand into a pocket. "Do not forget the magic of the dragon circle."

"Those dragons are alive, eh? They stayed hidden all this time without anyone ever finding them?"

Something about the curve of a woman's arm, even covered in supple buckskin, appealed to him, watching the rise and fall of Becca's arm as she combed her hair "Well, not exactly. A few learned of their existence."

"You?"

He nodded, deciding to keep the truth between them. "When you want to avoid detection, you hide in plain sight."

She set her comb in her lap. "Have you seen them?"

"Many times." He changed his mind about smoking and removed his hand from a pocket empty of his pipe. "And so have you."

"Me? How? When?" Abruptly her blue eyes lit with understanding. "Those strange dragonflies. They are the Guardians."

Once more, she demonstrated quick intelligence. He nodded. "They draw power from diamonds indigenous to Demit Woods. The gemstones are smaller than a grain of sand but are numerous enough and of a strength to work for the dragons. Some travel with us."

She clutched her amulet. "Sweet Luna, they're here? Where?"

"All around you," he said. "Naturally, while living in the dragon circle, they received the benefits of the enchantment. Some are ancient. Dragons have a life cycle much like a lizard's, although their adult behavior is far more complicated since they can reason as well as any human."

Becca peered around the campsite. "Why can't I see them?"

"I made them invisible." He poked at the fire with a stick, ashamed to meet her gaze. Sparks flew into the air. He was stalling and knew it. The Guardians had remained mysteriously silent throughout the conversation. Surely their silence was significant.

"Enough, wizard."

Relief exploded in him. The Guardians had been eavesdropping. He should have guessed. "Tell me more of your village, Becca," he urged, hoping she would comply.

"But the dragons…I want to see them."

"Listen, Becca, I'm sure you have dozens of questions, and I promise we'll talk of them later, after you have mulled over the importance of my revelation. Let's discuss the familiar. Or at least familiar to you—Froy."

She glanced at the horses nickering softly. "I have told you the essential details. Oh, there are a couple things you might find of interest about Froy, and the women in particular."

"Only one Froyan woman intrigues me."

She turned back, brows arched in surprise. "You don't wear beads in your hair. Nothing adorns a fine male like the beads he creates with his own hands. Males take great pride in the uniqueness of their beads."

"Where are yours? Did they fall out? You had some in your braid when we first met."

Her hair had dried to a light wheat shade. "I discarded them at the pool. The women of Froy are free to mate with as many partners as they wish. Our males offer them to women whom they favor. Some women take great pride in wearing the beads of numerous males. Others prefer only a few."

Cress could only stare at the beauty of Becca's face reflecting the moon's light. A sliver of jealousy heated his blood. By the gods, he couldn't remember if she wore different ones or if they'd been all the same. An oversight he wouldn't repeat. "I would think that causes problems if children are produced."

"Our women have the ability to control conception," she confided in a level voice. "We can take a man's seed within our wombs and hold it until we wish the pregnancy to proceed. We cannot control the sex of a babe, yet gender does determine by whom the child will be raised. Females remain with their birth mother, and male children go to the fathers. Naturally, a mother provides her own milk. Men use goats."

A warped society in his view, but he kept his comments to himself. "This ability has the ring of magic."

Becca's face flushed as pink as her lips. "Not magic. Not herbs. The power of our will."

Denial of the obvious. Cress studied the warrior woman when she heaved a log onto the fire. "Forgive me, but the ability to regulate pregnancy sounds like magic."

A flicker of comprehension hit Becca's eyes, and she raised her hand to brush her fingers across the cabochon necklace. "Mayhaps I am not explaining it well. All females wear an amulet similar to mine to honor the Great Mother Luna, but I recall a story about a dragon—a white dragon named Oyfele bequeathing us the ability to control pregnancy. I'd forgotten all about it…until now."

"Oyfele, the Savior," the contingent of Guardians whispered in Cress's mind. *"Ask the female more."*

"About what?" he shot back.

"Oyfele disappeared at the start of Great Dying. She made the greatest sacrifice any dragon could make. Gave up her lair and the treasure it held to carry our greatest treasure out of harm's way. We wish to learn of this tale."

"Oyfele," he repeated the name. "Tell me more of her."

"There is little to tell. We received this gift from her generations ago. Legend claims we once performed a favor for Oyfele. In turn, she granted us the boon of controlling our ability to breed."

"Makes sense," the guardians said. *"It confirms her ancestors were the priestesses of the last dragon king. They were trained sorceresses, and he sent them with Oyfele. Moonstone was Oyfele's gemstone. These sorceresses took it as their own."*

"Be quiet," Cress snapped. *"I can't concentrate if you keep interrupting Becca."*

"This is crucial information. Information we were never told. We cannot help ourselves."

"Really," he answered. *"I would never have guessed."*

Glancing at Becca, his heart skipped a beat. A tiny light of invitation glowed in the blue pools of her eyes. She sat near enough for him to catch her clean, fresh scent mixing with the hint of roses from the soap. The combination proved the most intoxicating aroma he'd ever encountered. When she licked her lips, he found himself wishing to taste her luscious mouth. Just a little taste. Just to satisfy his curiosity.

Then she looked away and the spell fractured like a broken looking glass.

"An intriguing story," Cress said, "and here I thought I was the one who would provide the entertainment tonight."

"You still can." She lay on her bedroll, stretching her limber body, patting the side for him to join her.

A small shock struck Cress. Passion warred with common sense, forcing him to battle the awakening heat in his veins. He swallowed the knot in his throat as she leaned forward, a smile of invitation widening on her mouth.

It didn't matter they shared nothing in common—unless he counted the fact they both cared for other people, had someone depending on them, and would do whatever it took to aid those they loved. How could he not consider those things?

All the same, he suppressed a niggle of concern from his conscience. He'd coveted bedding Becca since first seeing her battle the forest fire. Dare he consider setting aside centuries of responsibilities for a night of passion? The idea of exploring Becca's curves proved tempting. More than tempting.

"I cannot pledge myself to you," he whispered to Becca.

Disappointment raced across her face. "I'm not requesting an allegiance. Just an exchange of pleasure between two people. Will you lose your magic if you couple with a woman?"

"No, not that," he said.

"What then?"

Direct and to the point, admirable qualities. "Becca, I haven't made love to a woman in over a thousand years, and I'd be lying if I said I wasn't tempted, but I'm sure of one thing."

"And that is?"

"When I do take you," he said, "it will have to mean more than entertainment. It will be forever."

Chapter Sixteen

The silky texture of the wizard's voice tickled Becca as though feathers brushed across her skin. The sound stimulated more than another man's touch. If only he would caress her.

"Can I not warm your bed even for one night?" she asked, unfazed by the rejection.

"One night or a hundred," he replied, flicking at a speck on his robe. "Choosing a partner is easy and complex, and making love is no small thing. There is strength in it. Magic. Love has threads of power that cannot be broken by any means. For me it is the ultimate expression of commitment, the joining of two bodies into one. This might seem odd to you, but I want a woman to love me—only me...As I will love only her."

The rational part of her wanted to scream at his idiocy. *Love only one woman.* Yet another part—the part considering the outlandish idea of monogamy—knew he spoke from a deep-seated belief and found the idea secretly tantalizing.

"What a strange man you are. You have the oddest ideas I have ever heard. To attach such importance to coupling is...is beyond comprehension." Moonlight gleamed in his eyes, casting the Great Mother's light back at her. The sincerity in his expression rocked her to the core. "Do you realize how opposite your view is from mine? Your words shake the very foundation of traditions I have learned over a lifetime."

"Questioning antiquated beliefs is never wrong," he said, "especially if better ones appear."

"The women of Froy might disagree."

Her mind raced in circles, nearly making her dizzy. She never imagined men and women possessing deep feelings for one another. She wondered if this how people outside of The Wilds conducted their lives. Surely he uttered a delusion caused by years of isolation.

The wizard gave her much to consider. She tossed and turned until sleep took her.

Becca woke from a restless slumber. Even though she suspected wizards led complex lives, she couldn't believe how easily Cress confused her.

No, mystified her.

First, exposing the dragons' existence. Then speaking of commitment!

In the bright light of a new day, both ideas seemed ludicrous. To believe his tale about dragons meant reconsidering the validity of his words about a male wanting to share his life with only one woman.

Folding up her bedroll, she stole a covert glance to where he tended the horses and mule. His movements were quick and efficient. As though sensing her interest, he glanced over his shoulder. He skimmed her with a sharp eye.

An urge struck her to get busy. She doused the few coals with water when a breeze rippled the long tops of prairie grass and a funnel storm of larks exploded across the sky, flowing in perfect unison. It was too early for the annual migration of birds to start. What flushed the flock from hiding? A prairie hawk zoomed across the sky. The larks would find no safe haven in the air.

"Best we get started," she said.

Cress looked over at her curiously. "As you wish."

"We still have a long road ahead of us, but at this rate, we'll make Froy in no time."

Becca mounted and clucked her mare forward into the bright sunshine. A massive herd of wisents grazed ahead. Either they'd caught up with the original herd or a completely different one. With the wind at their backs, it carried their scent right at the wisents.

Cress reined in his mount. Becca allowed the delay, for one never knew where the capricious animals would be found next.

A wisent cow at the outer edge of the herd jerked its shaggy head as if sensing danger. Unexpectedly, ropy tails shot straight up, and the herd stampeded in a dark thundering wave—straight for them.

The earth shook, and a roar overpowered all other noises.

Instinctively, Becca inserted her horse between Cress's and the horde of charging animals. Could the wizard perform magic? She didn't have time to spare and dare not wait.

Swallowing down fear, she stood in her stirrups and prayed to the goddess she possessed enough arrows even as she unslung her bow, nocked the first one in place, and fired.

The closest wisent went down in a sickening, crunching tumble. She loosened another arrow and another and another. Never before had she fired so many, so fast, and still the herd rolled past.

The muscles in her arms burned and felt ready to fall off, yet she didn't relax her guard. Dust fogged her vision. With sheer will, Becca shut down all emotions, afraid to ruin her concentration.

When the last of the dark beasts stampeded on either side of them and their terrified, quivering horses, she slumped in her saddle.

"Becca."

Cress. She blinked when the air cleared. "What?"

"Is it over?" he asked.

Stacked in front of them was a wall of dead wisents, an arrow buried between each one's eyes or chests. A few stragglers stood on the fringes, panting, heaving their massive sides, and bellowing in a daze of desperation.

"Blessed Luna, I hope so," she responded. "Why didn't you use magic to protect us? You were able to lift the mule on the cliff. Why not lift us out of danger?"

"On the cliff, I hardened the air beneath the mule. He climbed onto the trail on his own. Besides, you were doing a great job on your own."

To her surprise, his praise contented her. She had deemed it her duty to protect them. She patted the quivering neck of her mare before swinging a leg over the saddle to the ground. She took a step, and her legs started to crumble.

"Are you all right?" Cress asked, beside her in a blink to steady her.

Looking deep into his eyes, Becca swore his soul stared back at her. Vibrant. Alive. Wanting. She trembled so long and hard she feared the sensation would never cease. Then warmth flowed through her.

Her cheeks burned.

She broke the connection with a shake of her head. "I'm fine."

"You were wonderful. So brave. So fearless."

"I did what was necessary," she said, wishing her body could melt into his. "Nothing more, nothing less."

Cress shook his head. "Accept the compliment, Becca. I do not give them freely. I should have assisted with magic, but the way of wizards is not always straightforward. One of our supreme objectives is to maintain the natural order. A wizard has a great responsibility and must never be tempted to use his power for dark purposes. That means, for me to kill with magic is wrong. I must resist the temptation."

His hazel gaze swept over the tall grass swaying in the breeze. What did he see? Did he hear something she could not? A furrow developed across his brow as though he focused on a hidden entity within the swaying grass.

He uttered an ancient chant. Tendrils of magic brushed over her skin, leaving her momentarily aching for their loss as though an old friend departed this earth. When Cress's lips stopped moving, a dozen or so brilliant yellow and black butterflies burst from the grass and flew in their direction. They encircled her wrists like living bracelets.

Becca stared wide-eyed at the amazing sight and felt the faint tickle of powdery wings on her skin. "Oh, my, they're magnificent. A gift such as this priceless."

Chapter Seventeen

Cress needed no thanks other than the look of pure joy on Becca's face. He remembered glancing at her through clouds of dust while crazed wisents thundered past them like a dark, living river. A feral grin claimed her face while she loosed arrow after arrow. She had been in her element and accomplished a near impossible feat. It only proved the warrior woman hailed from a much harsher environment than he, and the insight struck him like a blow.

Every wizard knew nature required balance. It compelled him to counter the savagery of the wisents' death with the magic of butterflies.

Just as his request last night for commitment had been balanced with silence. Becca had stared at him, mute, then lay down and went to sleep.

He shaded his eyes from the glare of a harsh sun with his hand. "How much farther?"

"Be strong, wizard. Emulate the human female," Guardians said with a hint of mockery, hearing his complaint.

Cress growled under his breath. *"What do you mean?"*

"Nothing, wizard. You have a suspicious nature. We admire your companion. All we do is offer advice."

Frowning, he wished he wasn't intrigued. *"I don't need your advice. Leave me alone."*

Becca looked up from regarding the butterflies to him. "We're nearly there. At Froy, you can rest."

Cress sighed. Carrying on simultaneous conversations proved draining.

In a swirl of yellow and black, the butterflies lifted off Becca's wrists and disbanded.

"Might as well get some easy meat." She headed for the slaughtered animals with purposeful steps. "The carrion birds and wolves can have the rest. In days, only bleached bones will remain in the sun. Nature will not waste a thing."

Cress stared in wonder as she removed her knife from its sheath and peeled back the hide of the nearest wisent to slice a huge chunk from one of its haunches. She wrapped the meat in a clean oilcloth to protect it from flies and other insects before retrieving her arrows. Without a wasted motion, she ran her fingers over the fletching, giving each one a quick check. Years of being alone must have affected him more than he realized because he would never tire of watching her.

They remounted and rode hard and fast, stopping only to rest the animals. On the third day, they came upon a divided animal trail. Becca started to turn left.

"Follow the ley lines," the Guardians mindspoke to Cress. *"They will shorten the journey by many leagues."*

Cress reined his horse to a stop. *"How? I cannot see them."*

"They exist. We see them. Go straight. We will guide you."

"Hold on," he called to Becca. "We should head straight."

She glanced at the direction he indicated before

turning back to narrow her eyes. "I think I know the way to Froy. I'm retracing my original trail, after all."

He empathized with her confusion. "Straight is quicker."

Becca's knuckles whitened on the reins. "Sweet Luna, you've never been here. How…? I hope you know what you are saying."

Dragons buzzed with delight.

"Me, too," he said. "Meanwhile, the sun's setting. Let's make camp here. I'll set up while you scout the area."

Becca opened her pretty mouth to protest, only to clamp it shut. The more he antagonized the warrior woman, the more appealing she became to him.

"Be tactful, wizard," the dragons intruded.

"As tactful as you." He untied cords at their saddles and tossed their bedrolls to the ground when Becca left. Next, he dug out the cooking pot.

"The warrior woman deserves respect."

He cocked his head to focus on listening for a twig breaking or a pebble being kicked to identify the route she took. Nothing. A cacophony of fluttering wings became the only sound he heard. *"I would never do anything to offend her…or anyone. All are entitled to consideration until they prove otherwise."*

"We admire tact," the tiny golden dragons mindspoke. *"We trust you. You should trust us."*

"You toss me a few sweetened words and expect me to swallow them as though they are the tastiest meal I've ever eaten."

"Is it our fault you cannot discern truth from falsehood? A human weakness. We confess that trait has bothered us for many long years. Diligence is

113

required. You can split fact from lies upon arrival in the female's village."

Smiling, he feigned disinterest at the babbling dragons as he gathered fist-size rocks and set them into a circle. Sufficient twigs and small branches littered the ground for a cooking fire. As he worked, the tension in his shoulders eased.

Cress straightened, his vision straining to perceive a trail, while his mind tried to penetrate to the bottom of the dragons' motives. He found neither trail nor answers. *"Why? Do you expect trouble?"*

"Not expect. Humans are unpredictable. You agree? Best to prepare for the unexpected."

He crossed his arms over his chest. The Guardians could be devious, but they'd never lied to him. At least, not to his knowledge. *"Tell me one thing…"*

"Clarify," two dozen voices spoke as one.

"Why did you not object when I told Becca that Guardians survived?"

"Could we have stopped you?"

The question held a certain amount of merit. *"If you had protested, I might have considered your request."*

"The decision is long past. Do you seek our approval?"

"I wish for an answer." He closed his eyes. *"You have kept your existence a secret for thousands of years. Why reveal it now? Why Becca?"*

"The answer is awkward."

That was all he received.

Silence surrounded him.

Chapter Eighteen

Wisent Flats lay days behind them. The temperature climbed steadily until it exploded with heat and humidity to an uncomfortable potency. They neared the marshes with bulrushes growing in profusion. Two and a half full months had passed since leaving the sanctuary of the dragon circle, and in that time, Becca had come to respect Cress.

In turn, she felt compelled to be open and forthright, qualities she hoped he admired and raised her higher in his estimation. Whatever reason lay behind telling her about the dragons, she appreciated his trust. She'd spent time compiling questions, rejecting them, adding new ones until her head felt close to bursting.

The horses and mule trudged with their heads hung low. Nowadays, they spent their energy swishing their tails against the masses of flies and insects eager to torment animal and human with equal vengeance.

Earlier that morning she found clumps of tufted lemon grass and broke off the sharp-edged blades to crush them into an oil essence to use as a repellant. She smeared the gooey concoction on Cress's and her faces for gratifying relief and dabbed the ointment carefully around the horses' eyes to give them a measure of protection.

Descending into a deep, narrow valley, they

approached the blackwater swamp, a mahogany-colored water stained by rotting vegetation. Cattails and marsh fern grew in abundance. The temperature climbed. Humidity pressed down on them, making their movements as sluggish as the river.

Becca inhaled deeply. Sulfur permeated the air with rank putrefaction, along with the scents of decaying vegetation and moldy stagnant water.

"Luna give me strength," Becca murmured under her breath. Swamps were vile places, filled with sinkholes and deathsand capable of sucking a person down in seconds. Snakes slithered through the brackish water, bullfrogs called to each other, and bugs polluted the air.

"We should probably give the horses a break." She dismounted, her boots sinking into the muck. "Let's walk them a while."

Cress wiped his brow and reapplied lemon grass oil to his forehead. "Good idea. I could use a stretch myself."

Pleasure rippled through her at his concurrence. "I swear this is the worst part of the journey. After this, we are near our destination."

The wizard nodded. "Good news to my ears. I will be happy to never see another swamp."

"Unfortunately, we have to return this way and cross it again. Unless you are freeing me from my vow to return with you."

"I am not," he said with a finality that brooked no rebuttal.

Besides the deathsand and sinkholes, they needed to stay alert for the great river lizard she'd seen on her way to find Cress. The enormous creature had taken an adult wisent between its mighty jaws while the herbivore quenched its thirst, and the lizard had hauled it into the murky water to drown.

"I need to find a place to cross safely," she said. "It's deeper since I last traveled this way. Keep a sharp eye out for logs or anything moving in the water."

Cress glanced at the sluggish water covered with greenish-yellow scum. "What am I really looking for?"

She stared at him as if for the first time. Quick and intelligent. And so handsome. Her attraction to him startled her. She didn't want the distraction.

She pressed ahead, alert. "I don't know the creature's name. It's big, scaly, and deadly. I saw one grab a wisent's leg and drag the bellowing cow into deep water. I have no wish to rescue you from such a creature."

"What if I use magic to protect us?"

"Trust him, child."

Becca sucked in a great breath. *"Great Mother?"* she asked in her head.

"It should be obvious. The wizard has your best interests."

Intuition screamed at the wrongness. The voice contained several different pitches. She frowned, thinking about it. The Great Mother was a single individual.

"What say you, child?"

"Faithfulness doesn't mean I follow blindly," Becca countered mentally, disliking the challenge in the voice's question. *"Lives are at stake. Considering all my options is the responsible thing to do."*

"Becca, what is it?" Cress stared at her with worry creasing his face. "You went pale as a ghost."

She shook her head. "I'm fine. The Great Mother spoke to me. She has honored me with advice."

He cocked a dark brow and brushed long brown hair out of his face. "Do tell. What did she say?"

She recognized doubt lacing his baritone voice. How dare he! She inhaled a long, angry breath, letting anger sustain her. "I always seem to be telling you what someone else said. The goddess told me to trust you. I assume she means your magic. So, any magic you can conjure will be greatly appreciated."

"In that case, a simple spell should do the trick," he said.

The wizard halted at the water's edge, raised his arms, and muttered words she couldn't catch. Hundreds of tiny stars tumbled out of nowhere, each full of the colors of a rainbow. They combined to form a solid looking ribbon of lights and streaked toward the swamp.

"What are you doing?" she asked, astonished. "I can feel—"

"Hush!"

She fell silent. The luminous lights were a delight to watch as they swished back and forth over the swamp until the dark, murky water slowed to a stop.

Cress motioned with his hands, and the lights disappeared into the water as they nudged it apart. A sickly sweet smell of rotting vegetation and fecal matter increased until the steady drip of water escaping from the sides sounded like chimes. Magic had cut the swamp in half, exposing primordial mud.

Cress stepped beside her. "Simple enough for you?"

Becca glared at the exposed ground, all muddy and

full of puddles. "Is it safe to travel?"

His hazel eyes turned warm and inviting as a summer day. "Well, of course. It's magic. The sides are solid. I'll go first if you're worried."

He dismounted, blindfolded his gelding and the mule, who sensed the strangeness and balked at entering the crossing. A squishing sound came with his first steps, followed by the thud of hooves. "Are you coming?" he called, once on the other side.

She took a tentative step. "Sweet Luna, protect me."

She blindfolded her horse and told herself it was safe. From the very start she had warned the wizard of the dangers of the swamp. The man was great and powerful. She shouldn't be surprised he conceived a plan to neutralize their danger.

Halfway across, a vertical slit-shaped pupil the size of her fist stared at her from the other side of the shimmering lights. Gasping, she stared at a great water lizard, then swallowed her fear and quickened her steps to the other side.

Cress muttered in a low, deep voice, and the ribbon of lights reappeared. They flashed over the open area, collapsing the sides with a crash as water reunited in an unstoppable rush.

Something splashed in the water.

"Look! See!" She pointed to a greenish-gray tail as the creature slithered into deeper water.

"A real monster. You were right for concern." Cress's voice filled with awe.

She smiled to herself at his concurrence as she removed her horse's blindfold. Over the journey, she'd learned to appreciate how different the wizard acted from the males of her village—not subservient—full of confusing viewpoints. He caused her to question many long-held values. Not to mention her feelings. His presence affected her emotions in ways that would take years to figure out.

If ever...

Chapter Nineteen

After the swamp, they turned west and made good time through rolling hills and valleys with hidden streams. On this day, a grove of pine trees added a summer baked leaf odor to the air that made Cress ache for Demit Woods.

"Something's been troubling me," he started after hours of hard riding ticked by. "I believe you hold the key to something happening with the Guardians. Tell me about yourself. Not about Froy. Not the Council. But you."

The warrior woman pursed her lips. The motion pulled in her cheeks, and Cress saw the harsh toll the journey had taken on her. Becca had lost weight. "You want to talk about me. Like what?"

"Everything. When dragons show interest in an individual, that very behavior merits investigation."

For a moment she smiled, obviously pleased, then reined in her horse. "They are interested in me?"

"Unusually so."

"Why? I'm no better than the next hunter."

Cress grunted at her modesty. "I doubt that. From all I've seen, you are extraordinary. An affinity exists between you and the Guardians. They claim you are special. So, aye, I want to talk about you. Do you mind?"

Her sigh marked a concession. "I suppose not.

Though I doubt I have anything of importance to relay."

Leather squeaked when he adjusted his position in the saddle. Riding was never one of his favorite pastimes. He preferred walking. "I'll be the judge."

Becca burst out laughing. The sound rolled across the sparse landscape and evaporated like the morning mist on a hot summer day. "A male—making a judgment about me? I don't think so."

Cress laughed back. "Be forewarned, Becca. You think you know about dragons, but you haven't a clue about their true nature. First and foremost, they are opportunists. But this is about you. I suspect their interest is important and vital. Let's start with how you were able to speak with Trell."

"I'm not sure…" Her voice slipped away.

He let her pause for a moment. "Surely, something was different, out of the ordinary. Is it common for the women of Froy to speak with enchanted beings? Or just you?"

"Not that I am aware of. The subject has never come up before."

The vague answer left Cress pensive. "Something must be different. Does anything stand out?"

"No, not really. I…Wait!" Blue eyes lit with excitement. "The first time I heard Trell, something brushed over my skin with the faintest touch. The hairs on the back of my neck rose. I thought it was a breeze, but perchance it wasn't."

She rode alongside him, her legs bumping into his. He fought against the tingle that erupted in his blood. "Good, good. That's a start. Have you ever felt that sensation before? Or heard voices?"

Becca nudged her mount into a trot and frowned.

"Voices? Aye."

"Explain," he demanded as a speck of curiosity arose.

"In my cave. At least I call it mine because no one climbs Tayvl's Tower except me. Most consider it haunted by spirits of old."

Cress's muscles tensed. Again. "Describe this tower."

Becca scanned the distance as though bringing the familiar sight into view. "It rises above the surrounding grassland and forest like a rocky sentinel. Everyone teased me, saying it was inaccessible to anything without wings."

Interesting. In her soft, poised tone, contentment rang clear, causing Cress to attempt to visualize Tayvl's Tower. "But you climbed it?"

Riding to one side, Becca smiled at him, her blue eyes magnified by the memory inside. "Aye. Hand over hand I crawled up the chimney with my belly pressed against cold rock. About three quarters of the way up, I found a cave. It was dry, dusty, and no one had entered it for years, if ever."

A cave—a favorite habitat of dragons, he told himself.

"Aye, aye," mindspoke the Guardains. *"Get her to expand about this tower."*

The rapid click of horse hooves over packed earth sounded. Cress let out a long sigh. *"Silence."*

The pinprick of tiny claws tightened on his shoulder. *"Make her talk."*

"That's where I first heard voices," she added in a mere whisper. "You're the only person I've ever told about them. I feared others would think me addled."

Cress jerked in his saddle. How could anyone have a single negative thought about her? "It's only natural to worry about one's sanity in such a case, but there's nothing wrong with you, Becca. I suspect the voices are real."

"How can you be so sure?" she asked, her eyes wide.

Cress grinned. "Because I'm positive there's a connection between your cave, the dragon circle, and Trell."

Becca cocked her head. "Trell's voice is clear. The voices in my cave are a jumble of whispers where I sometimes catch a word or two."

"Only sometimes?" His heart beat faster. "What do these voices say?"

"Help. Save us."

A shiver ran down Cress' spine. "What did you do?"

"Do?" Becca snorted. "I was only twelve that first time. I got out of there as fast as I could."

Cress laughed. He would have done the precise same thing.

"Ask more," the Guardians demanded. *"We require details."*

He sensed the rest of the tiny dragons looming around him. Their intrusion came as no surprise. In fact, he expected them to interrupt far more often.

"I think you've hit upon something important," he said to Becca. "Such openness deserves a reward. Behold! The Guardians!"

Chapter Twenty

Glittering specks of lights materialized close enough for Becca to reach out and touch them, but she stayed her hand. She sat transfixed as a cantata of leathery wings beat the air to cause a light breeze to brush her face.

Dragons!

She tracked the fast-moving creatures as they flew, darting in and out—sometimes hovering, sometimes flying away. She tried to entice them to land on her arm by holding it out.

Finally, two shimmering golden lights touched down on her arm. The prick of tiny claws tightened on her forearm. Their eyes sparkled like red diamonds.

She grinned at Cress, unable to contain her enthusiasm. "Please, tell me I'm not dreaming."

He returned her smile. "They're very real. You made a conquest, I think."

"Hello, there," she whispered to the dragons.

"Hello, child."

"I know that voice!" she rounded back in mindspeech, her tone accusing. *"So I haven't been speaking with the Great Mother?"*

"We regret our deception, but it was necessary."

What did she think, letting herself be fooled so easily? She'd blindly believed the voice belonged to her goddess. Sad and mad, both equal in intensity threatened to overwhelm her. *"How could you deceive me? How can I trust you again?"*

"We beg forgiveness."

"Was the wizard in on your duplicity?" she inquired, calmer, but insistent.

"Absolutely not! He knew nothing."

Tense muscles instantly relaxed. In truth, she'd come to admire Cress, and something inside her hoped he hadn't played a part in the trickery.

"Good," she said, spotting him swing his leg over his horse's flanks and begin to set up camp for the night. The dragons lifted off her arm. She dismounted as well, watching Cress's efficiency, and found an enticing warmth curling in her belly. Her attraction to him had thrown her off from the very first day they met. *"Can he hear us now?"*

"Conversation is not private, if others can hear."

"You have a point," she answered the voices in her head. Her brow creased in concentration. Something strange about them…something that reminded her of the voices in her cave.

"It is possible to include him in our conversation. Link together. Do you wish that?"

Standing mute for a moment, she gazed at the fabled creatures, fighting an urge to bow toward them. *"Link? What is that? I don't understand."*

"It is the ability to speak together. One, or both, or none at all. Is that what you wish?"

"Aye, I do."

"Good evening, Becca," came a new voice into the bewildering mix inside her head.

"Cress?"

"At your disposal," he said, his tone full of

amusement. *"I see you are finding my friends as frustrating as I do."*

She peered at the man hunched before the fire, feeding sticks to the growing flames. His rich baritone voice filled her head, though his lips never moved. How could he behave so casually about such marvelous creatures? Worry seeped into her mind. Were the dragons aware of her growing feelings for the wizard? Surely, creatures with the power to speak into her head could read thoughts as well.

"We will keep your secret," they answered her thoughts.

Astonished, Becca swallowed with relief. "Are dragons always difficult to get a straight answer from?" she asked Cress in regular speech instead of responding to the tiny creatures.

"I'm afraid so," he said. "They can be very annoying."

"We protest. Our dealings with humans have been fair and honest."

Becca tried not to laugh. She couldn't tell how many creatures she spoke with, but they sounded like one great beast. "And what dealings are those, if I may ask?"

Golden dragons fluttered in the air, a third of their number rising high, the balance swooping down and spinning around the wizard's head in tight circles. *"Our only contact for a thousand years was with Wizard Cress. No others."*

Standing, Becca brightened. She glanced at Cress to find him smiling at her, his expression warm with pleasure. "Look, ah…honorable beings…What should I call you?"

"Our name for one and all is Guardians of Secrets."

She counted twelve creatures but wasn't positive of her tally. "How many are there of you?"

"Hundreds. Thousands, but only twenty-four here."

"I confess all these voices in my head is confusing. May I call you Guardian?"

"It is our name."

Never one to waste time beating the bushes, Becca went right to what bothered her. "Why confide in me?"

"We want your help. Need, actually."

Suspicion mounted rapidly. She couldn't help wondering what Cress thought of this development and glanced at him again. "Do you know what they want?"

He gestured with his palms up. "I wish I could enlighten you, but I can't. We may never know what they're up to. Only time will tell. Dragons are naturally inquisitive. Sometimes they'll study a thing for centuries before taking action, and sometimes they just stare. You'll learn that the Guardians do as they wish."

Becca dragged her interest away from Cress to the red-eyed dragons. "You cannot control them? Are they not your pets?"

Tiny hisses erupted from the golden dragons.

Cress rose and planted his feet on the pebbly ground. "Certainly not! It would be like me trying to control you. Dragons are individuals, like humans. However, these Guardians have existed and worked as one for eons so that this is how they prefer to think of themselves. They often behave as a single entity, much as bees do. Moreover, I have no desire to control them, even if I could. And like bees, they can sting if threatened."

His deep voice sent a tremor of desire down her spine, and she let herself savor it before fixing her concentration on the creatures flying around the camp. *"*Why are you here? Are you coming along to help the wizard?"

"We will lend assistance, if he so requests."

"I hear hesitation," she said.

Silence followed her utterance. Struck by the anticipation filling her, she shifted nervously. What was taking them so long to answer*?*

"We wish knowledge," the Guardian said.

Cress lifted a dark brown eyebrow at the easy capitulation.

Becca wanted to learn as much as she could. "Why?"

"Why not? While the existence of The Wilds is known to us, it is also new to us. No living Guardian has visited it."

The dragonfly-sized Guardians flew back and forth between them, dipping and tilting in unison. Their scales flashed in the firelight, reminding her of fish swimming frantically in a school as they tried to evade a predator.

Becca sighed, sensing a much deeper mystery. "What kind of information do you seek?"

This time the Guardians hesitated.

Her gaze sought Cress in the lull. He wasn't like other males. She realized her attitude toward him had changed. For days she hadn't even uttered a derogatory remark about males. Maybe he had grown on her. Or had worn her down.

As a wizard, maybe he used magic on her.

Wood popped and sent sparks shooting into the night air, breaking her line of thought. The glowing dragons flitted around the camp.

"We seek what is ours."

"And that is?" she pressured.

"We cannot enlighten you."

"But you know the answer to Becca's question?" Cress rounded on the tiny creatures.

"Naturally. We are dragons, all-knowing," the Guardians responded.

"If you want my help," she joined in, "I demand to know exactly what you're searching for."

"We will consider your request. For now, we will leave the link in place."

So saying, the Guardians soared high in the air. They appeared to wink out of existence like campfire sparks.

Cress stretched his long legs before the crackling fire and settled in, apparently believing the conversation at an end.

"Everything comes back to the dragons, doesn't it?" Becca asked.

"I guess it depends on what you consider 'everything.' "

Such a cryptic answer. Were Cress and the dragons aiming to trick her? For what purpose? No sooner did the questions form than she scoffed at the crazy idea. She seriously doubted the dragons were evil. Mischievous. Secretive. But not evil.

Besides, Cress came to help Froy.

Otherwise… "Doesn't it strike you as odd that the Guardians want our help," she demanded in return, "but refuse to tell us what they're looking for?"

He blinked, grinning wickedly. "Not particularly. More significance should be put on the reason they need you. I've never known them to require any human's assistance."

"What are we going to do?"

The smile left his mouth. "Nothing. The Guardians will tell us when they are good and ready."

Chapter Twenty-One

The Guardians' refusal to respond to Becca gnawed at Cress all night. He raked back his hair, securing it back with a tie, while frustration overflowed like a flooding river. He had expected a more deferential treatment of the warrior woman than they showed him. Years of being companions had made them comfortable with each other. He'd counseled Becca to use patience—something in all honesty that he needed to exercise himself.

Golden sparks swooped and dove around them the next day. The sight of the little dragons acted as a reminder of his failure to free Trell. He'd left them visible. A mistake. Freeing an exasperated breath, he squeezed his eyes closed.

The valleys and streams fell behind them. Once again, the temperature warmed, but this time the air lacked the heavy humidity and moisture of the swamp. Small hummocks dotted the terrain. Everywhere he looked the ground appeared as baked and cracked earth. A relentless sun beat down on them. This place was hot and dry—a high desert.

Sweat beaded across Cress's forehead as he sat upon his horse. One bead rolled down his neck and slipped beneath his tunic. The aroma of desert sage awakened by the sun struck his nose. Not long after that he caught the scent of moist sand, followed by earthy oak and fleshy cottonwood bark. This northern land proved no more to his liking than the dangerous swamp. He yearned for the cool shade of Demit Woods with its endless hectares of forest—to stroll among the giant trees, not scanning every step for hidden danger.

Distant mountains looked naked and seemed subjected to whimsical color changes. He'd read about lands changing from tender blues and purples to warm yellow and crimson in rhythm with the slant of the sun. He imagined the season for blooming trees and shrubs had passed. In the more temperate climate of his home woods, flowers provided splashes of color throughout the year.

"What are those?" He pointed at two horns rising out of the valley's floor. Their shapes reminded him of dragon horns, only hundreds of times larger.

Becca swung her gaze to where he directed. "The Twin Kammas. Giant limestone towers carved from wind and rain. Against the backdrop of mountains, they seem small, but do not be fooled. Plus, they mean we are less than a week from Froy."

Cress kept his tone neutral. "Good."

Becca's gaze met his squarely. "Once we reach Twin Kammas, mayhaps two days more. We have to travel over the flats. Froy is on the other side of River Kelt."

Finally. "You must be excited about being so near home," he said.

She raised her hand to keep loose strands of hair out of her face. "I don't know what I'll find. I've lost count of the number of times I've woken up from a nightmare with images of my village full of the dead and dying."

The sultry breath of a desert wind caressed his face. Cress wished he hadn't opened this vein of conversation. Guilt pounded at him for reminding her of the danger. "Caring about people makes you feel responsible. Vulnerable. I didn't mean to upset you."

She stretched over the short distance between their mounts and laid cool fingers atop his.

"It's fine," she said. "I just wish I hadn't dreamed it. It always seems so real. All the familiar faces staring up with vacant eyes, accusing me."

Her description let a gory image leap into Cress's mind. "More likely your fears are for naught."

"The burden is mine to carry. I didn't mean to trouble you."

He sucked in a breath. "I'm not like most men. I am more willing to shoulder your burdens."

Becca smiled. "Thank you."

It warmed him to see her happy. She had proven to be a complex woman. He suspected little in life brought her joy while the sight of her smile brought him much, for it reminded him of a field of flowers sharing their colorful faces under a summer sun.

They forged on through miles of low growing bushes and shrubs.

Slow movement caught his eye. Suddenly, he whirled his horse and galloped a short distance away. He jumped to the ground and snatched his prize off the ground.

"Tonight's dinner." He held up a domed tortoise. At the look of disgust on Becca's face, he teased her by saying, "Even men can be useful some time."

"But a tortoise?"

He hadn't missed the fact that her rebuttal targeted

the animal, not men. He tucked the animal into a traveling pouch. "Is there a prohibition about eating them among your people?"

"Just the opposite, Cress," Becca replied as if teaching a child. "Many claim its meat gives long life, and besides, the shell makes a good bowl."

This time he snorted. "I certainly don't need to increase the length of my life."

For several heartbeats, her gaze settled on him. Focusing on the muted steps of the horses in the gray sand, he could almost feel her embarrassment.

"It won't be long now," Becca declared, breaking their silence. "I know you are eager to reach Froy and perform your magic to the best of your ability."

"I do not guarantee to prevail," was all he could think to say to her.

"You will be successful. I am confident."

Cress studied Becca. Her tone had softened, like she trusted him not for being a wizard, but for himself. He couldn't explain it, and the realization warmed his insides to know she thought of him in friendlier terms. "Remember, once Froy is safe from the plague, we return to Demit Woods."

"Of course, that was our agreement," she replied. "I imagine there is much you wish to discuss with your sister."

"Talking is the least of my desires. Freeing her is higher on my agenda."

"See what I mean?" she said. "You care."

He did. She knew him well. No one suffered anxiety as he did. He had an obligation to discharge. Save Becca's village, then save Trell.

Chapter Twenty-Two

Becca woke to the predawn light chasing Luna's shadows from the world. Thoughts of Cress filled her head. The wizard confused her. She had never met a male like him. Their journey neared an end, and as it did, regret filled her. It seemed strange to have a male care about her feelings. Strange and comforting. She'd learned much about the wizard. More competent than any male she ever thought possible…let alone like him.

Sitting up, she stretched, rubbed gritty sleep from her eyes, and pulled on her long leather boots. The morning's mild temperature felt good, but soon the sun would climb high and turn the day blistering hot.

Guardians flitted between Cress and her like inquisitive children. Their antics amused her while she and the wizard broke camp. She mounted her horse and aimed a smile at Cress when he did the same before spurring her mare into a fast pace, at last understanding an animal's eagerness to return to the barn. The same pull tugged at her heart.

They rode until they came upon a giant cactus, aptly named "prickly misery" in the center of a forked trail. Cress's suggestion to go straight had proven right on the mark. One way led north, the other west down a dry gully and then up through low hills. Becca nudged her horse forward on the westerly path, preventing the trotting mare from coming into contact with inch-long cactus barbs. The plants were bristly horrors because the slightest touch embedded spines into tender skin or thick hide.

Sunlight glinted off the golden Guardians darting in the air. Becca swore draconic laughter echoed in her head.

Cress swatted at the closest ones, clearly displeased with their teasing behavior as though he heard the same.

Sweet Luna, she prayed, *give me strength. Cress must succeed. He must.*

"Do not forget us," the Guardians chittered. *"We will help save your village. Fear not."*

The intrusion startled her, but she recovered quickly. *"Thank you, Guardians. Your offer is appreciated,"* she answered, wondering if the tiny creatures could perform magic better than the wizard. *"If Cress fails, I most certainly will call upon you."*

"We await your summons," came a chorus of voices as one. *"It is an honor to serve."*

Cress's words about the dragons having a purpose for accompanying them rolled through her head. *"Why?"*

"Never enough friends, child. We are your friend. We will seek a solution to your village plague."

She snuck a glance at Cress to check if he knew she communicated with the dragons only to find him studying the surrounding landscape. Amazingly, his conduct reminded her of a well-trained hunter. It showed intelligence to anticipate problems when entering new territory. The wizard puzzled her. He was male, but he seemed…different. Better. *"Are you making this offer because you doubt Cress's ability?"*

"Absolutely not!" they responded instantly. *"The*

wizard is highly skilled. He will resolve the problem."

She sniffed the air as if she could smell home. Smoke from laurel trees carried for miles on the currents. She sighed, hoping to catch a whiff.

Soon she would be home. Soon.

****

The next morning Cress woke to a drenching rainstorm soaking his skin. The storm came up so suddenly he'd had no chance to use magic to counter Nature's mood. Crouching beside Becca, he put his arms around her to shield her from the worst of the cloudburst.

He halfway expected her to object to his protective manner, but she hadn't. Oh, she tensed at first, but soon relaxed against him and seemed to find comfort in their closeness. He certainly had.

The deluge disappeared as abruptly as it materialized, leaving wet rivulets running down both their backs. He snapped his fingers, and their clothes dried instantly. Becca's smile of gratitude made the gesture worthwhile.

They mounted, and he hunched over his saddle and studied the stunted trees along the unhurried river they paralleled. Tiny reeds clothed the bank, along with tumbleweeds and cheatgrass. Tamarack saplings invaded the weeds.

For hours, they rode over low hills. A jagged rawness filled the area. Mighty convulsions from a distant past twisted the land, breaking rocks and pushing segments skyward with cataclysmic force. There were signs of landslides that had caused unstable boulders to crash down, then wind and rain eroded the landscape to give the rugged place its name: The Wilds.

Surviving in this inhospitable land took a hardy and energetic people. Cress tried to imagine Becca's ancestors finding their way here and struggling to stay alive. If they were a group of priestesses, they would have been accustomed to an easy life. For them to subsist in this land without assistance would have been a nigh impossible task, yet not only did they survive, they flourished and built new lives.

"I wonder where are the hunters?" Becca asked, breaking the silence encouraged by the inclement weather. "I deliberately chose this path because it is a favorite among them."

"Mayhaps they made a big kill and don't need to hunt for a while." He gave what sounded like good justification.

Becca turned her face away in disgust. He'd seen that look before.

"Game is scarce. Small parties constantly search for it." Stress lines marked the corners of the warrior woman's eyes. "No one has been here in ages. Look at the blinds. They're choked with weeds."

Cress studied the ground in the fading light. No trail or solitary footprint crossed this way.

Dusk fell rapidly, but Becca pushed onward. The clouds parted to allow stars to twinkle in the night sky. An hour later, a full moon shed silvery light to give him his first sight of Froy. He reined his horse to a stop to study it. The silhouette of a village sat on the other side of the river. He counted thirteen large huts of mud and daub with conical roofs sitting in a semicircle. Other structures were scattered here and there, and animal pens appeared situated away from the main village, but those thirteen huts held a high place within the society.

His attention remained fixed on the village. "At last, we've arrived."

Becca didn't answer him. Instead she scowled—a strange reaction for someone in such a rush to return that she practically threatened him.

"Smoke isn't coming from the center hut," she finally said.

The edge in her voice set his nerves on alert. She'd gotten them this far through dogged persistence, and now she hesitated. It set off a warning in the fine hairs on the back of his neck. "Is that significant?"

"Laurel leaves are burned in honor of Luna. It is our duty to see that the fire is never extinguished. The wind's blowing in our direction, so even if we don't see the smoke, we would smell it." She turned in the saddle, her eyes narrowed as though irritated that she needed to explain. "Nor is the Council's standard hanging over the roof. And where are the sentries? I know every location they should be stationed. Gette, my second-in-command, would not amend my orders without good reason. I don't know what's going on."

In the moonlight, Cress swore Becca trembled. Genuine concern rolled off her body, which ignited his own worry. "Then we should proceed with caution."

She drew her bow and set an arrow. "Not me. The best defense is to catch the enemy unaware."

Chapter Twenty-Three

Cold river water splashed Becca's leather leggings to soak her calves when she plunged into the river and galloped her horse across. Cress entered behind her not quite at the same speed with the mule in tow. She expected the thunderous hooves to bring hunters on a run. Nothing. No one. Only the sound of her own breathing and the gurgling river filled the night air.

She hated to criticize the first thing upon returning, but someone deserved to receive a tongue lashing for dereliction of duty. Where were the sentries? The people? What happened?

Small black and gold dogs caught their scent and rushed forward with hackles raised and lips drawn. At the first warning growls, she hissed the last password. The dogs fell silent. Since hunters pursued game at night, the dogs were trained not to bark immediately, only to investigate. If they sensed danger or found strangers, then they sounded the alarm. At least that remained the same. Small consolation, and her fears eased the tiniest bit.

One long-legged creature with a jagged scar across his broad skull approached cautiously. "Tulle, old friend, good to see you," she called softly.

The dog responded to her greeting by leaping forward, his bushy tail wagging as he jumped against her horse's side in an attempt to lick her hand. The roan mare skittered sideways at the dog's antics. Becca calmed the horse and ordered the dog to stay down. The others padded away, going back to whatever they were doing before she and Cress arrived home.

Home. A sudden rush of nostalgia swept over Becca. How many nights had she ached for this moment? How many times had she fretted, afraid of failure?

Was her mother dead? What about her sister and brothers?

Or am I being foolish? Maybe she had nothing to fear.

Someone hacked a cough in one of the structures. A child cried in another. People survived.

"We'll go to my mother's hut first. If she lives, she'll explain what's going on," she announced in a whisper, hoping she spoke the truth.

They stopped in front of the third hut from the center and dismounted. Humming from within elicited a smile from Becca, and she pushed aside the leather flap on the doorway. Inside, warm air smelled of wood smoke, spices, and her mother's familiar scent.

Moonlight leaked into the hut to reveal a lone figure with her back to the door.

"Mother," Becca said, moving aside to let Cress enter. The leather covering dropped down, swaying as though disturbed by the wind.

A muffled cry escaped from the woman. She leapt up and rushed forward with an enthusiasm that vanquished Becca's fears. "Becca! Sweet Luna," her mother said, enveloping her in an embrace that brought a rush of happiness and a sense of safety. "Is it truly you? I feared to never see you again, daughter."

Months of anxiety melted away. Becca sagged with relief against her mother and inhaled a familiar scent from childhood. Nothing could be amiss if Quinta d'Firn was thrilled for her return. "Oh, Mother, I can't tell you how often I've dreamed of this moment."

Becca spared a quick glance at Cress's dark shadow.

Quinta's gaze followed, but she remained silent. Instead, she brushed Becca's hair with a mother's gentle touch before releasing her. "Let me start a fire."

"That isn't necessary," Becca said.

Her mother moved away. "Then a light."

Quinta struck a flint. The lantern's wick flared. A yellow glow lit the hut's interior to reveal her mother's long curved bow decorated with feathers and beads propped against a wall painted blue with a yellow moon and tiny stars.

Her mother clutched Becca's hands, flicking a glance at Cress. "Honorable Wizard, are you hungry? I have some bread, cheese, and milk."

"Call me Cress."

She nodded, then turned her attention back to her daughter.

"I have succeeded and brought the wizard, but what has happened? There are no guards," Becca said, trying not to sound critical. "And aye, we could eat."

"I knew we chose right to send you, daughter. No one else could have succeeded."

Becca didn't have the heart to remind the older woman that she'd volunteered. Like most people in power, if a plan worked well, they forgot the origin of the idea. Her mother released her hand to retrieve food from a medium-sized domed chest, and the three sat on the thick furs.

"What has happened here?" Becca repeated. "Did the plague decimate the hunters' ranks that none could be spared as sentries?"

Quinta frowned as she handed out mugs of milk. "They are no longer needed."

Becca leapt to her feet. Milk slopped from the cup she dropped. "What? Who repels invaders or defends the village against danger?"

"Becca," Cress cautioned, "let your mother speak."

With a grateful glance at the wizard, Quinta set aside the chunk of bread that she'd torn off the loaf. "If we are attacked, the men of Froy can rebuff the assault."

"Men—" Becca began, then fell silent, her lips squeezed shut.

"If you think I've lost my senses, you're wrong," her mother continued in a voice edged with authority. "The plague hit right after you left. It swept through the village, taking children with the ease of water running through your fingers. I don't know the exact details as I was tending the sick, but when Pire's son was—"

At the mention of the blacksmith, Becca hissed through clenched teeth. She never liked the loudmouthed male. She visualized the large man— arrogant, heavily muscled with a thick neck, blotchy skin, and brows that beetled over his eyes, making his eyes glint like steel.

"—was stricken, his grief became inconsolable," her mother went on. "He yelled, demanding the Goddess Luna return his son. In a rage he threw his anvil into the fire, overturning hot coals. Maine dragged him out, but the fire spread to the granary. We lost the smithy shop and granary."

Nightmares materialized, although not exactly as Becca dreamed, but close enough to make her shudder.

Cress glanced at both of them, his expression schooled in a blank facade. What did he think of this dilemma? Was he as confused as she?

With a shrug, Quinta went on. "After the fire was extinguished, the men demanded equal rights."

"Heresy," Becca whispered. "Surely the Council objected."

"Naturally, and the men dispersed without argument." Quinta paused to rub her eyes. "They returned with swords in hand. Men and hunters fought. The Council saw the futility of the situation and called for the hunters to stop. The men were too well armed, and they knew how to wield the weapons."

"Hunters don't surrender," Becca said with a clenched fist raised. "I would have fought to the death."

Sighing, her mother shook her head. "The men insisted a vote be taken to determine who would govern Froy."

"Since when do males give orders?" She couldn't stop her resentment. "More importantly, who won this farce of an election?"

"Pire."

Men ruling Froy. It was sedition. Becca could scarcely encompass the concept. She cast a glance at Cress and knew instinctively he would never back such an action.

Becca placed a hand over her thumping heart. "How can you calmly sit and tell me you accept this change? You are a member of the Council."

"There is no more Council."

Dismay filled Becca. "Surely, you intend to rectify this…this abomination of men ruling Froy." She voiced her dissention aloud.

Quinta shot a commiserate look over the rim of her mug. Lowering the mug, she sopped a torn piece of bread into her milk. "The plague went away after the men took over, and Asa suggested that the plague might be tied to women ruling."

"Asa is loyal to Luna, and Luna would never side with males, not against the Council. Pire stole the Council's power."

"You've been gone many moons, daughter. Younger hunters bonded with the men," her mother said as if it explained the Council's defeat.

Becca felt the pull of a frown on her brow. What did Cress think of the situation? Did he believe the males weren't at fault? That the hunters were derelict of their duty? "Name the traitors."

"Gette, for one," her mother whispered, "but she's no traitor."

At her younger sister's name, Becca gasped. Sweet, reliable Gette. "Noooo."

Quinta nodded. "Pire's son was Gette's, too. She loved the boy with all her heart. Gette always favored Pire and had shown great joy bearing his son."

"I can't believe this," she said without qualms, noticing her mother's conical hat with gold beads in the corner. The older woman always wore it for special ceremonies. It broke Becca's heart to think her mother would never wear her prized possession again.

"You have to," Quinta said. "It is our way now."

Frustration burned through Becca like a knife. "But Gette! I can't believe she would do…How…how could she do such a thing?"

Her mother patted her hand. "The deed is done, and she is breeding again. To replace the child they lost."

"What of Nald and Quinn?" She named her brothers. "Surely, they opposed Pire."

Quinta shook her head. "Alas, my sons…your brothers helped hide the swords. I had no inkling of their dissatisfaction. Their betrayal cut as deeply as Gette's, mayhaps more because I repeatedly tried to show them favor, even though their father raised them. Now, they are off negotiating with the village of Norly."

Cress sat frozen, his body tense with rapt fascination. It pleased Becca that he listened and made no attempt to interrupt. His confusion must be as great as hers, maybe greater after listening to her berate men throughout the journey.

"Pire sent them as envoys," her mother went on. "For what purpose, I know not. I am not privy to all his plans."

Becca held back a sob. "What would you have me do?"

"Do?" her mother asked. "Why nothing, daughter. This change has come about, and I have accepted it. The men have worked ceaselessly since the fire. A new smithy has already gone up, and a new granary. Our ploughed fields have doubled. Never have I seen males achieve so much in such a short amount of time." She glanced at the wizard briefly. "A wise woman understands the necessity of seeking other people's support. But not even wisdom can defeat a village of armed men who believe they have shed the shackles of an unjust rule."

"They will not get away with this uprising," Becca said, frustration and anger sprouting out of control with the speed of weeds.

"The Council discussed this very prospect many times," her mother announced. "Though none expected it during our lives and rule."

Becca glanced at Cress. She remembered his look of surprise when she'd told him about men having no vote or say in the affairs of Froy. Now, she saw something else. Compassion? She should be upset but wasn't. Not with him. Never him. He possessed integrity. It set him apart. A man worthy of trust.

Still, she refused to accept males ruling Froy.

"Others will agree with me," she finally said, her voice trembling with excitement. "All I have to do is get them to talk with me."

Chapter Twenty-Four

Cress listened to the women, disturbed by their conversation. While his heart ached for Becca and the changes that had occurred during her absence, he couldn't blame the men for rebelling and overthrowing the Council. They had lived under the women's thumbs for generations.

Maybe he wasn't being objective.

Maybe Becca wasn't being objective either.

He stifled a sigh rising in his chest. Best to hold his counsel about Froy's leadership.

Becca shifted on her cushion. "All is not lost, Mother. It was wise to wait for my return before taking action. I'll handle Pire. He'll have to face me or reveal his cowardice before the entire village."

Quinta's color drained. "Your sister is married to Pire. How can you want to destroy their happiness—or the other couples'—for a return of life most are ready to forget?"

Becca's brow furrowed. "I must rid Froy of male rule. And with Luna's help, I will."

Cress stared at Quinta, whose blue eyes sparkled with a light that reminded him of Salida. He suspected the older woman wanted her daughter to consider the consequences before acting rash. Not that he blamed her. Sometimes Becca acted like a belligerent child.

"Becca, is that wise?" he finally asked, against his

better judgement. "I'm sure you're in shock. Mayhaps you should let it go."

Becca snorted. "Our society is based on the hunting cats of the plains. The females hunt and protect, while males remain behind to tend the young. That is the way it always has been."

"Pire has many supporters," Quinta said. "Your brothers. Maine. Women as well as men, especially the younger ones. Many have taken men as husbands. The time was ripe for change."

"Surely, Mother, I can count on you and other Council members. Side with me. Show the others."

Quinta shook her head. "Oh, Becca, can't you see? I am old. Tired. I have an easier life in this new way."

The friction between parent and child turned palpable. While Cress empathized with Becca's plight, being defiant and argumentative never solved a dilemma, nor did he believe a face-to-face confrontation would help.

Becca lifted her chin. "Gette's not old. I'll speak to her. I want to hear her betray herself with her own words."

"Do not be harsh on her," Quinta said. "A pregnant woman is emotional. Becomes overly wrought at the slightest thing. Do not distress her. It would crush her if she lost this babe. She has always been more fragile than you. Another loss might destroy her."

"Have faith, Mother," Becca appealed. "No harm will befall her. Or the babe. She will listen to me. I know she will."

"And if Gette doesn't?" Quinta asked with calm reassurance. "What then?"

Cress finished his cheese and washed it down with

a gulp of milk. His thoughts mirrored the older woman's. He swore Becca's lip curled, but he couldn't decide if she sneered or smiled. Mother did her utmost to persuade daughter, and he sensed a slight shift. The problem—which way—to stop or push forward.

Becca wet her lips when she turned to face him. "Could the people be enchanted? Can you sense any magic?"

"Not the slightest ripple."

She scowled, clearly finding his answer distasteful. "You're positive?"

"You doubt the wizard after bringing him all this way?" her mother asked.

Becca sat back, red blotches staining her cheeks. "Of course, I don't. Him, I trust."

That gave Cress pause. She trusted him. Since when? Nothing but negativity poured out of the warrior woman's mouth about men since meeting him.

Quinta looked surprised as well. "A little understanding and compassion for the people of Froy wouldn't be amiss right now. Investigate first? Hold an assembly?"

Becca jumped up, her voice shaking when she spoke. "I'm done talking. The situation requires action."

Much more slowly, Quinta stood as well. "Pire has shown himself to be a good leader, Becca. Give him a chance to show you."

"Mother! How can you say such a thing? It's traitorous."

"Hardly disloyal." An undertone of calm radiated from the older woman. "Merely not what you wish to hear. Change takes time getting used to. We fought it at first, but after six months, we have adjusted. You've only returned. Give yourself time."

"Becca," Cress said, looking up. "Hold your temper and heed your mother's words. She has a point."

The warrior woman swirled toward him, her face set in a scowl; then she brightened. "Cress, you are a powerful wizard. You could destroy Pire and restore the Council."

"You ask the impossible. I will not kill for you. Do you forget that negative magic has consequences to the user? While I sympathize with your predicament, I am here to find a cause for the plague." He chose his words with care. He cared for Becca, but she needed to understand his position in the order of things. "My mission is to save people, not murder them. Furthermore, if wizards used their magic to overthrow unpopular regimes, how long do you think wizards would last in our world?"

Quinta let out a weary sigh. "The man has a point, Becca. His focus should be on the plague."

Lantern light revealed Becca bracing herself against further arguments. Her chin inched upward. He recognized that stubborn tilt—she loathed being wrong.

Blue eyes flashed with an inner fire. "I'm not afraid to face Pire. Or any male."

"I never meant to imply you were," Quinta replied, but sounded less certain than when she started. "If you start issuing orders, no one will listen. For sure, not the men nor the women loyal to them."

"Why did the hunters surrender? Did they stop caring about Froy?"

"They care," Quinta said. "The men were winning the fight. The Council ordered them to put down their weapons."

Becca breathed deeply. "Tell me where Pire is, and I'll be on my way."

"Don't be rash, dear daughter. Prejudice is blinding you. You were the greatest leader of our hunters. Rather than confronting him, use those skills to win him to your side. Stalk your prey. Choose where to attack. You know I'm right. Believe me, I'm thinking of your welfare. Meanwhile, sleep here this evening. The night is half over. Pire will still be here in the morning."

Cress smiled. Clever woman. She layered her persuasion with the sweetest coating—praise and genuine concern.

"I realize that, Mother, and value your counsel," Becca said in a softer tone. "Come dawn, I'll seek out Pire. Meanwhile, I'm going to take care of the animals."

"I'll help." Cress rose alongside Becca and put his hand on her shoulder in hopes the warmth of his touch brought a measure of peace. She jerked free and stomped outside.

"Forgive my daughter, Master Wizard," Quinta said. "She is often outspoken, and I'm afraid this change is upsetting to her. Once she realizes how Froy has improved, she will see things differently."

****

The next morning dark-bellied clouds scudded across the sky. Stepping out of the hut, Cress smelled wood smoke and heard insects chirping. Pigs, goats, and chickens roamed between the huts and pens. A newly constructed granary lay a distance away from the animal enclosures and the blacksmith shop built into the hill.

A sleepy-eyed girl of five or six wandered to the river with a bucket in hand. Men and women stood talking to each other, glancing in his direction.

He swallowed hard. He'd grown accustomed to living in the dragon circle with Salida as his only company and Einer as an occasional visitor. The last time he'd been in the company of more than three people was when he's spied a Fezners' caravan, riding in their colorful wagons, laughing and singing as they journeyed from town to town. He'd stayed hidden within the shadows of the trees.

Shouts erupted when Becca stepped out of her mother's hut behind him. The loudness of their voices came as a surprise. Women flashed smiles, but the same could not be said for the men. They scowled, some appeared afraid, and two or three reflected open hostility.

Staring at the people, his concern for Becca's safety grew. He gave her an anxious look, whispering, "Not exactly the reception you expected."

"Nay, it isn't," she said in the same low tone.

Uneasiness stirred inside him. "Proceed with care, Becca."

A subtle shrug made her braid sway. "I appreciate your advice, Cress, but you don't grasp the seriousness of the situation." She waved her arm to include the village. "Order must be restored."

"It looks fine to me."

She frowned. "Not to me."

He shook his head. "If Froy isn't to your liking, then let's return to the dragon circle. Your mother made no mention of the plague returning. It might have passed, and the problem facing my sister still remains."

Becca stared at him, her face draining of color. "The plague is still a danger. You vowed to investigate. Before we depart, I need to make sure my people are protected."

"I wondered who visited Quinta," a powerfully built man with black wiry hair called in a booming voice.

He bouldered his way through villagers. His chest was the size of a water barrel, and he strode on muscular legs. The heavy leather apron draped over his front did naught to hide his massive size. Glancing at the man's hands, Cress judged his fingers could easily wrap around the thick handle of a belt-slung hammer meant to bend steel to his will.

Becca rushed up to the man's face in less time than it took Cress to blink. "Have you come to gloat, Pire?" she demanded. "I hear you are leader now."

"I came to welcome you back. The same as these good people would do if you'd stop scowling at them. Your horses were spotted in the corral, and everyone speculated on who arrived in the middle of the night. I'm glad it's you. We have all worried. Your family and me, more so since you are my sister-by-marriage."

Becca studied the area. "Speaking of Gette…Where is she? What have you done with her?"

Pire bowed his head. "She's resting."

Becca snorted with disbelief. "Why? Have you beaten her?"

The blacksmith stepped back a pace as through struck. His broad face darkened with anger. "Hardly. By this hostility, I assume the changes to Froy are not to your liking. None of what happened was done with malice."

A shiver ran down Cress's spine. He'd come to investigate a plague, not become enmeshed in village disputes.

Yet, he'd grown to care about Becca, and forced himself to remain at her side, ready to leap to her defense. His fingers tingled with magic. The Guardians, though invisible, flapped in the air, their wings sounding like angry insects. They might be small, but their fire breath could easily inflict painful wounds.

"Of course, you would say that," she answered the big man. "I will bear no grudge against you or any man if leadership is restored to the Council this very day."

"I cannot do that," Pire said. "Even if I wanted to, a new order has been established. If you are expecting me to repent my actions or the others, I refuse."

Two girls—no more than six or seven—ran past carrying bows. Giggling, they pretended to shoot invisible arrows. Cress decided Froy could use a dose of carefree spirit.

Becca glanced at them, then back to the blacksmith. "I challenge you to battle me."

"What?" Pire gasped.

"Becca, is that wise?" Cress mindspoke to her. *"Remember, honey draws more than vinegar. Smile. He expects trouble."*

Her eyes widened, clearly forgetting the link the Guardians had established between them. *"I thought to catch him off guard. Now let me continue."* She turned to glare at Pire. "I will show you the real mettle of a hunter. Once I defeat you, people will return to the old ways."

In those few seconds, Pire thrust his bushy brows together. "We have new laws now, Becca," he answered her. "New ways."

"You refuse to fight me? Your lack of willingness heaps more shame on your actions. You are a coward!"

Several men hissed at the insult.

The blacksmith's nostrils flared as he peered down at her. "I don't fight women. You're upset because hunters no longer reign supreme. Men defend Froy now."

"Bold words," she sneered. "What proof do you have to back them up? Has this bravery been put to the test?"

"Not yet," Pire admitted, stepping closer. "Our mettle will show when the time comes."

Cress looked at her and offered a small grin of support. The smile she returned warmed his insides, then she turned to face Pire again.

"I see," Becca said. "Then you won't mind if I keep my bow."

Pire took a breath and relaxed a bit. His muscular arm swept around. "Do whatever you wish. No one will stop you."

"So you say," she scoffed. "Somehow, I'll feel safer with it near me."

"You jest," the blacksmith answered with a grin. "A good sign, I think. Or mayhaps you have a guilty conscience. When you settle down, we can talk."

Male laughter rippled from the spectators.

Cress edged closer to Becca. "Introduce me."

Chapter Twenty-Five

The blank mask on Cress's face made Becca wonder if his stoicism stemmed from the fact he'd lived for centuries. She blew out a long breath. "Wizard Cress, this is Pire. Pire, the Wizard Cress."

The spectators gasped.

The big blacksmith's mouth widened to reveal a toothy grin. "Welcome to Froy, Master Wizard."

"Thank you for your welcome," Cress said.

Pire turned to face her. His leather apron contained scorched spots, and she smelled the coppery hint of heated metal on his clothes.

"I'm glad you succeeded, Becca," he said. "I worried you might have gone to meet the Great Mother or found a place you liked better than Froy."

Becca cringed inwardly. She'd made a tactical error revealing her opposition. Her mother had been wise to counsel caution. Sadly, she didn't listen. "No place is better than home. I traveled a long way and ran into several difficulties."

Pire scowled. "What difficulties?"

"Nothing I couldn't resolve. We're here, aren't we?"

"Tell me of this plague," Cress asked as though to separate them. "I am eager to resolve the problem before it returns."

Anguish passed over the blacksmith's face so fast

Becca wondered if he thought of his deceased son.

"We pray the pestilence never returns," Pire whispered. "It seems to start with young boys and—"

"Why did you revolt, Pire?" she butted in, unable to control herself. The sight of the man curdled her stomach. No way would she credit him with qualities belonging to good and decent women.

His gaze arrowed in on her in a flash. "For a better life."

"Not for power? Did you covet leadership of Froy? As I recall you were always inciting the other males. Tell me. Unless you're afraid to admit your motives."

Pire shook his head as though to clear it. "I told you—for a better life. Any fool can open their mouth, but a wise person knows when to speak and what words will have the most effect on those who listen. You are wrong about me, Becca. I fear nothing. I knew the consequences of my actions. Failure equaled death. Still, I took the chance. I know you're confused right now. Upset. Even afraid. I understand that and will give you time to adjust to the changes."

Her fingers clenched at her sides. Her bow slipped, and she repositioned it on her shoulder. "I fear no man, especially you. How can you, a blacksmith, lead Froy? How can you expect to equal the accomplishments of the Council?"

His brow furrowed. "All I can do is my best. My first concern is Froy. If I need advice, I have friends and advisors to call upon."

She gritted her teeth. She never liked participating in futile arguments. He presented an answer for everything. His quickness surprised her. "What of experience?"

Straightening to his full height, the muscles in his thick arms tightened. "Thirty years of being subjected to the Council's will and observing should suffice."

"You will find observation lacks substance compared to action."

"Froy was founded on a lie," he said.

Finally. The man erred. "Who lies now? Our ancestors established Froy because they were escaping death and destruction created by men like you. The old tales claim men grew greedy for dragon treasure and killed those magnificent creatures. The priestesses of Luna tried to save them. Led a few chosen away. Some males accompanied us as servants. We are the descendants of those brave people."

Soft murmurs emanated from the women. Becca's heart quickened. They listened. The truth shall set the hunters free. Maybe Pire's tenuous hold on her village cracked. Maybe the simple reminder of why they came to The Wilds was all they needed.

Villagers watched, waiting. The air thickened with expectancy.

Pire scowled at the shifting, murmuring groups. "An old myth is another issue we differ on. Dragons never existed. Hence, no treasure existed. Those tales entertained gullible children on cold winter nights. You judge me unfairly. But that said, you brought the wizard. Let me show him around the village. He can check for causes of the plague. Or, if you prefer, escort him yourself," he suggested. "Otherwise, there is no reason for him to remain here."

Nervousness undulated through the villagers like a stone's ripple on a lake.

She caught him in a lie. The Guardians were real.

She narrowed her eyes, trying to decide if she should speak of them. Would the tiny creatures reveal themselves to put fact to Pire's lie?

"Let me go with him, Becca," Cress's rich baritone whispered in her mind. The warmth of his voice spread through her like a sweet wine. The sound offered comfort and gave her courage. *"The Guardians are not going to reveal themselves. Not yet. Mayhaps never. Searching for clues might aid me in discovering the plague's cause."*

Becca wanted to protest, then decided she could best use her time to gather evidence of Pire's wrongdoing. She needed to keep him occupied.

The two girls with practice bows raced back through the open area. Their laughter cut the tension among the trio. Becca glanced at the pair who barely looked old enough to have been presented their first bows.

"I'll be happy to look around the village," Cress volunteered.

"Fine," she replied. "Go with Pire. I have other people to see."

In front of a new blacksmith shop Becca recognized Maine sharpening a sword. Sparks flew off metal in all directions. He sat on a small stool, bare-chested, sweat gleaming off skin tanned to a golden bronze by the sun. The sight reminded her of the Guardians, and she realized they'd remained silent since Cress and she entered the village. Cress had been accurate in counseling that they wouldn't reveal themselves.

"You know my wishes. Just be careful," Cress mindspoke to her, then said aloud, "I would be

honored."

"I promise."

"Much is at stake, Becca," Pire said. "I wish to be your friend, not your enemy."

She glowered at him. "You've already proved differently."

Pire shook his head and led Cress away.

Nearby people glanced at each other. She recognized several hunters, and except for the two young girls, they had exchanged their leggings and studded tunics for long shifts belted at the waist, and not one of them held a bow or arrows. Seeing unarmed women hunters cut Becca worse than she imagined, but she refused to let disappointment show.

It explained the blacksmith's confidence and lack of fear to confront her.

She spun away from the gawking people and walked up the hill toward Maine. Gette could wait. Maine glanced up from his low stool at her approach and flashed a crooked grin. That grin triggered a warm tingle as she studied her one-time lover. He'd always been her favorite. One of the tallest males in the village, mostly solid muscle, she'd always found him careful with his great strength.

Several thick, jagged scars ran over his shoulders and across his chest. He'd received them from a glossy black hunting cat that dared to attack the village's cattle. Maine choked the beast to death with his bare hands, and afterwards she had tended his wounds.

Now, he sprouted a short, trim beard. While she never cared for men with facial hair, the style fit him. She smiled at him with genuine affection.

"Hello, Maine. How are you?"

His large hands criss-crossed with fine scars from his pitched battle with the cat moved with precision as he sharpened the blade. The honed metal shone deadly bright in the morning sunlight.

"Welcome back, Becca," he greeted. The whetstone slowed as he stopped pumping the paddle that spun the wheel. "It gladdens my heart to see you once again."

"I never thought to see swords in Froy," she said. "Swords have only one purpose—to kill another person. Hand to hand fighting is foreign to hunters. Our method of defense is to rain arrows on the marauders and not allow them to get close."

Maine's handsome face wrinkled in puzzlement when he adjusted his grip on the leather-wrapped handle. "You better hope our sword arms never fail." He sighed. "I have no wish to argue with you, Becca. I saw you speaking with Pire. He's a good man, and I'm sure he explained what is best now."

"Pire? I'm sick of hearing his name and people's exalted opinion of him. He does not deserve admiration." She spat her words as if venom. "The Council should be in charge."

Maine's expression hardened. He stood to straddle the stool and tower over her. "It no longer exists. Nor does anger suit you."

Cold dread made her tremble. He knew her well. "I know. It is just hard for me to accept what has happened."

He flashed an apologetic smile and sat back down. "You were gone so long. I feared you dead. People were afraid. The plague struck, and the fire destroyed all our extra supplies. It was difficult to face the unknown."

"Why not speak up?"

"And say what? Stop! Wait! Becca will return. What guarantee did I have? None. I lost hope. Many did." His outburst over, he grinned, the tension in the air easing. "You never were very good at hiding your dislike for Pire. You faulted him whenever the chance arose."

"I see plenty of fault right now. And not just in Pire."

"I deserve that," he responded, sadness filling his deep voice. "Go ahead and lash out at me if you wish. I'm sure you blame every male in the village for overthrowing the Council."

"By *destroying* the Council?" she corrected.

He grunted at the different choice of words. "You shouldn't be surprised. Our fathers should have rebelled decades ago."

"If you were unhappy, why didn't you present your case before the Council?"

"As if they would listen," Maine answered, his tone heavy with scorn. "Name one time your precious Council listened to the pleas of men."

Becca narrowed her gaze in disbelief. "They would have."

He stopped and ran his thumb over the blade's edge sharpened to the width of a hair. A bead of bright red blood pooled on his rounded pad. He sucked it off. "You never did. I tried to talk to you. Do you remember?"

"I took your concerns to the Council! They chose not to act on them."

His eyes widened in surprise. "You never told me."

"I should have."

Comprehension suddenly dawned on her. Each time, after a night of carnal pleasure, Maine had whispered in her ear about the men's dissatisfaction. One time, she had grown so bored listening to him that she threatened to never accept his beads if he didn't keep silent.

"I don't mean to upset you, Becca. We men…" With a groan, he stopped and straightened his posture. "The rebellion wasn't planned. I swear. After the fire, we went to the Council to request certain rights, but they refused to heed us."

"With swords in hand?"

His lips tightened in protest. "The first time we came unarmed, our hands extended in friendship, and were thrown out! The Council refused to take us seriously."

Becca started to object, but Maine's expression stopped her. His brown eyes gleamed with conviction, and he seemed unrepentant. A new assurance gave him poise. She remembered the look on his face after they'd made love—contented, supreme, and subdued. He appeared the same, but different.

He took a deep breath. "Pire forged the swords in secret to use against marauders. They were brought out to show the Council we could do what we pledged. They ordered the hunters to strip us of our weapons. We had no desire to raise swords against the Council or the hunters, but we refused to surrender them. We wanted to contribute to Froy's defenses."

Her stomach turned. "Where did these ideas come from?"

Anger flickered in Maine's eyes for just a moment,

but he never lost his concentration while running his finger down the sharpened edge of the blade. "The traders' men told us who rules the outside world. Men! Not women."

"Sweet Luna, you believed strangers over people you'd known all your life? That proves how foolish males are. Trusting strangers. Had anyone from Froy traveled outside The Wilds and returned? No. Never. You rose up against the Council on conjecture. Women wouldn't have done that, Maine. A woman considers all the options first. We would have investigated before we acted."

Her own words stopped her. Maybe she overreacted with Pire. Exhaustion and fear had weighed on her shoulders for months. It seemed only logical for normal patience to dip low. She tried not to blame herself for committing the exact folly she preached against.

Maine switched his sword from one hand to the other, testing its balance. "We like our new freedom. No man will go back to the old way."

The conversation digressed. "Do you know where Gette is?" she asked, unwilling to continue the argument. "I would like to speak with her."

"She should be in your old hut," he answered immediately.

"My old hut?" Anxiety instantly rose in Becca. "Isn't it still mine?"

"The huts were reallocated, except Quinta's. Your brothers claimed it and asked her to stay. Pire and Gette took yours. Meetings are still held in the center hut."

"I suppose they divided up my belongings as well."

He sighed. "You'll have to speak to Pire or Gette.

Mayhap they chose your hut to keep it and your belongings safe until your return. I chose the one to the right of Pire's when I took Landa as my wife."

"Landa! She's the worst hunter in the village."

A slow smile spread across his face. "She loves me. She always has."

Becca felt a pang of what…regret? Jealousy? The news should have devastated her. Oddly, it didn't. Only a void. She didn't care Maine chose to wed another. What bothered her was he had selected such a poor hunter.

In slow motion, she stroked the yew bow on her shoulder, feeling the wood grow warm at her touch. Nothing comforted more than the familiar texture of the dependable weapon.

A few moments later, the play of children ground to a halt when she approached the hut she once called home. Standing before the entrance, Becca wanted to cry.

For herself.

For Froy.

For those she loved and thought loved her.

Chapter Twenty-Six

Cress walked alongside the muscular blacksmith. When sizing up an opponent, he preferred one-on-one far more. Dogs barked, sheep baaed, children laughed, men talked in small groups, and the occasional shout of a woman to a child rose above the din. He recognized the dog Becca called Tulle following on their heels.

Seen by daylight, the village didn't compare to Brenalin—no walls, no marketplace for merchants to barter goods from around the world, no barracks for soldiers. The conical huts were constructed of animal hides and poles. Small gardens next to huts were lush with cabbages and onions. A lazy river meandered left of the village, and ploughed fields appeared on the right.

In the distance, Becca talked to a tall, bearded man. He couldn't help being curious.

"That's Maine," Pire said, noticing his attention centered on the couple. "My second-in-command."

"Why tell me?"

"I thought you'd like to know. He's Becca's ex-lover."

To his chagrin, Cress latched onto the phrase ex-lover. The meeting meant nothing he told himself. Then he remembered Quinta mentioning the name. Had the older woman been passing a message to her daughter?

Pire directed him across the open area. They passed

a newly planted orchard. Pears and apuls had bloomed and set fruit on spindly trees. Fall would bring a small, tasty harvest.

Pire stopped where a pile of wood lay black and charred. An acrid smell still hung in the air. "A fire erupted at the start of the last plague. This is all that remains of my old blacksmith shop and the granary. The fire was my fault." He uttered the statement without shame and started walking again.

A candid man, Cress decided, *to admit guilt. He should be commended. Especially considering the circumstances.* "My condolences at your loss."

"We can ill afford to lose a single person to the pestilence. Buildings can be rebuilt. People cannot," the blacksmith said in a solemn tone. "In a few months, my wife will give birth again. No child can replace our first born, but the emptiness in our hearts will be eased when a new babe fills our arms. Children bring great joy and laughter into life. It is our responsibility to make them safe. They are the future, if Froy is to continue and prosper."

Cress took stock of the blacksmith. The piercing blue eyes beneath dark, bushy eyebrows burned with the fire of intensity. Listening to him, Cress wondered if events created this passionate man or if he had always existed.

Tulle sniffed at the ashes, sending up black puffs of air.

"Your requirements are no different from anyone else's," he answered. "People are much the same everywhere. All they desire is to live in peace and raise their families without fear of war or sickness."

Pire pursed his lips in objection, then heaved a

sigh. "I swear to you as one man to another, it wasn't always that way in Froy. For centuries the Council nurtured a conflict…a social difference between men and women that shouldn't have existed. To have you here, a man from outside The Wilds, and be revered is a sight I never expected to see in my lifetime. Traveling with Becca, one of the Council's staunchest supporters, must have made your journey interesting, if not outright challenging. She usually holds males in little esteem. Now, we'll make your stay as comfortable as possible."

"She treated me fairly," Cress said, biting down his irritation for the man to assume Becca would treat him with disrespect. He found her stubborn, hard, but fair. "Why does she dislike you?"

"I have no idea," Pire said, his tone neutral. "Ask her."

"I just might."

Pire shrugged. "Tradition is deeply engrained with Becca. Change is about control and is difficult to accept. The sooner she sees how people are prospering, the better."

"You took away her chance to decide," Cress countered.

A flicker sparked in the man's eyes. "You are very welcome here, Master Wizard, but I would appreciate you keeping your opinions to yourself."

"A fair request." Cress halted beside a patchwork of fields separated by rock walls. Half the fields sprouted barley and oats while the other half lay fallow with cattle, pigs, and chickens roaming about, dropping manure as fertilizer, a method of farming commonly used in Brenalin to increase yield. A sign that different cultures were the same at the core.

"We have doubled our fields," Pire went on to explain. "We have learned how to coax a harvest from the poorest soil, but do not be deceived by the arid look of our land. It is fertile here. All it requires is water, and the river provides plenty. With an oxen team, a man can plough an acre a day. We take turns behind the oxen, so no man feels abused. I work more days in the smithy, but that is by choice, and I will train any willing to learn the trade."

"You should be proud of your accomplishments."

Pire waved away the praise. "It took everyone working together. We've had a few years of drought, but the last two winters were snowy, followed with rainy springs. It is what has made our crops so abundant." He hesitated before continuing. "The fire set us back. We pitched together, men and women, to rebuild both structures. The Council would never have considered working as a team. We moved the granary closer to the fields. When our crops ripen and are ready to harvest, it will take less time to cart to the granary. Our winter spelt was plentiful and the last cutting extremely good. Already men are out seeking buyers for the excess."

Cress wondered why the man told him all this. To impress…or to convince? "I admire your ability to coordinate people. You must have a talent for it."

Pire's chest swelled. "I prefer things organized. I learned a long time ago in my shop, if tools are out of place, accidents happen. They should always be where I expect them. I am trying to apply the same principle to Froy."

Cress agreed with the blacksmith, even though the thought felt disloyal to Becca. "I came to assist your village against the plague. Nothing else."

"Aye, the plague," Pire repeated. "I can probably tell you more about what doesn't work than what does."

Cress pondered the man's round face. The weathered lines of his features implied arrogance and pride were deeply embedded within him—something he missed the first time he'd studied the blacksmith.

"Any detail might be significant."

"Charms don't work. We tried smoke on those who got sick. That didn't help. It seems to start with a simple runny nose. Breathing becomes labored. Then death."

"Any particular people afflicted first?"

"Mostly the boys. But no one is safe."

"I'd like to look around before drawing any conclusions," Cress said with a touch of sharpness. He found himself liking the man and preferred to remain loyal to Becca. "I'm sure I'll have more questions."

"Let me show you the new smithy. We moved it west of the original location."

The blond man sitting at the whetstone wheel with whom he'd seen Becca speaking had left by the time they arrived. A shame. Cress would have liked a closer look, to take the man's measure.

Tulle bounded over the hill, and the two men followed.

Within the blacksmith shop, the floor consisted of fine gravel for protection against wayward sparks. Pire headed to the forge with the confident steps of a man who knew the place well. Cress accompanied him, only to retreat when the blacksmith pulled a lever on the bellows and a wall of flames sent searing heat washing over him.

Even with the double doors open not all the warmth could escape. When the flames settled down, the gravel under Cress's feet crunched as he stepped forward again to see what the blacksmith heated in the coals.

A narrow piece of metal radiated bright red and yellow.

Cress raised a single brow, questioning. "More swords?"

An easy grin raised Pire's lips. "A scythe."

People owed their furrows and friable soil to hoes and rakes produced in a smithy's forge. Out here, a smith would be a treasured citizen, and his words would carry great sway. No wonder people did as he bade.

"We have established teams to plow each parcel, and more strips of land will be tilled next year, and more the year after," Pire continued.

"An ambitious strategy," Cress said, impressed with the scope of effort. "Did you figure this all out before or after rebelling against the Council?"

The blacksmith's face reddened. "No woman of the Council would admit this, but Froy was near collapse. Change was required."

"You speak lightly of revolt. How can you be sure it was the right thing to do?"

"Why do you ask?" Pire challenged.

"Do you trust me?"

Pire frowned. "You are a stranger to me. I don't know you well enough to trust."

Cress shrugged, aware he came down hard on the man. "A fair and honest answer. If you want me to find a cure, you're going to have to learn to trust me."

Chapter Twenty-Seven

With a hunter's stealth, Becca slipped inside her old hut. Her sister's recognizable form bent over a basket she wove. Her hands grasped the grass and wrapped the strips tightly against each other. The process could take hours or days, depending on the size of basket.

"What did you forget this time, Pire?" Gette asked in a teasing tone without turning around. Her dark blonde hair hung down her back in a single braid like Becca's.

"Gette." Becca grunted a sour greeting befitting her mood.

The woman leapt to her feet and spun around with dizzying speed, her belly rounding out her front. Her pale blue eyes widened in surprise, and her full mouth opened but no sound spilled out. She towered over Becca by two or three inches and was much heavier boned, yet the blood relationship between them was easy to recognize. Her round face had plumped out her cheeks and her complexion paled. She sank to the floor, barely missing a cushion of woven reeds. "Sweet Luna."

"The Great Mother can't help you, but at least you still believe in her." Becca hurried over, unhappy with the flash of worry that exploded within her.

Gette spread her hands wide, palms up. "Why

would you say such a thing? Oh, Becca, I feared to never see you again. Please. Sit down. When did you return? Were you successful in finding the wizard? Make yourself comfortable. Let me ease your thirst with some tea. I have your favorite."

Becca crossed her legs under her and laid her bow beside her, not softened by the offer. The tea probably came from her own stores to begin with. Then she narrowed her eyes. Shame rose as she realized how petty her thoughts were—below her dignity.

She surveyed the interior. Smoke curled from the low-burning fire in the center of the room. The spicy odors of rosemary and sage filled the hut.

Her muscles tensed. Where were her belongings? Tossed out? Appropriated? It wasn't right. Or fair. Losing her possessions and home seemed a poor reward for being the Chosen One and bringing the wizard to save Froy.

The only thing remaining the same were the walls—unpainted, as she left them. The plain walls surprised her since her sister liked color.

A pile of furs wide enough for two filled the far corner. An array of lead beads the size of small peas and large blueberries half filled a wooden bowl beside the furs. Pots hung above the fire pit in the center of the hut, and gourds of various sizes were strung along the wall—obviously, enough storage for a family. A crib, newly crafted from supple wicker, the stripped bark yet to darken, caught Becca's attention.

The sight squeezed at her heart. Concern rather than anger prompted her next words. "I can't believe you'd bred again."

A normal color returned to Gette's face as she

splayed a hand across her swollen belly. "It could be a girl."

"You almost died the last time. Why gamble with your life?"

"My son died."

Becca swallowed hard. "I never thought you were foolish. Did Pire force himself on you?"

"Pire and I love each other. I'll never find a braver, more honorable or noble man, no matter how hard I look." She paused and leveled her gaze at Becca. "Didn't you feel that way about Maine?"

"Nay, it was sex." Becca only wanted Froy to survive. She couldn't see it continuing with men in control. "Why start a family? Why marry Pire?"

"I didn't know I loved him until I got a chance to see the traders and their families. Pire took me to see them the last time we traded with them. I saw the strength in the bond when they committed to each other, and that inspired me."

Becca ground her teeth and forced herself to remain calm. Accusations did no good. They put Gette on the defensive. "I seem the only one upset over this change. Surely, another exists."

"None that I am aware of."

It took all Becca's effort to see the change in a new light…a better one…and failed.

"Where are my possessions?" she asked, changing the subject.

Gette rolled to her side and lumbered to her feet. She waddled to a medium sized trunk covered with lush furs. "I saved them for you." She lifted the lid, its hinges creaking, and made a grand, sweeping gesture. "Your things. Every last one of them. Untouched by me

176

or anyone else."

Becca's gaze went to the trunk she recognized as her own and then back again to her sister. A tiny crack formed in her frozen heart. "My eternal gratitude, Gette. But what of my home? Am I to sleep outside by the fire or with the dogs?"

Blue fire flashed in her sister's eyes. "Of course not. A proper place will be found for you."

"*This* is my home."

Gette poured heated water into small clay cups and sprinkled crumbled tea buds as though engaged in a perfectly normal conversation. "Claiming it is temporary. You can reclaim it when we move to the blacksmith's shop. Pire doesn't want to be leader forever."

Becca distrusted the statement. She wondered if her sister liked being married to the village leader. It seemed the only explanation to make sense for her traitorous behavior. "You've managed to excuse your theft of my home, but what of the hunters who died? Do you give any thought to them laying in their cold graves?"

"Bitterness does not become you, sister. Of course, I regret their loss, but they raised weapons against us. They killed young Draco and Phelps. We only defended ourselves."

"We? Us? I find it amazing you speak with the voice of your husband." She glanced at her sister's protruding belly and fought to restrain the bristle of her temper.

Gette's hand shook as she added a dollop of honey to one of the steeping cups of tea and passed the sweetened brew to Becca. She hadn't forgotten Becca's sweet tooth. "Pire and I are of one mind, and that is to raise our children together as a family. We weren't allowed to do so before. If we had been…mayhaps I could have saved our son."

Becca accepted the tea and sat back. A heady, floral scent of orchids wafted in the air. It reminded her of the powder Gette used to make from flowers for her son when he teethed. "I heard about the little one. I'm sorry for your loss. I never knew the babe meant so much to you," she said in a low voice. "But the past has no bearing on today."

"Doesn't it? You weren't always content with the Council. Admit it. You just weren't ready to commit."

Becca didn't believe in self-reflection. It made her feel vulnerable. "Everyone voices dissatisfaction at one time or another."

Her sister smiled timidly. "We broke with tradition because it was time. Equality exists now."

That came as a surprise. "Surely you jest."

Gette slurped her hot tea. "I am serious and beg you not to close your mind. Give Pire a chance. See if he rules fairly before taking action against him."

Solid misery rose inside Becca. Not anger. Not sadness. Only cold, desperate misery. "He's male. To even consider the possibility is wrong."

"That's evasion, and you know it," Gette said, a mixture of compassion and empathy on her round face. "I feel sorry for you, Becca. While I cuddle against the warmth of Pire's body at night, you lay alone. You will never experience the joy of a man's true love."

"Who lies alone?" Becca snapped, stunned to realize her sister's soft voice almost convinced her. "As usual, all you consider is your own welfare and call me envious. I am no servant to any man. Nor must I beg for one to pleasure me. The only time I am alone is by my choice."

"Froy is no longer one rule for the women and one for the men." Gette defended the change. "For me and the other women, being married means making our husband happy. Take the bearing of weapons—if hunters do not wish to carry a bow, no one points a finger at them for dereliction of duty."

Of all the ways for Froy's destruction—marauders, plague, fire, crop failure—never once did Becca believe it would fall for mishandling men.

"You think," her sister rallied, "since you're back, the hunters will follow you? I hate to disillusion you, but you'll be disappointed. Our future lies with Pire. He offers hope. People want order and structure. They believe he can lead them into a new future, a bright and successful one."

Becca's finger skimmed along the cup's rim. She had no business taking out her frustration on her sister, but the more resistance she encountered, the angrier she became. "Sheer speculation."

A frown settled between Gette's brows when she noisily sipped her tea. "Call it what you will. Everyone is happy with this new arrangement. If only you comprehended how much Pire cares about Froy and the people in it."

Becca harbored no love for the blacksmith or his radical ideas and listening only irritated her. Although she could well guess he didn't feel the same about everyone. Her, in particular.

Gette's gaze met hers. "Ask the hunters. Ask any of them. I dare you."

Silence filled the hut.

Becca regretted the pressure she applied, the hurt she inflicted. Unmistakable pain twisted her sister's face, and that tore at her heart. A queasy feeling settled in her belly. Setting her teacup down, she weighed the matter in her mind. Could her perception be so wrong?

No. The answer came loud and clear.

Becca shook her head and swept up her bow in her palm. At the door, she paused. "Don't you see the danger of men running Froy?"

Gette lumbered, big-bellied, to her feet. Sudden clinking filled the hut when her hand hit a bowl of metal beads, the same type of beads woven into her thick braid. "Great times are ahead for Froy. You'll see I'm right."

Chapter Twenty-Eight

Cress waved when Becca appeared from a hut near the center of the village. She adjusted her bow over a shoulder. Weeks of hard travel and whatever occurred inside etched her face into an expression of utter defeat. Thoughts of rushing to her side nearly overwhelmed him.

"Her brothers are due back any day," said Pire. "They'll be pleased she's returned, and hopefully she'll be happy to see them. The d'Firns always had a close family bond, which much credit belongs to Quinta. If Gette failed to convince Becca the new system is better, mayhaps they'll have more luck."

Cress wondered about the relationship between Becca and her brothers. He couldn't imagine her being close to brothers when she seemed to harbor animosity toward men. "How many brothers does she have? Did she get along with them?"

"Two—Nald and Quinn. Aye, she did. Or, at least, I thought she did. Though she'd be hard pressed to admit favoritism."

"Where are they?" Cress asked in an offhanded manner.

"Seeking buyers for our excess wheat. Nald's the thinker of the two. He'll study every offer before taking any action, while Quinn can charm a snake with his smile. Together they make a formidable team of negotiators. That's why I chose them to attempt our first pact."

"Gullible people are duped every day. You delude yourself if you believe people will buy what they can easily grow themselves," a voice said behind them.

Both Cress and Pire whirled toward the source. Their discussion had so engrossed them, they missed Becca coming up behind them.

Cress groaned. He caught her gaze, and she gave him a tiny smile. An awkward second passed. He doubted a change of heart lay in her immediate future.

Tulle trotted to her side for a pat on the head.

"So, you think I will fail," Pire said to her.

"One hopes," she responded in an even tone.

Pire's eyes bulged, his bushy brows lowering over his eyes. "Be honest with yourself, Becca. Your frustration isn't about Froy. It's about yourself. Your resistance stems from your own refusal to change. You've talked to your mother, Maine, and Gette. Would they lie? Change is vital to Froy's survival. It's good for everyone."

This time Becca stiffened. "I wish to call a formal assembly to present my case before the entire village. Do you deny my request?"

A jolt went through Cress. Trust Becca not to budge an inch. He murmured under his breath to summon his power. Circumstances mandated calm—he knew it intuitively, felt the serene emotion rise within him. His fingers tingled, and he tucked his hands into his robe's pockets. The light radiating from them could frighten the villagers. They might need a wizard's powers, but they weren't used to seeing magic performed. No need to frighten them.

The muscular blacksmith took a deep breath, his bulky muscles visibly relaxing. "You truly do not understand, do you, Becca?"

"Understand what?"

"It's not up to me."

She looked around, a frown darkening her features. "You are leader."

Cress dropped his hand to his side. Becca might not curb her temper, but fortunately the blacksmith controlled his.

Pire hesitated before he answered, "A leader doesn't order people. He guides. Makes suggestions. A good leader follows. The full moon arrives in five days. Call your meeting for then and the people shall come."

Cress frowned to himself. Men encircled the trio. He fought his unease of crowds. A few women lingered in the back. The growing crowd's voices buzzed his ears.

Becca's mother pushed her way forward. Quinta looked stunning in a mature way with streaks of gray in her brown hair and fine lines at her eyes. Neither one took away from her beauty. Rather, they added character to a woman he suspected lived a wealth of experiences. Sunlight beamed on her head and spun the gray to silver.

Becca smiled at her mother. "I thank you for the concession, Pire."

The blacksmith raked his bushy hair, acknowledging the older woman with a polite nod and answering Becca at the same time. "Not everything has changed. Luna still holds our hearts."

Cress resisted temptation to contact Becca through mindspeech. While he did not particularly care one way or the other for Pire, he maintained the man wasn't as evil as she alleged.

At the same time, Cress admired the core of Becca's courage and, despite himself, mentally pledged her his support. He doubted anyone else had the tenacity to cross The Wilds to find him and successfully return.

A man in the crowd snorted. "These days we do things differently, and we like it. Pire is our leader. He saved us from the plague."

Becca spun on her heels to face a man of small stature with dirt smeared on his face. Her bow slipped a notch and she shoved it back into place. "Let the hunters tell me themselves. I would hear their betrayal in formal assembly."

The man extended an arm to take in the crowd. His fingers were unusually stubby. "An assembly. My, my, don't you think highly of yourself."

"Watch your mouth, Legget," Pire snapped. "Becca has the right to call one, if she so wishes."

Another man, quite elderly, wrung his hands before he found the courage to face the ex-leader of hunters. "Why, Mistress Hunter, do you want an assembly? Pire's leading us, well and good. No one has any complaints."

"I might disagree. I have complaints," she answered, but her tone lost its harsh edge, replaced with a hint of respect for the elderly man.

Murmurs rippled through the crowd. Cress bristled at the sound. Were the people preparing to join the first man? The anguish on Becca's face tore at him. Couldn't these people see her pain?

Legget, the man with the short fingers, nodded at

the men around him. He stepped forward to face her.

Cress inched closer to protect her.

"You only want to make trouble," Legget said. "How come you want to do that, eh? Eh?"

Pire's chest puffed out as he glared at the man. "You're a fool, Legget, for thinking she'd answer you with your ugly puss shoved in hers. Leave Becca alone. She's not irrational. Give her time to adjust to the changes. She'll see what we've accomplished."

"Are you certain? Or are you just saying that because you're wed to her sister?"

"Men aren't the dullards she likes to believe. Well, except for you. You, she seems to hold in a higher esteem," Pire rebutted. "Have some sympathy for her. A lot has occurred for a hunter to accept in one night."

Cress agreed, wishing Becca saw the situation in a new light. She had great insight. All she had to do was let it shine through.

"I'll leave Froy before I let a woman control me again," Legget cried. "You delivered our salvation."

Becca smirked at Legget. "I'm sure you and the rest of the men would defend him."

Cress cringed. Blind determination drove Becca. Her focus had concentrated on saving her village for so many months that she could not release the obligation. To return and discover the village she adored gone—not from plague, but rebellion—must be a devastating blow.

Grumblings from the mostly male crowd grew hostile.

Pire raised his arms. "Enough. All of you, listen carefully, now. Becca has the right to make her plea before the entire assembly. If she can sway the majority, our law says we must follow her."

"No!" a dozen men cried, their faces dark with scowls.

Cress's stomach knotted as he worried danger would erupt any moment. A crowd could quickly become a mob, and mobs were uncontrollable. Time to get Becca out of there. Even if she didn't realize it, he did. She played with fire.

Even so, he shuddered with a pang of regret for these men. They only wanted to live as equals with their women.

Pire held up his hand. Mutters, sputters, then silence fell. "Calm down!" he demanded. "Listen to me. Each side will have a chance to speak and be heard on the night of the full moon. Five days is not long to wait to resolve the matter that will affect us for the rest of our lives."

Quinta hooked arms with the blacksmith. "Pire speaks true. Begone. Go back to your chores."

A few men elbowed the person next to them, a clear signal to disband.

Cress's lungs burned from holding his breath during the debate. He gulped cool, fresh air when the last villager left. "Becca spoke of a storyteller. Perhaps this person will entertain us with a tale. There's nothing like a few hours of amusement to bond people closer together."

Quinta's eyebrows quirked up. "A good notion, wizard, but unfortunately the woman speaks only when she deems the occasion appropriate. It is a privilege that comes with the position."

Cress paused, curious.

Pire waited, too, before turning to Becca. "It would

be safer if you kept your opinions to yourself until the assembly," he told her.

"Is that an order?"

"I only speak for your protection. Most will heed my words, but there is always the danger of dissent."

"He gives good advice," Cress seconded.

A gasp sounded, but he dared not look to see which woman uttered the sound—Becca or her mother.

Pire gave him a terse nod and left without a backward glance.

Becca anchored her hands on her hips, her chin raised. "Fools. All of them."

Cress straightened his robe, trying to decide whether to pull his pipe from a pocket. Tobacco always calmed him in stressful situations. "Granted, but promise me you won't antagonize them. You'll wait for the assembly."

"A distasteful request," she grumbled. "And I've got to tell you, it won't be easy."

"You're stronger than you know. I have the utmost confidence in your abilities," he said, relaxing. "Besides, the sooner we return to Demit Woods, the better I will feel."

Becca's gaze swept around the open area. "I haven't forgotten our bargain."

Quinta touched her daughter's arm. "What bargain is that?"

"I pledged to aid Wizard Cress break a spell." She looked around again and shrugged. "I overheard Pire say Nald and Quinn are due back any day. Wizard Cress and I will need different quarters."

"Take Mother Asa's hut. No one will object. It hasn't been used since her death."

"What?" Becca cried. "She's dead? How did she die?"

Becca blanched with horror. Cress ached to hold her and offer sympathy. Only the knowledge that she would probably knock him off his feet kept him from reaching out.

Quinta cleared her throat. "She was the last person the plague stole from us."

Glistening crystal tears welled up in Becca's eyes. "It's not fair! I should have been here. How was she buried?"

Quinta patted her daughter's arm. "Asa was buried in the hunter-warrior pose, on her back, with one leg straight and the other bent at the knee as was her due. Her bow, arrows, and extra arrowheads were included in her grave. Along with her mirror, silver bowl, and her gold beads."

Becca nodded, clearly satisfied the elderly woman had received the proper honors in death.

Cress continued to stare at her, a lump rising in his throat. The crestfallen expression on her face twisted his insides. The urge to wrap her in his arms intensified. He wanted to comfort her and promise her the world.

Except, he couldn't promise a thing.

Chapter Twenty-Nine

Darkness fell as Becca guided Cress to Mother Asa's hut. She didn't know what was worse—accepting the fact that the senescent woman had passed, or facing the joyous memories she expected to find inside.

She entered and took in an explosion of glorious colors decorating hide walls—dramatic streaks of blues and black, swirls of gold and silver representing the sun and moon in their lustrous glory. Here and there animals were depicted in various poses. Becca remembered helping the old hunter paint the lighter blue swirls during a particularly long winter. The familiar colors and patterns were a sight from her childhood, and seeing them freed a dam of silent tears.

She struggled to collect her thoughts as Cress peered around the colorful interior. "Mother Asa was the oldest female in Froy. All the children feared her. When I was younger, I thought she was too mean to die."

He swung to face her. "What a terrible thing to say."

Becca closed her eyes and murmured a prayer for the departed to quicken her journey to the goddess. "I don't think it matters now. She's dead of plague."

Cress dropped his travel bags to the floor. "She befriended you as a child. Mayhaps there are others she did as well. I'm sure her loss is felt by all who cared about her."

Becca inclined her head, embarrassed. "That's possible. I visited her on a dare. After receiving my first bow, I snuck into her hut. She lay unmoving on her back with furs tucked under her chin, her arms straight along her sides. I thought she'd died in her sleep. The sight nearly sent me to an early grave. I found a feather on the floor and put it under her nose to test her breathing."

Cress dug into his robe's pocket and pulled out his pipe. Strangely, it was already lit. He puffed on it as he lowered himself to the furs. "What happened?"

"She shot upright and pointed a bony figure at me, crying out, 'Luna, save me. I'm being suffocated by demons.' "

Laughter spewed from Cress. "What did you do?"

"What do you think?" She shot him a grin, enjoying the sound of his amusement. It warmed her insides. "I ran out as fast as my legs would carry me, covering my mouth to keep from screaming and waking the whole village. For days afterward I feared Asa would expose me and I would be punished for disrespecting an elder."

"But she didn't?"

Becca waggled a finger at him just like the old hunter always did as she set her bow and quiver down. "Years later Asa told me it took great courage to enter her hut and spy on her while she slept. I carried her praise close to my heart for a long while."

"I gather you became friends."

"Dear friends." Becca glanced at Cress. Her heart pounded heavily when his dark hazel eyes filled with compassion. She smiled again and received one in return as a reward that left her breathless. "I learned to heed her counsel and was rewarded many times for doing so. In her day, Asa was a great hunter and warrior. She had much wisdom to share, although her delivery sometimes lacked finesse."

"A trait I gather many people here share. It's nothing to hold against her. I wish I could have met her."

"She would have liked you."

"Me?" A white puff of smoke curled around his head as he unlaced his boots, depositing to them near his bags. "Why is that?"

"Because you're male. She favored men in general, especially handsome ones."

Cress hung his wizard's robe on an antler hook. Large hands, broad shoulders, long legs. Such an amazing body—a sinewy build that drew her eye. Beauty existed in the way he moved, and she would never tire of admiring him.

"Come here," he said, returning to the furs and slumping down.

Becca started to protest—partly because she sensed his inner strength and partly because complying with his request thrilled her.

Cress considered her for a moment. "Don't look at me like that. You have nothing to fear from me. I'm going to hold you while we sleep. It's been a long, trying day. Someone needs to offer you comfort, a little kindness. Who better than me? I mean you no harm. I recall you telling your mother that you trust me."

He wasn't offering beads, but instincts shouted to accept his proposal. The pounding of her racing heart filled her ears. Becca swore the wizard heard it as well.

She sank down beside him and inhaled deeply. His male scent proved powerful and alluring.

Sighing, she snuggled against his warmth and let the knots in her muscles fade away. "I did and I do."

****

Three days later Becca had talked with nearly every hunter in the village. A fat lot of good it did her. Not a single one showed interest for a return of the old ways. Everyone steadfastly dismissed her arguments as though they didn't care.

She spotted Maine's wife at the entrance of a hut next to her old one. The thin woman smiled and waved.

Landa was the last person in the world Becca expected a warm greeting from. She headed toward her. "Nice to see you, Landa. I've wondered where you've been keeping yourself."

"I heard you were going around the village." Landa's lips thinned. "Seeking to sway the ex-hunters to your side and by all accounts, without success."

Becca's guard went up. "Keeping tabs on me, are you?"

Bitter laughter rippled from her slender, birdlike throat. "Your absence hasn't changed you. Some thought a long journey with a male might make you more accepting. Personally, I always doubted it would. Too bad your failure hasn't taught you humility."

"Humility wouldn't hurt you, either," Becca replied instantly, recalling the number of times she'd chastised Landa for poor hunting skills. "It might make you tolerable."

The woman pointed a finger at her. "Watch your mouth! I am wed to Maine now, and he is second in command. That makes me wife to a commander in high standing. Beware, Becca. Your blustering makes you appear silly. Quit now."

"Quit." A shard of irritation braced her spine. "Never."

"You'll not win," Landa boasted, whipping the leather flap aside to whirl inside the hut.

Over the last few days, an insidious depression crept into Becca like a bloodsucking demon to drain away optimism. She took in her surroundings for several drawn-out seconds, then realized she stood in a village of strangers. A chill seeped through her body. People, once considered friends, had become foes.

It came to her she did not feel that way with Cress. He was a friend. Her only friend. He had eased the rigors of their journey, made it comfortable, enjoyable.

A tow-headed toddler waddled past holding a sticky loaf of bread, surrounded by dogs jumping for a chance to steal an easy meal. The little procession lifted the heaviest portion of Becca's melancholy. The girl bit chunks out of the loaf with crumbs falling onto the ground for the dogs to gobble up. She tottered along, holding her prize over her head to keep the more aggressive canines from snatching it away.

Suddenly a cry of panic sliced the air. The toddler stumbled into the pack's midst and disappeared from sight.

Becca raced to save her, but a man tending a nearby garden arrived first. Swinging his hoe, he hit anything with fur that moved. Becca could only stand and watch as snarls and yelps merged with the child's screams. Within seconds, the dogs crept away to lick their wounds.

The man rushed in and scooped up the girl. "There,

there, sweetheart. Everything's all right. I've got you."

"They stole my sticky bread." A hiccup erupted between sobs.

The man brushed blonde-white hair from the girl's face. "I'll get you another. I promise."

Amazed at the show of compassion for a girl child by the male, Becca stepped up, ruffled the weeping child's head and gave the man a nod of approval before slipping away.

Two days before the assembly, a longing to visit her cave called. Maybe there she would find the answers to defeat Pire.

With the idea sprouting, she cut between the huts to Mother Asa's. Gette waved at her and took fast steps toward her, not the least bit acting like a woman heavy with child. Today, she wore a yellow shift and a leather belt with the eight phases of the moon carved on it stretched over her bulging middle. The pale color turned her complexion sallow as though she held a lion's tooth weed under her chin.

"Should you be moving so fast?" Becca asked, voicing her worry.

Gette's round face flushed. "I swear I'm carrying two! I don't recall being this huge during my previous pregnancy."

Becca glanced around the village center for a sign of Cress. They'd been apart too much, and she ached for his company. "Is something amiss?"

Gette dragged Becca away by the corner of her leather tunic. Metallic beads clicked in her sister's braid with each step. "Nay. Nay. It just we haven't had a chance to speak since our first meeting, and I want to hear about your travels. You must tell me what lies beyond The Wilds. Did you meet anyone else beside the wizard?"

"I deliberately stayed away from people. I did meet one couple," Becca said, studying people as they passed. Most avoided eye contact. "The male was most impressive, a true warrior who hunted and fished at night the same as hunters. I offered to mate with him, but he declined. I suspect it was because of his fellow companion—a woman. She was the softest looking being I've ever seen. Couldn't hunt. Knew little of cooking. But her weak appearance did not fool me. Within her beat the heart of a true hunter."

Gette kicked a pebble with her toe. "Oh, tell me more. What did she look like? Did she wear fancy clothes?"

The tip of Becca's braid flipped over her shoulder when she cocked her head. "She had hair lighter than yours, which she wore loose and flowing. I shared the road with them for only two days, and not once did she braid it or wear beads to show she'd bedded her companion."

"Mayhap she was too ugly for a male to offer beads?" Gette suggested, reaching for Becca's thick braid. "Speaking of which, where are yours?"

A harder question than she wanted to admit. "I removed them, but you asked about the woman."

Tiny claps sounded when Gette slapped her hands together. "I did, indeed."

"While I found the behavior odd, the man acted very protective toward her, and she seemed to appreciate his attentiveness," Becca said. "I think she was glad to see me leave them. I sincerely believe she would have fought for him, if I had found a way to mate with him."

Gette squeezed Becca's free hand as though the physical contact drew them closer. "In all the months you were gone, you met only this couple? No one else?"

"I already told you, I avoided people as much as possible. I did meet Cress's housekeeper and the elderly master wizard of Brenalin who visited them. Brenalin is the largest town closest to the great woods. The young couple was traveling to it."

"Oh, I wish you had visited this town, too. How big do you suppose it is? If I had been the Chosen One, I would have made a point to see as much as I could, tasted the different fares offered by new places, and fetched a bounty of items to share."

Becca gritted her teeth. Gette's remark struck a nerve. Why did the Council let her volunteer? Had they been aware of the men's dissatisfaction and were ready to hand over the reins of leadership? The implication hinted at more than she could bear.

Two women walked by, deliberately avoiding eye contact.

"I stayed within the great woods where the wizard lived," Becca said. "He was my objective, after all."

The reminder caused Gette to lower her gaze. "I know, I know. Duty comes first with you. It always has. But what was his housekeeper like? Young? Old? Did she wear fine clothes?"

These same, frivolous questions had been a favorite topic of the other hunters she'd spoken with as well. They were all curious about the luxuries in the world beyond The Wilds. Or, had the revolt triggered this vanity in them?

Becca sighed. Smoke curled from cooking fires within several huts, bringing the aroma of citrus and bacon and frying fish wafting in the air. Children herded goats and pigs back to their pens for the night.

"You think my questions are silly," Gette prompted when Becca didn't answer immediately. "Say what's on your mind. Are you still angry? Have you not come to realize the wonderful benefits of having men as our equals?"

"Neither. Others have asked me the same, and I'll tell you what I told them. I seek the true cause of the rebellion. Not a surface reason. This goes much deeper. The catalyst of Pire losing his son…" A crushed expression flashed over Gette's face, and Becca hated herself for reminding her sister of the loss. "Forgive me. Dorral was your son, too."

Her sister's face crumpled. "Are you? Really?"

The accusation broke Becca's heart. Once Gette sided with her on everything. "Think what you wish." She refused to show her sadness. After all, her sister had a right to choose her own path—even if wrong. "I'm sorry, Gette. The assembly starts when the moon is full, and I need to prepare for it. If you'll excuse me."

"Of course, sister."

A barrage of emotions increased when Becca hurried away. Duty. Tradition. Family. They were all being tested, strained beyond limits.

Pausing at the entrance of Mother Asa's hut, she dusted off her tunic in case Cress had returned before she had. Realizing her actions, she stopped primping and entered.

The fire burned low and Cress sat before it with his long hair unbound. Water droplets dripped and sizzled on the rocks as if he'd just returned from bathing in the river. Something she had intended doing herself until Gette intercepted her.

He glanced up and smiled. "I think I've made a good start on the source of the plague. Or rather, it's what I haven't found that is important."

Hope flared—the first good news in days. "Oh, Cress, that's wonderful. Are you sure?"

"When I lived in Brenalin, some people drank foul water and suffered intestinal problems. Totally different symptoms. Because of this, I've eliminated the river. But to make sure, I walked up and down both banks for several miles, looking for dead animals or dying vegetation and saw no signs. I did find one stagnant pool but found nothing unusual around it. Nor were there an undue number of insects. No infestation of spiders or snakes. At least, none that I noticed.

"No one is currently displaying a runny nose, nor is anyone coughing. I am confident the people of your village are hale and hearty."

Becca shook her head. "The plague has struck two years in a row."

Cress tied his hair back. "What of traders who visit? Did the outbreak happen after they departed? They could have carried the disease. Whenever an influx of strangers visits Brenalin, outbreaks of illness seem to increase."

"The plague hits in the spring, and traders arrive in late summer. I wish Mother Asa still walked among the living. She was an excellent observer. And she would have agreed with me about the revolt."

"Your mother said Asa counseled tolerance."

Becca snorted. "She didn't mean it. All it would

have taken is one person on my side, then others would—"

"Just a moment, Becca," Cress interrupted, murmuring

Protect this hut.

Protect us.

Protect our words from other ears.

"Now you can speak freely without fear of being overheard. I spelled the hut."

She swallowed uncomfortably. "Was that necessary?"

He shrugged. "Merely a precaution. If we're discussing plans, it's best they stay within these walls."

For her, steeped in Froyan tradition, the revolt made no sense. She felt compelled to disrupt Pire's plans, to force the men back where they belonged.

Nonetheless, her estimation changed about one man—Cress. Their relationship had altered in subtle ways. He changed. Or had she? It had gone from her being indebted to him for agreeing to aid Froy to friend, companion…and maybe more.

"Let's change the subject for a moment," she said.

Cress angled his head, eyes wide with silent curiosity. "If you wish. What would you like to talk about?"

"The Guardians."

His mouth dropped when he stood. "Has something happened?"

"I'm unsure. They haven't mindspoken since our arrival," she replied. "At least, not to me. Have they spoken with you?"

"Hmmm." The width and breath of his shoulders seemed to fill the hut. "Nay, now that you mention it."

"Don't you find that odd? I wonder what they are up to." She approached within arms' reach of him. A musky clean scent swirled in the air. The odor made her fully aware of his maleness, of her desire for him. "Are they still with us? Mayhaps you should make them visible again, just in case."

"To be perfectly honest, I was enjoying their silence. One never knows what a dragon thinks, and the Guardians have been around for a very long time."

"You aren't curious? Worried?" Becca pressed.

"If their silence bothers you, of course, it concerns me. I care about you. And I would wager you care about me." His dark brows rose in a questioning arc that delighted her. "A little, perchance. Let me prove it to you."

So saying, he stepped closer, cupped her face in his hands, his thumbs resting on her cheeks, his exploring fingers spread into her hair.

He bent forward and kissed her on the lips. His long hair tickled her face, and intensely aware of his hard body, she let his strength call to her. His gentle tone tugged on heartstrings she never knew she possessed, and the sweet warmth of his touch lured her to lean into his hand. This close, his eyes were intense flecks of green, brown, and gold trapped within a black ring.

If he used magic on her, she didn't care. All thoughts of the Guardians vanished. Nothing mattered. Only them. Only Cress. He created a longing in her that overshadowed everything else.

Her heart quickened and pulsated in a nice way. Maybe she could add lover to their relationship. A delightful shudder of anticipation rippled through her.

She wanted this particular man and placed both hands on his chest, charmed at the strong beat of his heart. A wealth of promised delights—real and imagined—popped into her mind. What if they mated? Sweet Luna. Yes. Trembling with a fierce need, arousal stirred her senses.

"At dawn tomorrow," she whispered in his ear, then pressed a kiss against his mouth. "I leave for my cave. Come with me. We can have complete privacy there. To do whatever we wish, without interruption."

Chapter Thirty

Reality hit Cress with the force of an avalanche escaping the peaks of Dragon's Teeth. Becca looked at him as a man, inviting him as an equal. The comprehension barely sank in when he shook his head. "I shouldn't. I can't."

Becca's eyes snapped open and a hard line pulled at her mouth. That same mouth moments ago had softened beneath his. "You refuse? Why?"

He held her within his arms, unwilling to let her go. Their kiss, a mere brushing of lips, promised deeper passion. He tightened his hold on her waist. Her luscious body seemed to melt against him. "As much as I would like to accompany you," he said, caressing her cheek, "I'd better remain here."

Her fingers slid over his head to cup his face. "Aren't you the least bit curious about my cave?"

"Curious?" His mind focused on her smooth skin. He wanted to run his hands over her subtle muscles but resisted the urge. "I thought we were talking about the Guardians."

She snuggled closer and made a soft, erotic sound, sending warm breath across his chest. "We are. And my cave. After all, it is the place where I first heard voices. Strange whisperings that beckoned me with words of encouragement. This is just a guess, but they might be why I can speak with Trell."

Trell. Nothing prepared him for the realization that he hadn't experienced a single thought of his trapped sister in days. Shame burned the tips of his ears.

"Mayhaps another time," he managed to croak out. Becca practiced seduction of the mind and body on him. His heart beat faster. His body warmed. She stirred his blood in ways he had not felt in almost a thousand years.

"You don't know what you are missing," she cooed.

"Oh, aye, I'm afraid I do. I need to expedite my search."

Regret flitted over Becca's face as she slipped from him and headed for her trunk. "Will a couple days matter?"

Moonlight snaked through the hut's smoke hole. He wondered if Luna spied upon them. "It could make all the difference. The plague might strike tomorrow. Or the next day. We must eliminate the cause before conditions are ripe for its return. Any delay could be disastrous."

"I hate it when you're right. But you are."

"Even apart, we are together," Cress mindspoke, unable to forget their kiss. *"Go to your cave. I'll be fine here. If you need me, I'll come wherever you are."*

"Such a strange thing, this mindspeech, but I like speaking this way. It makes me feel close to you."

Cress couldn't be happier. Becca might be quick to anger, but she forgave more quickly. Or so he hoped. *"We are. Our thoughts are one."*

A smile tugged on Becca's mouth. *"We should have been speaking this way all along. No one would have known."*

The intimacy of mindspeech affected him deeply. He had never shared it with another human being, and combined with Becca's kiss, the familiarity created something he was eager to further explore.

"How long will you be gone?" he asked aloud.

"Two days, one night." She walked to her trunk. "Don't worry, Cress. I'll be back in plenty of time for the assembly. My leaving is no whim. I've solved many problems in my cave."

He winced. "Whatever decision occurs in the assembly must be final. Will you accept that?"

Becca loaded her arms with sturdy boots, a blanket, several coils of ropes, and cloth squares used to wrap food. "I made no such agreement when I called for the assembly."

"Nay, but the men of Froy will not give up their newfound positions."

A look of irritation washed over her face. "Then I'll just have to come up with a good reason to change their minds."

"It might be harder than you think," he said, tying his hair back.

****

The next morning before anyone stirred, Becca filled goatskin bags with water. She left on foot, following River Kelt's meandering flow for several miles until a sandy clearing spread out from the banks. Energy tingled her nerves, and she turned inland.

The boulders and vegetation cleared, and gentle slopes gave way to the limestone spear. Scree littered the base. Bits of rock contained shell fragments marbled with darker color, the outline of tiny creatures that once must have inhabited the area.

Already she missed Cress and battled temptation to return to Froy.

Her first journey to the tower, she recalled, began the year after receiving her bow and quiver of arrows. She'd felt so mature being in the company of hunters searching for game, and in spite of their warning cries, scrambled part way up the tower to show them her bravery.

Unfortunately, or luckily, her small arms could not stretch far enough to reach ancient handholds scratched in the limestone. Every birthday, she returned filled with determination, and each year she managed to crawl a bit higher. After five years of trying, she finally succeeded. All her efforts proved worthy of every drop of sweat.

A chamber, nearly the size of her hut with a floor that sloped down slightly to the back wall, was three-fourths of the way up. Warm air, devoid of moisture usually found in caves, smelled faintly of rotten eggs, but along the lines of sulfur before igniting a fire.

Today, eager to reach the peace awaiting above, she slung her bow over her shoulder, knotted the thinnest of three ropes to her belt and the last and thickest around her pile of supplies, and started to climb.

Warm drafts swept around the tower, tugging at her braid and clothing, making the climb dangerous. She needed all her concentration every inch of the way. The pull of the ground never slept, waiting for a single slip. Thankfully, ancient handholds gave her fingers a solid grip. Time became meaningless, her breathing labored. Dusty pebbles cascaded beneath her boots. Tiny clinking erupted when they hit the ground. She gritted her teeth and clung to the monolith's side to keep her feet in place.

Her hand smacked the flat opening of the cave, causing dust to rise. She heaved herself up with renewed vigor. Inside the inky opening, a warm embrace wrapped around her.

Exertion made her sigh, and she slipped off her weaponry to lay back and savor the moment. Her eyelids burned with heaviness, and she closed her eyes, her muscles responding to the strenuous climb by quivering every once in a while.

The next thing she knew, she woke stiff and aching to starlight and a waxing moon. She loved nighttime because she looked forward to hunting or resting or listening to the village storyteller.

So why did she feel disappointed? And lonely. Because she missed waking up without Cress being near. They had traveled together for three moons, and she'd grown accustomed to having him near.

"So much for watching the sunset," she grumbled as she unknotted the rope attached to her belt. She pulled on the thinner rope until it gave way to the next and then again to the last and thickest. The bundle knocked against the side of the great tower as she drew it up.

Once she retrieved her supplies, she struck flint to tinder. A spark ignited a fire, and she sat back to survey the interior at her leisure. Rough brownish-yellow walls contained striations of red running through them. In spots, the texture felt coarse to the touch. In others, a fine powder left a film on her fingertips.

She'd always imagined the crimson earth contained the blood of two lovers who died inside the cave.

Poignant and appropriate. Now, her growing affection for Cress made it just plain sad. Those long-ago lovers' lives were unfairly cut short by tragedy.

A pile of four rocks stood as a reminder of her last visit. She'd stacked them atop each other herself. They remained upright. The area shook often, and she had devised stacking the rocks to give her a sign of knowing how powerful the tremors had been in her absence.

Peering out the entrance, the night spread out in a glorious display. The stars and moon always seemed bigger, brighter up here. She felt closer to the goddess and counted herself beloved by the Great Mother and hoped that still held true.

Luna's will, she thought, in a few days all will be set right.

"Help us. We beseech you."

Another voice followed in rapid order. *"Free me."*

"Help me," mindspoke a different voice, higher pitched.

"No, no, not her," squeaked another. *"Me, first."*

"Help me, human," ordered a deep voice. *"I will grant you whatever treasure you desire."*

"Ha! Do not believe him," mindspoke another, deeper still. *"He has no treasure. None of us do. I am being honest. Free me instead. Let me fly free in the sky."*

Shocked, Becca sucked in her breath. Never before had the individual pleas separated themselves from the masses. Dozens of entities clamored for her attention.

She clasped her hands over her ears to block the incessant pleas coming from the storm of voices. "Leave me alone. Go away!"

The voices quieted immediately.

A shuddering breath squeezed her chest. They'd heard her—obeyed her. What just happened?

"Tell us what you hear." New voices entered the battlefield for her attention.

Becca spun in a circle within the cave. *"Guardians? Where are you?"*

"Here."

"You followed me?"

"Do not object. Our curiosity could not be denied. We wanted to know where you were going."

She didn't answer. Instead, she listened to wind swirl up the tower, a soft whisper amplified and echoed as she peered around the interior.

"Do you smell it?" the dragons asked.

She frowned, puzzled. *"Smell what? The scent is the same, no matter the season. Does it mean something to you?"*

Leathery wings beat the air. A shame she hadn't known of their plans to accompany her. She would have insisted Cress make them visible.

"Your cave contains our greatest treasure," they informed her. *"They were put in a protective stasis, unaware of the world around them. We have searched eons for them."*

"And what treasure is that?"

"Dragon eggs," the Guardians answered. *"We accompanied you because we had never ventured here to find our eggs. Now, we can smell them, but they cannot contact us."*

Becca frowned. She'd confessed her secrets and fears, assuming they'd never be revealed to a living being. *"I hear them…and they hear me. Your eggs are very much aware. They speak to me. Well, they make demands. They want to be free."*

"That cannot be," they replied in an agitated manner.

"It's true. I've heard them whenever I come near this place. Tonight they are louder than ever."

Becca's tunic wrinkled as several dragons settled on her arm, their talons like needle pricks stabbing her leather top.

"Our last dragon king, Oriole, was not a strong ruler. He didn't want to wage war with the humans, though he did take precautionary action," the Guardians continued with their explanation. *"He commanded every pregnant female dragon to donate one egg for our survival. Then the most trusted priestesses carried those eggs into The Wilds with Oyfele."*

"Dragon eggs," Becca whispered in awe. *"It cannot be. There's nothing in this cave but solid rock."*

Chapter Thirty-One

For whatever reason, Tulle remained at Cress's side. He didn't mind in the least, finding the dog's company enjoyable. Another dog approached and Tulle growled. The interloper slowed before he turned around, tail tucked between his legs.

As Cress started to leave, a tug on the sleeve of his robe kept him from moving.

"You really him?" asked a small, redheaded girl with a dusting of brown freckles over the bridge of an upturned nose.

He glanced down. "Pardon?"

"The Wizard Cress."

"I am he," he said, his tone gentle. "How may I help you, little one?"

Round eyes blinked. "Can you bring my mama back? She got sick with the fever and died. I miss her terrible."

Cress's stomach knotted with sadness. "I am sorry…ah…"

"Re—Reba," she answered in a quivering voice. "I'm Reba. Mama's name is Dara. She has red hair like me."

The child's name had a familiar ring. Then, he remembered…Becca mentioned it. Kneeling down, he faced the girl on her level. "What happened to your mother?"

A shudder shook the girl's small body. She bit her bottom lip. "She started vomiting like the boys from the granary and couldn't breathe. She was overseer, you know. They wouldn't let me see her, but I snuck in anyway."

Cress sighed. "How very brave."

Her throat wobbled as she swallowed and pulled up her tiny frame. She glanced around the open area of the village. "I didn't care if they got mad at me. I wanted to see my mama."

He tried to follow the girl's conversation. "Who said you couldn't be with your mother?"

"A hunter. She told me not to disturb her. That she needed to rest and I would harm her if I disturbed her." Another shudder rippled Reba's body. "Do you…Do you think…Did I kill her?"

What an outrageous burden for a child to carry. Cress put his hand on her shoulder to give her a gentle squeeze. Anger toward the unknown hunter made magic crackle from his fingertips. He vowed to track down the woman and chastise her for the lack of sensitivity.

"Certainly not," he said, keeping his temper under control. "Do not blame yourself. You're a good daughter. Tell me, Reba, did you sicken?"

Red curls bounced back and forth as she shook her head, her gaze studying Tulle. "Oh, no. Mama says I'm healthy as a horse. That I eat enough for three girls my age. I miss her so much. Can you bring her back with your magic?"

Despair broke his heart. "I'm sorry, Reba. Magic cannot bring back the dead."

Tears welled up in her eyes. Her bottom lip

fattened and curled over on its own accord. "Why not?"

"You mustn't cry, sweet Reba. She's with you." Cress tapped the area over her heart. "In here. Close your eyes and remember her. You can do that, can't you? Start with her hair. Is it curly like yours or straight? What color are her eyes? Blue? Brown? Is she tall? Short? Can you see her? I bet she's smiling right now."

Reba squeezed her eyes tight, long auburn lashes fanning pale cheeks. "I'm trying to do it, but I can't see a thing. Wait!" Her brow wrinkled and the corners of her mouth lifted. "I see Mama. I do. Oh, Mama."

Cress smiled at the precious child. Sometimes the power of suggestion controlled the strongest magic. "As long as you hold her dear, she'll be with you."

The girl opened watery eyes and sniffled. "You promise?"

"I do," he said earnestly. "Give me your word you'll never forget your mother."

"Oh, I won't. I promise," she vowed before dashing away.

Cress stood. His amazement increased as a stunning realization hit him. Reba gave him the best clue for the origin of the plague. Could it be so simple?

"Let's go, boy. I need to talk with Pire," he said, hurrying away with Tulle at his heels. He located the blacksmith at his forge on the hillside.

The other man looked up and grunted deep in his throat at his approach. Sweat dripped off bushy brows. He shoved a shaft of metal back into the glowing bed of coals. "Wizard, what can I do for you?"

"We need to talk."

"Let's step outside where we can escape this heat."

Tulle lay down in the shade. Birds soared above the fields. Insects fluttered about on a day still containing lazy fall air although winter rapidly approached.

They went less than a dozen steps when Pire asked, "What's on your mind, wizard?"

"What else? The plague. I've come to ask you more questions about it."

Pire stared at Cress. "I've watched you eliminate the obvious. What's left, I cannot say."

Cress inclined his head. "It's my understanding the eruption ended when the smithy and granary burned."

"Correct."

"Tell me about that night."

Pire's gaze swept the area. "One of the hunters used a flaming arrow and it caught the granary's thatched roof afire. When that happened, the fighting ended. Everyone rushed to extinguish the fire."

"Quinta tells it differently. She claims you started the fire."

"A lot of terrible things happened that night. I accept blame for the smithy, but a hunter's arrow ignited the granary roof."

"Was there a particular reason for moving the granary from its previous position?"

Pire scratched his head. "Only the one I gave you about saving time during harvest."

Tulle trotted over to the men to nudge Cress's hand until he scratched the top of the dog's head.

"Were the stricken tired, nauseated?"

The blacksmith glared at him. "Aye, I believe so. The illness progressed from headache, sore muscles, to shortness of breath."

"I think I found the key to your plague. But first, has there been an abundance of mice around the village?"

Concern pulled Pire's brows into a solitary line. He straightened, clearly unsure about the line of questioning. "As a matter of fact, before the fire, a larger-than-usual number were spotted. Why do you ask?"

Cress stood taller, too. He eyed the blacksmith, determined to drag the answers out. "Years ago the granaries in Brenalin suffered a rodent infestation. Several people sickened. Their symptoms were akin to what Froy has suffered. That pestilence was traced to mice."

"So simple?"

Cress grinned, remembering his initial skepticism. "It's something to consider. Most mice probably escaped the fire, but with the food burned, there was no reason for them to remain. I recommend you set traps or get some cats to keep the rodents at a minimum."

"Poison should work as well."

Cress admired the man's quick acceptance. Once again, Pire proved the future of Froy was in good hands.

****

Becca slept a scant two hours when the sun spilled bright light onto the tip of the limestone tower. Standing and stretching, she walked to the edge of the cave's mouth. Far off in the distance dust rolled across the parched ground, creating an obscuring cloud. Briefly, she wondered what caused it. A wind devil? Animals? Traders? The possibility crept into her mind since Cress mentioned traders bringing the plague.

Last night, with the Guardians prompting her, she'd spent hours uncovering a labyrinth of passageways, complete with chambers once possessing thousands of dragon eggs. The sad thing, though, was that time had cracked hundreds, thousands.

She couldn't wait to get home and tell Cress of her fabulous discovery. Shimmying down the tower, she ran most of the way back to her village.

As she drew near Froy, the odor of pitch-covered torches drifted in the air. The Council always made them of sweet sandalwood so as not to offend the goddess. Eight poles flanked the meeting hut's entrance, four on each side. Each pole had a dragon head carved on top with black leather banners flapping in the breeze as though tying them around the neck. Each banner held one of the phases of the moon in its inky center.

Becca searched for Cress and found him in their hut.

"I have news," she gasped in mingled excitement and happiness.

He turned to look over his shoulder at her. "Me, too. But you first."

"Is the protective spell still in effect?"

"Aye."

"Good," she said, relieved. "Its best if we are not overheard. I need to talk to you about the Guardians. I was right to wonder why they accompanied on this journey. They followed me to my cave. Do you find it odd?" She leaned forward eager to hear his response.

He shrugged. "Not necessarily. They're curious beasts."

His casual answer discouraged her. "Cress, do you

truly trust the dragons? Are they as good as they pretend?"

A puzzled expression passed over his face. "I've known them for a thousand years, and they've never given me any cause to doubt them. The more accurate question is 'should they trust us?' Remember, humans wiped out dragons as a species."

She sank to the furs and sighed. "They were on a mission, too. They sought to find their lost treasure."

A pop of wood from the fire broke into her concentration. For a moment Cress seemed to ponder the erratic dance of the flames, then returned to settle next to her.

"The Guardians never acted like they craved treasure," he said. "Knowledge has always been their most coveted prize."

"Until now…Their mission to The Wilds was two pronged. They sought the location of lost dragon eggs. Those eggs were hidden in my cave. I've heard their voices ever since I climbed to the cave. Now, they want our help to bring them to Demit Woods."

Cress took her news calmly. Too calmly. "I'm sure they convinced you of that, but you don't owe them a thing. Not you. I do, for allowing Trell to exist in the dragon circle and letting me to live there until I could free her. What I find curious is why they didn't seek out these eggs before now." He waved his hand and tiny golden lights winked into existence.

"The location of these eggs were unknown to us until the female human arrived." Dragon mindspeech blasted both Cress and her. *"Her ability to speak with Trell gave us the clue that she might have been in contact with dragon eggs."*

"How is it that Becca could hear these eggs?" Cress asked while Becca tried to grasp his reluctance.

"Conjecture among us is that the unhatched eggs reached out to other hunters, but only the warrior woman climbed the tower."

"I've got a few questions, if you don't mind. What happens if these eggs hatch? Those dragonets will grow into huge beasts. Dragons will soar Feldsvelt's sky. What then, huh?"

"Sweet Luna, Cress, we can't desert them. You were the one who told me the marvelous dragon tales. You made them sound wonderful. You must care about them. You taught me to."

Brown eyebrows rose. "How many eggs are there?"

Guardians zigzagged in the hut. *"Forty-two survive. Only fifteen females."*

Cress groaned. A shadow passed over his face. Becca didn't understand his anxiety. The Guardians were his friends. Would transporting the eggs slow them down?

"Forty-two," he repeated a second later. "I assume there's a variety of sizes. I've heard blues are huge. How can we transport them all at once?"

Becca's voice dipped low. "We have no choice. Opening the chamber broke the protective spell. Those that are alive are in jeopardy if not properly tended to."

He took her hands into his. "Wait just a moment. I'm not ready to commit to this endeavor. After all these years, isn't it strange that you managed to break the spell now?"

She gave him an exasperated look. His touch sent tiny shocks of awareness up her fingers. "The spell protecting them has been weakening for years. The earth shakes by the tower. It has caused many to fall and break. The unborn ones told me which rocks to remove."

"I see," he said, eyes narrowing. "I might have a solution. I'm sure magic could make the eggs lighter than air. We could move them safely then."

Relief filled Becca until tears threatened to spill out of her eyes. "I knew my faith in you was justified."

Cress brushed a loose strand of hair away from her face. "This explains a great deal."

"What?" She leaned into the warmth of his touch.

"The Guardians are correct. If the voices in the cave were dragons, somehow you have the ability to speak with creatures under a spell—including Trell." He smiled down at her. "You make me proud, Becca. After the assembly, allow me to show you my gratitude."

The assembly! Sweet Luna, duty completely slipped her mind, her dream of Froy returning to its former glory nearly forgotten.

"We'll speak more of this after the assembly," she said. "I must make people revert to the old way."

"You could try tact."

She grunted to cover her embarrassment. "I'm a hunter. Tact isn't necessary."

Cress shook his head. "You want to wager on that?"

"You fret too much. Just watch me."

"With pleasure," he said, "but first indulge me."

He waved a hand over an empty bowl, chanting words she couldn't catch. The air within the hut shimmered. Her skin tingled. Becca always loved it when he practiced his magic. An iridescent light condensed over the bowl. The sound of something dropping into it caught her attention, especially when the luminosity disappeared and glittering beads resembling miniature suns overflowed the lip.

"For you," he said.

She cried out in awe and joy. Never did she believe Cress would offer her his beads. "Why are you doing this?"

He lowered his arm. "I'm not quite sure. But will you accept my beads?"

Her gaze lifted to his. "With pleasure."

She leaned close to his side and nuzzled his neck. A low moan of pleasure vibrated up his throat. Teasing him with her movements, she unplaited several inches of her braid and with shaking fingers, picked up a glowing orb. Rolling it between her forefinger and thumb to admire, she saw a tiny hole pierced its center.

He never looked away. Not until the last bead had been strung and she replaited the braid did Cress move.

He reached over and stroked the glowing orbs in her hair. "I thought beads were worn afterwards."

"I'm making a statement."

"Can we not stay and continue this…this conversation?" he asked softly.

She grunted in frustration. "Duty calls. For a male, you are unduly correct too many times for my comfort. On the other hand, you possess many attributes I find admirable. The contradictions are confusing."

Cress gathered her into his arms and smiled down at her. "Poor Becca, you have much to learn about men."

Chapter Thirty-Two

"If you're offering to teach me about men," Becca said, delivering a faint stroke to his jaw, "I should tell you, I'm a quick learner."

Emotions swelled within Cress and shook him to his core. This softer side of the warrior woman supported a creature of temptation. She sent his senses whirling in all directions. He wanted to wrap her in his arms, to kiss her lush mouth, and to taste the sweetness inside. He wanted to fill her with himself.

"I think I'm the one who will benefit most. You're ravishing, Becca d'Firn. I find you irresistible," he said, amazed at how he choked with emotion. That had never happened to him before. "A long wait will be agony."

Golden strands escaped her braid to dance around her lovely face. "For me as well. Meanwhile, we should hurry."

"Wait! I want to wear beads, too. That way people will know we belong to each other."

He picked up a couple glowing spheres, rolling them in the center of his palm where they shimmered like miniature suns.

Becca stopped his hand as if guessing his intent. "Only women wear beads."

"If sharing beads is the language of men and women, why can't both wear them? Let's start a new custom."

Becca chewed her lip. "I don't know."

The heat of her breath fanned his cheeks, and it sent a shiver of delight down his neck. "Trust me. I want your village to know where my affections lie, who holds my heart."

She laughed, the sound light and full of life. "Tonight, I can refuse you little."

He caught her mouth in a kiss. Pulling back, he grinned and retied the thong at the nape of his neck. Iridescent beads mixed with his long hair and clinked together at the end of the leather.

"Exactly what I wanted to hear," he said. "Now, how do I look?"

"Magically handsome."

"Good, then I'm ready to face the assembly at your side."

Outside, a moon hung in the night sky, full and bright. It threw silver illumination over the open area of the village. They hurried toward the Council hut. He couldn't convince Becca to leave her bow and now she clenched it in her hand.

The buzz of massed people reached his ears as they approached. So many people. Crowded places held no appeal for him, not after centuries of living in the serenity of Demit Woods. He steeled his nerves and stepped between the poles. Pennants snapped in the night breeze, some cracking like lightning, others soft whispers.

The center hut had been constructed of mud and daub, the ground packed hard by thousands of feet over countless meetings. Walls glowed with torchlight, and sharp whiffs of burning leaves mingled with the sour odor of sweat from the men and women gathered together.

Cress suppressed a sigh and looked for one man—Pire. No sign of the blacksmith. Strange. He should be waiting anxiously for them. Especially since Cress had unwittingly given him the ammunition to defeat Becca and strengthen his position as leader—the reason for the plague and a solution to keep it from returning.

Part of him sided with Pire and the men. Another part worried how it would affect his relationship with Becca if the assembly's outcome transpired as he suspected. His honor and loyalty were being split apart. And he didn't like the sensation one iota.

Cress glanced fondly at her standing next to him, her fragrance unique and alluring among all the others. Right or wrong, Becca held a deep-seated conviction that Froy must return to the old order.

More importantly, she held his heart.

She scrutinized each face, especially the women wearing conical hats that jingled with their movements. He assumed they were once council members. A ripple of wonder started, building in intensity when people noticed the glowing beads in Becca's hair. Several women cooed with delight. How could they not? Becca was the most beautiful woman present—a jewel among mere stones.

A thin woman, her frame rendered thinner by the extra-fine woolen shift she wore, elbowed her way through the crowd. A loose belt the width of a rope draped her waist and hung down to the floor. Crudely fashioned beads painted yellow were attached to her long braid. The woman glared at the shimmering beads he'd created for Becca. Her face gave off a green tint.

"I am so glad a man found you appealing enough

to offer his beads," she said, fingering her own yellow beads.

Becca graced him with a quick smile. He slipped her hand into his to offer comfort and show everyone he stood by the warrior woman's side in case his beads supplied insufficient proof.

"These are the Wizard Cress's beads, Landa."

"That's obvious," the woman replied. "But wearing magical beads will not garner you support tonight."

Becca's lashes swept down, pale blonde over tanned skin. "Envious of how pretty they are?"

The woman straightened. "Don't be ridiculous. You flatter yourself if you think the wizard cares for you. You are nothing more than a novelty to him."

Cress's chest expanded. An instant dislike for the woman flared within him. He flicked his long hair forward to reveal the beads he wore. Several people aahed. "You presume to speak my mind. Do you practice magic as well?"

The thin woman glared at him. "I—I am only saying what everyone is thinking, yet afraid to speak." She turned to Becca. "I've warned you once. I'll repeat it for everyone's benefit. Maine is mine. He'll not tolerate you giving me insults."

"Then don't give me cause, Landa," Becca answered.

All around them people avoided eye contact.

Ah, now Cress understood. The man's name, the same as the one Becca went off to see the first morning of their arrival. Had rivalry always existed between the two women? Jealousy, often the crux of many disagreements, could drive a wedge between the closest of friends.

His gut tightened. The thought of Becca favoring another man brought a rise of anger and resentment in him.

"Goddess help him," Becca said with a tight smile. "I almost feel sorry for Maine. He's going to be busy defending you against the slurs your sick mind will imagine."

Landa paled. "Mock me not. Nor put words into my mouth."

Becca lifted a shapely eyebrow. "Bless the Goddess Luna, I put ideas into people's head. That is the purpose of an assembly, after all."

The reminder brought a short-lived smile to the other woman's face. "Forgive me, Becca, I don't know what came over me. It must be that your objections frighten me. The ways of the village have changed, are still changing, and I am just enthusiastic about them. So is Maine. His beliefs are the same as Pire's. I probably approached you wrong."

The apology rang false to Cress. Malice filled the words, yet he left the decision up to Becca how to respond.

She fiddled with her braid, his beads glowing different colors with her touch. "My objective is to restore Luna to her proper place. That means women must reclaim control of Froy."

Cries of protest erupted from the male onlookers.

Landa heard the commotion and smiled smugly. "Do you hear? Your protest will have no sway among those gathered here."

The anger within Cress rolled into red hot fury. Glaring at the woman, he let his silence, more ominous than shouts or threats, speak for him. The woman flicked a glance at him and inched back. A sensible move, he thought. If the harpy spoke another word, he might silence her in a drastic manner. The men might not wish to be subjugated again, but this woman needed to learn manners.

Before he could act rashly, however, Quinta arrived in a swirl of grayish skirts, which enhanced the silver streaking her brown hair. "There you are, Becca. Cress. I meant to greet you as you came in. Unfortunately, I was delayed." She shot a dismissive glance to Landa. "If you forgive us, I have things to say to my daughter and her guest. Important things. Give us some privacy."

"And if I refuse?"

Quinta smiled. "Then I will ask Wizard Cress to turn you into a toad. After spending a minute in your company, Landa, I'm sure he'd be happy to do as I bid."

The woman's eyes widened, and spittle bubbled on her lips. She retreated quickly with her head held high.

Becca grinned. "Would you truly do that?"

"Nay, but sometimes threats work better," her mother replied.

Becca nodded. "Have others joined my side?"

"I'm afraid not. Maine made a mistake with her." Quinta reddened, apologetic. "I just wanted to get Landa away before she caused real trouble tonight. Her tongue can be as sharp as a prickly misery barb. What will you do tonight?"

Becca laughed. "My very best."

Cress glanced at each woman. "I suggest we get this meeting over with as fast as possible."

"Gladly, but where's Pire? Why isn't he here?"

Quinta affected a calm mien, using one hand to hold her conical hat in place when she tilted her head. "His tardiness is nothing to fret about."

"Doesn't that prove he lacks the skills to lead? A good leader arrives in a timely manner."

"Daughter," Quinta said, "there could be a perfectly good reason for his delay. Do not judge too hasty, lest you be judged."

Becca looked around the council hut, a thoughtful expression on her face. "Have you noticed how men are standing in little knots? What if there are opposing factions among them? Mayhaps they're unhappy with Pire's leadership. Surely—"

Cress put his hand on her arm. "Heed your mother's advice. It has merit. An unwise person jumps to hasty conclusions."

"I've been approaching the hunters, trying to convince them. What if I've been focusing my attention on the wrong people?" Her tone exposed her inner feelings.

"It's too late now," he countered.

"Froy is my home." Passion raised her voice and hardened her expression. "These are my people. Sacred customs I grew up with are being shed without any thought to the consequences. All I hear is there is equality now; but that's not true."

Several men chortled. Every male wore a sword strapped on their hip.

One man separated from a group. Legget. "Will you listen to her? She thinks it's her village. Her customs. Her people. Such arrogance! Is there no end to her sense of superiority?"

Quinta offered protection as only a mother's

presence could by moving closer to Becca. Her face set in a scowl and she glowered at the short man until he looked away.

Cress shook his head, aware a nice calm discussion was out of the question. Legget's fractious words incited the villagers, making everyone excited, too irritated to react rationally. Himself included.

Cress wove a chant that bore no resemblance to the spell he really wished to create—one that would cause all these people to disappear. He needed to layer the spell line by line, the more lines, the more complex the spell and the safer for Becca. After centuries of practicing, magic came automatically. Words of power spun the spell.

"Both females and males of this village are arrogant," the dragons mindspoke. *"They are blind and deaf to all except themselves."*

Cress's jaw muscles tightened. He hadn't expected Guardians tonight, and he didn't agree with the broad assessment. Not when it came to Becca and him. The men would never agree to being under the women's control again. *"Some, but not all."*

"We can influence their thoughts."

"Nay." His focus remained on Becca. By her expression, the dragons did not include her in their discussion. *"No matter how stubborn they are, if you interfere, you are no better than the villagers. They have the right to rule themselves. As soon as the matter is at rest, more important matters need attending—your precious eggs."*

His reminder silenced the Guardians as he hoped it would. Time to stay alert and concentrate on the actions of the people around him.

Chapter Thirty-Three

"Begone, little man," Becca ordered Legget, regretting the instant she spoke. Her remark about his stature antagonized him. She knew better than to engage him in debate. "I refuse to argue with you. You'll hear me at the same time as everyone else."

"As if I wish to hear your comments," he sneered, stubby fingers squeezing the hilt of his sword. "You never saw any labor performed by men as worthwhile. You were always critical. We'll show you how wrong you are. By the Goddess, we will."

Before she could challenge the man again, Cress snapped his fingers, creating an ear-splitting crack of thunder inside the large hut. "Enough. Wait like the rest."

Magic silenced the room like a heavy curtain had dropped. The temperature in the room increased as though fire ignited it.

Quinta glowered at Legget as she licked two fingers. She hissed at the short man and made a motion with her hand that Becca recognized as a d'Firn sign to ward off evil. She giggled and he clambered off scowling.

Becca had labored to bring the wizard home. Wild animals threatened her. Inclement weather tried to slow her. She endured a long, arduous journey, fraught with danger; but faith and determination to locate Cress so he could find a solution to the plague had kept her pushing forward.

She raised her gaze to meet his warm one. Her feelings for Cress swelled and left her more confused than ever. He was her only ally, and to think, once he objected to traveling to Froy. Firelight gleamed off Cress's features, the angles of his handsome face prominent. He appeared a different man than the one who began the journey with her. The way his hazel gaze swept the interior made him look predatory. Dangerous. She would not want to find herself on his bad side.

"My thanks," she said. "I could have handled Legget."

"I'm sure you could, but his voice grated on my nerves."

Becca accepted his answer with a smile. An immense pressure lifted when she looked around the hut. Within these walls she had known order, structure, stability, and friendly faces, all things that used to bring her comfort and peace. What right did she have to question Froy's new practices? These men only want the same freedom hunters enjoyed for centuries. Was that so wrong?

The question caused indecision to surge within her. This change hit close to home, felt too personal. Did she have the right to challenge this new order?

Her eyes watered when she searched the interior of the Council hut and found not a single friendly face in its midst. The very people she wanted to save demonstrated no interest in aiding her. They made her feel as an intrusive presence. Unwelcome. Worse, they treated her no better than a stranger.

Reservations packed her head and she realized her sentiments were flawed. Emotions were no match for logic.

Except the feeling persisted.

Too late, Maine's comments about the men's dissatisfaction returned to haunt her. She should have listened closer.

She chased the line of speculation. Only one time did she inform the Council. They had chosen to ignore her notification. Then, when the thrill of adventure called to her, she'd left Froy vulnerable for the seeds of revolt to sprout.

A cold shiver went through Becca as a terrible thought burst through her mind. Sweet Luna! Did that make her culpable for the disastrous happenings?

Probably. Doubtless. Absolutely.

The realization weighed upon her heart until shame and guilt filled her.

Sweet Luna, forgive me, I never realized.

Suddenly, a man banged the butt of his staff on the earthen floor several times in a call for quiet and to hail the entrance of Pire. The muscular blacksmith sauntered inside with Gette flanking his left. A motley group followed in their wake with Maine in the forefront, his dark blond eyebrows disappearing beneath a fringe of like-colored hair.

Pire had washed off the smoky odor of the smithy, revealing a lined face that Becca couldn't recall seeing before. He wore sable colored breeches, a loose shirt, and tall boots. Even his meaty hands looked well scrubbed, the black grime normally underneath his nails, gone. Without his leather apron, he appeared thinner. Were the responsibilities of leadership weighing him down?

Cress stepped alongside Becca as though he sensed her consternation and silently offered his strength. A flutter in the air stroked her very being, warm and caring. She smiled in gratitude.

One of Pire's cronies produced a lip-licking smile.

Cress leaned toward her, his voice low, full of concern, "What's the matter?"

"Pomposity was never part of the Council," she whispered. "We gathered together to honor Luna, not ourselves. Pire better not expect me to grovel at his feet."

The blacksmith stood tall, his chest puffed out. "Good news, my friends. The Wizard Cress has found the source of the plague."

Gasps exploded from the people within the assembly hut. A ripple of whispers carried the news to those still outside.

"Praise the Great Mother."

"How did he—" Becca blurted out, then shot a questioning look at Cress.

Pire cleared his throat. "He's a great wizard. If anyone could save us, he could. And we have Becca to give our thanks for bringing such a wise man to us."

"Sweet Luna, we shall never fear it again," someone in the hut said.

Another shouted, "The plague gone. Thank Luna."

Becca gulped and felt her throat flutter. She had only herself to blame. Cress wanted to share something with her when she told him of the dragons' cache of eggs. They'd run out of time, and he'd never gotten the chance. She seriously doubted he would have let her be caught off guard on purpose. Just poor timing.

"How?" Becca turned to Cress, more wistful than angry, then to Pire. Her curiosity stuck on Gette when her sister took his arm.

The man bestowed a warm smile on his wife before stating in a loud voice, "Mice brought the plague."

"Mice?" a shout rose from the safety of the back.

"Hold your tongue until I finish," Pire countered in a booming voice. "That is what Wizard Cress claims, and I believe him. Mice are always present. We've all seen them around the granary. They were living there, breeding, growing fat on spelt and fouling our grain. The fire either killed them or drove them away."

"Wait a minute!" Becca flicked another glance at Cress. He nodded concurrence. "Mice are around the granary even when people aren't sick."

"The child Reba gave the wizard the clue he needed," Pire stated calmly, ignoring her denunciation. "Without her, he would still be looking."

"Bless Luna for the children," a woman murmured.

Smiling widely, the blacksmith continued, "After eliminating the logical sources, he followed the trail of those who took sick. The wizard discovered the boys who tended the granary were usually felled first, and from them it passed to the weakest in their families. When Reba told him her mother, a young, healthy woman who oversaw those boys caught the plague, he figured out the common thread—the granary. He'd already learned Mother Asa took ill after a meal had been delivered to her by one of those same boys. When I told him no new cases appeared after the fire, he said it was the only thing to make sense. Control the mice and you control the pestilence."

"That simple?" asked a man in the crowd.

Pire nodded. "I believe so."

"Good news, indeed," said another.

Maine shouldered closer. "That settles it. Let us celebrate the moon's fullness with friends, drink, and entertaining stories."

"Drunkenness does not honor Luna," Becca countered.

Pire stepped forward. "Many of the old ways are still prized, but changes were necessary for our survival. Think about it. Men and women work as partners now." He locked his gaze on her but addressed the crowd. "I'll say this only once, Becca, so best you listen. By bringing the great Wizard Cress, you have accomplished a deed no one believed possible. I personally wish to thank you for your service to Froy and its inhabitants. We are grateful for your efforts and want you to know all here are in your debt."

Her scalp prickled. What transpired behind his beady eyes? "You have a strange way of showing your appreciation, Pire. I called this assembly to expose your lie of equality."

"We can read his thoughts," dragons mindspoke to her.

"You would do that?" Becca asked, instantly tempted.

"Give the word and we shall try."

She glared at Pire and drew a long sigh. Knowing his thoughts would give her a definite advantage. She mulled over the offer for a moment. No, she would not sink to his level or use deceptive means to gain an upper hand. Cheating wasn't her nature. *My thanks, Guardians, but I will defeat him without outside assistance,"* she mindspoke before the tiny dragons took it upon themselves to read his mind.

"The plague took many innocent lives," Pire reminded her, his dark eyes pleading for understanding, "and the Council refused to take action. Oh, I know you were sent to find the wizard, but the Council sought no resolution, except to bemoan the situation."

"Luna would have protected most until I returned," she insisted stubbornly.

"Like you, the Goddess refused to heed our pleas. If she cared about us, she would not have allowed a plague to run amok in the first place."

"Speaking of Luna..." Becca said, determined. "You cannot turn your back on her."

"We didn't."

"You show her no respect. Men running Froy is an insult to her and an afront to everything she stands for."

Pire raised his hand to silence men near the door. "That's false, as you well know. Even though we suffered greatly under her, we honored her with offerings, the same as the women. Nothing has changed our devotion to the Great Mother. She is our Goddess and always will be."

His assertion rang false to her ears. "Tell me, Pire, were you guided by Luna when you lead the revolt against the Council?"

His eyes narrowed. "I succeeded, didn't I?"

"You could say that again," a man shouted.

"He did the right thing," yelled another. "Luna blessed our deeds."

The man was intelligent. Becca gave him that. And wily. His words inspired the men, and he let them applaud his exploits rather than boast himself. It allowed him to appear humble. Even so, she could not bring herself to agree with him.

"Does she now?" she asked. "Prove it. Has the Great Mother spoken to you?"

"Becca's right," a woman's quivering voice rose from the crowd. "The Goddess has never spoken to a man."

At last, an ally. "Step forward, Honored Mother," Becca said, positive an ex-Council member spoke.

"We have forsaken Luna," came the same voice.

"Hush, foolish old woman," a man criticized in the back.

"Call me foolish," the elderly voice objected. "I've a good mind to club you with my stick."

The anonymous man laughed. "Be off with you. We've enough trouble without having to listen to your fabricated worries."

Becca raised a hand, halting additional words from anyone. "I called this assembly for hunters to see that men running Froy is a sign we have been forsaken by Luna." She refused to let herself be led off course. "Granted, men speak favorably of the Great Mother, but your actions prove otherwise. Take tonight—the full moon is our time to celebrate the fact she summoned life out of the great water, not settle disputes or call for drinks. We are supposed to honor her efforts. She bequeathed us with many great gifts."

"Such as?" called a man out of sight.

"The ability to control our pregnancies for one."

"Incorrect statement," dragons mindspoke to Becca. *"Birthing gift was not from your Goddess. You received that ability from Oyfele. Birthing comes from the power of the moonstone. Oyfele passed that along to your ancestors as thanks for aiding her with the dragon*

eggs."

Becca never moved. *"My thanks, little ones, but we can discuss this later."*

Pire missed her distraction. "We honor Luna. Our storyteller will start the proceedings with…"

Wispy dragon wings flapped in the air near Becca. *"This meeting is a waste of time. The sooner this assembly is over, the sooner we can retrieve our eggs,"* the Guardians said. *"Let us dispose of him."*

"Don't tempt me." Becca wasn't in favor of using bloodshed to settle the discord. She wondered if the Guardians' attitude stemmed from her aversion toward Pire. Or, did they know something she did not?

Luna, help me, she prayed. *I have to make these people understand.*

"Your Goddess cannot hear you, child," the dragons mindspoke. *"We doubt her existence. Since we have lived on this world no deities have ever come forward. Your ancestors existed to care for our dragon eggs."*

Luna not real! Impossible. It went against everything she believed in. A shiver traveled up her spine as she fought against the blasphemy and tried to stay calm. *"If you cannot aid me, little ones, please do not hinder me in my task."*

"As you command," came the response.

She turned to Pire again, considering him.

"Do not our successful crops, the negotiations with our neighbors, prove the changes were right?" the blacksmith ended.

"Women work harder than the men ever did," she rebutted, needing to express herself as eloquently as possible. She would never be given another chance.

"You keep saying there is social equality, but no woman holds a position of power in this new rule. None govern jointly with you."

"That's untrue." Quinta stepped forward. "I am part of Pire's inner circle of advisors. He actively seeks my opinion."

Becca's world crumbled with her mother's words. Her line of argument was doomed to fail. "Why didn't you tell me sooner?"

"Would you have listened? You must believe me when I say our interests are being heard."

"This didn't happen overnight. Many wanted the changes, but feared to speak up," Pire added.

Cress stepped forward. "Why can't you come to an understanding?"

Betrayal swelled within Becca. Her stomach clenched. If her sole ally questioned her stand, all was lost. "What do you mean?"

"You cannot answer a question with a question," he said. "Otherwise this debate will go on forever. It must cease before hostilities erupt."

Pire's perpetually singed eyebrows wiggled. "Explain your meaning, Wizard."

"If you can't come to a satisfactory resolution, being deadlocked is the least of your worries," Cress said. "It will only be a matter of time before Froy splits itself apart. Already men threaten to leave if there is a return to old ways."

Silence fell when he finished.

"Becca," Cress continued in mindspeech. *"The Guardians want to talk with me away from the village. I haven't heard them so frantic before. They say danger is coming. I hate leaving you, but they are insistent. Do*

you mind?"

"*Go,*" she answered him. *"They are your friends."*

"The old way was for women to provide fresh meat and protect Froy against surprise attack." The blacksmith frowned as his gaze followed Cress as the wizard wove his way out of the Council hut. "Women no longer need to hunt. We grow our own fare. There are plenty of sheep and pigs, and we plan to increase those herds. Wild game will supplement our stores, but not be our primary source."

Becca winced. Give up her bow? Not hunt?

"As far as protection goes," Pire went on, tossing a glance around the hut, "men can defend Froy with their swords. We carry the heaviest load because we are free to make the choice. We are dedicated to preserving Froy for generations. Not one man shirks his duties. Nor will our women be worked to death. Don't you see, Becca, this is your home. No one disputes that fact, but you can't change what now is."

"Why not?" she replied at once.

Pire shook his head, studying her. "Be reasonable, Becca. Accept the change. The rest of us have."

Becca's mouth pinched closed. What else could go wrong? Thinking the worst turned into reality. A piercing shriek shredded the night.

Outside the Council hut, voices rose in fear. "Marauders! We are under attack."

Chapter Thirty-Four

"To arms!" Pire's voice rang true and strong.

"Hunters, to your bows," Becca yelled right after him. "Defend Froy."

Pire glowered at her. "Men to arms," he repeated. "Send the raiders back where they came from."

Swords scraped from leather scabbards as men poured out of the Council hut with bloodcurdling screams. Becca had never heard Froyan men sound so vicious. A tremor of pride filled her, and her voice joined their cries. She followed on their heels through the door, grateful she carried her bow. If only other hunters had done so.

Spears and arrows flew in their direction and thudded in the ground around her. Villagers who remained outside had scattered. The first man out of the Council hut dropped dead with a marauder's arrow piercing his heart. Froyan men froze at the sight.

"Fight, or die, you fools," Becca shouted at them.

"Do as she says." Maine's voice came loud and clear.

"Fight!" Pire hollered, fury blazing on his broad face. "Defend Froy."

The blacksmith used the same words as she. In the blink of an eye, she swept the bow off her back and fired her first arrow. Warmth filled her when she spotted women racing to their huts to fetch their

239

weapons.

The angry buzz of Becca's arrows, like roused hornets, packed the air. Nothing seemed to stop the flow of raiders as scores rushed out of the darkness. Combatants sparred in the square with deadly blades and axes as they cut air and bodies with equal flair. Grunts and cries of pain came from everywhere.

Not all villagers carried swords. Many males wielded scythes that slashed muscles and tendons and broke bones with the same ease as shafts of wheat. They were not trained warriors, but they fought for something far more important than glory or plunder—they fought to protect their homes and families.

The village's dogs dashed between legs, snarling, biting, and occasionally yelping in pain. Tulle sank his teeth into a raider's calf and received a swift kick for his efforts.

The battle surged around Becca. The clang of swords waxed and waned as she loosened arrow after arrow in quick succession at clear targets.

Her veins filled with gratification spying armed hunters tiptoeing to the outer edge of the fighting where they could fire arrows at the raiders without fear of hitting villagers.

A shadowy movement caught Becca's eye. Gette slipped from her old hut, trying to appear inconspicuous, a difficult task for a woman heavy in her pregnancy. She nocked a shaft on the bowstring as she skirted the worst fighting.

A man in a wolf vest skulked behind her sister. Becca whistled a warning. Gette dropped, rolling to her side, and Becca freed an arrow to catch the man in his neck. His mouth opened, his eyes bulged, and he dropped his sword, pitching forward, dead.

Gette waddled to Becca's side and divided the arrows into two. "My gratitude, sister. I didn't see him."

"No need for thanks. We always protect those we love."

Standing together, they fired with equal precision, making sure they had a clear shot of the enemy, neither wanting to hit one of their own.

Becca's heart swelled with pride. It felt good to have Gette alongside her. Just like old times.

A blade sang nearby, and a marauder with long hair matted with grease went down. Pire gave a deep-throated cry of triumph. At the sound, Gette turned and caught her husband's eye. They shared a quick smile.

Becca recognized Maine's yell for help, as did Pire. Three raiders in metal-linked tunics and padded leather breeches pressed her ex-lover. The blacksmith dashed to his aid and together they battled the group.

In the midst of fighting, three marauders pointed at her, her glowing beads a beacon that singled her out.

She reached for another shaft, only to discover her quiver empty. A quick glance at Gette showed her sister with one arrow left.

"Give me your shaft and I'll hold them off. You flee," Becca ordered.

"I can't leave you alone."

Becca ground her teeth. "Get more arrows."

Her sister bobbed her head and darted toward her hut.

Three men approached. Tackling the biggest fellow on the right one-on-one would be impossible. He towered over his companions and outweighed her by a half body. If she had any chance of surviving, he needed to be taken out first. Becca waited, firing when the trio were twenty feet from her. Her aim proved perfect. He went down with an oof. Then she drew her small knife from her boot. Let the other two come. She'd demonstrate the mettle of a true hunter. Waving her knife at the remaining men, she indicated her readiness to face them.

They glanced at each other, laughed, and charged.

Overconfidence would be their downfall. Becca leapt to the left, pretending panic. The closest man lunged, and she switched her knife to her left hand. A little closer. *Come a little closer*. She planned to sink her knife into his belly when a man's voice distracted her.

"You are not alone, Becca. I'll protect you."

Legget rushed in, swinging his sword in a whistling arc.

The trio of men met several feet in front of her.

Blades slashed and clanged. Dust cloaked the air. Becca followed the blur of motion. Legget gave a good accounting of himself until a yelp sounded and he staggered sideways with blood gushing between his stumpy fingers. He lost his grip on his sword handle. A raider's blade stuck deep into his belly. He looked at Becca, eyes huge and sorrowful.

No time to mourn Legget's sacrifice. In the next instant, Gette returned clutching a fistful of metal-tipped arrows. Becca grabbed two and took aim with a prayer to Luna for vengeance. She willed each shaft to seek an enemy's heart. The Goddess blessed her efforts, for each arrow found its target.

Amid the chaos of battle, the smell of blood, sweat,

and urine rose up. Shock of the raid and her outrage over the negligence of no sentries intensified when Becca searched the area for Cress. She couldn't see him anywhere. Where had the Guardians taken him? Did they know of the attack in advance? He couldn't have gone far. Had he already fallen? Her stomach rolled at the thought. No. She refused to believe that. As a mighty wizard, defending himself should be easy. Besides, if something happened, she would have felt his loss. Her heart would have broken. Still, fear wrapped around her and squeezed the air out of her chest.

"Cress?" she screamed in mindspeech.

"What's wrong?"

"We're under attack," she said, relieved. *"I need your help."*

"Hold on. I'm on my way."

****

Cress ran, fear giving his feet speed. Why had he followed the Guardians? He should have remained at Becca's side.

The dragons told him they needed those eggs. Had they deliberately led him away? They were the historians of dragon history. If there were no dragons, they would have nothing to record. Their numbers were diminishing. Over time more and more Guardians chose to leave the protective dragon circle. They were dying. Soon the Guardians would be gone…forever. They needed the eggs. They gave them purpose.

No amount of berating eased his burden as his long strides devoured the ground and he left the Guardians behind. His chest burned as he raced to the village.

What could he do with his bare hands? The wrongness of using sorcery against people vacillated inside him. He'd vowed to never use magic to harm another human being—not since Bonner's spell backfired and left Trell enchanted over a thousand years ago.

The fighting must cease. It meant he needed to use magic, even though it went against everything he believed in. More importantly, he must keep Becca safe. He had no choice.

Murmuring an enchantment, his fingers tingled, and his hands and arms began to glow. He summoned power. Sparks leapt out in an ever-increasing stream. The light grew brighter, blinding.

He ran on. The clash of fighting grew louder, rumbling off walls, drumming in his ears, throbbing in the very ground. Concentrate. He gathered his power into a single entity just as he burst between the huts where madness enveloped everyone.

He swept his arms upward and screamed out a spell. Magic shattered over the battlefield. A deluge of tiny sparks plunged downward, touching everyone, paralyzing them.

Arms outstretched, knees bent, the grim-faced villagers and marauders froze where they stood and fought. Faces pinched in fear, most would have trembled if granted the ability. The stench of blood and guts polluted the air.

"Becca!" he shouted through mindspeech. *"Where are you?"*

"Cress," she answered shakily.

Relief nearly overwhelmed him as he cast around the battlefield for her. He spotted her not so far away. She stood with her legs spread protectively over her sister who'd fallen to the ground.

His heart thumped with relief. She was alive. Unhurt.

Hurrying to her side, he touched her arm. "Be free."

Her gaze snapped toward him the instant the spell broke. She gasped, sucking in great mouthfuls of air. Her knees started to buckle, and he caught her in his arms.

"Are you hurt?" he asked, suddenly worried.

She dropped to her sister. "Nay, just exhausted."

"It's over," he said, touching Gette and freeing her from the enchantment. "No one else is going to get hurt this night."

Village dogs sniffed around frozen legs, hackles raised. He muttered soft words into the silence, freeing villagers, but not the forty or so raiders left.

"Let's kill them! Kill them all," shouted a villager.

"Nay!" Cress ordered, his voice ringing through the crowd. "I'll not allow you to murder vulnerable people!"

"They would have killed us," someone called out.

Although the marauders couldn't move a muscle, Cress left them the ability to see and hear. He could well imagine the fear of being butchered while defenseless to stop the violence.

"There's been enough death this night," he said, striding among the crowd. Villagers inched aside, seemingly afraid to let the hem of his robe brush against them. "Let it be known throughout this land that Froy is protected by magic."

Cress inhaled. He pointed at a marauder wearing a bear pelt and sprouting a beard knotted with sticks and leather ties. He waved his hand and the man fell to his knees with a moan. Eyes wide, he glanced around, considering flight.

"Who is your leader?" Cress demanded. Tulle trotted to his side, and he scratched the dog's head.

"Ontello." The man pointed at a figure in a metal-link vest frozen with a bloody sword in his hand, his eyes bright with commitment and his arm raised in the midst of dispensing a killing blow.

A golden stream of magic leapt from Cress's fingertips. It undulated like a living rope to the leader and encircled his powerful body with bands of light.

"Yield or die," Cress demanded.

Ontello's wide shoulders slumped. "I think we made a mistake."

"A mistake?" Not the answer Cress expected. "Because you've seen the power of my magic?"

"Aye. We didn't know a wizard lived here." Ontello squirmed against the bands encasing him.

"Stop! The more you struggle, the tighter they'll become."

The man ceased moving and bowed his head. "I yield."

Cress glanced at Becca. Her expression gave no hint about what she thought. "A wise decision. You and your men will never threaten this village again. Is that clear?"

"Aye, master wizard."

Cress sensed the villagers' restlessness. "The reason I'm letting you and your fellows live is to pass along a message."

"Message?" Ontello asked.

"Aye. Come to Froy with hostility in your hearts and receive my wrath. Tell anyone who will listen if they wish to trade in peace, they are welcome. Those who do not, will die."

A smile escaped Cress's lips when he gestured, his fingers spread wide. The bands holding the man prisoner vanished. He freed the other raiders next. Magic should be respected, and he believed these men had learned their lesson.

Ontello knocked his fist against his chest with a thud. "It shall be as you wish."

"Leave this place now," Cress ordered. "Take your wounded and dead. We want neither here."

The man grunted and sheathed his sword.

"Nay!" Cress said. "Drop it."

"But—"

"Learn to live without weapons. I'll not provide you with a means to attack another village."

En masse, the raiders dropped their weapons and moved off warily. When they deemed themselves far enough away, feet beating the ground sliced into the night as they raced for the safety of The Wilds.

Froyans whooped and hollered. Pire strode to the middle of the square with Gette and Quinta at his sides. He raised his sword and waved it over his head. The two women followed with their bows held high.

Cress remained where he stood, giving the villagers space for their festivity. Both men and women had fought bravely in defense of their homes and loved ones. They deserved to celebrate.

At last, Pire shouted for quiet. "We owe Wizard Cress another debt of gratitude. First, he solves the cause of the plague, then aids us against raiders. Nor should we forget those closest to us. We wouldn't have succeeded without our wives and women fighting beside us."

"We fought well together, didn't we?" Gette added.

Cress's gaze flew to Becca. The consternation on her face became easy for anyone to read as she battled personal demons.

Pire smiled. "A valuable lesson has been learned this night. The hunters were correct to place sentries around the village. I erred in not following their example, and it cost us dearly. Henceforth, sentries will be posted after dark."

The concession confirmed Cress's opinion about Pire. A man willing to make such a public admission couldn't be all bad. "People make mistakes. Didn't anyone ever tell you that?"

"People change their minds, too," Becca proclaimed loud enough for all to hear. "I concede this new order has survived its first test."

"That's not enough, Becca," her sister responded. "Pire cares about the wellbeing of Froy. He's the not villain you imagine him. Oh, aye, he is stubborn and bullheaded, but kind and caring, too. All characteristics you should recognize."

"Me?" Becca practically growled.

Cress watched, curious, when Gette nodded. "Aye, sister—you. He's just like you."

Becca stood scowling, then ever so slowly a smile softened her features. "I find myself in a quandary, for I should have given this change a chance to work before casting judgment."

"We understand each other," the blacksmith admitted.

Stunned by the concession, Cress suspected it was gigantic for Becca. As he watched, she turned and smiled at him. He smiled back. Had the battle with the marauders and the sacrifices she witnessed by a united village shown her something new and wonderful, something worth altering her opinion?

"It really was our decision to give up our weapons," Gette added, hearing the change in her sister as well.

"I suppose I should believe you," Becca replied with even more concession in her voice.

Relief spread over Gette's round face. Cress wondered how much the pregnant woman anguished over her sister's resentment and lack of acceptance. He couldn't be prouder of Becca.

Wrapping his wizard's robe around him, he glanced up at the full moon. Becca had called it Luna's Delight. Tonight they would be together and could share a delight of their own.

Wanting Becca nearly undid him every time he thought of her. He wanted her close, to prove to himself and her that life had purpose. Tonight he planned to tell her how important she'd become to him.

No, not just tell—to show her.

Chapter Thirty-Five

Several Froyans died, but the loss of one above all others bothered Becca the most. Legget's sacrifice touched her deeply—a Froyan male dying to protect her, especially him. Memories of the obnoxious man left her confused. If she thought long and hard, she recalled him being shiftless and unworthy. Yet, he'd stepped up to shield her.

Her opinion of him had been wrong—a valuable lesson for her—and she vowed to hold him in her memory forever and honor his name for as long as she lived.

Cress hurried off with Quinta to tend the wounded, for he carried Salida's gooey medicinal potion. Becca knew the powerful mixture, having benefited from its effects in the past. She noticed Tulle followed them.

Another loss affected her nearly as deeply—Landa. Marauders had cornered the hunter while Maine fought beside Pire. She fought well before being cut down. Her knife had been found in the chest of a dead marauder.

Becca started to head toward Maine to offer condolences, but a dozen women converged on him and led him away.

Froy had changed. Not outwardly, for it appeared the same. Women no longer made every decision. Men and women worked and ruled together now—and while she would like to blame one male in particular, Pire, her protest lacked substance.

Froy was no longer her home. Not anymore. It had transformed. So had she.

Staring at the inner circle of her village, Becca stood silent. She no longer belonged in Froy. Her promise to return to the dragon circle with Cress gave her purpose. She would help him break the spell that held his sister prisoner.

"Becca." Pire broke her reverie. "Becca? What ails you?"

She shook her head to clear her thoughts. "Admitting I was wrong isn't an easy task."

"I make mistakes all the time," he said in return. "Trust me. Being honest and acknowledging a mistake is far easier than defending an erroneous one."

She studied the blacksmith's earnest face. "I never liked you, Pire. You were too loud, too brash, too full of yourself. You took every opportunity to put yourself forward. I felt like we were in competition, even though you were a man and had no right."

His bushy brows wiggled. "You're not far off, Becca. I felt the same about you. Gette has it right. We are alike. You paraded around here with your head held high, just because you thought you had no match, but we are equals now, and I would very much like you to accept my hand in friendship." He stretched out his arm.

Becca stared at the extended hand. She fought the temptation to bat it away. Was he expressing genuine gratitude of her acceptance or was this a male trick?

"You will probably find this hard to believe," Pire went on, his arm still extended, "but it will sadden me greatly if you withhold your blessing. Your sister sets great store by your opinion, and out of love for her, I am willing to do anything to make her happy."

Becca's resistance melted instantly. She let her mind, rather than her heart, consider the situation. She'd seen no weakness on the men's part. They'd shown courage during the fight with the marauders.

She took his hand and gave it a firm shake. "I was wrong to cast doubt on your ability without first giving you a chance to prove yourself. For that I apologize."

An odd weight lifted from Becca's shoulders. Being truthful proved easier than she expected. Indeed, she had expected shedding years of bias would prove difficult, but she found herself conceding to Pire. Again.

His expression remained sober. "Let bygones be bygones. Truce?"

"Truce," she answered.

"Does this mean you accept my right to lead Froy?" he asked, hope etched over his features.

"Let us say I acknowledge you as the current leader, Pire. Rule well and wisely. Otherwise, you can be voted out."

The first hint of a smile lifted the corners of the big blacksmith's mouth. "I'd better do a good job then."

"I would say so. And since we're discussing certain matters, I urge you to take care of my sister. I will not tolerate her being mistreated."

"Fret not. She has my heart. Friends, then?"

"Not that," Becca hedged. "Family."

A genuine smile flashed across his face, and the blacksmith wrapped his thick arms around her. "Even better, sister."

He swallowed her within his hold. Sweet Luna, the

man did not know his own strength. He squeezed the wind out of her. Gasping, she tilted her face up to the luminous full moon seemingly watching her. Did the Goddess approve of her decision?

"The position will soon be vacant if you continue to crush me," she managed to choke out.

"Ah, sister, forgive me," Pire said, releasing her, stepping back, his expression mortified. "I forget my strength in my happiness."

Becca stumbled backward, grateful to take a deep breath without pain. She'd feared the man would break or crack her ribs. His apology rolled in her mind. He couldn't have faked his response or made his eyes gleam, if insincere. At least she latched onto that hope. She doubted she would fully understand men in this lifetime. Or, the next.

Thinking of men…where was Cress? More than an hour had passed. He should have returned from tending the wounded by now. During their journey to The Wilds he'd become her rock and she needed him.

Almost magically, as she thought of him, he strode across the open area, his billowing robe covering his long, lean legs. The sheer brawn of his masculinity thrilled her. And she wasn't the only woman who followed him with regard. Several younger, unattached hunters stopped their tasks to whisper among themselves when he made his way to her side.

Becca didn't blame them. Cress cast a handsome image. Virile. An aura of strength surrounded him that had nothing to do with magic. It was the man himself. When women had converged on Maine, she'd mentally wished him well. However, when it came to Cress— jealousy and possessiveness jumped to the forefront.

Tonight they would speak the language of the beads. She grew warm at the thought.

"You must be exhausted." Cress came to a stop in front of her and wrapped his arm around her shoulder. "Are you ready to retire?"

She smiled at him. "Aye, although it's not rest I require."

****

Cress stood next to Becca in the center of the village. He never discovered the reason the Guardians insisted he leave the assembly, for they refused to answer his questions no matter how much he demanded, threatened, or cajoled. Dragons were the stubbornest creatures in existence.

"The bloodshed is over. We are glad," Guardians mindspoke to him. *"Humans are fools to fight amongst themselves."*

"I am human."

"You are unique among your species. Fighting solves nothing. It creates heartache and sadness. There would have been much grief if you hadn't become involved. Your solution saved many lives."

"Then you approve?" How could he focus on Becca with the dragons pestering him? Which made him wonder why he answered them with a question when it only prolonged the discussion.

"Well, naturally," they returned. *"Why learn magic if you do not put it to good use?"*

Becca's slender body swayed when she shuffled her boots in the soft earth. He tightened his hold to prevent her from leaving his side. Her wide-eyed expression told him she wondered why he postponed their departure to their hut.

"Go away," he ordered the dragons. *"Don't disturb me again."*

"We need to discuss our treasure."

He waved a hand. *"Not now. You want our help. First, we trade. Give me your word that you'll give us privacy tonight. Tomorrow we'll return for your eggs."*

Silence greeted him. He took it as an affirmative. Still, he uttered a visibility spell. It wasn't that the Guardians weren't honorable beings. They were dragons. He wanted to make sure they didn't intrude on his time with Becca.

And thinking of Becca…

He visualized them together. After months of traveling together, he refused to wait another minute. His heartrate increased and his stomach tightened at the thought of being with her. The desire of discovering the mysteries of her womanly form, to immerse himself in the softness of her body made him ache with want. He'd dreamed about her, lusted after her, and tonight he would claim her as his.

Becca stared at him, an expression of hope and excitement on her face. "Do you intend to stand here all night?"

"Of course not. I—"

She rested her finger on his lips with the lightest pressure. The scent of her warm skin teased his senses. "Shhh, no more. Come."

Promise rippled through her words, and his heart raced faster. "Do you believe the paths of people's lives can be woven together like strands of a tapestry?" He took a firm hold on her arm and accompanied her from the open area. "That they can be bound together?"

She peeked at him beneath long lashes. "I haven't

given it much thought."

An occasional villager passed, acknowledging them with a nod or smile. Tulle followed, tail wagging.

"I have," Cress said, buoyant and optimistic. "I believe we were meant to be together. That we belong with each other."

The soft padding of their steps became the only sound he heard. Her silence prompted a flood of worry. Had she changed her mind because of his delay?

At their hut, Cress inhaled deeply, longingly, holding the leather flap aside for the warrior woman to enter. Time to confess his true feelings. "I care about you, Becca," he said in a low voice.

She stilled, one foot outside the entry, the other inside.

Holding the flap with one hand, the fingers in his other ached to brush the fine golden hairs circling her face. Had he overstepped his bounds? Preposterous. Nerves made him doubt himself. He'd never encountered a woman like Becca, and despite his walls of protection not to get close, she'd crept inside.

"It seems strange to admit such a thing because I never expected to find a woman to love. I feared my entire life would be spent trying to free Trell. Now, I don't know. I'm a wizard. You're a warrior woman. Can we find happiness together?"

Becca looked at him, blue eyes sparkling and bright in the dim light. "Foolish, foolish male. Just kiss me."

"Now, listen here, Becca d'Firn." He grinned, his worry vanquished by her words. "Once I start kissing you, I plan to do much, much more."

She clutched the edges of his robe and drew him

closer to her. "Well, I certainly hope so. Prove to me you are a man worthy of—"

"There you are," came a familiar voice.

Disappointment flickered within him when Becca released her hold on his robe to face the newcomer.

"Mother," she said.

"Quinta," he acknowledged the older woman.

"A halo encircles the moon, and I see six stars," the older woman stated with a smile. "Rain will come tonight and last for six days."

Cress groaned with frustration. This wasn't the time for a weather superstition, but courtesy demand he remain polite. "How do you know this, and why do you feel compelled to tell us now?"

"More than sorcery exists in the world, Wizard Cress," Quinta said. "I learned long ago observation is a powerful tool."

"Forgive Mother's interruption," Becca mindspoke to him, and he never thought he would be grateful to the Guardians for granting them the ability. *"I am sure she will leave shortly. She only wants to make sure we're unhurt."*

"Her timing is in dire need of improvement."

Becca laughed softly. *"I agree, but you should know that maternal interference is a common fault among Froyan women."*

Quinta glanced from him to her daughter, her leathery face warm with affection. "All is well?"

"We are fit," Becca answered, grinning at her mother and him. "Not even a scratch from the raid. Although, I need to clean up. Excuse me." She gave him the smallest nod. *"Obviously my mother approves of you. She has never bothered with any of my other men."*

He chuckled. At any other time, Cress would have enjoyed an in-depth discussion with someone of Quinta's intellect, but anticipation of making love to Becca created a strong motivation to follow her inside. *"Seconds apart from you will seem a lifetime,"* he mindspoke back. "Now, Quinta, I am sure this is no social visit. How may I help you?"

"How astute, Master Wizard. A mother always worries about her children, even after they grow up. I value my daughters, and each deserves to enjoy her life. Gette has achieved happiness. I came to tell you that it's Becca's turn. She cannot hide her emotions from me. I suspect you have captured her heart. A mother has the right to approve of her daughter's choice."

"And do you?"

"I do."

"Then I'll do my best not to disappoint you, Quinta."

She snorted an odd sound, suspiciously like muffled laughter. "It's not me you must impress. But I wish you good dreams." She gave a parting wave. "Have a fine evening."

"I shall." He swallowed his relief when Quinta left and would have called her back to hug her if movement inside the hut hadn't caught his attention. He ducked within.

Becca waited for him in the center of lush furs, a secret smile curling the corners of her mouth. A magical moment, not created by sorcery, but magic nonetheless.

"At last, I have you to myself," he said.

He muttered a quick spell, and rose petals

materialized out of thin air to float onto the furs and add their heady fragrance to the air.

"I heard my mother," Becca said, her tone teasing. "If you're planning on sleeping at all tonight, you'll be sadly disappointed. I don't intend to let you catch a single wink."

Becca dragged him down to the furs by a hand. He willingly complied and knelt, facing her, beaming a big grin at her.

"You are so beautiful. Perfect in every way," he said both aloud and in mindspeech.

She reached for his robe, her hands gliding over his chest and arm muscles. *"I find you so remarkable— warm and hard—you remind me of heated stones,"* she answered him in the same seductive manner.

"I like you touching me." His fingers traced the curve of her mouth. *"Your lips are smooth and soft. Let me show you what a man not of Froy can do. How he pleasures a woman he desires. I promise not to disappoint you."*

"I've wanted to mate with you since we met," she uttered aloud.

"That was your first mistake, Becca," he said, following her example. "I'm not going to mate with you. I'm going to make love with you. A big difference."

A muscle fluttered in her throat. "Show me…now."

He gathered her into his arms and simply held her against his burning body. He wanted her selfishly but resisted the temptation. "What happens tonight will be at my pace. Not yours. And, I have to warn you, I'm a very methodical man."

Eager passion crept into her gaze. "You really

259

intend to dominate?"

"Domination has no place in this hut tonight. I intend to seduce you." His fingertips traced her chin, neck, and down between her breasts. Beneath his hands, her sleek figure quivered with muscles and soft contours, a stimulating combination.

In seconds, her breathing increased. She arched her back on the furs in a position as old as time. No matter how much she tempted him, Cress would not rush the night. Her expression softened and contained all he wanted—longing and love.

Another spell ignited dust motes to sparkle and dance around them in a faint golden sheen.

"Tell me what you want," he whispered. "I need to hear you say it."

"You," she gasped. "All of you."

"Good, that's exactly what I wanted to hear."

Chapter Thirty-Six

Shivers of excitement rippled through Becca when she met Cress's warm and knowing hazel scrutiny. She'd seen the inviting look from men before—looks that raked her curves with male appreciation, and never before had she been so pleased to see that expression on a man's face.

Cress leaned forward and kissed her face, her lips, the top of her eyelids, her temples. He left no spot untouched. His kisses reminded her of summer rain, warm and tender. She let her heart guide her limbs to tighten her arms around his neck. His hands glided over the curve of her waist and down her hips in agonizingly slow motion.

Oh, sweet Luna. She cried out in sheer joy to her goddess.

No man commanded her on the furs, yet to her surprise, letting Cress have his way proved provocative and tantalizing. His kisses demanded participation, and she cooperated willingly. He was so close that she felt the heat of his body and heard his breathing over the sound of her own.

This felt different. Deeper. More meaningful. Becca normally asserted herself during mating, only this time she wanted to give pleasure as much as receive.

Cress gathered her into his arms and nibbled on her

ear. *"Mayhaps I should kiss you again."*

"Oh, aye, I like your kisses very much."

"I like yours, too. You taste of mint and honey, fresh and sweet."

She could barely catch her breath. *"Then, please, kiss me."*

"Oh, I intend to, Becca."

"I want you to know how I feel," she whispered through the mental link. *"You make me tremble with delight."*

His fingers crept over her body. *"I've got a pretty good idea how you feel. I feel the same way."*

Riffling through his long hair, she inhaled clean, inviting, enticing pine. Strong and unbending, Cress reminded her of the mighty trees of his forest.

He cradled her head in his hands, covered her mouth with a kiss that teased and tormented at the same time. His lips were soft and sweet. He kissed her deeper, harder, his tongue parting her lips and making her senses leap higher.

His hold adjusted as his velvety lips sought her neck, working lower until he found a breast and suckled a taut nipple.

A wild rush of sensations swept through her like a flooding river. The last of her warrior inhibitions dashed to smithereens. She arched her back again and offered her body to him.

Somehow they'd stripped off their clothes. She wore only her moonstone pendent. In the firelight, Cress turned into a vision of lean muscle and sinew with a sprinkling of dark hairs running down his flat stomach. His nakedness excited her. The temptation to let her fingers play over his rippled muscles nearly overwhelmed her. He fascinated her in ways that made her want him all the more. His hard, pulsing arousal pressed against her bare leg. She wanted him, all of him, and she reached for his member to guide him inside her.

He stopped her hand with a growl, although a shudder rippled through his body. *"Not yet, Becca,"* he mindspoke, his words rolling through her. *"We have all night to pleasure each other."*

"I want you. Why do you torment me so?"

"I torture myself, too," he murmured under his breath.

To her elation, colorful stars twinkled within the hut. Laughing, she tried to grab them, but they dissolved in her hands.

Cress became busy, too. He peppered his way down her front with more kisses that created a pure torture of delight. When he stopped, the wet trail left her skin on fire.

His hands replaced his kisses, caressing her skin, making it tingle, kneading where sore muscles tensed. Resistance became impossible. She gasped out a desire so intense, so complete that she knew it was right.

He rolled atop her, belly-to-belly, his erection hard and hot against her bare skin.

"Now?" she whispered, spreading her legs, positive he wanted the same as she.

"Aye, now," he answered, sliding into her.

She gasped, savoring the fullness and need within her. Seconds stretched while the golden sheen filling the air thickened in the hut. Magic tingled on her skin. Soft chimes sounded.

Cress filled her—hard, hot. She clutched his broad

shoulders as her body throbbed with a raw need she'd never experienced before. She reached around and grabbed his buttocks with her hands.

A wild recklessness heated her blood. She burned with need. "I can't take any more. I have to move. Please, Cress."

And she did. She climbed and soared, clutching Cress closer—pleasure jolting through her body. Crying out again, she didn't care who overheard when her hips lifted and she flew to the heavens with joy, tears burning her eyes.

In the next breath, Cress's breath turned rapid, with low panting sounds in his throat. His hard body tensed as he propelled himself forward. Faster and faster. The explosion of his release rushed inside her, and pleasure suffused her when he buried his head into her shoulder.

Becca touched Cress's face—moist with perspiration—and she savored his weight, the warmth of his skin, and marveled at the contentment curling through her body. It wasn't her nature to release control or surrender to a man. Never did she imagine such a thing would bring an immense feeling of freedom. Only Cress could have caused it.

When he brushed his mouth over hers in a feathery kiss, she wrapped her arms around his neck, her legs around his.

"Can we do that again?" she asked with a smile.

****

The next morning Becca's muffled cry woke Cress. He jerked upright, then realized no danger existed. He glanced down at her, the golden flood of her hair spread out on the winter pelt of a fox.

"Are you all right?" he asked softly, kissing her

throat, tasting the hint of salt on her skin.

Her eyelids fluttered open and she grasped her pendant. "Forgive me. I was trapped within a nightmare."

He winced. "That shouldn't happen after a night of passionate lovemaking. Tell me about it. Speaking of it will ease your suffering."

"I dreamed Froy was gone. Destroyed…I don't know how, but not a single hut remained standing. It was as though the village never existed."

"Ah, Becca, you have been through a lot of turmoil. Think about it. All your life your only goal was to keep Froy safe. That has changed. You are no longer responsible."

"But—"

"Nay, no buts. Now you have much to look forward to. Let me help you forget about that nightmare." He leaned forward, intending to kiss her, but she looked up at him, eyes wide with hope.

She touched his cheek, her fingers scraping the stubble on his chin, a reminder he needed to shave. "Last night was perfect, Cress. I shouldn't burden you with my nightmares. They aren't your fault."

He rolled onto his back, tucked his hands behind his head, and stared at the ceiling. Raindrops pelted the roof. Quinta's prediction had come true. "If they bother you, they bother me."

"I've always been prone to them."

"What we shared last night should have given you pleasant dreams." He rolled on his side, noticing how her breasts rose and fell with her breathing. He silently moaned. "Should I begin again this morning?"

"An offer I am more than willing to accept." She

smiled, and the warmth of a perfect summer day heated their hut. Her fingers tripped lightly over his bare chest.

His lower body responded to her touch. He started to tug her on top of him.

"Cease! Enough!" Guardians objected through mindspeech and flew through the smoke hole in the hut's ceiling. *"Our treasure awaits. We must tend our eggs now. No more dallying with your human needs."*

Cress frowned. *"What do you expect from me?"*

"You must ask? Really?" a dozen Guardian voices merged as one, indignant and irritated. *"We must save them. They represent the future."*

Becca sat up slowly. *"Please, Guardian, we'll do whatever it takes. I promise."*

Dragons left him to hover around her head like sparkling yellow diamonds in her hair. *"Today?"* they asked.

"Aye, today," she told them.

"Our sincere thanks. At least one human has the proper attitude. The wizard should take lessons," they admonished.

Cress shook his head. He'd been surprised and concerned about Becca's nightmare. His responsibility would never ebb for those he cared about—Becca or Trell.

Trell.

His sister's name signified a thousand years of failure. A thousand years of frustration and not seeing her bright smile. Trell wasn't responsible for what happened to her. He was! Whatever the sacrifice, he would do whatever it took to break the spell. Her needs came before his own wants.

Even before making love to Becca.

Becca represented his means to communicate with Trell for the first time in centuries, a luxury he looked forward to. As part of their bargain, Becca agreed to talk with his sister for him until they found a way to break the spell.

With the enigma of the plague solved and Becca's acceptance of the changes in her village, they would collect the Guardians' precious eggs and head for Demit Woods.

Contentment filled Cress. He was going home. The trials and hardships endured thus far were worth the price. Only the slightest annoyance tweaked his conscience, for once there, Salida and Einer would demand all the details of their travels. Being alone with Becca would no longer be an option. Although he did have the long hours of being on the road with her—especially the nights to look forward to.

He chose not to glance at Becca, otherwise the temptation to remain in their hut—dry and warm—and make love at their leisure would supersede all other yearnings.

"I suppose we should rise," he said, despite his personal wishes. "If we intend to travel to your cave, best we make preparations."

Becca lunged playfully for him. "For shame, Cress. We still have the morning. Are you truly ready to leave our little nest so soon?"

Warmth exploded within him. She desired the same thing he ached for. He trapped her in his arms. "Well, if you insist upon continuing last night—"

"Wait! We are ready to depart now," the dragons interrupted, buzzing and dipping at his head.

Reluctantly, Cress rolled off the furs and gathered

up his leggings. "I suppose we should count ourselves lucky. They left us alone last night. We might not be so fortunate in the future. Dragons are persistent creatures."

"All right," Becca said, the inflection in her voice hinting at disappointment. "There is little we'll need for the journey. We can be ready in an hour or less. Although in this rain, I can't guarantee we'll be able to climb the tower. It might be too slippery to chance."

"Forgive us." The dragons offered as an apology, flying around the ceiling of the hut. *"We are eager to begin."*

"Aye, that is obvious," Cress said, smiling.

Tulle greeted them with a soft woof when they exited their hut. He followed on their heels while they gathered food, water, and empty baskets to carry the precious dragon eggs.

"You've got a friend," Becca said.

Cress patted the dog's head. "It appears so."

During the night, rain washed away all traces of the battle. No blood stained the ground. Footprints disappeared into puddles.

By late morning, for better or worse, they set out for Becca's cave. Tulle started to follow, but Becca ordered the dog to sit. The animal refused to obey until Cress commanded him to stay. Head down and tail tucked between his legs, the spotted dog slunk back to lie outside their hut.

Rain fell in a steady mist. Cress made no attempt to stop the inclement weather. Even to his unexperienced eyes, he saw the thirsty land soak up the drizzle. The vegetation glistened under the rain.

A lizard skittered across their path. No other

animals or birds were visible. Cress thought they were the smart ones. No sane creature would venture in weather like this. So, why was he?

"For us," Guardians answered his thoughts.

"Stop that. I've warned you before about reading my mind. It's an invasion of privacy."

"We did not do so. Long association makes understanding human expressions easy."

By the time they reached their destination, both Cress and Becca were soaked.

Becca pointed at a craggy spire. "We're here."

Cress peered upward. A vertical spire stretched hundreds of feet in the air with columns of rocks dividing it. A jagged point topped the monolith to remind him of a broken tooth. At the base, bits of white chips spread over the land to add to the illusion.

His steps rattled the loose gravel. Bits and pieces scattered with each step. He never expected to find dragon eggs housed in a tower composed of limestone. "We climb now?"

"Aye, carefully." Becca touched the surface. "It won't be easy though. Climbing on slippery rock is dangerous."

"We will dry the tower with fire," dragons chorused.

A sizzling crackling erupted above his head, and Cress gasped. Guardians shot fire against the tower. Steam rose from the heated rock. A low groan preceded pieces of limestone splitting, cracking, and falling off.

Cress stared. Had the efforts hindered or aided them? He hoped for the latter.

Becca smiled, then nodded at the dragons flying up and down the vertical spire. "Isn't that sweet of them to help?"

A lone dragon dove down to hover in front of Cress. *"Hurry,"* it ordered. *"You must hurry and pray to your gods that we are not too late."*

Cress recognized Parr's voice as he wondered "too late for what?" Ages had passed since the tiny Guardian deigned to speak with him individually. *"We can't rush. Safety first."*

Parr rested on Cress's shoulder. His head bobbed on his long neck as tiny red eyes glowed with indignation. *"Why dally? Do not be slow."*

"All you have to do is flap your wings," he reminded the tiny dragon. *"Give us a few moments to study the path we must cross. Familiarity will increase our odds of traversing it safely and allow us to reach your precious eggs without mishap."*

Becca snapped her fingers with a pop. "I have an idea! Can you gouge out deeper hand and footholds with magic, or better yet, elevate us right to the cave?"

"I wish it were so simple. Unfortunately, even magic has limits. Or, rather a wizard's strength does. Performing magic has a price. It drains my energy. I have limits. It doesn't happen often, but between my spells against the marauders and the magic I used in our lovemaking, most of my powers are spent."

"Are you all right?" Compassion softened her expression.

A wave of warmth heated his insides at her concern. "I'm fine." He studied the vertical monolith. "All I need is a nap."

Chapter Thirty-Seven

"Sleep later," the Guardians complained.

"Hush," Becca demanded in mindspeech. She faced Cress. "I won't lie to you. This climb is dangerous. While I have completed it hundreds of times, it took me several years of trying to reach the top. Of course, I was only a child when I made my first attempt." She smiled in an attempt to reassure him. Maybe the wizard didn't like heights. "Just watch and follow me. Put your hands and feet where I put mine, and you'll be fine. Whatever you do, though, don't look down."

"Right, don't look down."

She decided, if it gave him courage to sound sarcastic, she would not argue. "There's nothing to be ashamed of, Cress. Even the bravest can become dizzy at heights. If you keep your eyes focused directly in front of you, you won't suffer the effect as much."

He stared at her mouth for several seconds, as though intrigued. She'd had her choice of lovers— being a hunter—but none had found enough favor to have a child with…until now.

Tender feelings washed over her. Cress was different. Special. Maybe he planned to kiss her. Her wanton thoughts fixed on his lips. She wondered if she'd insulted him. That had not been her intent.

Then he rubbed his eyes and frowned slightly. She

swore that he wanted to kiss her, and she wished he would.

Why wait? Why deprive herself? Being a hunter, even if the other women of Froy abandoned their roles, she had not. It was only natural for her to take control. She clapped her hands on either side of his face and kissed him—deep, satisfying, and full of passion.

"I'm tempted to take you right here," Cress said, his breath ragged, "but I only have enough strength to climb or make love to you. Which would you like?"

"That's an unfair choice. I would prefer to make love. But the Guardians need our help," she replied, shoving disappointment aside and looking at the tower again. Water condensed in shallow pockets. The rain stopped, save the fine drizzle wetting the back of her neck. She sank to the ground and began tying the different ropes together. Fastening the lightest one to her waist, she tied the thickest to the bundle of supplies and water.

As always, the climb caused her heart to beat faster. Still she considered the safest route to proceed. Straight up made the most sense, but Cress's inexperience prevented that. Zigzagging over the slippery surface would be safer.

She sighed, dug her fingers into a crack, and pulled herself up. Her feet sought dents to keep her from shooting straight back down the rock face. "Follow me."

Golden sparks fluttered over the tower. Bursts of yellow flames hit the rock. Occasionally a sizzle gushed high above and a metallic twang of burnt rock teased her nose. Tiny dragons labored to dry the limestone, but they fought a losing battle until the rain completely stopped.

"Guardian, mayhaps it would be best if you keep to the handholds we are about to use, rather than those high above us," she mindspoke.

"We will follow your wishes."

Her foot slipped at the easy compliance. Below, Cress muttered as loose pebbles pelted him and clattered to the ground.

"Careful," the dragons warned. Several dove down around her as if to catch her if she fell.

Seven or eight feet to the right, a crack yawned. Becca remembered once believing the tower a smooth surface. A misconception on her part. A tapestry of parallel cracks divided the rock into columns in a pattern no artist could recreate.

She dug her fingertips into a gritty crevice. *"Don't worry about me. Just make sure Cress's handholds are kept dry."*

"Naturally. The wizard is important to us."

"I'm certainly glad I count in a small way," Cress joined the conversation, exertion making his mindspeech sound tight.

Becca wished she could ease his labors. *"Not much farther, Cress. Just a little higher."*

A tug pulled on her waist when the second, thicker rope scraped against the rocks. The sound measured her progress—more than halfway. Her fingers cracked and bled from digging along shallow ledges. In two handholds she'd reach the point where the great monolith's steep grade changed, sloping in, making the climb easier.

Additional stones cascaded down the side. She fumbled for a handhold, swallowing a gasp and gaping at Cress. He leaned inward, his head tucked tightly against the limestone. His long hair, tied in its familiar leather thong, swirled at his back like thousands of miniature whips.

Handhold after handhold, fingers crimped hard into folds of rock. Nearly at the mouth of the cave, the nauseating smell of sulfur saturated the air.

A surge of energy replaced exhaustion, and she hastened her progress to squirm into the cave's gaping mouth on her belly. The putrid smell had become much stronger since she'd brought the eggs into the main cavern. Her eyes watered. She fervently prayed to Luna that the odor of death and decay did not foretell an ill omen for the creatures' survival.

She rolled back to the opening and grabbed Cress's wrist the instant his hand touched the cave's floor.

****

Once inside the cave, a mound of eggs in a variety of sizes—large blues, medium-sized reds, green, white, small bronzes, golds, blacks, and tiny brasses covered the floor. Cress knocked powdery dust off his clothes and steadied his legs before staggering over to inspect the pile.

The blues shimmered with mottled hues from the sky to the sea, the reds ranged from a fiery hue to reddish gold and looked hot to the touch, the greens had huge spots of emerald to lime, and a few metallic ones were covered with swirls that remind him of lustrous threads.

Only the whites appeared as a solid color, yet upon closer inspection he discovered an error in his judgement. Lines ran over the shells that were barely discernable to the naked eye.

Tiny brasses, close in color to the golds, lacked the intense shine of the precious metal.

A solitary copper egg, the size of his thumbnail, gleamed with an incandescent color somewhere between orange with a pinkish luster.

"Are they not beautiful?" Guardians mindspoke as one. *"But such a shame."*

Cress and Becca glanced at each other.

"What's a shame?" he asked.

"Out of thousands, these few survived," they answered. *"Not even dragon magic can last forever. Time was our enemy. Every female dragon donated one egg during the Great Dying for the preservation of our kind. Usually female dragons form links with embryos during incubation. For many of the females, the emptiness was so great, they just lay down and died."*

"How awful," Becca said.

Cress stared at the multicolored pile. *"So few. Yet so significant. A new beginning."*

Half the Guardians left their hovering over the eggs to fly around the cave's interior. *"Your understanding is much appreciated. We have a saying, 'All life comes from the egg.' Now we must act fast to save these precious few.*

"The protective spell is gone. Each dragon species requires unique conditions to hatch. We must duplicate those environments in order for them to survive. For that, we need your assistance. Both of yours."

"How much time before they hatch?" Cress asked out loud, imagining a future with wagon-sized creatures flying the skies of Feldsvelt. "And just how big will these dragons grow?"

"Hatching varies, depending on the dragon. We

275

don't know what effect the suspension in this cave will have on incubation. Normally, it takes two to five years for a dragon egg to hatch. Blacks and greens have the shortest gestation. Less than a year. The average takes about two years," Guardians answered without any hint of guile. *"Their growth depends on the individual."*

Cress noticed a huge hole at the back of the cave. "What happened here?"

"That's where I broke through the cave wall," Becca told him. "The embryos told me which rocks to loosen and remove."

He studied the pile again. What had he expected? Chicken eggs? He'd never actually seen dragon eggs before—not even those belonging to the Guardians of Secrets. Here, now, were so many. Some would fit in the baskets left at the bottom of the tower...but not all. "I guess we'll have to find a way to get them down to the bottom."

"I wish I had your confidence," Becca said. "I can't imagine trying to transport something as fragile as eggs."

"Fret not," Guardians said. *"Dragon shells are like leather—thick and sturdy with some pliability. We will join our magic with Cress's to lower them to the ground."*

"A good suggestion," he said. *"Let them meld their magic with mine."*

"Let us begin," the Guardians said. *"The sooner we start, the sooner the journey will be over."*

"Tomorrow is soon enough," Becca spoke up. "Night will be upon us shortly, and it's unsafe to descend in the dark. The climb down is even more difficult. One is constantly searching for safe footing, and it's murderous on knees."

Cress nodded his appreciation. "If we remain, I'll have time to inspect the cave."

"Why?" the dragons demanded.

"Let him do as he pleases," Becca said.

Cress smiled at her, appreciating how she came to his defense. "To assure that not a single egg is overlooked. I'm sure Becca's search was limited with only a torch. I can create a brighter light."

"All you will find is death and destruction," the Guardians said together.

They resented the delay. He expected as much. "Let me find out for myself," he said and conjured a ball of light that floated over his palm.

"Don't mind them," Becca said. "I'll help you."

A hot tickle raced up Cress's spine in response to her support. He couldn't fathom what lay ahead, although he appreciated the bright sphere that chased away the shadows in the cave to reveal a path which angled slightly downward. He stepped through the gaping hole with Becca flanking him.

Heated air flowed over his face and hands, warmer than what should be natural within a cave, reminding him of the uncomfortable heat emanating from Pire's forge.

And the smell. He wished he could hold his breath forever.

In the outer cavern, at least fresh air kept the worst of the stench at bay. The swamp where the great river lizard lived smelled like the sweetest rose in comparison. Here, an obnoxious odor one associated with rotten eggs or flatulence saturated the air.

The path dipped steeper and became more

complicated to negotiate—narrow and twisted with blind corners. He stopped, listening, shifting his regard to Becca. He didn't know how long he could hold his breath. Uncertainty tempted him to turn back. Then he shoved the feeling aside and resumed his search.

His feet crunched to an almost musical cadence, yet the dryness of the cave absorbed the majority of the sound. He started to mention the unusualness when he happened to glance at his feet. Blood drained from his face.

They were walking on broken shells of all colors. Hundreds. Thousands. Over the eons, eggs had fallen, cracked or broken. His insides clenched at the waste. The sheer numbers tallied in the thousands. In places, the rubble of shells created mounds a foot thick.

The devastation was nearly impossible to comprehend. What led to this disaster? Earthquake? Freak accident? How could so many eggs have broken?

"We believe they rolled off their perches or were crushed by fallings rocks. This land is unstable. Oyfele was unaware of its destructive potential. A regrettable lapse."

"But the shells?" he demanded. "You said they were tough like leather. What happened?"

The Guardians hesitated. *"Dragon eggs are not indestructible. If the shell is damaged or cracked, it turns brittle like ordinary eggs."*

"This isn't right," he said. "Such a waste. They shouldn't have perished."

"You speak the truth, but there is nothing we can do now. Forget the dead. Dragons do not mourn."

"I don't understand." He shook his head sharply. "I thought you said female dragons grieved so hard that they died."

"The bond of mother and child is unexplainable. As Guardians of Secrets, our strength lies in looking forward. The only thing that matters to us now is for these eggs to survive. They are the promise of the future."

"We still have one small thing to do." Cress's voice quavered despite his best efforts.

Becca looked at him. "What's that?"

"Make sure all the eggs have been found."

"We appreciate your thoroughness," the dragons said.

The admission surprised Cress. Dragons commonly refrained from expressing sentiments of gratitude. He waited a little to see if they would add more. They didn't, and he squinted down the path. The darkness seemed to swallow up his hope. But he refused to quit.

He'd never given up trying to save Trell. Even if he didn't know how to break the spell. Oh sure, his confidence wavered from time to time. He refused to dwell on failure. Not when disappointment could eat away at a person's self-belief.

He yearned to connect with his family, his sister. He rejected the idea of deserting Trell. He'd gladly carry the burden of responsibility to save his sister. He must. Just as he must complete this mission.

"Come," he whispered to Becca, venturing farther down the steep path. "There are numerous places in this limestone where an egg could be hidden away."

"It's not much farther."

An urgency filled him that he did not question. He forced himself to ignore the destruction and staggered in Becca's wake until they reached a high-ceilinged cavern. He glanced around, grateful for her willingness to aid him without probing his reasons. The magical sphere cast a cold light—glowing bright.

A burnished flash caught his eye. "Stop!"

She whirled around, knife in hand. "What's wrong? What is it?"

"Be easy," he said. "I saw something. An egg."

"I don't think so," Becca said, disbelief filling her tone. "No voice is calling me."

He indicated the faint glimmer of pinkish-orange tucked into a niche on the wall. A small copper egg rested on a ledge too high for her to have seen earlier. Anticipation made his heart beat faster. As he approached, sweat beaded his brow.

"Is it alive?" she asked, extending her view by rising up on tiptoes. "Why didn't it call to me?"

Guardians flew so close together they appeared to form an oversized golden egg themselves. *"Cress is correct. There is an egg. We sense it. Let us see."*

"It's very pale, but a bit of color still remains." Cress curled his fingers around the egg with great care. It felt cold. Icy. Devoid of life. His disappointment left him nauseous as though an invisible fist hit him with a swift blow to his gut.

"Let me see." Becca held out her hand. She put the egg to her ear. "Sweet Luna, it's there, but it's faint. If I concentrate, I can hear the embryo. We have to save it."

"Give it fire. It needs that to live," the Guardians said.

Cress's heart thudded hard. He discarded the orb of light and drew raw fire magic from the depths of the earth and trapped it in the form of a flame in the cup of his hands.

"What now?" he asked.

Three Guardians flew into the fire and out the other side. *"Coppers require heat. Immerse the egg in the flames,"* they said.

At Cress's nod, Becca set the fragile egg into the flames. A miniscule weight barely registered in his hands.

Becca stared at his burden, then raised her eyes to him. "Should we continue to look or head back?" she asked.

He glanced around the cavern. Indecision allowed a swell of acidic bile to rise up his throat and leave a sour taste on his tongue. Helplessness was not new to him, yet he hated the sensation. He offered up a grim little smile. If this egg lived, it meant two rare coppers survived. "Apparently we should go back."

"At last," the Guardians said.

Chapter Thirty-Eight

When Cress insisted upon searching for additional eggs, Becca wanted to object, but staring into his hazel eyes, she'd didn't have the heart to refuse him. He'd forgotten her ability to hear the dragon embryos, forgotten they'd guided her to themselves. The man never realized how pointless his quest, nor would she tell him. No, she couldn't tell him. He must discover the futility on his own.

Or so she told herself until he found the pale copper egg that he gingerly carried in magical flames. She hadn't listened to her inner voice and now gratitude filled her.

A magnificent view spread out before them in the main cavern upon their return. For as far as the eye could see, green grass and low-growing shrubs stretched out below them. A gray sky blanketed the land, and the silver ribbon of River Kelt wrapped over the countryside as it gushed from the higher mountains. Becca imagined the bubbling sounds the water made as it tumbled over rocks. The Wilds made her proud to call it home.

She wished time existed to appreciate the beauty before her. But it didn't.

Cress placed his precious cargo into a small bowl, his compassion a joy to see. Becca tore her gaze away from him and turned to solving the problem of all the eggs.

How could they lower their treasured cargo? They needed to find a safe way. And then?

Then she would return to Demit Woods to fulfill her obligation. She vowed to communicate with his sister until the spell broke. Afterwards…she'd be free to do as she pleased.

But what did she want?

Return to Froy? Likely not. The challenge of finding the wizard to save Froy changed her. For better or worse, she couldn't say. A chance for excitement, to venture into the unknown.

And now? she asked herself. While The Wilds looked the same, her beloved homeland had forever altered.

Froy no longer represented home to her. Her home had vanished. She pulled her brows together as she mulled over the transformation. She didn't like it one bit, but she could do little to bring back the old ways. Those were gone…forever.

What if she left and never returned? An odd pang of sadness swept through her with such force that she wasn't sure if it was real or not.

She glanced at the stack of rocks she'd piled in the corner of the cave. The top one had fallen off. Three remained. Did she knock it off toting the eggs or had the earth moved? Did it matter anymore?

"Do you have any other plans?" she asked Cress.

"Tomorrow I'll be able to use magic."

"If you're not too tired."

The faint flutter of leathery wings filled her ears while she waited for his reply.

"I am a wizard."

No emotion in his voice, not a hint of censure, yet Becca's heartbeat increased. "Which doesn't mean a thing. You said it yourself—you needed to replenish your strength. You used the last of your reserves to save the copper."

"True, but I recover quickly."

She leaned against him, testing him. "In that case, seducing you should be easy and will be my pleasure."

A slight scent of pine rose from his skin and treated her nose to a heady fragrance with a deep breath. He'd shown how passionate a man he could be the other night, and she ached to repeat that potent, intimate experience.

In truth, being near him set her on fire.

****

Cress blinked as morning sunlight peeked over the far horizon. Becca had touched him, and the lonely recluse he'd once been had melted away. Now, listening to her gentle breathing, he savored her curves as she snuggled against him. His fingers glided across her ribs to wake her. A tingle sizzled up his fingers and urged him to move faster. He fought the compulsion, repositioning his hand to trace the length of her bare hip, deliberately avoiding touching her intimately.

She stirred, a purr escaping her lips. Last night her cries of pleasure filled the cave, and they had been the sweetest sound he'd ever heard. He remembered how her nipples hardened into delightful beads. The sight drove him crazy.

She stirred again, arching her hips on the pallet of blankets. Did she dream of him? Did enough time remain to make love before they tackled the job of lowering the dragon eggs?

"Absolutely not!" Guardians snapped in his head, reading his thoughts. *"Human copulations expend too much time. Dragons waste no effort to procreate. We must insist on no more until our eggs have been rescued."*

"That's the difference between humans and dragons," he answered in mindspeech to keep from waking Becca. *"It's not just a physical act between us. It creates an intimate bond."*

"As much as I would enjoy spending another passionate hour or two with you, Cress," Becca whispered as she yawned, "they're right. We need to act. Now."

To his chagrin, the mindspeech from the Guardians had included Becca. "You were awake the whole time."

"Should I have let you know? It would have been a shame since you were having such fun arousing me. I was curious how far you would go."

"Satisfied?"

Becca smiled coyly. "A poor word choice. But to expound on it…Not yet. I would have you continue."

Cress leaned over her. "As you wish. Lie back down and let me do as I please."

"Enough," Guardians interrupted.

"Shush, you meddlers," he mindspoke, his fingers grazing along Becca's arm. A familiar tingle went up his arm, and so did his desire.

"Meddlers!" Guardians fluttered at the cave's ceiling in sharp agitated motions. *"We do not have difficulty with timelines—you do."*

"All right, if you are adamant, I've come up with a spell that will work."

"What is it? Tell us."

Cress gave up. He'd never have any peace of mind until he satisfied the Guardians. He stood.

Keep these eggs light.

Keep these eggs out of sight.

At his words, the pile of eggs rose in the air. Even the tiny, copper eggs wrapped in their protective coating of flames floated from the bowl. Puffy and white, a cloud formed out of the air. It expanded and covered the suspended eggs.

"Looks are deceiving," he went on to explain. "While my creation resembles a real cloud, it is solid enough to move, and the eggs within it as you wish. Test it."

The Guardians flew toward the cloud, disappearing into the opaqueness. The cloud inched forward.

"It works!" they shouted happily through mindspeech.

Cress did his best not to chuckle out loud. While he was distracted, Becca slipped into her leggings and tunic, and braided her hair with his beads. The sight of the glowing beads caused his chest to fill with more than fresh, clean air. Pride made him grin.

It took an hour to lower the eggs. Only when they were safely on the ground did Cress scale down on his belly in a controlled slide. Bloody cuts covered his scraped hands, and his knees burned with an intensity he'd never experienced.

"You can leave Froy tonight," he told the Guardians. *"Follow the winds."*

"Too dangerous. The ley-lines are the shortest route. We can see them, but your magic can control the winds in the right direction. While the eggs are few, there are too many for us to protect. We'll need your

assistance on the journey."

Cress glanced at Becca. She gathered their supplies. From her actions, the dragons did not include her in the conversation. *"From what?"*

"Unknown," Parr said. *"For safety's sake, we must remain with you."*

An unfamiliar sensation of mistrust shivered down his spine. What were the Guardians not telling him? Frowning, he extracted the heaviest items from Becca. She smiled her thanks. They covered the return trek to Froy in record time.

Occasionally, along the way, one of the tiny dragons flew out of the cloud as though taking bearings.

"Someone comes," the Guardian said.

"Who?" he asked.

"The dam of Becca."

"I wonder what she wants." Becca looked up at the cloudy sky. "And what about them?"

"They'll be fine. They'll blend in perfectly, and on a sunny day, a single cloud won't draw undue attention."

"Welcome back," Quinta said upon reaching them, then rotated to face him. "I'm glad you survived your visit to Becca's cave. You are the first to have climbed it with her."

"It was an interesting experience," he said.

"Come, then," the older woman said, slipping her arm into his and dragging him toward the village. "Some men brought down a deer this morn, and we're going to celebrate by listening to a tale from our storyteller. It has been ages since she has graced us with a tale."

Cress stayed alongside the older woman. "Becca

has told me much about your storyteller."

"I promise you'll not be disappointed," Quinta said.

The trio drew near the center of Froy. People rushed around, shouting, "A story! We're going to hear a story. Everyone. Hurry!"

The cry spread through the village. The biggest woman Cress had ever seen waddled into view. Her braid hung to the small of her back, a thin rope of brown sprinkled with gray. She dressed like most of the women in an open neck shift that brushed the ground as she strutted past without giving them a second look. The crowd parted for her, and she disappeared into the ex-Council hut.

Cress and Becca followed Quinta inside. She led them to the right, very near the middle.

The littlest tots formed a circle on the hardpacked ground, faces bright with anticipation. Next, older children sat. Cries of pain and objection mingled as one as they jostled for position with their elbows. Women came after and muttered to the disruptive children. Their warnings silenced most. One boy seemed unaffected and continued to torment those around him until a woman leaned forward and tweaked his ear with a twist. He yelped and promptly obeyed. Lastly, men stood at the fringe. Several couples gathered in the far back. Cress spotted Pire and Gette. The blacksmith rolled a barrel inside and insisted his wife sit upon it. When Maine spotted him, he flashed a grin at them, then at the unwed women around him. He whispered something into their ears, and titters of silly laughter erupted from the women. If the man proved his rival for Becca's affection, he certainly wasn't behaving like he cared. Unless he deliberately tried to make her jealous. A possibility.

The enclosed hut grew hot, the air thick. Tension sprouted within Cress like toadstools on the forest floor in cool fall weather. So many people. His chest tightened. The room seemed to shrink around him. The thought of leaving popped into his head. Or, at least, to excuse himself to stand near the door.

A late arrival, Reba slipped into the hut and upon spying Cress, shrieked with joy. She wove through the crowd right for him. "Wizard, can I sit on your lap?"

"That depends on whether you can keep quiet and still."

"I won't move a muscle. Pretty please."

Refusal became out of the question. Cress wondered what it would be like to have a child of his own. "It would be my pleasure."

Reba settled her small frame on him.

Becca grace him with a seductive grin. "Looks like I have competition."

The storyteller eased her ponderous bulk onto a stool with a heavy sigh. She smiled and revealed a gap between her teeth. "Who has brought me a gift? No tale worthy of my time and ability can begin without payment."

A woman wearing a conical hat, whom Cress recognized as an ex-Council member, wove forward with a jug that sloshed with liquid. He had the distinct impression the woman performed this ritual on numerous occasions.

"I have brought something," the ex-Council woman declared in a forceful, clear voice. "Will you accept this jug of apul cider as payment?"

The storyteller grinned, brushing back gray hairs that escaped her braid. "Gladly. I thank you for this gift. What story would my eager listeners care to hear?"

"What about the great bear that menaced the village many summers ago?" someone shouted from the left.

"Ahh, you speak of old Tasha, the honey licker," the heavyset woman replied, nodding with approval. "Fond of sweets and mischief she was. She stalked Froy the last year of her life. She bore no cub that spring and decided to torment humans for fun."

"Not that silly tale! Tell us about the year of no summer," protested a voice from the other side.

The storyteller pulled her shoulders in and hugged her flabby arms as she pretended to shiver. "That was a terrible year. Two winters joined together. Not much snow, but ice coated everything. Lakes never thawed. Freshly shorn sheep froze to death. It was—"

"Nay, stop," cried someone else. "Dragons! We want to hear about dragons."

The storyteller's smile widened. "So be it. Dragons...I will be happy to tell you how dragons lost the opportunity to rule over the world and how our ancestors rose above all other creatures."

Becca leaned closer to Cress. "That's one of my favorites."

"Mine, too," Reba piped up.

"This will be new for us. We are curious to hear," mindspoke a chorus of Guardian voices.

Cress didn't respond, for he wanted no distractions.

The heavyset woman glanced in their direction. "First though, to have an ending, we must start at the beginning. Imagine..."

The single word worked like a suggestion. A strong image appeared instantly, and Cress nearly missed the beginning.

"…when the world was new, a world where gemstones cried to the heavens for someone to hear them. Only one species heard those cries, and those creatures were dragons," she began in a low voice. People leaned forward as though afraid of missing a single word.

Cress and his group did the same, along with everyone else.

An occasional soft whistle of air escaped between the gap in the storyteller's teeth. "Fierce, magical creatures. They came from all over the universe and descended from the heavens."

"That's where they live now," a small voice came from a girl.

"Aye, child," she said, smiling, "but that is a different story. Today is about how the great beasts fought amongst themselves. The roar of their challenges filled the skies. The earth shook. Battles to death, they were. Fierce and bloody, those fights went on and on for days. Whatever their motivations, no one knows. Dragon reasons." She paused to let her audience envision the battle and draw their own conclusions. "One dragon, an ancient black male named Obba, was wise above all others. Obba had grown old when inspiration struck, his ebony chin turned gray, and many of his scales resembled hematite rather than his true obsidian coloring.

"Obba, the immemorial one," a Guardian mindspoke to both Cress and Becca.

"Though old, his great and powerful voice would

not be silenced," the storyteller continued. "He claimed the earth would not pour out its gifts of gemstones if dragons weren't wise and patient. He warned them that their lives and existence were too precious to be lost to such silliness as fighting amongst themselves and dared them to form a society to prevent more deaths. Otherwise..." The storyteller took a deep breath, her expression sad. "...otherwise, when the last dragons perished, the memory of their existence would fade into obscurity. We all know that didn't happen, don't we?"

Heads bobbed in confirmation.

The storyteller bent over with a grunt. She picked up the jug, uncorked the lid, and took a swallow. "They went on to become myths to frighten small children into obeying their parents, didn't they?" A teasing note entered her tone. She wiped her chins and set the container on the ground where the hem of her shift revealed thick ankles.

The nearest children giggled nervously.

The heavyset woman held up her plump hands for silence. Cress noticed no veins showed. She didn't lower them until a soft cadence of expectancy filled the air. "Obba's words must have struck a chord. Those early dragons ceased fighting with each other, formed their first society, for they had more than one, and elected the wise and beautiful Soluna, to rule over them. But that wasn't the last trial for dragons. Nay, nay, nay."

Cress listened, letting the words and images fill his head, positive the woman spoke solely to him. He suspected her mannerisms and vocal inflections were rooted in history, passed down from generation to generation. Looking around, he saw everyone's face reflected the same engrossed intensity he felt.

"It is said Soluna descended from our Goddess Luna," Becca mindspoke to him. *"That is why we honor dragons."*

"Trouble erupted once more," the storyteller went on. "In the chaotic world of long ago, whilst early humans were barely evolved higher than the animals, humans and dragons preyed upon one another. Dragons, ever wise, sought a way to bring order to this realm." She widened her eyes until the whites seemed to gleam, and then she looked around the hut, making eye contact with each and every person. "The dragons, their chests adorned with every precious gemstone imaginable, summoned the giant sand bears and ice wolves to a race, and they included humans. They formed an enormous circular path outlined on the prairie. The winner would rule the world and all living creatures. The dragons assumed with their immense size and wings that they would win the contest.

"But the race turned into a mad frenzy as contestants ran around and around." She raised her hands again and this time drew circles in the air. "The ground sank, forming a mountainous bulge amid the circle. That bulge burst and showered the racers with debris. Many creatures died. Only the humans survived in any number, and they claimed the right to rule the world."

The tale came as a new one to Cress.

"A true accounting," Parr whispered to Becca and him as though surprised a human tale could be accurate.

"You left the eggs?" Cress asked.

"They are safe. I was curious how these humans would describe events of the past. I must say, the oral

perspective is accurate."

"The remaining dragons retreated to their lairs with their pride wounded. The other animals went back to their habitats. Time passed. Humankind busied themselves with building their civilizations, though they never forgot about the dragons' treasure. Eons passed, and once again humans preyed upon the great creatures, destroying them. But do not fear—legend claims one day humans and dragons will work together to save the other. Who shall save whom is a story yet to unfold."

Cress looked over Reba's bright red curls at Becca. *"Well, part of that legend is coming to pass,"* he said in mindspeech. *"We are living proof."*

She smiled back at him. *"It would seem so."*

Scattered applause erupted into full blown clapping when people realized the tale had ended. They leapt up, cheering. Cress set Reba on her feet and joined the revelers.

"Marvelous!" he said to Becca over the noise. "I can truly say I have sat in the presence of a master storyteller."

Becca nudged him and Reba toward the door. "Why so surprised? Did I not say our storytellers prided themselves on their ability to convey accurate and entertaining tales?"

"That you did. I'll never doubt you again."

She laughed. "Can I have your word?"

A woman came up and took Reba's hand. The little girl cocked a finger at him to bend down. Her small arms wrapped around his neck. "You're my friend," she said in a low voice.

A heavy lump formed in his gut. "You're mine,

too. Forever and always."

Becca squeezed his hand. "Children are precious, aren't they?"

"Indeed, they are," he answered, recognizing his earlier discomfort of being in the crowd had vanished. "Do you realize the historical significance of what we just heard? Your storyteller disclosed a truth I never suspected. Dragons lost the opportunity to rule our world because of a race."

The reminder of humans and dragons once being rivals caused Cress to frown. It could be significant. He wasn't sure. Privately, he wondered what kettle of fish retrieving the dragon eggs opened.

He and Becca finally made it out of the hut. He inhaled a few breaths of cool, refreshing night air. They barely took a step when a male voice halted them.

Chapter Thirty-Nine

"Becca. Wait."

She and Cress turned to catch Maine propelling his muscular frame through the crowd without his troupe of admirers. He appeared oblivious to the remaining villagers hurrying out of his way. Becca frowned. The behavior seemed out of character for the gentle giant.

"Don't like the looks of that," Cress said next to her, his scrutiny locked on Maine.

"You sound jealous."

"I'm not. I'm…" Cress stopped as though unwilling to utter a word he might regret later.

Then she saw it. A green flash of jealousy sparked in the wizard's eyes.

Most people had departed for their own huts and sleeping quarters. Deep inside, she wished they didn't wait. "I suppose we have to see what he wants."

"I'll stay with you. I don't want you facing him alone."

What had Cress heard? Was he worried? "All will be well."

"Hello, Becca. Wizard. Thanks for waiting," the other man greeted them.

She craned her head at the tall blond. "What can I do for you, Maine?"

He stood motionless, staring at her for a few seconds. A frown pulled his brow together as his gaze flicked from the glowing beads to her face. "Becca, I need to speak with you about an important matter. In private."

"Tell me here."

"It's about Froy's future. Our future."

She locked her attention onto his. "What do you mean?"

Maine glanced at Cress. Clearly, he wanted the wizard to leave. The stern expression on Cress's face revealed his intention of not budging. The two men looked so different—one tall and fair, the other slender and dark, one high-spirited and cheerful, the other serious and moody—yet they were much alike. And each mulish in their own way.

"Bringing order is never easy," the big man started out. "People resist change. I want to make sure the new Council promotes cooperation and harmony. Doing so is difficult. You always sought expert advice whenever faced with a problem. Can I do any less? I seek the most qualified person I know for the answer—you."

"Me?"

"You always swayed people to give their utmost for Froy. Pire doesn't want to be leader forever. He'd rather work in his smithy creating tools or teaching his craft to anyone who shows interest. Eventually, he wants me to take over leadership. I need to learn how to wield authority for the common good. And I need someone at my side who—"

Cress coughed, hacking like he choked. Becca shot him a glance. Maine ignored the rasping sounds. Male posturing, if she didn't know better.

Maine continued in a sincere tone. "Froy is your home, Becca. It's where you belong because you will always care about its welfare."

She swallowed hard. His voice softened, appealing to a part of her, the same way in their youth. A memory flashed in her head—an image of the two of them skipping rocks over the river. Competitors, friends, lovers. In truth, she'd avoided encountering him since Landa's death. The impulse seemed silly now. The corner of his mouth tilted up to grin at her.

She glanced at Cress. "Mayhaps I should talk with him alone. Wait for me in Asa's hut. I won't be long."

A stern look froze on his face. "I'll stay."

His tone brooked no opposition. Did he consider Maine a rival? "Really, it's fine."

"Isn't it strange for him to seek you out now? He's barely spoken to you since returning."

"Go," she said softly, wishing Cress would offer for her, all the while knowing her secret optimism only created false hope. "I need to do this myself."

Cress clenched his fists at his sides. She halfway expected him to launch an attack or use magic against Maine before he calmed.

"Nay," he said. "Where you are, I'll be."

Both men cornered her. "Fine, stay." She turned back to her ex-lover. "Speak, Maine. I won't wait forever."

A smile lit up his face. "You were always direct. I like that."

She returned his smile, remembering all the times they'd talked, argued, and made love within a single hour. "Keep talking then."

"You and I can be the rebirth of Froy."

The declaration stole her breath, even though she halfway anticipated it. "Why would you say such a thing?"

"Because it's true. Everyone would benefit. You were always the best hunter. The quickest to solve a problem. You could regain a position of leadership." He reached for her arm. Cress growled and stepped forward.

Men! They were touchier than a hunter during her moon cycle. Tension filled the air as the two postured over her.

Each man represented a different way her life could go. In truth, neither one was a bad choice. Each possessed good qualities. A part of her wanted both. Though, after the last couple days of splendid lovemaking, she leaned toward Cress. He'd taught her so much, opened her eyes to delights she never imagined.

As much as she believed a future might exist with the wizard, she worried none did. But one might with Maine. She couldn't reject the possibility.

Did she have a choice? Probably not.

"The wizard and I leave in a few days, and we have much to prepare," she announced, wondering if she would miss Froy like she did the first time.

"Why must you guide him back?" Maine asked, his voice cracking with despair. "You've done your part and more. Someone else should be sent in your stead."

"I brought him here. It's my responsibility to return him to Demit Woods. Besides, he and I have an agreement."

"What agreement?"

An eerie calm possessed her. "That's between him and me. What would you have me do? Break my word? Neglect my duty?"

"What of your duty to Froy?" Maine pleaded. "Your friends? You have a family that loves you."

She held her arms out as if to hold him off. "All that's important. But this is not the time to speak of such things."

"I missed you," he whispered, ignoring Cress standing inches away. "I don't want to lose you again."

A sigh fell from her lips. "Once I believed returning to Froy and saving it from the plague the most important thing in the world. I thought I could fix any and every problem, but I was wrong."

"Nay, Becca, not you. Me," Maine said, his tone conveying an edge she'd never heard before. "I admit it now. I was wrong."

"About what?" she asked. Her gaze swept over his face, from his blue eyes to trim beard.

"Don't judge me too hard." His rugged features revealed a grimace. "I should have waited for your return. I shouldn't have wed Landa. I wasn't strong enough to believe you would be successful. Let me prove myself to you now. Trust me, Becca, please."

"Trust you? For what purpose?"

A grin flashed over his face. "If you must leave, this time I promise to wait. You know I am fond of you. And I think you care for me."

Becca flicked a glance at Cress. Fury darkened his expression.

Maine's words hung between them, a promise, a new chance, and unexpectedly, they held no appeal. "Don't waste your time waiting for me. I might not return."

"Life would never be dull with you." Maine went on as though not hearing her answer, his brow rising in

a teasing challenge. "Will you wed me?"
****

Cress trembled as he stood beside the river listening to Becca and Maine. Magic tingled in his fingers as pent up rage tried to find an escape. He couldn't let his emotions control him or he would use conjuring power in the worst way against the blond giant.

His heart urged him to speak up, but his tongue refused to cooperate. *I want you for all eternity. Tell that man you want nothing to do with him.* He almost sent the imploring message through mindspeech, but before he could Becca answered Maine.

"You honor me," she said.

The blond main grinned.

The world tilted for Cress. Fear and dread clawed at him, shredding his insides between passionate desire and desperate need for the woman he loved. Tension filled the air—tangible, palpable. He declined to think of Becca in Maine's arms, but he couldn't stop himself. If she returned to Froy, they would wed and rear a brood of muscular sons and independent, beautiful daughters. Those children would become the pride and joy of the village, the best hunters, the finest defenders.

"Your agreement is all I desire," Maine declared, standing straighter in anticipation of winning Becca's fidelity. "Men and women are pairing throughout the village. It is the way of the future."

Becca shook her head. "A future I am unsure that I will fit into. I am a hunter, through and through. I—"

"Wait! Don't answer me this moment," Maine interrupted. "Think about it. You know my heart, Becca. All I ask is that you consider my offer. And if it

301

helps, just know that I'll be waiting for you."

Cress flinched at the intensity of the enormous man. Somehow Becca had become his richest treasure. As though lightning struck him, he understood why dragons coveted treasure. He wanted to show her how much she meant to him. He didn't want to live alone. Not since finding Becca. With her, he felt whole. Those children he imagined should be theirs. They should be his sons, ones he could train as wizards, and daughters Becca could teach to become warriors and hunters. Cress never expected to fall in love, but since he had he intended to prove himself worthy of her affection.

Chapter Forty

Becca and Cress stayed in Froy two more days, gathering supplies for their journey. The subject of Maine never came up, which suited Becca just fine. On the final day she wandered through the village. While the trek was difficult at times, she recognized places she had seen all her life and wondered whether or not she would ever return. Maine provided her with a reason to come back.

Was it enough?

"We must leave," she told her mother that last night outside the older woman's hut. "Autumn's cusp is fast approaching. We risk not reaching the mountains until winter."

Quinta's expression fell. "Your brothers are due back any day. They will be sad to have missed you."

Becca bowed her head. "I'm sorry, Mother. Cress kept his word. I owe him a debt of gratitude. And I will not break mine."

A mixture of sadness and acceptance passed over her mother's face. "We are all in his debt."

The next morning, a light rain dampened the land. Becca stepped out of Asa's hut to find Cress waiting for her. They had not made love since returning from the cave and encountering Maine—two whole days and even longer nights. The wizard considered her impulsive, headstrong. Time to demonstrate her patience. Whatever his reason for withdrawing, she would allow him time and space.

At his smile, though, gratitude filled her as she changed into soft leather riding boots that went up to her knees and a tunic decorated with animal motifs. She wore one of her best, and she wanted to look good for him. With his appealing dark looks and his long wizard's robe flapping around his legs, he stood apart from the men of Froy. Something carnal about him spoke to her.

Behind him, the entire village waited in the center to bid them farewell. Pire, along with Gette and her mother, stood in the forefront.

"Pire," she said loudly, wanting everyone within range of Asa's hut to hear their conversation. "I can't blame you for what happened here. Not anymore."

His mouth dropped open, then he clamped it shut again.

"You brought reform to Froy," she went on as raindrops dribbled down her neck. "I see that now. People are happy. The crops are flourishing. You established a unity between men and women that didn't exist before. You made Froy whole."

Incredulity filled Pire's dark eyes, as did pride. "High praise, coming from you, sister dear."

Quinta stepped forward. "It takes two to reconcile. You make me proud to call you daughter, Becca."

Gette smiled. "Me, too, sister."

The tribute stymied Becca's breathing. She never expected easy forgiveness for her earlier hostility. She glanced at Cress and saw him smile. Warmth filled her, and she grinned back. Turning to her mother, her smile widened and she kissed her sister's cheek. "I'm positive many consider me a troublemaker, but no longer in the way they think."

The huge blacksmith stepped forward and swallowed her in a hug. "Take care, Becca."

"The same to you, Pire." She swung onto her roan mare who'd grown fat grazing on lush grass. "Recently, I've learned regret of the past is a waste of the present."

Pire put his large palm on her horse's neck. "When will you return?"

"I'm not sure I will."

Pire stepped close to her horse. "There is someone who will be pleased to see you again," he whispered.

Becca's grip tightened on the leather reins when she glanced around at the various faces. She did not see Maine among them. Intuition told her the lone figure on the rise where the old forge once stood belonged to her ex-lover. She'd known him all her life. He was of Froy. And, most important, he wanted her.

Could she love him? Would the heat and passion that once existed between them reignite? Maybe time away would help her make the right decision.

The crowd edged forward as if to embrace her.

Cress mounted, looping the mule's lead to his saddle horn.

"Farewell," she said, kicking the mare into a trot.

"May Luna protect you," her mother called after them.

"Tulle's following," Cress said as they forded the River Kelt. They watched the dog bound up the bank, tail wagging as he cleared the tall cattails with ease.

"Let him. He's attached himself to you. Besides, he can flush birds for me to shoot for our meals."

They rode away in a mist of rain. The dragons and

their precious cargo hid in a little cloud strafing the belly of gray ones above. Shallow creeks tugged at the horses' and mule's hooves as they crossed one after another.

They made incredible speed, and the first night they traveled numerous leagues before making camp beside a stream that seemed days away from Froy. She wondered if Cress tapped into the magic to add swiftness on the journey back.

Tulle stayed close to Cress as he tended the horses and mule while she built a sorry fire that sputtered and jumped in the rain. She didn't mind the dull covering of clouds during the day, but at night they created a barrier to the stars and moon. It seemed they blocked the goddess's view from her.

"You are content about leaving those you care about? If you wish to return, we will aid the wizard with our eggs," Guardians mindspoke to her as she bedded down.

"Don't listen to the old ones." New voices entered the conversation.

Becca's eyes flew open. *"Eggs?"*

"Who else?"

"Why do you advise against your elders?"

"They mean well, but they are jealous that we speak with you, and not them."

That made sense to Becca. *"I appreciate the notification. I can handle them."*

"As you wish," the dragon eggs said.

She mindspoke to the Guardians. *"I will return to Froy when I'm ready."*

"What if it takes many long years to free the wizard's sibling?"

"I suppose it could," she responded. *"*
"This male human called Maine...he is good?"
"Aye, better than I remembered."
"You are fortunate to have him wait for you."

Confusion grew because she couldn't decide between Maine and Cress. The Guardians added to her bewilderment. Why would they try to sway her into returning to Froy? And why would the dragon eggs counsel against it? Who should she believe?

After a week, the rain ended. Bursts of color from the rising of the sun greeted them with the promise of a warm day. As the day progressed, only one small cloud marred the wide expanse of blue.

The fair weather let them ride hard and fast, resting each night by a hastily built fire. At each stop, Cress stomped around the camp, sullen and surly except when Tulle appeared out of the darkness to lay by his side. Only for the dog did the wizard smile.

Becca wondered what bothered him but refused to press him. She'd kept her promise to return with him. What else did he want? Did he want her to make the first move? After all, she did not understand the ways of wizards and magic.

She did know how to arouse a man though. Sinking down beside him, her hand touched him intimately.

He sucked in a breath, a soft excited sound. "What are you doing?"

"I want you. You've pleasured me at the cave, wizard. It's time I return the favor. I've thought of nothing else for days."

His erection pulsed beneath his leggings against her palm. Her fingers enveloped him, tightening, and his manhood grew longer and harder and hotter, reminding her of the fire crackling next to them.

"We shouldn't be doing this," he said. "What about Maine?"

"Sweet Luna, what does he have to do with us pleasuring each other?"

He coughed or chuckled—she couldn't tell which—and then leaned over and kissed her. Breaking the kiss, he pulled down his leggings to expose himself to her view. And what a magnificent specimen he was. The one part of every male's body that differed the most. Cress's manhood was long, thick, his skin flushed purplish red, and his sacs were drawn up tight.

"You are beautiful," she said, stroking him, going faster, squeezing, until a drop of liquid appeared. He instinctively bucked against her hold. "You respond well, too."

"Exquisite torture," he panted.

"I am not done."

She lowered her lips and took his shaft in her mouth. She wanted to give him pleasure, to make it perfect. He groaned as she went slowly, licking and sucking. His muscles tightened as her fingers raked his inner thigh. Suddenly he jerked as his essence poured from him.

He inhaled deeply. "Now it is my turn."

Sparks suddenly burst from the campfire, and she wondered if Cress used magic. As she looked at his handsome face in the undulating light, she tried to imagine for a moment what it would be like to remain with him—how her life would change—if she dared.

He joined her on the bedroll and slipped his hand beneath her leather leggings, over her belly, and down to her sex. His hand burned against her skin. She shuddered when his fingers rolled the nub of her arousal. Hot. Tingling. Wonderful. His touch became magical. Exactly what she wanted…needed. He slid one finger inside, a second, and a third. Her senses were swamped with pleasure.

She rode his fingers, her body demanding release. The sensation built, exploded, encompassed her. A cry ripped out of her, and she threw her head back when shudders of delight pulsated through her. Peace and courage wrapped themselves around her as she gathered her thoughts.

Dim moonlight bathed them in an incandescent light as Becca lay next to Cress, resting on his arm with his other draped over her stomach. "It feels good being in your arms," she said, "but we need to talk. You haven't commented on Maine's proposal until a few moments ago. Why is that? Aren't you the least bit curious about my answer?"

Tension hardened his arm that she lay against. "Becca, I didn't want to interfere. Maine has offered you a future in Froy. I should never have kissed you."

She eyed him, unsettled. "Perchance, I shouldn't have let you."

The next night, without a word of explanation, Cress set their bedrolls on opposite sides of the fire. Tulle curled beside him to sleep. The traitor.

Hurt, she felt ambushed. She had sought his affection. Made the first move. Cress gave her his answer and she hated it.

It took the better part of the week to trek across the boggy land of the great swamp. Once again Cress parted the water to allow them safe passage. They blindfolded the horses and mule to lead them across.

Tulle trotted up to black swamp's edge. Becca watched him sniff the ground but refuse to cross.

Cress, the restive gelding under him, waved his arm at the dog. "Tulle, come."

The black and white spotted dog whimpered in response.

"He's afraid," she said.

"Of what?"

Sweet Luna, he remains silent for days, but speaks to me about a dog. She wanted to scream. "He senses the great river lizards in the water. All creatures fear them."

A Guardian flew out of the magical cloud. *"You and the animal belong in Froy. We urge you to cross back while you can. We will guide the wizard home."*

Becca could tell the dragon spoke only to her. *"I already gave you my answer."*

She searched the sky for the small white cloud. It appeared a league or two ahead of them. Did the eggs tell her true? Guardians certainly weren't acting like grateful creatures, but then they were dragons.

"I'll get him." Cress dismounted and walked into the opening, his boots sloshing until he reached the middle of the swamp. Water oozed out of the walls' sides held in check by magic.

She enjoyed the timbre of Cress's rich voice; watched his long strides, knew the strength of those sleek muscles hidden by the brown folds of the cloak he wore.

Remembering the delights they'd shared on the furs drove her crazy. Her body warmed with desire, making her nipples harden beneath her tunic. The pounding inside her threw her off balance, and she nearly slipped off the saddle. Jerking upright, she stared at Cress. A part of her ached to express her feelings, to let him know she approved of him, but how to do so without appearing less than a hunter. Hunters did not grovel.

Logic called for her to remain patient. Maybe it was a good thing he'd never offered for her. At the thought, she inhaled sharply.

Cress approached with Tulle snug in his arms. His piercing gaze darkened. "What's wrong?"

She glanced at the water's surface, trying to bury the embarrassment of her body's reaction to him. "I thought I saw a great lizard."

"They are trapped in the water."

He set Tulle down. The dog loped off. Cress remounted, and they continued on their way. The swamp gave way to Wisent Plains. The time between summer and fall left the land dry and browned. The prairie appeared empty and desolate, much like how she felt inside. Cress continued to place his bedroll on the other side of the fire and spoke only the barest amount to her.

The roar of wisent bulls announced their presence before the herd came into view. Lumps of dried mud clung in thick clumps on the long hair of their forequarters, heads, and beards, making them appallingly hideous creatures. Rutting season had concluded, but bulls still chased cows and fought with each other for the right to mate.

One morning after they had eaten a meal of quail and grouse, a scuffle between two bulls occurred yards from their campsite. They faced each other, pawing the dirt and throwing it over their backs, their bloodshot eyes rolling—one massive with dark reddish mats of hair containing much lighter streaks that reminded her of Maine, the other slightly smaller with dark hair almost black like Cress's.

Which would best the other? The crash of their heads rolled across the grassland. The bigger bull thrust this way and that, his sharp hooves straining for footing, his great and powerful shoulders pushing.

The smaller bull held his own, twisting his thick neck to rake his opponent's side with sharp horns. This would be a long and arduous battle, the outcome determined by fate.

Somewhere hidden within the massive herd, another bull bellowed, a deep, low chant. Bulls picked it up and echoed until the sound rolled over the plains, constant, throbbing and entering the bones of all who heard—Becca and Cress included.

"We'd better leave," she advised, turning away from the battle. "I have no desire to get caught in another stampede."

"Agreed."

They struck camp and headed east. After two weeks they reached the base of the mountains, far faster than Becca expected. They stood and looked up at the barrier of rocks and dirt looming above them. During their travel fall caught most of the land in its grip, yet the needle-high peaks were dusted in white. Winter crept closer.

The horses' and mule's hooves clinked on stony ground as they wove and twisted up the mountainside in a circuitous route. Trees changed from thick copses of pine and spruce to random stands of windblown and stunted fir. As she exhaled, Becca's breath formed ice crystals in the air. She felt cold inside and out as if all the exhaustion in her reflected Cress's silence more than the miles.

That day a skiff of snow fell along with the temperature. Becca and Cress dismounted and led their animals around a gap in the trail caused by an avalanche that had occurred since they last passed. They reached Dream Pass in the middle of the next day. Soon frost would glisten silver on branches and ice would form at the water's edge.

"Dare we stop?" she asked, fatigue pulsing through her.

"We're so close," he answered. "We could reach the bottom of the mountain by day's end. Let's keep going. I know you miss your mother and friends."

"Why would you say that?" she asked.

"It's true, isn't it?"

"Aye, but—"

He put up his hand to stall her. "I don't know how long it will take to break Trell's spell. Remember, I haven't been able to do so in a thousand years."

"You couldn't talk to your sister. I can."

"What can she tell you?"

"I have no idea. She might have a clue. All I can do is ask."

Glancing into his eyes, Becca kept her expression impassive. That didn't prohibit her heart from racing. He smiled at her, and his lips parted as though he wanted to say more. She mentally urged for him to speak.

Enticing memories stirred in her mind. Why didn't he pull her into his arms? She wanted him like no other male. A true hunter took what she wanted. She did not ask, beseech, or humble herself. However, Becca would show him that she possessed the patience to wait for him to come to her.

Far below, the vast evergreen swath of Demit Woods beckoned. The forest would retain its verdant color throughout the winter.

Guardians zoomed through the air, their golden bodies shimmering. The artificial cloud inched forward.

Becca and Cress descended, their pace escalating.

"Is it my imagination or are the horses going faster?" she asked Cress.

He responded with a smile. "They sense home is near. Haven't you ever noticed how a horse picks up speed on any return ride?"

"I have," she said, enjoying seeing him happy.

The journey took them past the clearing scoured by the fire Becca attempted to contain and was then dowsed by wizard magic. In the months since departing, new grass and other vegetation had sprouted among the blackened stumps.

A sign from the goddess that life goes on? She'd been so near Cress, yet received simple, curt responses. The last few moons were the longest in her life.

Chapter Forty-One

The hum of dragon wings greeted Cress a half day's journey from his final destination. Home. Trell.

And the Guardians of Secrets.

Hundreds.

Thousands.

And here he thought they were declining in numbers. When it seemed the air could hold no more, still more of the tiny dragons swirled like rays of twinkling lights. The entire colony must have flown out to welcome them home.

Tulle barked, leaping on his hind legs. His jaws snapped as they did on their journey when he flushed birds for their evening meals.

Cress reined to a stop. Complications between Becca and him preyed on his mind. The night they satisfied each other before reaching the swamp was seared into his memory. He hadn't wanted to argue afterward, but it seemed the safest thing to do. His dedication to Trell rested in one hand, while his affection for Becca lay in the other. Every time he looked at her, his body heated in response. He wanted her. Could he enjoy a happy future with her if his sister remained trapped?

He shook his head. Lustful thoughts drove him insane. Guilt swelled because he'd bedded the warrior woman without offering her a future.

"Welcome back, wizard. Becca. We have been anticipating your arrival. We are indebted to both of you for your efforts."

"Thank you, Torka," Cress answered, recognizing the voice of Parr's mate. *"I did very little. Thank Becca. She found the eggs. They spoke to her."*

"We suspected the female's ability to speak to Trell was because our eggs taught her. Embryonic dragons reach out to their dams and other creatures around them." Radiant flickers bobbed in the air. *"We have readied a cave beyond the dragon circle in advance of your triumphant return. First, though, I wish to see those that represent so much. Wizard Cress, please remove the spell covering our eggs."*

"As you wish."

Cress waited while two dozen Guardians pushed the cloud down. He inhaled a soft breath and muttered the words to terminate his spell. The opaque cloud faded away, and the eggs within drifted slowly to the ground. The pile grew to the size of a small wagon. Hues of green, blue, gold, and silver glistened in the fading daylight. Even the protective flames that surrounded the copper eggs burned bright.

"Do you need my help transporting them to the hatchling cave?" he asked, concerned.

"It is our responsibility, and we gladly fulfill the task. However, your assistance is required to recreate conditions for proper incubation."

"It will be my pleasure. Let Becca and me continue to the dragon circle. It has been a long, weary journey. After we have rested, I will come."

"So be it," Torka said.

Guardians swooped in on a command not meant

for him to hear to carry the smaller eggs away and roll the big blues.

A whiff of wood smoke scented the air as it escaped from the chimney of his home. He nudged his mount into a ground-eating trot. At their destination, Cress dismounted to seek the Ossa pine of his sister. Tulle followed him. Both mature and unopened pinecones littered the ground at its base.

A thrill of relief ran down him. Trell was safe. His sister and he had been close. He recalled her as a budding woman at the time of the accident. He remembered every little aspect about her—the way she laughed or wrinkled her nose or wept if a patient died. Trell preferred the tactical method of hands-on learning while he loved reading. As children, after the candles were snuffed, he used to retell the stories he'd read. The bond made them close. A day didn't pass when a memory of their childhood wasn't triggered.

He never liked discussing her dilemma. Never had.

Regardless of his loyalty toward Trell, he snuck a glance at Becca, then back to the tree. If not for his stupidity of competing with Bonner, this tragedy would never have transpired. He owed his sister loyalty, no matter how much happiness it cost him.

"It's good to see you once again. The journey to The Wilds has provided new tales for you," he said, then sighed. "If you know anything about Bonner's spell, you must tell Becca. It's the only way you will be free."

Branches swayed, and an especially long one dipped low to brush his shoulder. The sweet scent of vanilla fanned the air around him. He savored the fragrance as Becca dismounted and led her horse in his

317

direction.

"Hello, Trell," Becca said. "Do you remember me?"

Ossa branches swayed.

The warrior woman cocked her head, and her braid fell forward to dangle in front of her. The glow of his beads appeared like miniature suns in her hair. A flash of guilt hit Cress as he wondered if his sister recognized the significance of the beads.

"I guess we should begin figuring out how to free you," Becca said. "What can you tell me about this spell?"

Silence seemed to fill the dragon circle. Becca cocked her head as if listening. He wondered what his sister said, especially when a tiny frown turned Becca's lips down and her eyes narrowed with a stern look.

Cress's gut tilted in a sickening lurch. "What does she say?"

Becca held up her hand to silence him. "Shush. Of course not. He hasn't offered. I swear."

"Swear what? What is happening?" Becca licked her lips, wetting them and turning them a rosy pink. Desire quivered through him. "What does my sister want?"

She leaned against her horse. "I don't know myself. I'm confused. I—I need to think."

She gathered his reins and the mule's lead rope, and then led the animals away.

Cress ached to go after her. Instead he worried until Tulle's pointy muzzle rubbed his palm. "Wait a moment," he called. "Why won't you tell me?"

Becca spun around to glare at him. "It doesn't concern you. It was personal."

He swallowed hard, bristling. Personal? For whom? He was positive Trell wanted freedom. And Becca? What did she seek? To return to Froy? Wed Maine? A commitment from him? The future could go in different directions for the warrior woman, and he doubted she controlled the patience to last long.

"I won't accept that," he replied, surprised at his own persistence. Talk about patience.

"That's all I'm going to say."

His fingertips tingled with magic as he fought the urge to smash something. Nothing had been resolved. He simply stood there, feeling helpless, letting her go.

The creak of a door opening sounded like the clap of thunder. Salida and Einer stepped through the doorway. At least the sight of the elderly couple lifted his spirits. He swore they held hands, but upon spying him, released their grip. His housekeeper's oval face glowed with joy, her eyes filled with love and affection. Einer's colorful cape billowed like a banner in the wind, and his staff struck the ground with a soft thud and the jingle of tiny bells.

"I was beginning to worry you'd never return. What took so long?" Salida demanded, hurrying over.

He didn't answer. Instead, he wrapped her in a hug. How he missed her humbling brusqueness. "It was a great distance to travel. Magic isn't a cure. First, I needed to find the cause of the plague before I could fix the problem. Surely, Einer could have told you that."

"I have. Many times," the silver-haired wizard answered. "The mule she sometimes imitates refused to heed my words of wisdom."

"Mule!" Salida smacked Einer on the arm. "How dare you compare me to one of those creatures."

319

The white-haired wizard rubbed the spot, smiling at Cress. "You see! I hope the same never happens to you. Do you remember those tomes I used to talk about when I came from Brenalin?"

Cress frowned, confused. He couldn't recall what his friend referred to, then the fog lifted from his memory and he nodded. He cast a glance at Becca disappearing into the barn, wanting to call her back, to express his inner feelings that she returned with him. Loyalties split between her and Trell silenced him. No matter how much his body burned for Becca, his sister's freedom came first. The gods knew how often he wanted to explain to the warrior woman her importance to him, only to choke on his own words.

Was his failure due to the Guardians? They constantly harped to let Becca return home. That his behavior smacked of selfishness for keeping her from the ones she loved.

A heaviness settled on his chest. "You'll never convince me the solution to breaking Trell's spell has been there all along."

Einer grinned. "I've told you thousands of spells are in the library's tomes. Bonner could have used any one of them."

"Why haven't we found it yet?" Cress scowled, his blood slowing to a crawl in his veins.

"I didn't say uncovering the truth would be easy." Einer scratched his long white beard. "Nor do I have any evidence to point at and say, 'see'. Trell was alone with Bonner for several moments before he cast his spell. We do not know what transpired between them. It could be of vital importance."

The conversational tone retained such misleading

mildness that Cress nearly dismissed it, yet he knew better. The old wizard like to make people think. "What do you have in mind?"

"Such matters should be discussed in comfort," Salida interjected, stepping between the pair. "Enough talk. Why are we standing outside when I have fresh sweets ready in the house? Get inside, now."

"There is the crux of my dilemma. Her treats make up for the lack of respect," Einer said.

Cress laughed and the trio headed inside.

Salida fetched a platter of honeyed apuls and nuts. Cress and Einer settled into the chairs around the table.

When the door opened and Becca entered, Cress's breath caught. Though she'd only been out of his sight for a few minutes, he missed her terribly. Salida and Einer greeted her with welcoming salutations. Their gazes met during the exchange, and he considered looking away only to find he couldn't. Her cheeks were flushed, shimmering with a healthy glow. She looked happy. Sad.

Becca leaned her bow against the table and sat.

"Eat," his housekeeper told them. "I didn't labor over these treats for people to just ogle them."

"I don't need to be told twice," Becca said, reaching across the table. "I love sweets."

Becca and Einer snatched up a treat at the same time. With their mouths full and crystallized granules crusting their lips, they looked at each other and laughed.

"Communication is key, Cress," Einer said, stuffing a second delicacy into his mouth. "If Bonner used the word heartblood, it means the spell is tied to you and Trell. It's in Becca's hands now."

She nodded. "Doing nothing invites doom."

Cold dread swirled through Cress at her words. He said nothing…nothing because he suspected doom loomed in his future.

Chapter Forty-Two

The next morning, Tulle gave Becca a soft woof of hello and uncurled from his bed next to the door. She awoke before the others stirred and headed for the Ossa pine swaying in a gentle breeze, branches creaking. Or was it a groan?

"I'm sorry, Trell," she began with an apology, "that you are unhappy with my presence. Nor do I have any intention of confessing that to Cress. Call me selfish, but I gave my promise, and a hunter does not break her word. You can talk to me or remain silent. Either way, the decision is yours."

"*My brother is hurting. I sense a tension between you and him. What have you done to cause him pain?*"

Becca blinked. Being chastised by a tree never happened to her before. "Nothing. I swear."

"*I know Cress. A deep sadness is inside him and you are the cause. Leave.*"

It was one thing for the Guardians not wanting her around. Now, Trell. "I know there is tension, but I have no idea what is the cause."

"*Silly, silly woman. He cares for you. Have you rejected him?*"

"Of course not. We have mat—" Becca stopped. She started to say mated, but what Cress and she shared went deeper. He captured her heart, soul, and love.

The tree bombarded her with pinecones. Tulle,

smart dog that he was, raced out of range. Becca dodged the missiles. After a few moments, the downpour ceased. She stood there, motionless, waiting to see if the girl would speak. Nothing.

"I'm sure," Becca went on, determined, "it would be a great help if you told me why you think you no longer need me. Did something happen while Cress and I were away? Did the Guardians do something? Have they learned to speak with you?"

More silence.

Frustration welled up inside her. "If you were human right now, I'd treat you as a novice hunter. You're behaving like someone who needs many lessons before they can roam free and hunt on their own. You think you know everything, but you are wrong. Foolish girl. Until you accept your ignorance, you are a danger to yourself."

Becca stared at the tree. Insults didn't work. She'd have to try another tactic.

"What about Bonner?" she asked. "Tell me about him. What kind of wizard was he?"

"*If you are done berating me, first tell me of what importance is Bonner. He is long turned to dust.*"

A breath gushed out of Becca. She wanted to scream at Trell. Scream at a tree. "It matters. Knowing the people and circumstances surrounding an incident is of vital import," she huffed, struggling to remain calm. "Now, if you want my help, tell me about Bonner."

"*Not much to tell. Cress and I grew up with Bonner. He lived on the neighboring farm. Neither he nor Cress had any desire to become farmers like their fathers. They shared a fascination with wizardry.*"

Becca perked up. "You jest! Cress a farmer? I find

it hard to imagine."

"*So did he. He hated it.*"

Becca lowered herself into the slight dip Cress had created over time. Tulle curled beside her, and she rubbed behind the dog's ears. "Who was the better wizard?"

"*Probably Cress.*"

"And Bonner didn't mind being less talented?"

A branch hit the side of the Ossa. "*Of course he did.*"

"So, he could have been jealous of Cress," Becca said. Rivalry made sense. Hunters competed with each other to be the best, though there were never hard feelings. "Einer mentioned heartblood. Have you heard of it?"

"*Sorry. No. I wish I could be of more help. Have you asked Cress?*"

"He's told me as much as he remembers."

"*An illustrious destiny awaits the wizard,*" a Guardian mindspoke to Becca. "*He must dedicate himself and concentrate for it to happen.*"

The tiny dragon landed on her arm. Its red eyes burned into her. "*Sweet Luna! You startled me.*"

"*Humans frighten easily. There is still time for you to return to Froy before winter sets in the mountains. Go, while you can.*"

Frustration seeped into Becca's bones. "*Sometimes I find myself half wishing I could.*"

"*Leave then. We will aid the wizard.*"

She stiffened. "*What's going on? Trell wants me to leave. You want me to leave! Why? What are you not telling me? Are you so sure I will fail?*"

"*What is it?*" Trell asked.

Becca hesitated only a brief second. "A Guardian is pestering me."

"*I should have guessed. They have teased and tormented Cress for eons. Even though I am eager to meet the creatures, be careful around them. Dragons are crafty.*"

Becca's gaze followed the glittering path flitting among tree limbs. The tiny dragons' behavior chafed at her. "I suspected as much," she said to Trell. "Shouldn't we concentrate on the task ahead—you and breaking the enchantment? What did Cress do when the spell was cast on you?"

Tree branches snapped back. "*Why?*"

"I need to know what motivated him to enter a magic contest with another wizard," she said. "Cress doesn't come across as a competitive person. His skill is so superior that he has no need to show off. He has more sense than that."

"*My fault.*"

"Yours?"

"*A lapse in judgment. I was young. Foolish.*"

Becca knew about self-recrimination. "All three of you were young."

The Ossa swayed slightly, rustling branches and dropping long needles. "*True.*"

"Do not blame yourself. You are not responsible for the actions of others," she said as kindly as possible. "Cress definitely does not fault you."

Trell offered no further comment.

Becca closed her eyes, pondering the long silence. Positive no further comment would come, she rose, and Tulle followed her steps to the hut.

"Well?" Cress inquired when she opened the door.

He stood in the empty cooking area where crystals dangled from the ceiling and a flowery sweetness of treats hung in the air. Salida had banked the fire in the great hearth and the elderly couple had yet to rise from their beds.

Becca wanted to reassure him of a happy future. That he had nothing to fear. That she could break the curse.

"Nothing, I'm afraid," she said.

A flicker of disappointment sped across his features. "Are you going to tell me what Trell said to you last night?"

"No," she answered. "Is that why you rose early?"

Surprise sped across his face. "I wanted to tell you that game is plentiful in Demit Woods. You may hunt at your leisure."

"My thanks. I'll speak with Salida to see if she is partial for anything in particular."

She never took her gaze off him. A frisson of desire rose up inside her. Did the air crackle between them? Could he harbor the tiniest fondness for her? Would that be enough for her to remain once Trell's spell broke?

She opened her mouth, but Cress's curved into a frown and he turned away, disappearing down the hall. Tears welled in her eyes. Rejection cut deep into her soul and she prayed to Luna for strength.

Days became routine. Becca spent the majority of daylight hours with Trell. At night, she hunted when the housekeeper requested fresh game, to break the repetition. Otherwise, the nights left her with trying to decide which man she wanted—Cress or Maine. No insight offered peace from her torment.

****

Dusk fell when Cress remembered what Einer had said all those months ago. *Love never fades.* He latched onto those words thinking of his sister, but now...now they applied to Becca.

He scrutinized the dragon circle. Guardians had been absent of late. No surprise there. They tended their precious treasure of dragon eggs. He had created environments as close to their natural environments to give the unhatched eggs the best chance at survival until fatigue overwhelmed him on that first night.

Movement near the Ossa pine caught his attention. Becca sat in his favorite spot, her long braid draped over her front. He smiled to himself, seeing glowing beads woven through her golden locks. She hadn't tossed them away like those yellow ones. He hesitated, not wanting to intrude, then decided his sanity required being near her.

"Want some company?" he asked.

Surprise flitted across her delicate features. "By all means." She patted the ground. "Sit here."

A branch lowered to touch his shoulder. He ran his fingers across the needles. "Have you learned anything?"

"Much is still a mystery, although I have learned a certain risk is involved."

His eyes widened, and he frowned. Unexpectedly, he found himself annoyed. "Don't give me excuses."

"Being uninformed isn't an excuse," she answered, her voice steady. "It is admitting my lack of knowledge."

Cress hated himself for acting like a lout. The behavior was out of character. "Forgive me for being short with you. The delay is nerve wracking. I assumed, mistakenly, talking with Trell would provide a means to break the spell."

"Trell isn't in danger. You are."

A jolt of surprise pierced him. "Me? Explain."

Becca looked into his eyes and shook her head. "The heartblood Einer mentioned is yours. It must be spilled."

Icy coldness wrapped around him. "What? How you do know? How much heartblood? All of it? Or just a little?"

"We forbid it. Refuse!" Dozens of Guardians swarmed out of the woods. Their bodies shimmered in the branches, vanquishing the shadows. *"You are too valuable, wizard."*

Stunned by the protest, Cress composed his fears, hopes, and emotions. *"You have no say in the matter. I'll do whatever it takes to save Trell. Have no doubt."*

"Impudent human."

He leapt to his feet and faced the mass of glittering dragons. *"And I thank the gods, I am. This is not your choice. Now begone."* Determination grew stronger. He waited until the last Guardian departed before turning to Becca. "Tell me what I must do."

"I don't know yet."

"Ask Trell. Mayhaps she knows."

"I know you can hear us, Trell. What can you tell us?"

The tree shuddered at the request. Branches swayed so hard a breeze disturbed nearby trees.

Becca shook her head. "She claims not to know."

"You say that as if you have doubts."

"Somewhat. She's definitely your sister and very

protective of you. She has refused to cooperate from the start. I—I think she knows how to break the spell but won't tell me."

Cress didn't hesitate. "Trell, please heed my words. Do not worry about me. I am willing to face any danger to free you. I beg you, please tell Becca what she needs to know."

Long seconds of strained silence filled the circle, then the Ossa quivered and shook. Hard. Violently. Pinecones pummeled the ground. Needles showered the air. The very ground split at the base of the tree, and massive roots lifted.

Cress stood dumbstruck. "What is it? What's happening?"

"You made her cry," Becca said, "but she will help."

He put his hand on the tree trunk, feeling the rough bark. "Forgive me. I didn't mean to. I'll try to be more understanding." He took Becca's hand, stroking the top with his thumb. She didn't pull away, which pleased him immensely. Everything about her appealed to him. He loved her with all his heart and regretted putting her in such an unpleasant position.

"You are a male. You have a thick skull."

Cress shook his head realizing little light remained from the setting sun. "We should probably go. Salida will have dinner ready. She frowns upon tardiness."

Becca rose. "Before we go, have you noticed anything strange about the Guardians?"

She spoke so low Cress wasn't positive he'd heard her. "The Guardians? They've been extremely busy with their treasured eggs. Minding over forty consumes all their time."

"Aye, I suppose it does. My hunter's instincts are positive they're up to something."

He'd had similar thoughts but waited to hear her suspicions. "They're dragons. Intrigue is second nature to them. What worries you?"

Becca's brow furrowed. "I find deceit discomforting, no matter who perpetrates it. You should as well."

Cress permitted magic to rise within him, letting the ancient power soothe him. "I'll see if I can figure out what's going on."

"Don't take too long. It might be important."

With that, Becca left, her confident stride muted in the soft loam. He started to follow.

"The warrior woman is stubborn," tiny dragons spoke through mindspeech. *"Remember how she refused to take no until you submitted to do her bidding?"*

He stopped short. *"Eavesdropping again, I see. So what? Why bring it up now?"* His gaze trailed after Becca until she disappeared inside.

Guardians swept out of the woods to dip and swoop before him. *"Free the warrior woman from her pledge and let her return home."*

He glared at the dragons, their allusion sharpening his interest. *"I thought you wanted her to help me."*

"We do not mean to be critical. Stubbornness is her strength. Her people need that."

"What about Trell?" Even as he spoke, thoughts of Becca leaving made his heart lurch sickeningly.

"We can help with your sibling. We are learning to communicate through our nascent eggs."

Their reply sounded weak. He would have sworn

satisfaction laced their tone. Why? *"Why didn't you mention this before?"*

"Patience, wizard. We did not know until now. Our eggs are more powerful than we imagined."

"Cress!" Salida called from the cottage door. Einer stood beside her.

Questions filled Cress's head. The Guardians flitted like golden flakes among the dark trees. Occasionally red eyes gleamed at him.

Cress debated ignoring the summons, then with a shrug walked over to the couple. "Sorry to be late."

This time Einer held his housekeeper's hand within his age-speckled one. Salida wore a long cloth belt loosely knotted at her thick waist that glowed the same way as the older wizard's multicolored cape. Clearly, the pair had set aside their bickering, using their time together in pursuit of other things. Cress smiled to himself at the happiness his friends discovered with each other. Companionship at any age was good.

Salida craned her neck, and she tracked the Guardians' movements. "Those beasts are up to something."

"You, too? Becca suspects them as well," he answered without censoring his words.

His housekeeper cocked a gray brow. "Dinner will be served shortly. Becca's washing up. But first, we have matters to discuss."

Einer nodded in agreement. "Aye, we do."

Cress scowled. He didn't need more problems. They already knew what happened to Trell—though he had never articulated his feelings at any length with either of them.

Stars studded the night sky with the brilliance of

white diamonds. A sight that normally brought him comfort…Until now.

He felt alone. Which, of course, proved false. Salida and Einer stood before him, the soft jingle of bells on the older wizard's staff fading away.

"Such as?" he asked with deliberate self assurance, knowing he'd erected a wall on his emotions. "Do you doubt Becca's ability?"

Blue fire flared in the older woman's eyes. "Of course not," she denied, a slight catch in her voice.

Cress frowned. "Mayhaps you should. She hasn't been successful yet, and the Guardians claim they might be able to speak to Trell with the help of their eggs."

The housekeeper appeared thoughtful. She glanced at Einer before giving him a cool, appraising look and responding in deadly seriousness. "Really?"

"I know that tone. Why so suspicious?" Cress asked. For all her gruffness, Salida cared for him and his sister.

"It depends," she said. "It depends how much you trust the Guardians. It might be time to readjust your thinking, I believe."

"What my lovely is endeavoring to say is that you need to be more circumspect when it comes to the Guardians. They are dragons, after all. You have considered being around them as rewarding, but I wonder if that is wise," Einer said softly. "By their very nature, they are not benign. Time has given them ways to plot and contemplate conundrums that no human can imagine."

The discourse reminded him of the discussion he and Becca shared, yet much darker. "You would not speak thus without reason."

Einer and Salida exchanged a sidelong glance.

"Glad to see you haven't lost your talent to grasp matters quickly," the silver haired wizard said, his tone amused. "You are not the only one the Guardians are speaking with, you know. They have been encouraging Becca to leave."

Cress stiffened with shock. His pulse raced, and his fingers tingled. If anything, he thought the dragons approved of her. His mind swam with confusion until he shook his head to clear the stupor.

"Told you he wouldn't like it," Salida said, her expression softening.

"So you did, love," Einer continued with his usual calmness. "But what will he do now that he is aware?"

"Do?" Cress searched the dark, shadowy dragon circle for any sign of Guardians. Churning coldness warred with hot rage for the betrayal he felt. "Why I'm going to confront them."

Chapter Forty-Three

Cold white moonlight slanted into the room Becca used for sleeping. She lit a candle, washed up, and changed into a clean tunic. She undid her braid, removed Cress's beads to admire the glowing orbs nestled in her palm before brushing her hair. When she finished, she wove the blonde length into a braid. Several times her stomach growled in anticipation of Salida's meal.

She checked the mirror and wondered where heartblood could be found. In the heart, of course. But where else? Her hand stayed when her gaze locked on the large vein in her neck. It seemed logical for blood to flow from the heart to the head. Heartblood. An arrow aimed just right might spray the Ossa with enough heartblood to break the spell.

A shiver raced down her back even as her feet set into motion.

Her steps scuffed over the stone flooring. Grinding sounds that reminded her of gears and pulleys were faint within the hut that turned into a tower. Her amazement seemed misplaced. Cress was a mighty wizard, and she should have expected nothing less from his home.

She headed for the cooking area. Salida loved to concoct new dishes, and Einer always seemed eager to sample her experiments. A pot simmered in the hearth where the aroma of basil, garlic, onion, and possibly a gray-green flower that the housekeeper called lavender emerged. A brisk scan revealed an empty room.

Where was everyone?

Movement outside the window caught her attention. Cress stomped across the open section of the dragon circle. He stirred her senses even at a distance. He headed for the nesting cave. Why now? No matter how much the wizard defended the Guardians, she suspected they were up to something.

Stepping outside, she met Salida and Einer staring after the wizard with the hint of satisfaction on their aged faces. "Where's Cress going?"

Einer turned toward her. "To confront the Guardians."

"At this time? What could be so important?"

A grin popped out of Salida's wrinkled face. "You should be asking Cress, dearie."

Becca studied the pair. A deeply engrained respect for the elderly rose in her, and being discourteous wasn't in her nature. "I would prefer to hear the reason from you."

"And if we have no wish to tell you?" Einer interjected.

She shrugged. "I wouldn't press."

"Even if it concerns you?" Salida asked.

Her heartbeat skipped. Surely they teased. "I won't press if you feel a need to keep quiet. But, out of friendship, I wish you would explain. One of you."

"Seems the Guardians, the little buggers, haven't been honest with Cress or you," Einer pointed out. "If there's one thing that upsets the boy, it's dishonesty."

Being right about her suspicions gave her no

satisfaction. All along she'd known the Guardians were being deceptive. "Tell me."

"Mayhaps you should follow him to find out, dearie," Salida said with a chuckle.

She swallowed hard. "Mayhaps I will do just that."

****

"You evil…despicable…What have you done?" Cress couldn't utter another word. Anger tied his tongue in knots. All around him Guardians flew about the cave, tending eggs. He'd trusted them. Assumed they were his friends. He couldn't believe they would betray him, that they worked against him to make Becca leave.

"We are not good or evil. We are dragons. To lie and deceive is our nature. Why are you so surprised?"

Why indeed? Was it guilt? Anger? What did he feel? For turning his sister into a tree? For murdering his best friend? For not declaring for the woman he loved?

Now Cress faced a dilemma he wasn't sure how to correct. Dare he confess his feelings, and risk exposure? Did he stay silent and let the dragons ruin his life?

He made a decision. *"You went too far! You had no right to interfere in my life. I want nothing more to do with you. You betrayed me. All I did was aid you."*

"Preservation of our species comes before all else," dragon voices answered him calmly, without regret. *"We told you on the journey back to send the warrior woman away."*

Cress paused. The narcissistic creatures needed a lesson in humility. *"I can't forgive your meddling. How would you feel if I smashed your precious eggs?"*

Dozens of Guardians flew in agitated circles. *"You*

would not dare!" they protested, fear filling their voices.

"Guard them well!"

"Tell him what he wants to know, or I'll make you regret ever being born," Becca said behind him.

Cress whirled around. *"Do not interfere."*

"I'll do as I please. This concerns me as well."

"The truth then." Torka's voice came through clear and steady. *"Our actions were based on selfish reasons. When the spell is broken, your sister will no longer be a tree. Trell might wish to leave the dragon circle. If she goes, you'll be tempted to follow her. But we still require your wizardry skills."*

Cress seethed. Silence stretched. Never in a million centuries did he expect treachery from the very beings he'd co-existed with.

"So, all along, you never intended to free Trell."

"Mayhaps, after a while," the dragoness answered.

Disappointment made his gut rise and fall with sudden sickness. *"A long while. It's been over a thousand years."*

Becca put her hand on his arm. "Betrayal is trust broken. It hurts. I'm sorry. You cared about the Guardians as much as you did Trell. To learn that they had ulterior motives is devastating."

He glanced around the cave that he'd created with magic. Eggs rested in various conditions suitable for hatching. He'd helped them over and over. Yet they repaid him with disloyalty…or it felt that way.

Pain stabbed at him. The emptiness in his gut went along with the heaviness in his chest. "I would have done anything for them. How could they betray me?" he asked, surprised his voice worked.

"You said it yourself," Becca said. "They are dragons. Confirmation of what we consider normal is the dragons' curse. If possible, we should forgive them."

Cress regarded her directly. The paranoia that threatened to overtake him eased as he stared at her suntanned face with freckles dancing across the bridge of her nose. "Why should I forgive them?

"Forgive them for me."

He drew in a breath of heated, sulfur-laden air and glared at the flickering creatures who listened to every word.

"Do not come to me again," he mindspoke, *"Unless I call for you."*

****

Einer and Salida stepped out the door without holding hands upon Cress's return to the dragon circle. The smiles on their aged faces were similar in width, the sparkle in their eyes held the same brightness and merriment as though they'd spent decades together. Einer leaned against his staff.

A flicker of uneasiness stirred within Cress while he stopped before them. "I hope you bring better tidings than your last."

Salida smiled widely. "Knowing is half the battle."

He resisted her smile. "I didn't see the Guardians' betrayal. They deceived me. It caught me totally by surprise. The pain is difficult to bear."

"This type of treachery happens more often than you know. You cared about the Guardians. Time will ease your pain," Einer said. "And Becca's company."

Through an opening in the trees, the person whose name was just spoken approached. Salida and Einer

339

excused themselves to disappear inside the cottage before the warrior woman reached him.

"I've missed you." A riot of emotions rose up inside him.

"I see you every night while we sup."

The thought of her strong body snuggled against his awoke swirling emotions. The heat of their skin touching, the heady scent of lovemaking. The image elicited pangs of arousal until he ached. How could he expect Becca, a warrior woman, to want to stay with him? Why did it have to be so hard to speak his heart? Couldn't she see how he felt? He swore he wore his emotions on his face. Life without her meant nothing. She mattered to him.

"It's not the same thing," he said. "You know what I mean."

Becca looked at him expectantly. "Speak straight."

"I have a darkness in me." He kept his tone light, hoping she thought him jesting. "Mayhaps the reason I never discovered how to break Trell's spell was because the gods found me undeserving."

Becca's eyes widened. "Sweet Luna, I don't believe that for one moment. Share your burden with me. Together your guilt might not seem so heavy."

"I am sure you believe that, but you don't understand."

She reached for his arm. "Are you so sure? The Guardians tried to use me, to make me leave because they knew I could guide you to make the right decision."

Her touch made him tremble. He must be mad to want her, but he couldn't help himself. He had never given any thought to the consequences of falling in love and sharing his life with someone at his side. Freeing Trell had always been sufficient for him.

Chapter Forty-Four

Becca had every intention of remaining a hunter. Too long her feelings for Cress had stymied her behavior. No more.

"Becca—"

She hushed him. "You have spoken, let me now."

Releasing a sigh, she caressed Cress's lean face—the light stubble, rough beneath her fingers, a delight to touch. "I know how to break the spell."

Joy and fear exploded on his face. He sucked in a sharp breath. "What? Why didn't you tell me sooner?"

"Because I just figured it out." She motioned for them to step away from the hut. "It calls for heartblood to break the spell. Stabbing you in the heart is out of the question. But here..." She stroked the side of his neck where a thick vein pulsed. "Your heartblood flows from here as well. I know males. They think differently than hunters. I sincerely believe this other wizard didn't seek your death, but he wanted to challenge you. To test your courage, your strength, your love for your sister."

"Give me your knife." Cress held his hand out, palm up. "I'll slice my throat myself."

Becca nearly screamed. "Are you a fool? That's not what I meant. It's not that simple. I suspect you were never meant to decipher the spell or inflict the injury. You've said this wizard was a friend. Right? He wanted you to place yourself in the hands of another—

probably him—to free Trell."

Cress's eyes widened with understanding. "Nature against nature. Wood to wood," he muttered in a low voice. "I'd forgotten that part of the spell. What you say makes sense."

"My only concern is how much heartblood is enough?"

He graced her with the warmest smile. "We won't know until we try. Just nick me. Let's do it now. I see no reason to wait another moment. I embrace my destiny and put myself in your capable hands."

Becca flinched at his words. Her worst qualms were materializing. Worry wrenched at her very being. "I—I can't. What if I miss? Don't ask me to do it." Her voice held firm. "You could die."

Hazel eyes pleaded for her to weaken. "You are proficient with your bow and arrow. Just be quick."

"If forced to do this deed, I'd rather be accurate."

"I trust you."

Fear churned within Becca, but Cress's calm gaze soothed her nerves. She'd always admired the way they changed from gold to green. It seemed unfair for him not to shake with fear the same as she, especially when she held his life in her hands. She concentrated on the task ahead.

She and Cress had such a short time together. Barely six moon cycles. Not nearly enough time. The burden of this task weighed heavily. What if she missed, made a mistake, or her arrow went off course? She tried to remember the joy they shared—making love and discovering the dragon eggs. The hardships of their journey, solving the riddle of Trell's imprisonment. Accumulated memories nearly overwhelmed her.

"Ready?" she asked, unsure if she was.

Cress stood with his back against the Ossa pine that was his sister. Two branches dipped low to wrap him in a hug. He stroked the thick evergreen, his gaze glued to Becca. "I trust you, Becca. It takes a brave heart to do what must be done. Whatever happens, I accept my fate. You won't let me die."

Sweet Luna, if someone had told her…she, leader of the hunters, would be afraid to fire an arrow, she would have thought them crazed. "I wish I had your confidence."

"Don't stretch out the agony, my love."

The sincerity in his voice squeezed her heart until her eyes filled with tears. She blinked them back, hard, to clear her vision.

Everything Becca held dear depended upon her aim. She waited for the grays to turn into blue as dawn chased away Luna's shadows. The faint chill of the night lingered in the delay. Dew moistened the ground. She smelled the tang of dampness. Soon no further excuses would be left.

Cress stood still, entrusting his life in her hands.

Could she trust herself?

She tested the wind by dropping a blade of grass. A delaying tactic. A soft east wind ruffled her hair and her cheek.

Becca eyed her target, the right side of Cress's neck. Such a narrow spot. The steady pulse of his heartblood beat with a strength she hated to see end.

She pulled against the tension of her bow, her arms quivering, then used her thumb and finger to adjust her hold ever so slightly. Her breathing slowed.

"Ready?" she repeated.

"Aye," Cress answered. "Fret not, my love. I have confidence in your skill."

A hard knot tightened in her belly, and she offered him a faint smile. She pinched string between her fingers and sighted down the shaft. She released the tension on her bow and a ping sounded a second before her arrow flew. The spinning shaft devoured the yards with amazing speed.

What if the wind changed? What if her arrow veered off target?

Becca stared in horror as the stone-tipped arrowhead skimmed Cress's skin, slicing a gash that sprayed a crimson ribbon against the Ossa pine. A shrill cry ripped out of her throat. She flung her bow down and raced to Cress's side. Blood seeped between his fingers as he slid down the tree trunk.

Sweet Luna, she'd hit his jugular. A mortal wound.

The ground turned slippery with blood even as her knees lost strength. She sank down beside him. If he died, she vowed to follow him before night fell.

"*Noo!*" cried out Trell in pain to pierce Becca's mind. "*You killed him.*"

****

Everything happened at once. A wave of ancient magic surged over Cress as a voice from the past echoed in the air and Bonner's spell filled the air once again.

Let Trell stand proud and tall
Let Cress's pride fall
Let heartblood spill
Let love cure all

The dragon circle came alive with lights sparkling

with the brilliance of diamonds. Intense heat wrapped around Cress, nearly singing his exposed skin. Sweat drenched his body.

A thunderous boom echoed in his ears. Pinecones rained down on the ground. The earth beneath him shifted and lifted as roots loosened. Loud crackles filled the air. He looked up sharply. The entire Ossa pine shook as if about to topple. Branches snapped, twisted, and pulled into its mighty trunk. The tree shrank into itself.

He hurriedly rolled out of the way, even as he sensed a wave of surprise sweep through Becca. A quick look showed her blue eyes were huge and bright, her mouth a perfect circle. Debris stuck to his clothing. It wasn't sweat he felt, but blood. His heartblood had bonded with Trell.

He muttered a quick spell and wrenched a cotton bandage out of his robe's pocket. Next he conjured a gooey mixture and slapped it onto his neck to stem the bleeding. Magic couldn't cure, but it certainly could give his body the tools to heal itself.

"What's happening?" Becca asked, kneeling beside him.

"You did it," he said, recalling the sights and sounds of the original spell—hating them then, yet delighted to see and hear them once again. He wrapped his arms around her and found comfort with her familiar scent. "You broke the spell."

She touched his face. "I nearly killed you."

A groaning continued in the hundred-foot Ossa as it shrank to half its previous size. It glowed with an eerie light that grew dimmer with each passing second. Branches and twigs snapped and cracked and disappeared into one another. The deafening noise diminished. Thousands of yellow-green needle clusters littered the ground, giving off a slight citrus and vanilla scent when he stood and crushed them underfoot. Lichen which grew on dead branches floated down silently. The thick reddish-brown bark lightened, and the deep furrows smoothed before his eyes.

Becca reached out to touch the tree.

He restrained her arm with a gentle hold. "Ahhh, best not to touch."

She nodded, her eyes full of doubt. "Why not?"

"Magic is an art that leaves a lot to interpretation. Every spell is dependent upon the practitioner at the time of its creation. I don't know what kind of mood Bonner was in at the time. Better to be cautious than regret something that will have adverse effects."

"I thought you were an all-powerful wizard."

Cress took a breath, held it, then let it go. "I swear. Both Bonner and I were apprentice wizards when this occurred. I have no idea what will happen. I am in the dark as much as you."

His head swam with memories. He visualized Bonner, Trell, and himself on that fateful day in the dragon circle—Bonner and he competing in a silly contest, each trying to outdo the other with magic spells…the moment he fought Bonner. The crack of his friend's skull hitting solid rock.

The shrinking Ossa creaked and groaned. He shivered, knowing the sound would never be forgotten.

How could he possibly make up all the lost time to Trell? What if she didn't forgive his rashness? What then? Could he live with that?

A being—part human, part Ossa—stood barely five

feet tall. The conical crown once shading the giant tree resembled hair and swayed within the slight breeze. Two branches jutted out from the trunk. A thin bead of sap oozed where the arrow pierced the bark. The base split, and Cress swore the tree shape developed a human form. The process seemed identical to what happened so long ago, except in reverse.

He dared not look away. "Trell?" he asked low and intense...and oh so full of hope.

His stomach lurched when eyes, his sister's eyes, fluttered open in the tree trunk and blinked. At his side, Becca caught her breath.

The tree-like figure creaked and groaned as it attempted to step forward with painstaking movements. Chunks of bark split and fell away to reveal the very same gown of dark green velvet trimmed in brown along the hem and tippets of her sleeves that his sister wore the day she had been enchanted.

Trell lifted her leg and took an unsteady step. She stumbled. Cress jerked into action, clenching his teeth at the sudden burning alongside his neck that almost threw him off balance. He caught her before she collapsed. Beside him, Becca reacted with equal speed, and he smiled at her for the assistance.

"*At long last. Free. Hello, dear brother.*" Trell wrestled with a cough to clear her throat. "*I guess I am* out of practice talking." Her voice smoothed out as she spoke.

"Save your voice," Cress said.

"There's so much I wish to say," she answered, ignoring his entreaty. "I wanted to die when Bonner died. I loved him, and he loved me. To watch his death was the hardest thing I ever had to do."

Hot tears slipped down Cress's cheeks. He'd waited a thousand years for this moment and could hardly believe the vision standing before him. He couldn't decide what to say or whether to simply wrap her in a bear hug. His sister hadn't aged a day. At sixteen, plus a thousand years, Trell remained an adolescent. Could he manage a girl on the verge of womanhood? It didn't matter. He would try.

"We can talk later." His fingers twitched as they removed a fragment of bark clinging to her arm. "I…I had a fine speech all planned, and now I'm unsure what to say…except forgive me."

Trell peeled bits of wood off her face. Her fingers examined her bare skin in a tentative, almost exploratory way. He could only imagine what it would feel like to touch smooth skin instead of rough bark after all these centuries.

"How could I not?" Trell responded. "You stood by me all this time and risked your life to break the spell. Bonner's death was an accident. You didn't mean to kill him, any more than he meant to trap me."

Cress marveled at her words. He should have realized she would understand and forgive. Trell never held a grudge.

Holding her tight, he said, "I behaved foolishly."

Trell stepped out of his hold with a new strength and stood on her own. Her fingers trapped the velvet fabric of her gown and rolled it together.

"Thank you for staying with me," she said. "I'm not sure I would have survived without you."

"I would have stayed forever and am willing to accept whatever vengeance you wish to administer. What happened was my fault."

"Oh, Cress," Trell said with a shy smile, "I never blamed you."

A great weight of guilt lifted from his shoulders at her forgiveness. "I should never—"

Trell raised her arm to silence him, a solemn expression on her delicate features. "Haven't I listened to you pour out your heart to me over the centuries? Dear brother, it was a silly prank gone bad. Very bad. Bonner would never have enchanted me if he thought it would turn out as it did."

"Still…"

Trell shook her head, and her gaze flicked at Becca, who remained quiet while brother and sister reacquainted themselves with each other. "Have you forgotten what started the contest? Truly, you don't remember?"

"What?" Cress asked, confused, unable to dredge up a thing to ease his guilt.

"I dared you to best him. I taunted you until you gave in. You created a fistful of colorful diamonds from drab pebbles. Remember? Then Bonner changed a blackberry vine into a rose bush. I laughed at him. That's when he turned his magic on me."

"I had forgotten." He stared at his sister in utter amazement. So young. So wise. Briefly, he wondered if all those years as a tree gave Trell a wisdom no other human possessed.

He glanced at Becca and, as usual, drew comfort from her nearness. She gave him a sympathetic look and reached for his hand.

"Greetings, Trell," she said. "I'm pleased to make your acquaintance and glad I was able to break the spell."

"Your shot was guided by your heart," Trell replied, "not skill. It made your aim true."

Cress listened. If only his sister's face wasn't so pale and drawn. The sight squeezed his heart tight with worry. His gaze swept over her for the arrow wound. No blood. No wound. Not even a hole in her gown. Was she ill? Had the transformation injured her in some way unseen by mortal man?

"Are you all right?" he asked. "You look pale."

"The bark protected me." A frail smile moved Trell's lips. "I'm just tired."

"Let's go inside. There are people eager to see you," he said.

Trell brought her hands in front of her, palms pressed together, then brushed them over his arm. The touch reminded him of all those times she would lower a branch and skim the bough over his shoulder. Affection welled up in him for her.

"Oh, aye!' she said, her tone undulating like the breeze skipping through the treetops. "While you were gone, Salida and Einer read to me and told me all the old tales of Feldsvelt. In fact, it was a little detail in one of the stories that gave Becca and me the clue to breaking Bonner's spell. We live in an amazing world, don't you think?"

Cress laughed at her enthusiasm. "Come on, then. I'm sure Salida has some broth for you."

"Agreed, but first, give me a moment. I would like to stay outside for a bit."

"I'll stay with you," he offered, wondering at her request.

"Nay, please. I wish to walk around to gather my thoughts. I am used to being alone."

Pushing his sister into something she didn't want was the last thing he wanted to do. He let his arm drop and smiled. He grasped Becca's fingers in a firm and gentle grip, determined to win her heart and never let her go.

Inside the cottage, three kettles hung on the chimney crane—one with stew, one with broth, and one with water for tea. Trust Salida to make all the preparations. Trell would be unable to eat solids immediately. Einer propped his staff against the wall and followed his housekeeper. As Salida filled bowls, Einer carried them to the trestle table. They'd become a team.

Relief filled Cress when Trell entered the cottage, looking none the worse for wear for her brief sojourn around the dragon circle. He stared at his sister in wonder. Her pale skin held a tiny spot of color on her high cheeks now. In all honesty, she didn't appear to have suffered any adverse effects from her long confinement.

Her eyes, Langois eyes, golden hazel, studied the cottage. She'd never been inside. He'd built it after her enchantment, so he could remain close. "It's so noisy in here."

He smiled. "What do you expect with Salida and Einer clanging utensils?"

"I'm used to hearing the wind, gently whispering or howling angrily. Then there are birds, animals, even the click of insects. Sound was always around, but nothing as harsh as this."

"Trell—I'm so sorry this happened to you." Cress's voice was raw with emotion.

"I'm back now. That's all that matters."

Salida rushed over with a cup of broth. "Here you go, dearie," she said to Trell. "Drink this slowly, and you'll feel much better. Later you can try some stew."

Salida stood beside the table, and Einer joined her. They held hands. "I…we leave tomorrow afternoon for Brenalin," the older wizard announced.

Cress snapped his head up. He stared in disbelief. "You can't…I—I mean…"

Just then, Becca coughed. He went silent.

Einer gave him a small smile. "We know what you mean. Your concern is appreciated, but I received word Prince Duran's wife is due to birth their first child, and it is best we be close at hand."

Salida nodded. "We wish we could stay longer, but we talked this over while you were gone. I was born in Brenalin. I would like to enjoy my final days there. With Trell back and Becca here, you don't need a third woman. You'll have enough on your hands. I'm sure you'll want to spend time with your sister and Becca."

Cress leaned forward, his elbows on the table. "I most certainly do."

Trell's eyes struggled to focus. Her gaze went to the older couple, then to him. "I might have something to say on the matter."

The tone in his sister's voice raised the hairs on the back of his neck. Instinct warned him that he wasn't going to approve of what his sister had to say. Should he stop her before she began? "What is that supposed to mean?"

"It's simple, Cress. I'm not staying."

All four stared in shocked silence as everyone's attention focused on Trell.

Cress's breathing hissed through his teeth. Leave?

Had she lost her mind? He finally had her back, and she planned to depart. "You would leave?"

Trell's chair scraped over wooden planks as she stood. Her chin rose a notch in defiance. Cress knew his sister better than she realized. The Ossa's branches would stiffen the same way when she disapproved of what he said.

"There's no need to scowl at me," she said. "I've made my decision. We've been together for a thousand years. And remember, even in human terms, I am of an age to do as I please."

"I am not scowling," Cress said, his voice strained, incredulous.

Trell started to hold out her hand, then dropped it to her side. "I know you envisioned a different reunion," she began, her voice low, "but I wish to travel to Brenalin with Einer and Salida. I want to resume my healing education. Arguing won't change my mind because I've had years and years to decide what I would do once the spell was broken."

Cress's fingers clenched as he sat, shaking his head while his thoughts raced. "It is folly beyond belief, Trell. You have no idea how much Brenalin has changed during the past centuries. It is not the same place you remember."

Becca stood beside Cress and put a hand on his shoulder. "You are treating her like a child," she said, her voice rock steady. "She is a woman and has the right to make decisions about her own life. Show her your trust. Let her determine her destiny and fulfill her dreams."

"You know nothing of this," he snapped, feeling betrayed by his beloved as well as his sister. It rankled more than he cared to admit.

Becca tossed her blonde braid from her shoulder. "You devoted your life to freeing her. Now you want to keep her prisoner. Is that fair?"

Cress went cold. The irony of Becca's words settled on him in a disquieting manner. He remembered the happy girl with a laugh that made everyone smile. "All right, Trell, make your plea. I promise to keep an open mind before I make my decision."

Relief flooded his sister's face. "We both know I do not belong here. I don't know who I am. Oh, I am Trell Langois. Part of me is a six and ten girl, but a portion of me will always remain part of the elements. Look at yourself, Cress. Once you were only two years older than me, but now you are a man, a score and ten."

"It has been a thousand years, Trell. There were times I ventured from the dragon circle. I aged when I stepped outside the circle. Those times added up."

Trell smiled. "You have practiced your spells to become a full-fledged wizard. Let me go to grow as well." She stopped to catch her breath. "I want to become a healer. Or, at least, study to become one. I'm perfectly aware the healing arts could have changed during my absence, but that only makes me more curious. Imagine the developments and improvements the centuries have produced. Do not deny me the opportunity to learn who or what I'll become. Besides, no matter what you say, the choice is mine."

He gulped in a huge lungful of breath, trying to maintain a calm that did not exist any place inside him. He'd never thought of the consequences of setting Trell free. He just assumed she would stay with him. "Nothing I say will dissuade you?"

Trell shook her head. "Nothing."

Cress released a heavy sigh. To treat his sister any less than how he wanted to be treated himself seemed wrong. Becca proved right. He needed to trust and respect his sister's decision. "Then be happy, Trell. I wish you well."

Chapter Forty-Five

Salida, Einer, and Trell stayed an extra day. With the trio gone, the tower felt bigger. Emptier. At dusk, Becca stood silent, her eyes closed, and listened for any movement on the other side of Cress's door. He'd disappeared to his sleeping quarters the instant the others departed.

Becca sighed, careful not to make any noise before raising her arm. This would be their final time together. She'd decided being near him wasn't enough, and that meant she must leave. It broke her heart to love him and not have that love returned.

Cress yanked open the door. "Come in. I've been expecting you."

His eyes were pools of flashing green and gold, his mouth grim. Becca squashed a twinge of nervousness. Not the time for her hunter's nerve to desert her. She entered and inhaled deeply. The scent of pine and male filled her nostrils. "I want to talk to you."

He slammed the door shut. "Just talk?"

She fingered the magical beads in her braid. They continued to glow since she'd picked them out of the bowl and woven them into her hair.

"Well, to begin with," she went on, wanting to open her heart to him. "I want to explain why I sided with Trell."

Cress's hard gaze raked her in the flicker of a

solitary candle. "No explanation is necessary. You did the right thing. I was wrong to expect her to stay here."

A blush burned her cheeks. "Then, I should confess I did fib a little. I don't want to talk. I want to make love."

The man who held her heart gave no indication that he shared her feelings. Sweet Luna, let him not refuse. He peered so hard at her, keeping her in suspense for the longest time, Becca thought he tried to find her soul. A muscle twitched in his jaw. It fluttered, flexed, and fluttered again. A decision swirled within his head, more likely the single most important decision of her life.

Without a word, he gathered her close.

Her heart thumped with joy as she wrapped her arms around his muscular neck, careful of his wound. He tensed as she touched his bandage, but she refused to stop and lifted up onto her toes to kiss him. Slowly, his finely sculpted lips softened, tender and sweet, beneath her onslaught. She shivered as his kiss turned confident and sure.

"Help me out of my clothes," he rasped, low and throaty, as he untied the leather thong holding his thick brown hair back from his face.

"With pleasure."

She grabbed at the edge of his tunic and lifted it over his broad shoulders and head. She had the distinct impression he restrained himself, keeping himself from moving when her fingertips brushed his bare skin. The brief contact reminded her of tempered steel and made her ache to press her body against his.

His finely woven leggings proved stubbornly difficult to remove, clinging to his firm legs until she gave them a hard tug, freeing his arousal. He stood naked before her. Marvelously naked. Marvelously male.

Cress let her stare until he barked out a short laugh. "Now, it's your turn. I'll remove your clothes."

Her breath caught. She initiated this. He slid his large hands under her tunic, his fingers fondling and caressing her breasts with tender torture before stripping it off. She expected air to bite at her naked skin, but the temperature in the room rose as though magic heated it. She snuck a glance at Cress to find him intent on shedding her of her deerskin leggings. He peeled them down her legs, and his fingers played with the curls between her legs before sliding two fingers into the moist softness of her exposed flesh, in and out.

Gasping, she grabbed his shoulders for balance. "Oh, Cress, aye. Aye."

"You like that?" he asked, rising up and pushing his body against her belly.

She cradled the back of his neck with her hands. "Very much."

She pulled away from him just slightly. Nothing worse than a smug wizard, and she wanted to prove to him who was in command. This was her idea after all. Already her muscles and bones had gone soft and weak.

"Good. Now, I have another idea." He stared at her. "Climb into that bed, Becca. I am a man in dire need, but I vow to go slow."

"Not too slow, I hope," she teased him back.

When he joined her beneath the covers, the heat of his body sought her out and warmed her. Becca snuggled closer in the circle of his arms.

"This feels so wonderful," she cooed. "I don't

know what it is about the initial contact of bare skin against bare skin, but each time is like the first."

Cress laughed. "Personally, I believe it depends on who you are cuddling with."

The merry sound warmed and delighted her. Never would she tire of it. Or him!

He kissed her eyelids, her mouth, and then all the way down to her belly. She dragged his head back up until they were face to face. A long, leisurely kiss followed. Arousal hardened her nipples and created an urgency within her that only Cress could satisfy.

He hovered over her, his long hair falling forward to brush her breasts.

Her hands flexed, and the muscles on his back tightened as his shaft thumped against her thighs. Magic wasn't necessary for her to want or need Cress. He fulfilled all her dreams. She would never achieve this deep connection with another man again.

He smiled at her and entered with a swift, deep plunge. For a moment, they stared at each other. Then Cress began moving slowly, going faster and faster, bringing her closer to the ecstasy she'd never found except with him.

Becca matched his moves with her own. Pleasure took over, coherent thought became impossible as a sweet pulse beating in her core carried her higher up a mountain of sheer bliss.

Go on, the voice of desire urged inside her head. Breathless with her efforts to reach that elusive summit. *Faster. Race to the heavens.*

They both heard the words.

"Oh, Cress." She whispered his name like a lovesick woman as stars exploded throughout her body and lit the room with a magical light.

He caught her tight around the waist again as he joined her in the same erotic fulfillment. "Becca," he whispered, planting gentle kisses on eyelids, ears, down her cheeks until he reached her mouth. "I love you."

She kissed him back and snuggled into the warmth of his strong arms. He made her feel wickedly wonderful. Alive. Happy.

A half hour later, the glimmer of dozens of tiny flickering lights sparkled in the room, but this time it wasn't magic.

Guardians flew in through the open window. *"We have news to share."*

Becca and Cress sat up and watched dozens of tiny, golden dragons flit around the chamber, buzzing with excitement—the first time they'd deemed to make an appearance since returning to the dragon circle with their cache of precious dragon eggs.

"By the Gods!" Cress mindspoke to the dragons. *"I told you to never come back unless summoned. "*

Becca's insides warmed as he included her in the mindspeech. *"Remember I suggested you forgive them."*

"It won't be easy," he grumbled.

"We met Trell. We are happy for you," the Guardians mindspoke to them. *"We cannot overrate the importance of family."*

"Indeed," Cress answered them. *"How are your eggs doing?"*

"The first wyrmling has hatched. A black male. He emerged when Trell happened by before she left for Brenalin. She stayed to aid us in his birth."

Cress looked at Becca and with one glance he

knew she was unaware as well. *"She never mentioned a word of her involvement,"* he mindspoke back.

"Probably an oversight. The black's appetite exceeds all Guardians' ability to feed him. Soon three male earth dragons will emerge, and one of the females is near hatching. Meanwhile, we are constantly searching for food for the first wyrmling."

Becca smiled. *"I'll be honored to supply food for your dragonets until they can hunt for themselves. When can Cress and I see him?"*

"Our sincere appreciation." The Guardians buzzed around the bedchamber. *"Our apologies, too. It was wrong of us to attempt to influence you in returning to your homeland. We beg your forgiveness."*

"Talk about being honored. That's a first. The Guardians have never apologized for their actions," Cress whispered in her ear, nibbling as he spoke.

"Promise to visit the cave in the near future."

"We will," Becca and Cress said together.

The Guardians zipped out the open window.

Cress smiled and pressed a kiss into the warm hollow of each of her palms. Shivers of delights rippled through her body. She wondered what he thought. The same as she? How wonderful it would be to spend several days in bed.

He steepled his fingers to regard her through them. "I don't want you to leave."

Her heart squeezed tightly. "Cress…"

"What?"

His tone held a deadly seriousness and it broke her heart. Her knees quaked like a novice hunter on her first hunt. "After the hunting for the dragonets is over, nothing is left for me here."

Cress turned his face away from her. "I'm here. Don't go."

She reached out her arms to him and wrapped them around his neck. "For a great wizard, you certainly have a lot to learn about women. I don't want to go. I want to stay with you, Cress."

"I thought…" He stopped talking and moaned when she wiggled against him.

"I am in love with you. I have been waiting for you to make up your mind. Now cease talking and kiss me."

Cress's breath came soft against her hair. A flood of longing flowed through her body to nearly overwhelm her.

She inhaled, feeling the need to continue speaking, "Froy is no longer my home. Wherever you are is my home. All I desire is to remain by your side."

"I always wondered what love felt like," he murmured to her. "Now I know, and I wouldn't change this feeling for anything. Living without you wouldn't be living. All I want is to bind my life to yours. Not with magic, but love."

Sweet laughter, delightful to hear, bubbled from Becca. Her body responded to him in a hot, quick manner. "Show me."

The room shimmered as the air filled with a rainbow of colors. She smiled to herself. Magic definitely had its uses.

She remembered the first time they met. Smoke polluted the air. Lightning flashed across the sky. Thunder boomed. Fire burned around her.

Now fresh air filled her nostrils. No hint of danger existed. She felt safe, secure.

"Becca with the golden hair," Cress said, his voice

husky with desire.

She smiled, trying to visualize their future. "Aye, but will you love me when it's gray and I am old?"

"Silly woman," he said softly. "Once a man falls in love, he always sees the woman of his affections the same as when he first laid eyes upon her. You'll always have golden hair to me. Besides, most of our time will be spent in the dragon circle. Quite a few centuries will have to pass before we age."

"Come then," she teased. "We mustn't waste a single precious moment. Smoke dissipates quickly, and I do love the smell."

A word about the author…

Award-winning author Darcy Carson grew up reading everything her mother brought home from the library. Reading romances became her favorite topic. Eventually her love of those novels led her to start writing them. She resides in a Seattle suburb with her husband and a prince of a toy poodle.

Thank you for purchasing
this publication of The Wild Rose Press, Inc.

For questions or more information
contact us at
info@thewildrosepress.com.

The Wild Rose Press, Inc.
www.thewildrosepress.com

www.ingramcontent.com/pod-product-compliance
Lightning Source LLC
Chambersburg PA
CBHW051128030726
47504CB00004B/766